Ti...rope

WITHDRAWN

Tightrope

Simon Mawer

W F HOWES LTD

This large print edition published in 2015 by
W F Howes Ltd
Unit 4, Rearsby Business Park, Gaddesby Lane,
Rearsby, Leicester LE7 4YH

1 3 5 7 9 10 8 6 4 2

First published in the United Kingdom in 2015
by Little, Brown

A CIP catalogue record for this book is available
from the British Library

ISBN 978 1 51000 626 3

Typeset by Palimpsest Book Production Limited,
Falkirk, Stirlingshire
Printed and bound by
www.printondemand-worldwide.com of Peterborough, England

This book is made entirely of chain-of-custody materials

For Emma, first member of the next generation

PART I

ENCOUNTER WITH A GHOST

I hired a car at the airport and drove along the north shore of the lake. It was an hour's drive, skirting Lausanne and taking the road towards Montreux. At Vevey I saw the sign for the turn-off too late and had to go into the town and turn back on myself, cursing for not having asked for a satnav when I picked up the car. The girl at the desk would have happily obliged – she'd managed to persuade me into an excess waiver and a full tank of petrol besides the rate I'd paid online in England. What would another pile of Swiss francs have mattered?

The woman I had come to see lived up the hill behind Vevey, in a modern apartment block couched in plush lawns. Regimented vines marched up the slope on the other side of the road. Below was the distant glimpse of the lake, as blue as forget-me-nots. The whole scene looked as though it had been computer-generated by an architect's office but it was real enough – as real as you can get in Switzerland, which, living as it does on the fantasies of all the others, has always been the least real of European countries.

When I rang I could hear the doorbell inside but no other sound. I wondered whether she had heard it. I wondered – you do when the person in question is eighty – whether she was even alive to hear it. Maybe, even since my email of two days ago, age had finally caught up with her.

And then the door opened.

There was that moment of hesitation that you see in older people, a rapid shuffle of the cards of memory, but as quick as a card sharp in her case, so fast that you could hardly see it. 'Samuel,' she said. 'It must be almost fifty years.'

She'd done her homework. Get your story by heart. Make sure it's consistent. Make sure you don't have to think about your replies. But don't be too accurate. Being too accurate is suspicious. 'Fifty-one,' I said. We kissed, on both cheeks. Her skin was soft and powdery, the texture of old velvet.

'You look middle-aged,' she said, considering me at arm's length.

'That's because I am.'

I forbore to say the obvious – that she looked old – but it was true. Perhaps I could see the lineaments of beauty in her face – sharp eyes, a mouth that still possessed beguiling curves, the line of jaw and chin that hinted at the features of her youth – but she had stepped over the border into old age and beauty was no longer evident but rather something to be inferred. I can't deny a shiver of fear remembering what I had once felt for her. Now, there was nothing. Until she spoke,

4

that is. The voice was still the same. The same intonation which she had never been able to disguise, an occasional uncertainty in her syntax that betrayed the French origins lurking behind the English lady she pretended to be.

We went through into the sitting room. The windows looked out over the lawns and I realised that, had she been waiting there, she'd have seen me approaching. She'd have watched me all the way into the building. That pause before opening the door would have been deliberate, as would the hesitation on seeing me. She was still a consummate actress.

'So how are you?' I asked.

'As well as anyone who's reached eighty. What'll you have?'

The possibilities were plain enough, sitting on a side table: a bottle of gin and a bucket of ice and a neat squad of tonic bottles. 'It's a bit early for me. A small one. Lots of tonic.'

She laughed, as though lots of tonic was an amusing weakness. While she made the drinks, I glanced round the sitting room for clues. They were there sure enough, as I might have expected. A glass-topped box with her medals in it – the Médaille de la Resistance embossed with the cross of Lorraine and the bronze Croix de Guerre. And photographs, one of my parents for a start, holding hands and smiling into the light, my mother with her hair in disorder and a free hand raised almost in salute but actually to keep the sun out of her eyes. Then a framed picture of a figure that I recognised but had never known – Benoît Bérard, the man with whom she had dropped into France in the autumn of 1943. He was standing in front of a sunlit stone wall. The focus wasn't brilliant but you could see that he was a composition of smiles and manly rolled up shirt sleeves and careless hair. 'I suppose I loved him,' she'd told me once, wistfully, as if she couldn't quite remember. Next to this photo was a picture of Clément Pelletier, a studio portrait that made him look more handsome than he really was, and slightly untrustworthy. Or was that my own prejudice finding things that weren't obviously there?

As she handed me my drink, I noticed her hands, the fingers like crustacean limbs, swollen at the joints. They trembled slightly. 'Anyway, it's been a long time,' she said.

What, I wondered, was the 'it' in that sentence? Because everything was a long time ago now – her first encounter with my parents, her first meeting with me, those moments when she breezed in and just as suddenly out of our ordinary, domestic lives. She was twelve years older than me, which had meant a great deal then although rather less now. When she had first met us my mother suggested I address her as Auntie Marian and she had laughed the suggestion away. 'It makes me sound like a sixty-year-old spinster.' From the outset she'd been a strange, errant creature who had occupied my fantasies; later she evolved into a daunting, obdurate woman who had fulfilled some of them. She was the first adult I ever called by her Christian name, the first adult who ever seemed to regard me as a person to respect rather than a child to be condescended to, the first adult with whom I'd had an adult relationship. Somehow, whatever our difference in age, I'd always felt her equal.

Sipping her drink, she considered me with something like sympathy. 'They got you in the end, did they? As I warned you they would.'

I shrugged. 'It seemed a good idea at the time, more interesting than the Foreign Office, more exciting than the Civil Service.'

'And now?'

'Retired, of course.'

'Family?'

'Two children, both married despite their parents' bad example. We got divorced in the seventies and I never remarried.'

She picked on divorced. Was there a hint of satisfaction in her expression? No sympathy, certainly. 'I can't say I'm surprised. I didn't have you down as the – what's the word? – uxorious type. What about the children?'

'They lived with their mother.'

'They always do.'

'Stephanie used to tell me they missed their father. Personally, I don't think they really cared. I'm friends with Edward but I don't see much of Margaret. I guess she blames me for everything.'

But I didn't want to talk about my life, I wanted to talk about hers. When they spoke about what Marian did, my parents always talked in oblique terms. Some cultural exchange programme or other, working with the Soviet Bloc. All a bit strange, really. But what happened during the war wasn't strange – it was remarkable. She'd been dropped into the south-west of France as a courier for one of those special operations circuits that France was riddled with. WORDSMITH was its code-name. While there she'd been sent to Paris on some damn fool errand and she'd been arrested. The story was well known enough, cropping up in books and newspaper articles whenever there was a rush of interest in the French resistance – when that film *Odette* came out, for example. But I knew about it from my mother recounting it, thrilling my post-war child's mind with the words *Gestapo* and *Resistance*; and, I suppose, from Marian herself. What she never talked about was what happened after, when she had spent time in captivity in one of the concentration camps, and miraculously, like someone coming back from the dead, had survived. But how? How does one achieve such a thing? How does one cheat death when the dice are so loaded against you? Anyway, she had survived and she never talked about it. That's what my mother said. She was special, strange, both courageous and dangerous, a good friend and someone you wanted to treat with caution, exciting to know but shot through with a sinuous vein of delinquency. 'She's dangerous,' my father said, in an unguarded moment. He was right in that. She was dangerous all right. I can vouch for it.

'So,' she said, 'you've come to get me.'

I tried to laugh the accusation off. 'They dragged me out of retirement simply because I knew you—'

'But you never gave me away, did you?'

'Never. It's just that now . . . they want to close the file. There's no question of prosecution or anything like that. They just want to tie up loose ends. All in complete confidence, of course.'

She laughed at that. 'I suppose they wouldn't want to suffer further public embarrassment. From what I can see, your service didn't cover itself in glory during the Cold War, did it?'

'It's the mistakes that got the publicity. Most of the successes remain secret. That's the party line, anyway.'

Her eyes were hard and bright, still youthful within that aged frame. 'Was there a mole at the top, Sam? Is that part of your brief, to find out if I was betrayed?'

'It's all entirely unofficial, Marian.'

'Everything's unofficial. It always was. Unofficial and therefore deniable.'

'Something like that.' I nodded towards the glass-topped box. 'I see you've got your medals out.'

She got up from her chair and went over to them, picking them up and examining them as though she had only just noticed. 'At least the

French did better than the British,' she said. 'All the British could manage for us was the MBE. And they gave that to the Beatles.'

I had heard the story before: they'd offered her a civil list MBE and she'd turned it down. Nothing that I did was civil, she'd told them. So eventually the authorities relented and changed it to a military list award. But still only the MBE, the bottom of the range, the decoration you give to school janitors and charity workers . . . and pop singers. 'They were like that with all of us,' she said once. 'Except for the dead darlings.'

Who were the dead darlings? Noor Inayat Khan, of course, the fragile, ethereal daughter of an Indian sufi mystic. And Violette Szabo, the working-class girl from Stockwell. And the one surviving darling, played by Anna Neagle in the film: Odette Sansom, who became Odette Churchill, who became Odette Hallowes. They all got George Crosses, the highest civilian award for gallantry, and who's to say they didn't deserve them? And a couple of George Medals were dished out to one or two others. But only civil list MBEs for the remainder – is that an honour or an insult?

'It's dead and buried now,' she said. 'Water under the bridge. Milk that's been spilt. What other clichés are there?'

I laughed. There are many. The whole damn story is riddled with clichés, heroine being one of them. Traitor being another.

NORTHOLT, 1945

The airfield was slick with rain, the concrete hardstandings turned to mirrors, aircraft glistening like fish, the wind a damp breath. Flights had been delayed so Atkins had been waiting for almost an hour, sometimes sitting in the car smoking, but more often, when the drizzle lifted, getting out and standing on the concrete apron, as though just being there would bring the aircraft in. The corporal who had been detailed to accompany her had suggested she could wait in the officers' mess but she had turned the offer down. She wouldn't have felt at ease in the mess despite her rank and uniform. Flight Officer was nothing more than a sham, like the flag of convenience that merchant ships carry. Your flag might say you came from Panama but no one really believed it.

'Can't they give us any idea?' she asked.

'It's taken off, ma'am,' he assured her, 'and what goes up must come down. Sooner or later.'

The woman didn't smile.

'They say . . .' he added.

'What do they say?'

'They say there've been terrible things over there. I saw it in that Pathé News. Did you see it, ma'am? Them camps. Terrible it was.'

She didn't answer. She didn't want to get drawn into conversation, and certainly not with this corporal and certainly not about what was happening in Germany at the moment. Instead she listened, and finally heard something on the air – the sound of distant engines. There had been many aircraft moving around while they'd been waiting, aircraft taxiing and taking off, aircraft dropping down over the houses to the left and hitting the runway with a screech of rubber and a dash of spray, the sound of aero engines so loud in her ears that she could barely think. But there was something about this new sound, as though it came from far away. 'Is that it?'

'Might be, ma'am. You never know your luck.'

The sound drew nearer, somewhere over to the east; and then the aeroplane could be seen, dropping out of the cloud, a twin-engined machine with a sharp and almost eager look to it, as if it were straining forward over its swept wings.

'Yup,' the corporal said, 'that's the Dakota. 'Bout time too.'

They watched the aircraft fly downwind and turn onto the approach. It dropped onto the tarmac, bounced once or twice then settled down, running to the end of the runway, turning and taxiing towards them, chin up, with the tail snaking slightly to give the pilot a better view of the ground in front. An aircraftman made ritual semaphore with what looked like table tennis bats and the engines stuttered into silence. There was a pause before the fuselage door opened and passengers began to climb down onto the tarmac.

'It's a lady, isn't it?' the corporal asked. 'The one you're waiting for, I mean.'

'A woman, yes.'

The passengers were walking towards them, a mixture of Army and Air Force, all officers, one with gold braid on his cap. She remembered to salute and was surprised to get a salute in return. And then they had gone past and there was just the aircraft, with the door open and no one in sight.

'Maybe she missed the flight,' the corporal suggested.

'She's there,' said Atkins.

She had sat motionless in her seat while the uniforms left, hoping they wouldn't notice her. They'd watched her during the flight, whispering about her so quietly that she couldn't make out what they were saying, nodding if they caught her eye, even giving brief smiles; but once the aircraft had landed they made their way down the slope towards the open door and out into the daylight without casting a glance in her direction. Only the dispatcher, a middle-aged flight sergeant who had tended her with quiet care throughout the flight, came up from the tail and stooped over her like

13

a doctor and asked if she was feeling all right. Because it was time to go, ma'am. Was there someone waiting for her?

She hoped so. They had assured her there would be.

Did she need help unbuckling her seat belt?

She didn't. She could manage that. Like undoing the buckle on a parachute harness, wasn't it? She remembered that well enough although it was a long time ago, over a year ago, and in another world. She attempted a smile as she left her seat, carrying the suitcase they had given her at the Red Cross. It contained all she owned, which was a change of clothing and some washing things. Washing things were the wonder. A toothbrush, a tin of toothpaste, a bar of soap that smelled of carbolic sitting almost untouched in a metal box. A flannel. And a tube of lipstick. Treasures worth ten, twenty times their weight in food.

Pulling her beret down over what was left of her hair, she cautiously made her way down the slope of the fuselage towards the rectangle of daylight at the end. For a moment she stood there in the entrance, looking out like a small mammal at the opening of its burrow scanning for predators. She saw nothing more than a stretch of concrete, with a black car parked a hundred yards away and two figures standing nearer, waiting. Beyond that was just the stuff of an airfield: hangars, a low-lying building of some kind, a squat control tower with a glass box on top like an aquarium, where silhouettes moved back and forth against the panes. Watching her, perhaps.

Carefully she climbed down the steps to the ground. Her shoes were too big for her and she had to drag her feet when she walked. They were all the Red Cross had in the way of women's shoes. Her own shoes had been so ruined they'd taken them away at the hospital and she never saw them again. Anyway they were made of cardboard, whereas these were leather. More treasure.

'Here she is,' the corporal said. 'You were right, ma'am.'

'Of course I was right.'

The woman crossing the stretch of concrete towards them seemed shorter than her actual height, as though she had been crushed into a form that was too small for her. Perhaps the military greatcoat that she was wearing created the illusion. She was the first, the very first to come back but, Atkins hoped, not unique. It was difficult in those first weeks to calculate what the chances were of there being others. As things transpired, of the women, there would be only three others. There would be more men, but then there had been more men in the first place; and Atkins only felt personally responsible for the women. Her girls. Forty dispatched, twenty-six returned safe and sound, one way or another; fourteen arrested and missing. Until this moment. Doing the mathematics meant you could push the emotions aside; she'd long ago learned to suppress emotion because by denying it the remainder of you might survive more or less intact.

The two women met like formal acquaintances, Atkins holding out a hand almost as though to ward off any closer and more intimate gesture. If you were trying to guess you'd have suggested a woman greeting a prospective employee, a maid perhaps, come from the country. Or perhaps a social worker meeting a patient recently released from a convalescent home. Even the words exchanged had a distant formality about them:

'Marian, how good to see you.'

'Miss Atkins. I wondered who would come, whether I would even recognise whoever it was.'

'Have you had a good flight?'

'I slept a bit. I've grown used to sleeping in difficult conditions.'

Atkins watched her carefully. The younger woman's skin seemed stretched over her facial bones, giving her complexion a strangely luminous sheen. There was a darkness around the eyes, a sculpted hollowness to her cheeks. Atkins was reminded of a painter whose work she had seen in Paris before the war, a Norwegian called Munch.

'Shall I take your suitcase, ma'am?' the corporal asked.

Marian held the case to her as though if she released it she might never see it again. 'No. No, I'll keep it.'

'Your clothes . . .' said Miss Atkins.

'The Red Cross gave me some. I didn't really have much when they found me.'

'No, of course not.'

'The shoes don't really fit.'

'No, they don't, do they? We'll soon put that right.' But what else would there be to put right? Atkins wondered.

The corporal held the car door open for them. ''Scuse my asking, ma'am. But have you come from Germany?'

'Of course she's come from Germany,' Atkins snapped. 'The aeroplane came from Germany; Miss Sutro must have come from Germany.'

He looked from one to the other. He was young, barely out of school, and with a youthful insouciance that would get him into trouble in the service but maybe would be an advantage once he was back in civilian life; whenever that might be. 'Have you come from one of the camps?'

Atkins's face compressed with anger at his question. Marian looked back at him with an expression that was devoid of any real feeling. 'Yes, I have.'

He nodded. 'Welcome back, ma'am,' he said.

The inside of the car smelled of cigarettes and old leather. It reminded Marian of something. There were other memories of other cars but she struggled desperately to find this particular one, groping back to a world that seemed to belong to someone else – a time before the war when there was a young girl called Marian Sutro with the smell of jasmine and sandalwood in her nose, a fragrance that came from the first bottle of scent she ever owned. And then that smell of tobacco and leather, which was the smell of the Delage in which her family had toured the north of Italy. Remembering brought with it a little burst of further recollection: she had wanted to stay in Geneva because Clément was there, but of course she couldn't tell them that. So she and her parents piled into the car and set off for a two-week tour round the Italian lakes that was rendered miserable by her sulking. 'What on earth is the matter with the girl?' her father asked at frequent intervals.

'Women's problems,' her mother replied.

Two years later it was the same car that got them across France to Bordeaux and away on the last passenger ship out to England.

HOMECOMING

'Back to London, ma'am?' the driver asked. 'Oxford,' Miss Atkins said. 'We're going to Oxford.' She turned to Marian. 'Is that all right? We thought you'd want that.'

She shrugged. Where else might she go? Wherever she was sent, really. Choice hadn't featured much in her life recently. 'Yes, yes, I suppose I do.'

'That's fine, then.'

The car made its way through the regimented lanes of the Air Force station. There were rows of huts that awoke another memory, a more recent one, one she was already trying to bury like someone interring a body during the night – the camp. Rows and rows of huts under a leaden north German sky. A world of grey. As they turned onto the main road Atkins produced a cigarette case and they lit up, huddling over Atkins's gold lighter as though sharing a secret. Marian drew smoke in greedily and coughed at the shock. In contrast to her own eagerness there was something of a controlled ritual about Atkins's smoking. She tapped the cigarette, then wedged it carefully between her fingers before raising it to her lips like a communicant taking the host. Her fingers were stained with nicotine.

Marian pointed. 'Could I . . .?'

Atkins frowned. 'Could you what? Oh, the cigarettes. Of course.' She handed over the packet and watched while Marian hid it away in the pocket of her coat. 'Your cough . . .' she said. 'I assume you were seen by a doctor.'

'Doctors. More than one. American. British. Even a Swedish one from the Red Cross. The Red Cross deloused and vaccinated us. Typhus, typhoid, everything they could think of.'

'That's good, then. But we'll have you see one of ours.'

There was a silence. There were so many things that might be said but somehow none of them seemed appropriate. 'Buck sends his best wishes,' Atkins offered, as though it was a birthday celebration or something.

'Buck?'

'Colonel Buckmaster.'

'Oh, of course.' Marian tried to picture the man and failed. A smile was all that remained in her memory, an oleaginous smile like the Cheshire Cat's.

'Where were you held?' Atkins asked. 'By the Germans, I mean.' The question was almost casual, as though she was asking about a minor inconvenience, a mere delay in travel plans.

'A place called Ravensbrück.'

The woman nodded, but clearly the name meant nothing to her. 'And you escaped?'

'I was on a work commando at the Sicmens factory. One day they took us westwards. I think they were afraid that the Russians were coming.' She shrugged and looked out of the window. The outer suburbs of London – rows of semi-detached houses – gave way to fields and farms. Low hills and the occasional spinney. A small, delicate landscape.

'How did you get away?'

Marian thought about the matter. The question implied that escape was something willed, planned, decided. But nothing was planned and every moment was a moment in which you might die; that moment of escape as much as any other. She sucked in smoke and coughed again. 'We were being marched along this road . . .' Not *this* road running through the Chiltern Hills, but another road crossing cold flats, rimed with ice and brushed over with snow. Not a decorative little wood on one side but a dark forest straddling the way ahead. 'There was an aircraft. American, British, I don't know. Two engines, I remember it had two engines. It came down low and fired at us. And in the chaos we escaped. Three of us. Others . . .' Others were killed. Others died. Others vanished from her own little world, which now became that of the forests, a place where creatures hid and foraged, and died or survived according to laws that were impossible to determine. The laws of chance or nature or something. 'We spent some days in the woods and then hitched a lift on a Red Cross lorry. They took us to the Americans.'

'Do you know anything about any of our other girls?'

'Yvonne.'

'Baseden?'

'Rudellat. Yvonne Rudellat. She was there in the camp. She wasn't in my block but I saw her from time to time. She was using another name.'

'Another name?' Atkins had taken a notebook from her respirator bag.

'Jacqueline . . .'

'That was her field name.'

'But she called herself Jacqueline. I don't remember the surname. Galtier, something like that. Gaudier, perhaps. But she left the camp earlier, I think it was in February. I don't know where they went. People said some kind of convalescent camp. That was the rumour. We envied them.'

Atkins wrote: *Jacqueline Galtier? Gaudier? February.* 'Any others?'

'I heard stories. They said there was someone held in solitary, in the bunker. That was the rumour. A British parachutist, people said. Winston Churchill's daughter was one of the stories. Odille? I don't remember exactly.'

'Odette? She was arrested with Peter Churchill. Perhaps it was her.'

'Perhaps.'

'Anyone else?'

★   ★   ★

If she stares out of the window perhaps the questions will stop. There have been so many questions. The American intelligence officer asked her questions, dozens of questions that referred to a time that seemed so distant as to belong to another person in a different world. She had wanted those questions to stop but they kept on mercilessly:

'How did you get to France?'

'I jumped.'

'Jumped?'

'Parachute. I parachuted.'

'When was this?'

When was it? Time was dilated, the whole of her previous life compressed into a few moments, the last year in the camp stretching out into decades. 'I don't recall. October, I think. The October moon. Look it up in your calendar.'

'Last year?'

Was it last year? Days, months stumbled through her brain, the units of misery, the texture of her existence, a medium she struggled through, like wading waist deep through icy water. 'The year before. Nineteen forty-three.'

'You parachuted into France in the *fall of forty-three*?' There was incredulity in his tone. 'Where was this exactly?'

'The south-west. North of Toulouse. I forget the name of the place . . .'

'And who sent you?'

'I can't tell you that.'

'Why not?'

'Because it's secret. If you contact British intelligence they'll confirm my story. Please, do that. Please. I beg you.'

'And then you were arrested. Where was that?'

'In Paris. Near Paris, not *in* Paris. At a railway station.'

'Name?'

She shook her head. 'I forget. If you show me a map, maybe then . . .'

But he hadn't fetched a map. Instead he'd sent her to the place they were holding dozens of women, a whole congeries of women, women weeping and complaining, women arguing and shouting, women picking lice from each other's hair, women sitting huddled in corners waiting as they had waited for so long. 'I shouldn't be here,' she complained to one of the guards. 'I'm a British intelligence agent. I should be sent to the nearest British headquarters.'

The guard had looked at her with pity, as though she was mad.

'No one else,' she told Atkins. 'At least, I don't think so. There were thousands in the camp. Tens of thousands, maybe hundreds, I don't know . . . I don't know anything very much . . .'

'Perhaps later, when you're rested.'

Rested. It seemed so unreal, the idea of rest. When your life had been either sleep or waking, the one annihilation, the other a kind of hell, rest seemed a state of unimaginable delight. Hell or Hades? Hades was cold, wasn't it? Her father knew

24

that kind of thing. Hades, cold; Hell, hot. So both those places, Hell and Hades. And sleep was heaven.

They drove on towards Oxford, the conversation desultory, as though the two of them were vague acquaintances who knew little about each other; or relatives who knew too much. There were questions she should ask – what happened to Benoît? What happened to her whole circuit? And Yvette, what happened to her? – but somehow she couldn't formulate them into words. They lay there in her mind, ghosts of questions, mere phantasms skulking around her brain.

Where was she going?

She had to keep reminding herself – she was going home, wherever that was.

They passed a sign saying Stokenchurch and she wondered what a stoken church might be. There would be some arcane meaning. All place names meant something. Even Ravensbrück must mean something. Rabensbrück, maybe: the bridge of ravens, across which ravens walk into hell. There were crows picking at the fields, crows or rooks. Once she knew the difference. Her father had explained. Rooks were more social animals, he told her. They had bare faces which made it better for them to root around in rotting corpses, which was what they did, just like people in the camp. Carrion feeders. Ravens as well.

'Anyway,' Miss Atkins said, 'at least you are back.'

'Yes.' What was the expression? *Back from the*

dead. But she didn't say it because it sounded melodramatic. Instead she said, 'I wasn't Marian Sutro, did I explain that? I was Geneviève Marchal. She died of pleurisy and I swapped names. That was how I survived. Someone else dying for me.'

'Well, now you are Marian Sutro once again.' As if to confirm this remarkable resurrection, Atkins opened her case again and produced an identity card and two ration books. For the first time she smiled. 'And you've got these to prove it. Don't worry, they're genuine.'

It was a joke. She smiled. Cautiously, Marian opened the identity card. The photo looked back at her from the past – a thoughtful face she barely recognised. Almost beautiful. She had almost been beautiful. The realisation was a small shock. 'I don't look like this any more.'

'You will soon enough.'

'Will I?' She stared out of the window, through the vague reflection of her present face, and wondered where that girl had gone and what she had been replaced with. 'So what'll happen now?'

'Once you've rested we'll have you up to London to get the medics to check you over and to have a bit of a talk. Eventually, you'll have to write a report. We'll want to know exactly what happened. How you were arrested, how you were treated. Where you went, all that kind of thing.'

Marian shook her head at the passing fields. 'I'd rather forget.' But instead, insistently, the other memory of the other car is there – a narrow, black

26

car with chevrons on the radiator. A Citroën Traction. The same interior smell of leather and cigarettes but supplemented by sour sweat. And the perfume of the Alsatian woman, who turns round in the front passenger seat to look back at her. 'You think you're clever,' the woman says. 'But you've just been lucky. Up to now.'

'Where are you taking me?'

The woman doesn't reply. Her thin smile is like a hairline fracture in bone.

'Where are you taking me?'

The woman turns back and stares through the windscreen at the road ahead.

'Where are you taking me?'

No one answers. Marian can taste blood from her split lip. The men crammed in on either side of her shift their backsides on the leather seat. The car crosses the river and threads its way through a town. Orléans, she knows that. The Maid of Orleans. La Pucelle. Jeanne d'Arc.

Slowly, with the inexorable logic of physiology, her bladder fills.

'I need the lavatory.'

No answer. They are out of the town now, driving on through the flatlands south of Paris, a forest on the left and the road dead straight and empty but for the occasional horse-drawn cart or stuttering *gazogène*. She repeats her demand, insistently, like a child shouting at its mother. 'I need to have a pee. Do you understand? A piss. Otherwise I'll just go here in the car.'

It's the woman who finally relents. 'Pull over where you can,' she tells the driver.

The vehicle slows and comes to a halt. They are somewhere in France, somewhere on a long empty road with a line of poplar trees through which the breeze seethes like the sea raking a shingle shore. Marian holds out her hands. 'You'll have to take the handcuffs off. How am I meant to do anything if my hands are tied?'

'Be careful,' the Alsatian woman warns them. 'She's a dangerous bitch.'

The man on her left unlocks one of the handcuffs and clips it to his own wrist, then pushes her out of the car. The other is already out with his pistol drawn and pointing at her. Any chance of escape has vanished. Manacled to her guard she turns away and uses her free hand to pull her knickers down. The men watch. The woman smokes. Marian squats to let go a stream of yellow piss into the grass and down into the ditch. One of the men, the one who had hit her round the mouth, says something to the other. She only catches some of the words – *eine geile Fotze* – but she can guess the rest, more or less. There is laughter – that particular male kind of laughter, smeared with dirt. She tries not to appear to understand. Her knowledge of German may be an advantage, to be kept secret. Awkwardly she straightens up and pulls up her knickers. They bundle her back into the car and the journey continues.

For a while she sleeps, her head rocking from side to side with the motion of the vehicle, at one point resting on the shoulder of one of the men beside her. She wakes with a start and snatches herself upright.

He smiles. She looks away, past the other man, out of the window. Paris is coming upon them by stealth: houses, villages merging into suburbs, warehouses becoming factories, railway lines converging into shunting yards; and then familiar buildings standing shoulder to shoulder along the boulevards, tall blocks with mansard roofs. There is a glimpse of water as they cross the river, a glimpse of the Bois on one side, and suddenly through the windscreen, down converging parallels of trees, a view of the Arc. She knows where they are, the exact address to which they are going: 84 Avenue Foch. Paris Headquarters of the Sicherheitsdienst, the SD, the intelligence agency of the SS. She knows the addresses and the organisations – the Geheime Staatspolizei, the Abwehr – their uniforms, their ranks, their characteristics. Hours of lectures at Beaulieu have given her this, the intricate theology of enemy intelligence.

'My parents. Do they know I'm coming?'

The road passed through woods and breasted an escarpment, winding downwards to the plain below. She'd forgotten the smallness of England, its vulnerability. A small country of which she knew almost nothing.

'I telephoned them as soon as we had news of your arrival. I'd already written, when we first heard you were safe.'

'So they'll be expecting me.'

'Of course they'll be expecting you.'

'And my brother?'

'I'm sure they'll have told your brother.'

She thought for a while. 'It's going to be more difficult with family,' she said. 'With people who know me.'

'You'll find your feet soon enough.'

Find your feet. The feet were the most important part of the body, much more important than your brain. Women had scratched each other's eyes out over a pair of boots. In the evenings they unwrapped their feet and washed them with what little water there might be. Washed each other's feet, often. Tenderly. With love. Like Christ. Your feet were your life. With your brain you could only think, but if you had your feet you could work and if you could work you might survive.

The journey went on. There were houses now, the outskirts of Oxford, the road dropping down Headington Hill to the river. There was Magdalen Tower from where she had heard the choristers sing on May Morning in the second year of the war, a piece of England that she had barely understood at the time and understood even less now, a place of picture postcards, not a home. Bicyclists besieged them in the High Street and the Cornmarket. St Giles spread open as wide as a

Paris boulevard; and then they were on the Banbury Road and turning into the street that she had last seen in the early autumn of 1943, thinking that she might be away a few months, that she was going on the greatest adventure imaginable, that she would live or die. Instead she had achieved something different: neither death nor life but an existence between the two states, a kind of limbo.

The car slowed, turned into a gravel drive and came to a halt. Marian peered up at red brick and steeply pitched roofs, at a hint of turret, a suggestion of gargoyle, the intimation of an ogee window. She tried to evoke a sense of familiarity from the stew of her memory but the place remained strange to her – her family had only lived here for eighteen months and it had never become home, not in the way the house in Geneva had been home, not imbued with memory so that somehow you were moulded to it and it to you.

'Here we are,' said Atkins, as if to remind her.
'Of course.'

The driver came round and helped her out. She stepped onto the gravel just as the front door opened like some device in a stage set, to disclose her parents, or some simulacrum of her parents artificially aged as though for a theatrical perform-ance, her father quite grey and stooped, her mother small and stout where once, Marian supposed with a sudden rush of understanding, she had been petite and voluptuous.

There was an awkward moment of greeting, the

pair shuffling round her, neither knowing which one should embrace their daughter first. And she didn't know how to respond, how to conduct herself, how to navigate the treacherous waters of familial discourse. Two years had been enough to kill any instinct she may have possessed. 'Papa,' she said. '*Maman.*'

They fussed around her and made small exclamations of surprise and simulated delight and barely disguised shock – 'You're so thin. Frank, *elle est tellement maigre!*' – and kissed her as though she were made of something fragile and frangible whereas she was, Marian knew, as tough as rope.

'This is Miss Atkins,' she said, pulling away.

Atkins smiled. The smile never spread to her eyes. It was a social convention, like shaking hands. 'I'm glad I can deliver her back to you,' she told them. 'She's been very courageous. We're very proud of her. And now I have to get back to London, so I'll leave her in your care for the moment.' She might have been speaking of an invalid.

PARIS, NOVEMBER 1943

There are five floors to 84 Avenue Foch. With a man on either side to hold her arms she climbs the stairs, crosses expansive landings, passes reception rooms and drawing rooms, climbs smaller stairs to the narrower purlieus of the fifth floor where a central corridor runs beneath the mansard roof. Doors on either side give onto small rooms where servants once lived, the maids and the valets.

At the desk she is booked in as though it's a *pension* and she is staying the night.

'Name?'

'Follette, Laurence.'

'Documents?'

'They're in my handbag.'

Her escort places her handbag on the desk like evidence. They tip the contents out and make a meticulous list of all that is there, a pathetic heap of possessions that suddenly mean nothing at all. With two careful fingers, as if it might be contaminated, the man at the desk opens the identity card. Her photograph looks up at him, her right cheek just kissed by the edge of the Préfecture de

Police stamp. Carefully he copies the details. *Nom* . . . *Prénoms* . . . *Profession* . . . *Né le* . . . *à* . . . all the little lies scrupulously copied into his register.

'Your coat.'

She surrenders her overcoat. Someone goes through the pockets and comes up with a brown capsule of rubber, her L capsule, her lethal pill, the route to nirvana, which would have denied them everything. 'Why the hell didn't you search her properly?' the man at the desk demands of her escort, displaying the evidence in the palm of his hand. 'She could have swallowed it and we'd have a fucking corpse on our hands.'

Her escort make their excuses. The bitch was manacled. They had her held on both sides. She couldn't have done anything. And all the while the bitch stares straight ahead, as though she doesn't understand what they are saying. Better keep her German to herself. Better keep everything to herself that she can. Soon she will have nothing she can call her own except what is inside her head, and they'll try and take that from her just as surely as they are taking everything else, the litter of things in the handbag, the tube of lipstick, the nail file, the handkerchief, the powder compact of nine carat gold that Vera gave her at that moment in the barn at Tempsford when they said goodbye and wished her *merde alors!*

Merde indeed. Deep in it.

When the reception is complete they push her

into an empty room halfway down the corridor and slam the door shut. There's a bed and bedside table, a chair and a washbasin. The window looks out over rooftops and down into an inner court-yard. She can raise the pane a few centimetres before it blocks. Cool air comes in through the gap – a fragile contact with the outside world. Beyond the glass is a wire grille.

She sits on the bed and waits, thinking of a whole rush of things. How did they know to wait for her at the station? Had someone betrayed her or was it just a fluke, one of those things you cannot predict, cannot guard against? Thoughts and emotions merge, the one generating the other, fear awaking ideas of pain, anger evoking questions that have no answer: how did they know? how could they have known? Then: what about her cover story? Is there any point in that? Laurence Follette. That is what they have written into the register but it is not what the Alsatian woman called out as she dozed on the bench, waiting for the Toulouse train. Marian? she called out. Marian Sutro? Only Yvette knew that. But Yvette didn't know she'd be at the station of Vierzon. So why were they there? How much do they know? What do they know? Logical questions that will soon be lost in a world that has no logic.

She sits on the bed and waits. No one knows she is here. She is detached from her circuit, on her own and adrift in this murderous sea. No one knows and no one will ever know. The extraneous noises – people coming and going, doors opening and closing, the occasional snatch of conversation, the distant and irritant sound of a gramophone – all conspire to heighten her feeling of isolation. Outside there is a world going on. Inside there is nothing but these walls, this bed with a plain bedside table and a single chair.

In the early evening they bring food: a bowl of soup and a plate of lamb cutlets, carrots and boiled potatoes. She hasn't eaten so well since coming to Paris but what this excellent food signifies is unclear. No one talks to her. No words beyond the necessary minimum are uttered. 'What am I doing here?' she asks, but the man who attends to her offers no answer. When she demands to go to the lavatory he takes her to the end of the corridor and stands with the door open, watching.

'I need some privacy.' She says it in French but he just stares at her as if he hasn't understood a word. *'Privat?'* she tries, choosing her German carefully so as not to betray her true knowledge of the language. *'Geschlossen?'*

The man glances over his shoulder to see if he is being watched, then pulls the door closed. It's a small victory, the first time she has managed to bend one of them to her will. But what has it gained her? A cubicle smelling of disinfectant with no lock on the inside and a barred window. She squats on the bare porcelain and feels the world close in on her, a universe as narrow as a rat trap. Within a minute the guard is hammering on the

36

door and shouting, '*Dépêchez-vous!*' and pushing the door open just as she is pulling up her knickers. '*Komm!*' He grabs her arm and marches her back to her cell.

The first night is spent in a limbo of expectancy. She lies down on the bed in her petticoat and pulls the single blanket over her and imagination does its work, conjuring devils out of the dark. Sleep comes in snatches so her fantasies are magnified by repetition, each awakening being signalled by a renewed fear. When she sleeps she dreams, and the dreams are uniform in giving her hope that is dashed by each waking: she dreams of home, of safety and security, and she awakes always to this small space, this bare room in the attic of a town house in Paris, this anteroom to a universe she cannot yet comprehend.

HOME

They stood in the porch and watched the Humber ease its way out of the drive. Marian's mother held one of her hands and rubbed it as though it were cold. 'So thin,' she repeated.

'Don't fuss, *Maman.*'

'They treat prisoners of war like this?'

'I wasn't a prisoner of war, *Maman.*'

'What were you, then? A prisoner. It was war. Weren't you some kind of soldier? Weren't you?'

Her father muttered something about the Geneva Conventions, as though he were still there at the League of Nations, mouthing words of peace and rationality while the whole civilised world collapsed around him. She turned away from the discussion and made her way inside.

The smell of the house was familiar. She had so long been anaesthetised to smell, desensitised to corruption and decay. Shit had meant nothing to her; a swimming soup of diarrhoea alive with worms, nothing; the stink of blood and vomit, the pungent stench of decaying flesh, crawling with dying lice, nothing – and yet she could smell this scent, which was the scent of her own being and the people she had come from. Family. She felt the smell envelope her.

'I'll make a pot of tea,' her mother was saying. 'You take her through to the sitting room, Frank. See that she's comfortable.'

'I think I'd like a bath first. And a change of clothes.'

'Of course.' Her mother looked her up and down. 'Put some proper clothes on, not those dreadful things. I'll bring the tea up. Go with her, Frank. See she's all right.'

'I'm perfectly capable of looking after myself, *Maman*. Please don't fuss. And there's no need to bring anything up.'

'Go easy on the hot water, Squirrel,' her father called after as she climbed the stairs. 'Usual shortages, I'm afraid. Meant to be no more than five inches, although no one will be watching.'

Her bedroom was a sanctuary, full of things forgotten and things dreamed of but never longed for. Early in her captivity she learned that – never long for what you will never have. Your treasure became a scrap of cloth, a hair pin, a splinter of wood, your spoon; never things like these, carefully folded into drawers, laundered and perfumed with lavender, or hung like flayed skins in the quiet shadows of a wardrobe. Her mother had kept everything like a shrine to a dead daughter. But the dead had been resurrected after a fashion and now she looked at her things in wonder, took them out and held them against her to see how she looked in the long mirror. That was a shock. She had not seen her image, not the whole length of her, in almost two years. Curious, she pulled her beret off. Her hair was growing back. You might call the cut *gamine*, if the word or the style meant anything in England. Weeks ago she had just looked bald.

She put the dresses aside and took off her clothes. The naked creature in the looking glass was a caricature of the woman who left this room two years earlier, an anatomical model showing the joints and bones and sinew but little of the substance. 'You're not as bad as many I've seen,' the Red Cross doctor had told her. Inured to being naked before strangers, she had stood before him without shame while he listened to her breathing, tapped her back and front, placed a stethoscope on her chest to hear her heart, and on her belly to hear the movement of her bowels, then put her on the scales to weigh her. They'd given her some pills and calcium tablets, ointment for the sores on her legs. 'Just eat sensibly. Not too much meat, not too much of anything. Lots of starch and fresh vegetables and fruit if you can get them. You'll be right as rain in a few weeks.'

She wrapped herself in her dressing gown and padded quietly to the bathroom where she drew a bath much deeper than five inches, and washed, slowly and methodically, as though she might rid herself of the stink of the camps. But the smell remained there inside her, a fetid, sour reminder of what had been.

As she was drying, her mother knocked on the door. 'Are you all right, darling? Can I come in?'

There was a moment of panic. 'No, *Maman,* you cannot. Please don't fuss. I'll be down in a sec.'

She waited for her mother's footsteps on the stairs before opening the door. Back in her room she searched for underwear that would fit. The flannel underpants provided by the Red Cross were a novelty, a luxury, the first proper underwear she had worn in months; but the things she found in her chest of drawers were different, an almost forgotten species of clothing – cotton drawers she must have worn at school, but also pink and blue silk knickers with lace edges and Parisian labels, and brassieres designed to contain full breasts, not the shrunken paps that she possessed now. She tried on whatever fitted her and stuffed the brassiere cups with handkerchiefs, then found a floral frock with padded shoulders that gave her a bit of bulk and a fullness in the upper arms that suggested flesh where there was none. In the long mirror she looked thin, but no longer skeletal. The light jersey seemed to float around her, barely touching her flesh. Dressed properly for the first time in over a year, she felt naked.

She crept downstairs. In the drawing room she discovered her parents sitting among the teacups and the questions. What did they do to you? What

41

was the camp like? How did you manage? How did you survive? Questions that had no answers. 'I really don't want to talk about it,' she told them. 'I just want to get on with things. They'll want me in London—'

'In London?'

'I'll have to write a report. And . . .' She cast around vaguely, unsure what would be required of her.

'There'll be trials,' her father said. He had been on the telephone, calling on former colleagues. 'War crimes. They cannot be allowed to get away with what they've done. And they'll need witnesses.'

'Witnesses? I don't want to be a witness. I want to get on, not look back.' She handed her ration books to her mother. 'You'll need these, won't you, *Maman*? I've forgotten how everything works. Do you still have to register with each shop? Anyway, Vera thought of everything, as you can see. She's like that. Now tell me all your news. Tell me about Ned. How is he? Does he know I'm back?'

Her mother made that little moue of disapproval that she always showed when her son was mentioned. 'He's still the same. Barely lets us know what's going on. But your father wrote to him when we heard about you. He sent a postcard in return.' She handed it to her daughter like a barrister showing evidence to a witness.

Marian looked at her brother's familiar scrawl. Whatever he wrote was barely legible, as though words were a mystery to him. *Good. Tell her to get in touch when she's back.* That was all. 'Typical Ned.' It was a relief to laugh, a comfort to be back within the small, pointless difficulties of family life. 'And Uncle Jacques and all the family. Have you heard from them? Are they all right?'

'We've had a couple of letters. Everyone's all right. There's even been a suggestion that I should go and visit, but of course travel is still a problem. When it's all over, we'll go, won't we, Frank?'

When it's all over. You didn't need to say what. It seemed an impossible fantasy, to return to France in safety.

PARIS, NOVEMBER 1943

Breakfast is a bowl of milky coffee – real coffee – and two slices of toast with jam. She washes in the basin and, when she asks, someone takes her down the corridor to the lavatory again. Then she is back in her cell but this time the waiting time is short, for after a few minutes the door is unlocked once more and two men in grey overalls grab her and hurry her downstairs to the floor below, to a blank room furnished only with a zinc bath in the middle of the floor and a single wooden chair. Standing beside the chair is a small man with slicked back hair and a narrow face. He smiles and invites her to sit. The questions begin, questions floating on a threat of violence, the men waiting just out of her field of vision, the bath tub there in front of her.

Who is MECHANIC?

Who was the passenger in the aircraft?

When did you come to France?

Who were you going to meet in Toulouse?

She is wearing her blouse and skirt but she feels naked beneath their collective gaze.

Who is MECHANIC?

I don't know what you mean.

Who was the passenger in the aircraft?

I don't know what you are talking about.

When did you come to France?

I've always been in France.

Who were you going to meet in Toulouse?

I wasn't going to meet anyone.

When it comes, the change is sudden. Perhaps the man nodded. Perhaps he gave some kind of signal. But she didn't really notice. Just that, without any apparent warning, she's grabbed by the arms and lifted out of the chair and propelled towards the bath tub. Someone takes the neck of her blouse from behind and drags it down over her shoulders.

The tub is half full of water. It looks innocent enough. You might imagine a mother bathing a baby there, dipping her elbow to test the temperature. Marian is as helpless as a baby in the hands of these two men. Helpless and hapless as they hold her over the water.

'So,' says the interrogator. His French is good but the 'So' is entirely German. Zo. 'Who is MECHANIC? We know he is the man whom you dispatched to England. But who is he?'

'I don't know who he is.'

'But you must know who he is. You were most friendly with him. Affectionate.'

And instantly she understands the implications of what he has said. She tries to turn her head to look at her questioner but his hands grab her by the hair and hold her steady, facing forwards. 'How do you know that?' she asks. 'How do you know what we did or didn't do? How do you *know* we were affectionate?'

There is a silence. She needs to see his expression, but she can't. Her head is held as though in a clamp and all she can see is bare wooden floorboards, the zinc bath tub, the shimmering surface of water. 'Marian,' the man whispers, 'we know so much, so much. We know about Miss Atkins and we know about Buck. We know all your little London secrets. We know about the Orchard. We know everything about your organisation, where it works and what it is called. Now tell me, who was this man called MECHANIC?'

She says nothing.

It happens in an instant. No warning, no noise from the man behind her. One moment she is held there between the two men, facing the tub; next she is propelled forward and upended into the water.

The shock of cold. She holds her breath. Of course she holds her breath. Hands hold her down. The residue of air shortens. Still the hands hold her down. Although she doesn't want to, she struggles. Still the hands hold her down. And then she feels she is bursting and the air is fighting to get out of her and bubbles appear at her nostrils and her struggling expands to occupy the whole of her body. It isn't breathing *in* that matters, it is breathing *out*, getting rid of the exhausted air inside her, purging herself of its filth.

Then she is out and gasping, like a fish on the deck of a fishing boat. Soaking wet and gasping for the blessed benison of air.

And then she is back in. No option, no question, no warning. Back in. A gust of water in her face. She's drowning. Air and water blend in nose and mouth. Airways are waterways. Her lungs are riven with pain. Her mind, if she has a mind, is empty of everything but the terror of water and the fight for air.

She's out, gasping, vomiting, tearing at the small fraction of air she is allowed, grabbing bites of it like someone starved snapping at chunks of bread.

'Who is MECHANIC?'

'Where is your wireless?'

'What were you doing in Paris?'

Then she is back in the water. Air and water have become one thing, an element you desire and abhor, life and death. Her eyes bulging, her heart pounding, her mind drawing down to the narrow dimensions of survival. She is going to die.

Then out again, on her knees before the tub, held by the hands, breathing in and breathing out at the same time, convulsions of breath that seem to jam the air and water in her windpipe. And a moment's glimmer of coherent thought gives her one idea: she will drown herself. As she goes in the next time she'll draw a lungful of water and she will die.

'All you need to do is tell us who MECHANIC is. And then all this will stop.'

47

She gives no answer.

The hands plunge her forward. She will draw in a lungful of water and she will die. The water comes up and hits her face and the truth is made manifest: she cannot. She cannot force herself to drown. It is against the merciless logic of physiology. You fight for breath. You fight to keep the water out, you fight against the wall of water for as long as you have oxygen in your blood and in your brain. The laws of nature are immutable.

They heave her out once more and she is gushing water, vomiting water, exhaling water, fighting for air. She is an aquatic creature out of her element, dying on the dry land. She is dying and she wants to die and she cannot die.

'Who is MECHANIC?'

'Where is your wireless?'

'What were you doing in Paris?'

She lifts her hand. Gasping and gagging, she lifts her hand.

The men wait, watching. She is an aquatic beast lying in her own water, a fish flapping at the bottom of the boat. The words come out in bits: 'Place. De. La. Con. Trescarpe. Café. De la. Contrescarpe.'

They wait. 'Go on,' the man says softly. 'Take your time.'

'Radio,' she says. 'In the. Bathroom. The basement. In the bathroom. In the basement. The people there . . .'

'What about the people there?'

'They don't . . . know . . . anything. They don't know . . . anything about it.'

She has bought time with a fragment of truth. That is how she must live, feeding them fragments of truth.

Some hours later they return. She can tell the difference in the mood. 'This!' the man shouts at her. 'This!' He holds his hand out to display the two radio valves. 'Where is the radio? I want to know where you have put the *radio*.'

'It was there,' she tells them. 'Really, it was there. Someone must have found it. How can I help that?'

The blows begin. If it had been the *baignoire* she would not have been able to withstand it. But instead it is blows, slaps, punches and, when she falls to the floor, kicks to the head and kidneys. Perhaps things are breaking inside, she cannot tell. But she can withstand the hitting and the punching, she can place herself outside and watch it happening. The *baignoire* was different. It worked at the very fabric of her being, inciting her body to fight for life even as she willed it to end. But being hit is different. Pain is different. You can move through the agony into a world of detachment, above and beyond your assailants. Bloody of body, you can become bloody-minded.

'Marian,' the man says, putting out his hand and touching her on the cheek where it's bruised.

A different man, in a different room, one of those on the top floor just along from her cell. There are two chairs and a table. She is sitting in one of the chairs but he has come round to stand near her, to bend down and stroke her cheek. His fingers are soft, like a woman's. She wonders – one of those erratic, divergent thoughts – whether he plays a musical instrument. The piano, perhaps. His long, delicate fingers. Or maybe he's a surgeon, his hands softened like a girl's through over-washing. Scrubbing up, isn't that what it's called? 'Marian, what have they done to you?'

It was different when they were hitting her or when they were trying to drown her. There was something despicable about all that, something craven. And if you could despise them you could attempt to bear the pain or the gasping for air. But this man gently fingers the bruises round her eyes, touches the cut on her cheekbone and comes away with a smear of her blood. Lifting her chin he turns her head so that she has to look up at him. He is wearing eau de cologne. She can smell it. He has a kindly, thoughtful face, a look you might trust. She wants comfort from him, the touch of his hand, the consolation of his voice. And she wants him to kiss her. She wants to see him stoop towards her and touch her bruised and swollen lips with his. She wants him to lift her skirt and touch her there. She wants to please him.

'I promise you, Marian,' he says. 'I won't let them do anything like this to you again. As long

50

as you give me something to go on. I must have something to show them, something to convince them.' He strokes her cheek. 'It's us against them, Marian. Us against them.'

There's a pause while he draws up a chair and sits opposite her, close to her, leaning towards her and holding both her hands. 'Now,' he says gently, 'let's see if we can't sort some things out. First, the man you called MECHANIC in your final transmission. The one you made in clear. The man you took all the way to the landing ground. Tell me about him. Were you and he friends?'

She must give him something. In return for his kindness, in return for not sending her back to the other man, in return for being her protection. 'Friends, yes.'

'Were you perhaps, lovers?'

LONDON

Days of dreams. Nights of nightmare. Most of the time she kept to her own room, reading and sleeping. She found the bed too soft to sleep. Instead she lay on the floor with a blanket pulled over her, and then when she woke in the early morning she had to mess up the bed to make it look as though she had slept the whole night there. When she came down to meals her parents watched her closely, as if she were a newly acquired animal and they weren't sure what to feed her.

'You must eat,' her mother insisted. 'You must build yourself up.'

'I'm just not hungry.'

When she slept, her dreams seemed real; when she awoke the world appeared dreamlike, remote and alien, as though she was watching it all through a sheet of plate glass, as though it was happening somewhere else and to someone else. Someone came to visit – a cousin, an aunt – and she stayed closeted in her room.

After a few days – had it been the weekend? – the organisation sent a car, complete with FANY

52

driver and a conducting officer, to take her up to London, to the Central Medical Establishment in Cleveland Street where the medics were waiting for her. They X-rayed her chest and then attached her to a machine that produced a trace of her heart activity. Naked, she felt no shame. Shame was a luxury that had vanished long ago. Perhaps it would return with time and care but for the moment she lay there, gaunt and sinewy, her breasts mere pouches on the basket of her ribs, her belly a withered hollow, while the doctor hummed and hahed and prodded her here and there and listened through a stethoscope to whatever was happening inside. The sores on her legs and chest were caused by hypovitaminosis. They were getting better, weren't they? And her cough was nothing. It would be gone in no time. There was nothing on the X-ray to worry about.

The idea of a cough being nothing seemed remarkable – where she had come from a cough could be a death sentence.

'What about my periods? I haven't had a period since . . .' She could barely remember. Some time in prison. When was that? Years ago, centuries ago, that golden age.

'Oh, they should start again now your diet is back to normal.' He talked about a convalescent home, a place they'd set up where they could keep an eye on things.

'I don't want a convalescent home. I'm not ill, am I? I want to be with my family.'

He tapped his pencil on the blotter in front of him and chewed his lips thoughtfully. 'Perhaps that's the best thing under the circumstances. You'll have to have regular check-ups but considering the circumstances you are reasonably fit. I'll prescribe vitamin and mineral pills. Otherwise, just eat a normal, healthy diet. You'll get a ration supplement, of course. I'm pretty sure we'll be back to normal soon enough.'

We. Why did doctors so often resort to the collective pronoun? As if they might be able to bear some of the burden.

'You're due to see the dentist next and then I've got you down to have a chat with the trick cyclist.'

It was a joke but she didn't understand it. 'Psychiatrist,' he explained.

'*Psychiatrist?* Am I mad?'

'Good lord, no. Perish the thought. But you ought to see a specialist, to help you adjust.'

The visit to the dentist was less comforting – her teeth were decalcified, one or two compromised. They would have to be extracted.

'Will it show when I smile?' she asked, unsmiling. But the dentist smiled back. 'Don't worry, there are excellent prostheses these days. The men will still come flocking.'

The psychiatrist was a Group Captain, 'a neuropsychiatrist, as a matter of fact, but don't let that frighten you. It's just a fancy title, that's all.' He only wanted a chat really, about life in general. How was she sleeping? How was she feeling? Did she feel angry? Miserable? Depressed? Happy? Were there mood swings?

'I don't feel anything much,' she told him. 'I want to, but I don't. I just want to be left alone.'

'I'm sure you do.'

'Sometimes I feel afraid. For no particular reason.'

'That's hardly surprising.'

'And my parents . . .'

'Tell me about your parents.'

'They fuss. I think my father feels guilty that he let me go.'

'I can imagine that.'

'And my mother doesn't seem to understand. Neither of them understands. I just want to be left alone to pick up the pieces.'

'Do you feel you are in pieces?'

'Not *me*,' she snapped. She didn't mean to snap, but that's how it came out. 'Pieces of my old life, I mean. I want to go back to France. I want to see the places and people I loved. I want to love them again . . .'

He waited, head slightly on one side.

'But I don't.'

'Your parents, you mean?'

'Yes, my parents.'

The strange conversation went on. It was not unlike going to confession. She recalled confession from school, when they made up sins so that they had something material to admit to. And now? Where did murder and betrayal feature in the

55

confessional world of this bland neuropsychiatric specialist with his quiet manner and his carefully folded hands? She felt as though she was pared down, her whole personality cut back to a hard kernel, capable only of survival. No emotions, few appetites.

'I tell you what I'll do,' the Group Captain said. 'I'll put you in touch with a colleague of mine in Oxford.'

'Is it necessary? Is there something wrong with me?'

'I'm sure there's not. But you may want to talk things through.' He handed her a visiting card that said *Dr Andrew Morgan, Clinical Psychologist*. There was a little blizzard of letters after the name. FR this, MR that. Do letters equal ability? she wondered. How many letters did Ned trail behind him? Or Clément?

'Dr Morgan's a Welshman, but none the worse for that.' The Group Captain laughed, to show it was a joke. 'Worked with Rivers at Craiglockhart during the last war. Do you know about Rivers?'

She didn't. She didn't know about anything very much.

'Dealt with shell shock. Very advanced for the time. We've gone all American these days and now we call it combat fatigue.'

'I haven't been in combat.'

'It's just another name. Not a very good one. Anyway, I'll write to him so that he knows about you when you get in touch.'

When she was finished there was the car to take her to Baker Street, to number 83, which called itself Norgeby House and bore a discreet plaque on the outside announcing itself as the Inter Services Research Bureau. She had never been here before. She only knew Orchard Court, the flat in Portman Square where F Section always dealt with its agents. Now there was this office block with a uniformed guard and a reception desk and a chit to fill out for visitors, while the conducting officer and the receptionist exchanged a bit of backchat, complaining about working hours.

'It's being so cheerful keeps me going,' the receptionist said. The conducting officer laughed, but Marian missed the joke. It was like listening to humour in a foreign language where you understand the words but not the sense of the thing. Nor did she understand her reception on the second floor where the French Section was housed: as soon as she followed her escort through the door the clatter of typewriters was stilled and people left their desks and stood in the corridor to watch. She felt guilty, as though she had done something wrong and was being called to account and everyone knew. Like in school. Like in a dream, one of those awful nightmares where you find you are naked and walking in public and people stare. But these people were smiling so it couldn't be that bad. There was a smattering of applause, as though she was a star of some kind.

One or two even greeted her by name although she could not, for the life of her, recall who they were. Smiles and handshakes followed her into Colonel Buckmaster's office where he perched on the edge of his desk and looked benevolently on her as though she was a niece who had done something rather splendid, like winning a gymkhana. 'You conducted yourself in the finest tradition of the organisation,' he told her, but how did he know what she had done or how she had done it? And did the organisation have anything like a tradition? It was founded in 1940 and now, its *raison d'être* over, it was all but finished. So there was hardly anything traditional about it, was there?

'What about Le Verger?' Marian asked. 'Orchard Court.'

Colonel Buckmaster gave a little resentful laugh. 'Had to get rid of it. No further use. Now they're trying to push us out of this building as well. It seems they don't want to know us any more. Anyway, you're looking damn good, considering. The medics given you the once over, have they? Everything all right?'

'I suppose so.' She searched for something more to say, thinking of the Orchard Court flat, the meetings with agents that went on there amid the relics of luxury, the constant coming and going overseen by Parks the butler who always tried to separate one operation from another. She and Benoît had found refuge in the bathroom to rehearse their cover stories. She had perched on the edge of the bath, he on the bidet. 'Come on,' he'd said after a while, grinning at her as though the whole thing was a huge joke: 'Let's get out of here and go for a walk.' And they'd walked in Hyde Park and talked and talked and she'd never been happier in the whole of her life.

'What happened to Benoît?'

Colonel Buckmaster looked puzzled. 'Benoît? Do you mean Major Cowburn? How do you know Major Cowburn?'

'I don't know Major Cowburn. I've no idea who Major Cowburn is. I'm talking about Benoît . . .' But she had forgotten his surname. Memories came and went without pattern or logic, as though a premature old age had descended on her. 'He was part of WORDSMITH. We dropped together. And . . .' And what? What should she say? That they slept together? That they were lovers? That he was the man who took her virginity, in that other world where virginity was a concept that meant something, where *pudeur* was still possible and you weren't forced to stand naked in a crowd of naked women while the guards looked on and laughed. 'CÉSAR. His field name was CÉSAR. He hated it.' She tried a shrug but she had lost the knack of it. It felt like some kind of exercise, elevating her bony shoulders to achieve some physical advantage. 'We were friends, that's all.'

'CÉSAR, you say? Let me see.' Buckmaster leafed through some pages in a folder on his desk.

59

'WHEELWRIGHT . . . WIZARD . . . WORDSMITH. Ah, Bérard, is that the fellow?'

'That's right! Benoît Bérard.' Just knowing the name brought excitement. And memory of a kind, a sensation of delight and surprise that had lain dormant for so long. Benoît with his shameless smile. Benoît standing in the bedroom of the flat in Toulouse, stark naked. Benoît lying with her, clinging to her – who was clinging to whom? – calling her Minou and kissing her neck and telling her how lovely she was, how lovely she was, how lovely she was. Benoît deep inside her.

Buckmaster looked up. 'I'm afraid he was killed. In June 1944, just after the invasion. In action.'

'Oh.' The possibility had not occurred to her. She considered it for a moment. Benoît dead. Should she weep? Should she give vent to all those tears unshed for months, the tears that had been impossible when death was a commonplace? But there weren't any tears. None. She was as dry as bone. 'What about the others? What about Le Patron? And the pianist. GEORGETTE, was that her field name? Louise March, wasn't it? What happened to her?' But she didn't care about the others. Benoît was dead. She was indifferent to the fact that WORDSMITH had been a great success, the circuit achieving what had always been intended, harrying the German forces in the southwest in order to prevent their moving northwards towards the Normandy beaches, contributing to

60

the Allied victory by attacking convoys, blowing railway lines, cutting communications. And Benoît killed somehow – Buckmaster didn't know how – in one of those vicious little engagements, the great bull of a Panzer Division being stung by gadflies. Occasionally the flies got swatted. But at least Le Patron and GEORGETTE survived, repatriated in September after triumphant scenes at the liberation of Toulouse. 'That's what they were there for,' Buckmaster said. 'Mission accomplished.'

But what had her own mission been? And had she accomplished it? And Benoît, what about his?

'Yvette? Do you know anything about her?'

'She would be—?'

'Yvette Coombes. MARCELLE was her field name. She betrayed me. I think she betrayed me. Or Gilbert did, the one who arranged the pick-up.' She shrugged. 'Someone did, anyway.'

The mention of betrayal brought its own reward: a stillness, a clearing of a nervous throat. Treachery and the fear of treachery stalked the corridors of the headquarters. There were accusations, there was complicity, there was the desperate scurry of people covering their tracks like cats covering their shit. 'Ah, yes. Of course. MARCELLE.' Miss Atkins was consulted. Was anything known of the fate of Yvette Coombes, wireless operator for the CINÉ-ASTE circuit?

Nothing.

Marian nodded, and stared vacantly out of the window at further windows on the other side of

Baker Street. Lives went on there behind other panes of glass, lives that meant something precise and precious to each owner. It was difficult to imagine what was involved, though. Going to the office, writing papers, making assessments about things, recommendations, decisions, going to lunch, having meetings, returning home in the evening. Greeting the children. Greeting the wife, greeting the husband. The small triumphs and tragedies of domestic life. What people do. Not what Benoît did. Not what Yvette did in the cemetery of Père Lachaise, waiting for her to come while the Gestapo gathered. Not what she herself did, hurrying through the streets of Paris with the wolves all around.

'What are your plans now?' Buckmaster asked, ludicrously. Plans hadn't occurred to her. Plans were what you made when you controlled your own life, not when you lived at the mercy of others.

'I just want to get things back to normal.' But even that was a deception because she didn't know what normal was. She had been a girl barely out of school, and then a trainee, and then a trained agent, and then a killer and then a prisoner in the purlieus of hell. Normality was so long ago that she could barely recall it and certainly couldn't aspire to recovering it.

'By the way,' he added, 'we'll be putting you up for an award.'

'An award?'

'Can't give women medals, I'm afraid. Because

they're not recognised combatants. FANY and all that. So we have to go for a civil list gong. OBE or something.'

'What's an OBE?'

'Officer of the Order of the British Empire. Great honour.'

She contemplated *great honour* in silence while Buckmaster smiled his oily smile and clapped his hands on his knees. 'Well, I won't keep you any longer, Marian. I'm sure other people want to see you.'

'I really don't think I want an award.'

Did she say that or merely think it? Thoughts seemed to take on the strength of spoken statements, as though she had said to all these people what she was thinking – that they were part of a world that had ceased to exist, a world of bumbling possibilities, of meaningless plans and fatuous ideas. She lived, she died, she was resurrected into the real world, which was grey and drab and pointless. In pursuit of pointlessness her round of the offices continued. The finance officer wanted a quick meeting. There were monies due to her – a year and seven months of field pay at the rate of three hundred and fifty pounds per annum, which came to a grand total of five hundred and fifty-four pounds three shillings and fourpence. 'Mustn't forget the fourpence,' the accountant said and she wondered why it was so important to remember the fourpence, before understanding that it too was a joke and she must at least smile. 'Shall I give instructions to have it paid into your bank account? Of course now that you are back with us, you will continue to be paid at the normal rate. As long as you are on the strength.'

He looked round, as though there might be eavesdroppers, then leaned secretively towards her. 'I believe there is also some talk of an ex gratia payment in view of the hardships you have faced but as yet nothing has been decided. I'll let you know.'

He handed her on to Miss Atkins, Vera Atkins, the queen bee sitting in the midst of a hive that was being dismantled around her. Vera was immaculately turned out and yet there was something tawdry about her, as if she had been dressed by the wardrobe department of a repertory theatre and wasn't quite the genuine article. Nicotine-stained fingers shuffled papers on her desk. Smoke and floral perfume clung to her 'You're already looking so much better,' she said. 'Are they looking after you properly?'

'They suggested some kind of convalescent home, but I'm not ill.'

'Of course not.'

'So I'm staying with my brother for the moment. In Bloomsbury.'

'How convenient.' Vera wasn't really the kind of woman for pleasantries or chit-chat. In contrast to Buckmaster's languor she showed a sharp desire to get on with things. 'Tomorrow you've got a meeting in Bayswater with someone from the Security Directorate. If you're feeling up to it.'

'The Security Directorate? What's that?'

'They'll want to know about your arrest, I expect. All very tiresome but they insist. A car will come and pick you up, if you give me your brother's address. And there's this.' She slid a typewritten sheet across the desk. It was a list of names, some of them familiar, some unknown, Yvonne Rudellat's with *Jacqueline Gautier. February left Ravensbrück. Bergen-Belsen?* scrawled in pencil against it, another with *Ravensbrück* against it; and Marian's own was there in the middle. *Returned from captivity, 16 April 1945.*

'Our missing girls. You're the first to come back, as you can see. You mentioned Yvonne. We've now got a report that she may have been moved to Bergen-Belsen. We're looking into that now. I'd like any further information you may recall. Just so we can contact people in the right place. And so that I know where to look when I can get over there.'

'You're going to Germany?'

'Oh, yes, I'm going to find them.'

PARIS, NOVEMBER 1943

'I want you to meet someone,' the gentle man says. She knows his name now. He's called Freund. At least that is what he has told her to call him, but whether he just means that she should see him as a friend, she doesn't know. Although he smiles reassuringly, a part of her – a suppressed, ignored fraction of the frightened mess that is Marian Sutro – knows that he is not a friend, that every suggestion is a threat, every move a potential trap. Despite that she clings to him, feels a leap of delight when he visits her, wants him to touch her, wants him to talk to her and be with her and bring her comfort.

'Who?'

He smiles his lovely smile. 'You'll have to wait and see.'

They take her downstairs. There's a small room, empty but for a chair and a table. She is told to sit and wait. The waiting is the worst thing. Reality is brutal or painful or frightening, but waiting is a distillate of fear that corrodes and dissolves. She wonders who it will be. Her mind goes round the people who know of her presence in the city:

Gilbert, insouciant, careless, apparently at ease with everything he does. *Our air movements man in Paris. Capital fellow.* Or Claire, his assistant, with the remnants of beauty in her face and a hardened cynicism in her heart. Or dull, defensive Marie, the maid who mans the barricades of the Pelletier apartment and goes home every afternoon to attend to her ageing mother. Or Yvette.

Yvette, she decides. Yvette whom she ought to hate for her betrayal, but still loves for her fragile stupidity.

Or Emile, whom she knew in training, perhaps even tiresome Emile who is languishing somewhere in captivity like all the others of his circuit. Any one of these might step through that door.

Or perhaps it is one of the agents who came in with the Lysander – David or . . . the other name escapes her if she ever knew it. Looked like a bandit. Unshaven, moustachioed, wearing a beret.

Or maybe – her imagination shudders at the thought – maybe Clément himself, battered and bruised after being dragged from the wreckage of the plane that was intended to carry him to England. Perhaps that, the ruins of her mission flaunted in her face.

Or even Benoît. How could they have Benoît? Benoît is hundreds of miles away in Toulouse. How could they have him?

But they can do anything, can't they? They have power absolute.

Fantasy plays its callous game, changing one option for another, shuffling the cards, dealing a different combination each time, each one a losing hand.

Yvette. She decides it will be Yvette.

Then the door opens. Even though she is expecting it, the fact of its opening is sudden, a surprise, an abrupt enlargement of her own circum-scribed world, giving her a glimpse of the corridor outside. But most of the view is taken up by the three men standing in the opening. A triad, a hybrid beast, a trinity, a crucifixion with the middle man strung out between two thieves, his arms outstretched, his head hung down. His hair is wet, his shirt and trousers sodden with red. His feet drag behind him like the flippers of a beached fish.

She feels pain, a physical pain at the core of her belly, in her womb.

Someone grabs the crucified man's hair and pulls his head upright for her to see him and, presum-ably, him to see her. As far as he is able.

She looks into the ruined face of the man she knows as Julius Miessen. A potato face. Eyes swollen, cheeks bruised, lips split. Nevertheless she recognises him. His left eye watches her through a slit of swollen tissue.

Freund is there to ask the questions. 'Do you know this man?'

'No.' Which is truth of a kind, a white lie, the kind that carries with it no penalty. She always wondered about that. It seemed like deceiving God.

68

'Are you certain?'

'Yes.'

'This man is a murderer, Marian. Do you know that?'

'No.'

'Well, he is. He has confessed as much. He killed two members of the security forces. In Belleville, a week ago. Shot them down in cold blood.'

Miessen's single eye watches her through its narrow slit. A soul gazing out at someone else in hell. Slowly, lizard-like, he licks his lips.

'He will, of course, be executed for this crime unless new evidence comes to light.'

'I don't know what you are talking about.'

'You were in Belleville that day, weren't you, Marian?'

The lizard eye watches her.

'You were running away from the police. And this man was arrested there, shortly after two policemen were murdered.'

'I don't know what you are talking about.'

'They were shot down in cold blood. Nine milli-metre bullets, one through the left eye, one in the chest. The second man was dispatched with a bullet through the forehead. Expert shooting.'

Twice in her life she has held power of life or death over someone. Once standing there in the impasse in Belleville, facing the two men; and now, facing Julius Miessen. 'I don't know what you are talking about.'

Freund looks at her carefully. He turns from her

to Miessen, looking for a glimmer of a clue, then back to her again. 'Marian, you must be honest with me. Are you certain you know nothing about this killing?'

'I am certain.'

Miessen's single eye watches her, a small jewel of pale blue gleaming between the swollen lids. Can an eye alone have expression? What is it asking, what is it saying?

'What about you?' Freund asks the crucified wreck. 'Do you know this woman?'

There is a pause, as though the question has to go down labyrinthine passageways before it reaches his inner core, and then the answer must retrace the same pathway to register as a reply. His tongue moves to moisten his lips.

'No.'

'So why did you shoot the two police officers?'

Again the long and painful pause. The voice that comes out has a strange dignity to it, as though this is something formal, the kind of thing you might prepare in order to speak before a court. 'It was an act of war.'

'An act of war.'

'Yes.'

'And you don't know this woman?'

'No.'

Freund gives a slight nod and the wreckage that is Julius Miessen is dragged out of the room. The door is closed behind him and she can breathe again.

70

'What will happen to him?'

'What I said. He killed two agents. He will be executed. What do you expect?'

'How do you know it was him?'

'Because he admitted it.'

'You can get someone to admit to anything with your methods.'

'Do you doubt his confession?'

She hesitates a moment. Hesitations are what he thrives on, the small intervals of mendacity. Will he read this hesitation aright and see her lie? 'I don't know anything about it.'

NED

Her brother's flat was just as she remembered it. There was the same sense of impermanence and decay, as though he had bought things hurriedly from a junk dealer and was prepared to get rid of them at a moment's notice. Papers and books were strewn everywhere, records were scattered on the floor beside an ancient gramophone, the remains of a meal littered the dining table. Entropy tends towards a maximum, that was what he always said by way of explanation.

They made themselves some supper – omelettes made with dehydrated egg, a plastic substance called cheese, vegetables called greens. Somehow Ned had managed to conjure up a half bottle of red wine that announced Bordeaux on its label. The wine was brown and oxidised but the alcohol did its trick of lulling her into a sense of security. She talked, more than she ever had done or would do with her parents. Perhaps because it would interest Ned, she talked of the work she had done in the factory attached to the camp, the Siemens factory where they had made, the rumour had it, parts for flying bombs. Ned grew excited, of course.

'What did you do? Can you describe what you did?'

But she had no idea. 'It was soldering, just soldering. Electrical components but I've no idea what they were. You'd have known, I suppose. We did the same thing hour after hour and if they caught you doing it wrong you got beaten and returned to the main camp. One girl tried to sabotage things . . .' She hesitated, remembering – an officer being called, the item being held up, the girl being seized and dragged out. 'She was taken out and beaten unconscious. Not by the Siemens people. By the guards.'

There was a silence while Ned watched her. 'I tried to do everything right,' she admitted.

'Who could blame you?'

She sipped her wine and felt light-headed, as though she had been absolved. Perhaps that was why she mentioned the name that had been in the back of her mind the whole evening. Perhaps the wine had emboldened her. 'Clément,' she said.

Ned gave the little grunt of recognition. 'I was wondering when you'd bring him up.'

'What happened to him?'

'He went to Canada, to Montreal. He's still there as far as I know. They're building a research centre out in the wilds at a place called Chalk River.'

'What kind of research . . .?'

'It's all very secret.'

'But that project? We talked about it, remember? A super bomb. There's been no super bomb, has there? It was all a fantasy, one of your mad ideas.' Emotion began to break through the light-headedness: she felt resentful, as if everything had been Ned's fault. 'I went to France thinking there might be a bomb that would end the war and here we are, fighting to the bitter end.'

'It's not that simple.'

'You seemed to think it was. Did you see Clément? When he got to England, I mean?'

'Briefly. He told me . . .'

'What did he tell you?'

'He told me that the plan was for you to return from France with him. Up until the last moment he thought you were going to get in the aircraft with him. But once you'd got him strapped in you climbed down and left him there. And he didn't know whether to laugh or cry.'

'He said that?'

'His words. No one knew what had happened to you, Squirrel. It was almost a year later that the parents got a letter from some dubious person in Whitehall. "We regret to inform you that we have not had contact with your daughter for some time and must consider her to have been arrested." That sort of thing.' He glanced at her and she saw something like pain in his expression. Pain was not an emotion she expected him to suffer. 'In fact, Squirrel, we rather assumed you were dead.'

There was a silence. 'They arrested me the

morning after Clément left for England,' she said eventually. 'I was waiting on a railway platform, half asleep. I never saw them coming.'

'So you should have gone with Clément, shouldn't you? You could have got away.'

'I suppose so.'

'Father was ill with worry. I almost felt sorry for him.'

'That must have been a novel experience.'

He attempted a laugh. '*Maman* was a pillar of strength but he rather went to pieces. Wouldn't leave his room, wouldn't meet people, spent a lot of time close to tears. Strange how people react in unexpected ways.'

'Why should that make me feel guilty?'

'Does it?'

'A bit.'

'So why the hell didn't you get out when you had the opportunity?' The change in tone was abrupt. That was another of his characteristics: sudden squalls of fury or laughter. Perhaps it was the frustration of being faced with irrational human behaviour. 'Why can't you act *reasonably*?' he would scream when he was a child confronting parental decisions. But it was he who wasn't reasonable, working himself up into a rage at such provocation, going red in the face and throwing things.

She tried to shrug the question away. 'It's hard to explain now. We were on the landing ground in the middle of the night. Somewhere in the Cher

75

Valley, near Tours. The aircraft was standing there ready for take-off and I had to make a snap decision. I decided to go back to my job, the job I'd been sent to do.'

'But you didn't. You got yourself arrested.'

'I couldn't know that at the time, could I? For God's sake, isn't it obvious? I thought I was out of Paris and therefore out of danger.'

'Sounds pretty daft to me.'

'And I wanted to get away from Clément.'

'Get away from him?'

'I thought, if I went with him . . . Oh, I don't know, involvement or something.'

'Involvement?'

'Did he tell you he'd got married? And he's got a baby as well. They're in Switzerland.'

'So why might you have got involved?'

She looked at him, hoping to find understanding in his face, because she had none. What did involvement actually mean? She had forgotten the muddle of emotions that went with it, the fear and thrill of possession. 'Because I slept with him,' she said.

'You *slept* with him?'

'It's what happens, Ned. The tension we were under, the fear of discovery, God knows there were motives enough. Madeleine was in Annecy with his wife and baby, so we were alone together.' She laughed, feeling emotion returning, the first hints of normality. 'Why the hell am I trying to explain? Anyway, I feared what might happen if we went off together. Maybe I'd follow him to Canada. Maybe I'd get pregnant. Maybe he'd be consumed with guilt and dump me. I've got no idea, Ned. You can't predict the future, can you? But you can avoid it.'

Ned didn't say anything. It was almost as though he hadn't understood. Or perhaps he was remembering all those little moments before the war, the small jealousies and triumphs within the little group of friends, the days in Geneva and Annecy, the swimming and the skiing, the games and laughter – fragile moments that seemed, in retrospect, as translucent and brittle as porcelain. 'I suppose I'm not surprised,' he said eventually. 'I remember the way you were with him. And he with you, I guess. So what happens now?'

'Between us? He's three thousand miles away. How can there be anything?'

'When he comes back to Europe?'

'Look, Ned, it was an aberration, the kind of thing that happens in wartime. He's got a wife and child. He'll have to deal with that. And meanwhile, I've . . .' she spread her hands helplessly. 'I've got to get over what's happened. Christ, I'm barely a woman any longer.'

'Don't be stupid.'

'No breasts, no periods, no inclination.'

Her words embarrassed him. He looked round for distraction. 'So what *are* you going to do now, Squirrel? You've said what the parents want you to do but not what *you* want.'

'I don't really know. Once I get my strength back I want to do something useful.'

'That rules out university.'

She laughed, understanding a joke for the first time. 'The thing is, I don't have any skills. Well, I can strip and assemble a Sten gun blindfolded if that's any use. And parachute out of an aeroplane.'

'The circus, maybe?'

Another joke she understood. For a moment they laughed together and it was just like it had been.

DEBRIEF

So there you have her, returned to the bosom of her family, sleeping on the broken-backed sofa in her brother's flat, sleeping fitfully, besieged by dreams of the camp, of rows of huts rendered in grey and brown, a place drowned with rain and populated by shades. Among the prisoners of her dream there were people who had never been there in reality – her parents, her brother, even figures from her past who had no real part in her life: a teacher from her school in Geneva, a nun from her convent school in England, a boy she had once danced with at a party. Yvette Coombes pleaded with her to be her friend but her real friend was someone else, a familiar figure who held her in her arms, her Lagermutter, who looked after her, deloused her head in the evenings, slept beside her, loved her. Véronique.

She woke in the cold dawn, with the disappearing shadow of Véronique's body against her and the usual sounds in her ears, the banging of tin canteens, the shuffling of feet, the slop of a thin gruel, all of these transforming slowly and painfully into the sound of Ned banging around in the kitchen next door. And Véronique vanished.

'I've got a lab meeting this morning,' Ned said when she appeared at the kitchen door. 'Will you be all right?'

'There's a car coming for me. They want to debrief me. Sounds a bit strange. Like taking your knickers down.' It was the first joke she had made in more than a year.

The debriefing was in an anonymous building in Queensway. Debriefing is a good name, suggesting the reverse of something positive, an undoing, a cancellation, as though at the end you might be purged. But of course it wasn't like that at all. It was an interview at best, an interrogation at worst. It is all there on file, a dull, typed transcript that the National Archive stores like it stores so many things, mindlessly and without favour, the words giving nothing of the participants, the gaunt, wary figure of Marian Sutro on one side of the table, with, opposite her, the austere figure of Commander John Senter with his icy white hair and the icy manner of a barrister confronting a suspected child murderer. He was a Scot, from Edinburgh, but there was no gracious Edinburgh exchange of courtesies, no how are you feeling?, nothing that might put you at ease, at least nothing of that kind recorded in the transcript. Just the demand for details that she couldn't remember about events she had forgotten and no longer cared about if

80

she did remember them. That, perhaps, was her defence, the barrier that kept the demons at bay.

Could she outline the events after her arrest in the autumn of 1943? She must understand that this was important, to find out what happened, who was responsible, who might face charges.

'Charges?'

'Criminal charges. The illegal treatment of prisoners. Other offences.'

So she told him, dug up those memories she had buried, quietly, in the dead of night, like a murderer burying a corpse – her arrest on the platform at Vierzon station, the cramped backseat of the Citroën Traction, the drive to Paris – while Senter nodded thoughtfully, occasionally jotting notes on a ringbound pad. On the table between them a wire recorder wound its memory into the future.

Later the same day a car came to pick her up and deliver her back to Oxford where her parents were waiting with that attentive anxiety that annoyed her so. Was she all right? How was she feeling? How had it been?

'All right, I suppose. They wanted me to remember; I just want to forget.'

'Of course you do, of course.'

Her mother had been cooking, as well as she could, seeing that rationing was still in force. There was even wine that her father could obtain from the college cellars. 'Now all you have to do, darling, is rest and recover,' her mother said.

Recover seemed the right word with its hint of covering up, covering over, burying something as absolutely as possible. But the thing buried was always there, waiting for her as she slept, occasionally ambushing her when she was awake. At night she dreamed. She was in the camp, she was in prison, she was running through streets and alleys. People were pursuing her, hunting her, capturing her and locking her away. Sometimes they hit her but the blows brought with them no pain. Sometimes she was with Véronique and the others in the hut, dealing out scraps of food like an impoverished hand of cards; often she was alone, afraid and hungry while everyone around her was happy and content. Sometimes she awoke sweating and shouting, except that it seemed she had made no sound because no one in the house stirred. Through the door to her parents' bedroom she could hear her father snoring. Furtively she crept to the kitchen and discovered bread and margarine, knowing it was for breakfast, knowing she was doing wrong but eating it just the same. Her life depended on it. Once she had finished it, guilt consigned her to a dreamless sleep and a fetid, muggy morning in which she apologised abjectly for her theft during the night like a child caught stealing sweets.

So, like a prisoner gathering scraps of food and squirrelling them away, she began to gather up the fragile pieces of her past to put them back together into some semblance of a personality. She read a lot – but without much concentration – and slept a great deal. During the day she did small things around the house, little tasks that you might give to a child – arranging flowers, making biscuits, some weeding in the garden. Tedium was a positive thing, something to be treasured. It blended with safety and freedom, the circumscribed freedom of going cautiously to the shops with her mother – but waiting outside in case someone should draw her into conversation – or walking in the Parks with her father where it was easier because there were no people to stare at her. It became habitual, this walk, in rain or shine, as far as the River Cherwell before turning for home. He talked of what had been and she talked of what might be – how the old League of Nations had failed and what they needed now was a universal aim and belief, a belief in the rule of the people. No more rich, no more poor, everyone united in a future of shared achievement.

'You sound like a Communist, my dear,' he said.

She thought of Véronique. 'Maybe I am.'

Perhaps to distract from such dangerous ideas he mentioned that they had had a letter from Clément Pelletier.

'From Clément? Why on earth didn't you tell me?'

'I *am* telling you, Squirrel. That's what I'm doing now. It was posted in Canada, sometime last year. He said—'

'What did he say?'

'That he'd seen you in Paris.'

'Yes. Yes, he did.'

'He asked after you. I wrote back but of course I couldn't say because we didn't know anything. And even if we had . . .' His voice trailed away into the silence of official secrets.

'I got Clément out of France,' she told him. 'Did he mention that?'

Her father pondered this information. 'He more or less implied it. I feel he owes you a great debt.'

'I'm not sure what he owes me.' She felt a little snatch of excitement at being owed something, however nebulous. 'Do you still have his address? I'll write to him and tell him I'm back.'

'Your mother will have it somewhere. He was in Montreal, as far as I remember. Your mother always said—'

'What?'

'That he was soft on you. Then there was that business with the letters you wrote to each other when you were at school . . .'

She attempted a careless laugh but the expression didn't really work. Nothing much worked at the moment, all the little gestures of social intercourse felt awkward. 'It was a long time ago, Papa. He's married with a baby now. His wife and child were in Switzerland during the occupation. Probably they're back in France. Maybe he is.'

'Switzerland,' her father echoed, making the name sound like the land of Cockaigne, a place of sweetness and light. 'Maybe we should have stayed there. Maybe that would have been better for all of us.'

'For me, you mean?'

She glanced at him as he walked. In profile his face seemed old, sculpted by worry and age and something else she barely recognised in him: guilt. 'It's my fault, Squirrel,' he confessed. 'I blame myself entirely. I should never have let you go.'

'Don't be silly, Father. It was my choice.'

When they got back to the house her mother searched unsuccessfully for the letter. 'There was another one as well,' she added as she rifled through drawers and pigeonholes in her escritoire. 'I'd quite forgotten. Over a year ago. Now where did I put that one?'

'Another letter from Clément?'

'Not from Clément. No, it was about that nice French boy you brought to stay. What was his name? Benoît, wasn't it? I'm sure it's here somewhere.'

'A letter from *Benoît*?'

'Not *from* him; *about* him. Now where is it?'

Benoît. Memories were perceived through a kind of fog, shifting and folding and unfolding. She glimpsed things through it and then the vapour closed in again and they had gone. Benoît, sitting here in this room, plying her mother with compliments, only a few days before they left for France. He was wearing French uniform and looked wonderfully smart.

'Here it is!' her mother cried in triumph, holding

up an envelope. 'I knew I had it somewhere. Not the one from Clément. The other one.'

The postmark was Southampton and the letter was dated 14th March 1944.

Dear Mr & Mrs Sutro,

My name is Alan Walcott and I'm a pilot in the RAF. The reason I am writing is that I recently met a friend of your daughter Marion, who suggested that I contact you. I should explain that on operations last December over Belgium I was forced to bale out. Subsequently, with the assistance of many local people, I escaped through France to the Spanish border. On the way I was helped by the resistance group to which this friend of your daughter's belongs. He says you have met him and he told me to get in touch as soon as I got back to England. It has been quite a journey for me, but here I am at last, at home and with a bit of leave on my hands before returning to ops. The man's name is Benoit but I'm afraid I forget his surname. He says he stayed with you once and he knows your daughter well. He told me he didn't want to alarm you, but she went to Paris and has not been seen in his area for some time now. Perhaps she is working in Paris, he said. He said she is a wonderful girl and very brave.

If you would like more information please
do get in touch at the above address.
    Yours sincerely,
    Alan Walcott (Fg Off)

She sat there with the letter in her lap and
wondered. What might have happened chased
away what did. Benoît, whose death she knew so
little about, was dead. A mere letter wasn't going
to bring him back.

'That letter was the first hint we had that everything wasn't all right,' her father said. His tone
was accusatory, almost as if the letter were to
blame. 'I might tell you, we were pretty damn
angry that they didn't keep us better informed. A
month later we got a letter from that Atkins woman
confirming they had lost contact with you and you
had probably been arrested. And then nothing
more until just a few days before you came back
. . .' His eyes glistened. 'You can't imagine how
difficult it's been.'

Marian sat and watched him doing all those
brave and embarrassed things that Englishmen do
when ambushed by tears – coughing, breathing
deeply, looking away through the window as
though something outside had just caught his
attention. Her mother didn't move to show
sympathy or anything. A show of sympathy would
have merely compounded the embarrassment.

'You do *remember* Benoît, don't you?' Marian
asked.

Her father took out his handkerchief, a fine, white lawn handkerchief, and blew his nose. Her mother said, 'Yes, of course we do, darling. Such a nice young man.'

'Well, I was in love with him.'

Her mother looked at her with sudden attention. 'You hardly knew him, dear.'

'I knew him well enough. And now he's dead. Killed in action, apparently. Dead, anyway. Dead.'

She composed a reply to the letter about Benoît. Of course there was no certainty that this Alan Walcott was still at the given address, or even still alive. There was no certainty about anything any more. And framing the fact of Benoît's death in words of any kind somehow made the fact of it final, something etched in stone rather than just reported to her by Colonel Buckmaster:

Dear Flying Officer Walcott,

I write with regard to the letter of 14th March last year that you wrote to my parents – I am the Marian Sutro you refer to. Following my arrest, I have recently returned home after a period of detention in Germany. I regret to inform you that on my return I learned that Benoît Bérard did not survive to see the liberation of France. Shortly after the landings in Normandy he was killed in action while operating against units of the German Army making their way northwards towards the beachhead. I know nothing more than this, I am afraid, but he was a courageous man and was quite prepared to give his life for the France that he loved. Thank you anyway, for contacting my parents and letting them know about your meeting with him. Although I only knew M. Bérard for a short time we were quite close.

She paused, wondering about that last sentence with its hint of intimacy. Should she strike it out and start again? But she decided not. It would do like that. She signed the letter, addressed the envelope, and went downstairs to find a stamp.

The letter from Clément Pelletier only came to light some days later when her father discovered it in his own desk. It was, of course, in French and written in that impatient scrawl that she knew so well from letters he had written years ago when she was at school. He called her father '*Professeur* Sutro', which seemed absurd, and signed himself '*Votre ami*, Clément Pelletier'. What came between was curiously guarded. When in London he had spoken at length with Ned who would surely give them more details about his movements. In the meantime it only remained for him to say that he owed a great debt to Marian and tell them what they probably already knew, that she was a young woman of great courage. He hoped she would be safe.

Anodyne words, she thought. The address at the top seemed almost generic – *L'Université de Montréal, Département de Physique* – and the date was January 1944. She put the letter aside.

REPORT

Throughout that spring the other SOE survivors came back from the wreckage that was Germany. A handful of men, fewer women. In France General de Gaulle had branded agents of the SOE as mercenaries and expelled them from the country, while celebrating the achievements of the French resistance as though French men and women had acted alone. In Britain there was desultory interest in these denizens of the underground war – the occasional newspaper article, the occasional radio interview – but generally the story skulked below the horizon of public attention. Uppermost in people's minds were the struggles with shortages, the coming demobilisation, the forthcoming election.

Occasionally Marian travelled up to London by train, taking a corner seat in the compartment, burying herself in a book, trying to ignore the glances of the other passengers, braving the journey, the exposure, the sense of desolation and isolation, the fear. Once or twice she found herself in the company of my father. I remember his mentioning this. 'Travelled up to town with Marian

Sutro this morning,' he would say. 'She seemed in good spirits, considering. I've heard she's in line for one of their dreadful honours, a CBE or something. I offered to share a cab but she scampered away like a rabbit down a hole.'

The 'hole' was a watering hole, a bar in the station where she would have a glass of sherry before venturing out into the maelstrom of the city. Not the pills that the psychiatrist had prescribed for her. The pills made a sleepwalker of her; but alcohol, a sherry or two, worked just fine, making her light-headed and careless. I follow her in my mind's eye as her taxi takes her along the Marylebone Road to Cleveland Street where the doctors weigh her and test her reflexes and listen to what is going on in various parts of her torso and pronounce her fit as a fiddle. 'How are you feeling yourself?' asks the medic. What he means is, what is the psychological damage? What is going on inside that head, which we cannot see, cannot hear, cannot palpate?

'I'm all right, I suppose. A bit detached, as though nothing is real. And sometimes rather depressed. Occasionally I get . . . panicky. For no real reason.'

'Psychological stuff. Are you seeing the shrink?'

'Yes.'

'And how's that going?'

'It's useful, I suppose.'

'Jolly good. Just remember, we're here if you need us. Always here.'

Jolly good. Where did that expression come from? Jolly. She didn't feel jolly. Good she could understand, but not jolly, which suggested fat, middle-aged men and women, laughing uproariously over nothing much. Seaside postcards. Pantomimes. Not *joli* at all.

At the office in Baker Street she sat with a typist to complete her report. They needed it for the records. Just an outline. Field names only.

I have a copy of the thing in front of me as I write. The original sits in the safekeeping of the National Archive in Kew, in Marian Sutro's SOE personal file. The catalogue number, if you want such a dry-as-dust piece of information, is HS/9/1089853/2.

> Proper Name: Miss M. Sutro
> Field Name:ALICE
> @Anne-Marie Laroche @Laurence Follette
> Circuit:WORDSMITH
> 3rd June, 1945
>
> REPORT ON MISSION.
>
> I arrived in September 1943 in the S. W. of France as courier to ROLAND, organiser of the WORDSMITH circuit. I fulfilled this function for approximately 1 month before I was directed to travel to Paris to make contact with MARCELLE, a W/T

operator for the CINEASTE circuit. This order came from London, via ROLAND. Contact with MARCELLE had been lost and as I knew her personally, I would be able to identify her. I also had a further task, to contact ~~MECHANIC, a man~~ known to me before the war, whose code-name was MECHANIC. Both these people were to be returned to England.

In Paris contact was made with both MECHANIC and MARCELLE and a Lysander pick-up was arranged through the GILBERT circuit. However, I established at the last minute that MARCELLE was blown and was under surveillance by the Gestapo. Fortunately I was able to escape the trap set to arrest me and the Lysander pick-up duly took place from the GRIPPE landing field near Tours on November 10. MECHANIC was successfully taken to England.

The next day, while travelling to rejoin my circuit in the S. W. of France I was arrested by the Gestapo at the station of Vierzon. I was taken to 84 Avenue Foch where I was imprisoned and interrogated for some weeks. I was subjected to some physical violence and the baignoire but gave away nothing that could have been of any use to the enemy.

After Avenue Foch I was imprisoned at Fresnes Prison for eight months in solitary confinement. In August 1944 I was transferred to Karlsruhe civil prison and from there, in October, to Ravensbruck concentration camp. Here, with the help of a prisoner working in the 'hospital' I succeeded in swapping my identity with a French prisoner who had died of pleurisy. So I ~~became~~ was fortunate to be transferred to the sub camp serving the Siemens factory. I worked as a translator because I could speak German. Perhaps this saved my life as conditions in the Siemens camp were better than those in the main camp.

In late April I was with a group that was moved westwards away from the approaching Russians. On the road our column was machine-gunned by an American plane and in the confusion I escaped with two friends (French). Later we had a lift in a Red Cross lorry and eventually found US soldiers who took us to their headquarters. After interrogation I was transferred to the British forces.

The story of disaster rendered down to a few hundred words. I imagine her reading it over and pointing out a few things: 'We need to add an *aigu* to Cinéaste. And an umlaut to Ravensbrück.'

The accents are there, as evidence, carefully inked in.

Miss Atkins read it through rapidly and then put it to one side as if it was of no consequence. She drew on her cigarette and looked at Marian though wreathes of smoke.

'What about you? How are you getting on?'

'I'm all right. It's sometimes not easy, adjusting to the real world.'

'Of course it's not. Eventually you'll need a job, won't you? Do you have any ideas what kind of thing might suit you? Or are you headed for university?'

'I'd like to do something to give me a bit of independence. But I don't really have any useful skills . . .'

'I'll make enquiries if you like. I have contacts.'

'That would be very kind.'

VE

With the surrender on Lüneburg Heath, the war in Europe dissolved into something more resembling exhaustion than peace. 'We may allow ourselves a brief period of rejoicing,' Churchill cautioned on the radio, 'but let us not forget for a moment the toils and efforts that lie ahead.'

Marian walked with her parents to see the celebrations, people cheering and waving rather aimlessly, a bonfire at Carfax, a torchlight procession through the streets culminating in an effigy of Hitler being burned at the Martyrs' Memorial. 'I think they've got the associations wrong,' her father murmured as they watched the figure enveloped by flames.

Two days later one of her mother's friends came round for tea with her two children, a young daughter and rather older son. Marian wanted to hide upstairs in her room; instead she summoned up her courage and appeared like a ghost at the party, to brave their curious glances. There was, of course, no mention of what she had undergone during the war, but things had already been said, whispered comments between parents had been overheard. The little girl fixed Marian with sharp, inquisitive eyes. 'What was it like in the camp?' she asked. 'Did you live in tents?'

There was a terrible silence, broken only by her older brother's caustic sarcasm: 'Don't be stupid, Amanda. It wasn't a Brownie camp, it was a *concentration* camp. They killed people.'

The girl's eyes widened in astonishment. 'They *killed* people?'

'That's enough of that,' their mother snapped. 'Go and play in the garden or something.'

Of course the children did nothing of the kind, but stayed precisely where they were, watching and, in the indiscriminate manner of children, remembering.

Amanda and Sam Wareham; their mother, Judith.

Can I keep my distance from my own mother? It's a trick you learn as your parents diminish with the perspective of time. Judith Wareham, née Juniper, was a loose-limbed woman with chaotic blonde hair and a pair of spectacles as large as saucers. She wrote short stories for magazines like *John Bull* and *Argosy*, and attempted to learn French under the tutelage of Marian's mother; her husband Gordon, absent on this occasion, worked in the physiology department of the university and often travelled up to London where he sat on a variety of committees in the Ministry of Food. Judith always accused her husband of being more interested in fish, fowl and faeces than in human beings, although the truth is that later in his career he was to show altogether too much interest in one of his D.Phil. students, thus bringing the marriage to an abrupt end. But that lay in the future. In 1945 they were together and moderately happy, living in a flat in north Oxford in a state of bohemian laissez-faire with their two children, both of whom had been brought to the Sutro household on this occasion to impart some semblance of easy-going normality to the event.

Judith tried to move the conversation on. 'And what is Marian going to do now?' she asked Marian's mother, as though the subject of her enquiry were mentally deficient and unable to answer for herself.

'She doesn't really know yet, do you *ma chérie*? At present she's on paid leave.'

'Oh, that's nice.'

'No, it's not,' Marian said. 'It's not nice at all.'

There was another dreadful silence. She stood up and excused herself and went for a walk in the garden, knowing that would be construed as her being distressed by what the children had said or the Wareham woman's tactless questions. But it wasn't distress. It was just indifference, a sensation of estrangement from the ordinary matters of human contact. Conversation with anyone felt like trying to talk to people in a foreign language when you only have a fraction of the vocabulary at your disposal and half the grammar. People soon became bored and inattentive.

That, at least, was her memory of the encounter. My own is rather different, but clear enough, like one of those photos you find stashed away in the back of a cupboard – snapshots of people you half recall in places you don't remember. I see a tall lady – of course she was tall, I was a mere eleven years old; and of course she was 'a lady', because that quaint term was what I called women in those days, just as adults were 'grown-ups' and men were addressed as 'Sir'. So: a tall lady in a white blouse and green skirt, pinched at the waist with a wide belt. This lady reaches out and we shake hands. Later there's a vague memory of talk among the adults; and then nothing more until we leave – certainly nothing of the awkward conversation about camps and tents and killing. I presume this departure is part of the same occasion because I think, but only think, that she is wearing the same clothes. So presumably she came back from her walk round the garden in order to bid farewell to the departing guests. And as we take our leave, rather than offering to shake hands, Marian bends down to me, says something in French – perhaps, *on fait la bise, n'est-ce pas?* – and to my intense surprise delivers two kisses, one on each cheek.

She had a scent that was her own. It's hard to describe scents. Hers was dry and faintly sweet, of oatmeal and cut grass, a hint of moss, a breath of mushroom, enhanced by the perfume she wore but not drowned by it. I sound like someone struggling with wine tasting notes. She was a stranger to me and this smell was strange – foreign, enticing, disturbing for a young boy who hadn't yet encountered adolescence but who already knew the allure of sexuality. Perhaps it was also those two kisses and my subsequent fiery blush that etched the moment in my mind.

My sister didn't blush, of course. Six-year-old girls expected to be kissed by virtual strangers in those days. Not so, now. 'She's not nice,' she said of Marian when we were in the car driving home.

'Why not nice?' asked our mother. 'I think she's very nice.'

'I don't like her smell.'

Which was strange, because that was precisely the thing that stayed in my mind. Yet now I wonder whether Amanda hadn't unknowingly detected something, some residual stink of the camps that still emanated from Marian Sutro's body. Maybe it was always there, a subtle hint of corruption that can both attract and repel.

I didn't expect anything more to come of the visit. Childhood is like that – encounters with people you don't know, don't understand, never see again. What part could Marian Sutro, a tall, neurotic grown-up twelve years older than me, possibly play in my life? But we would never cast adrift from Marian because my mother held on to her, determined to help despite being rebuffed, determined to interfere. She always befriended waifs and strays, and probably did more damage than she

101

knew. So it was from her that I learned of Marian's careful reconstruction of a life. I heard about her creeping out into the post-war world, going shopping, braving the cinema, occasionally meeting people, becoming practised at talking obliquely and evasively about what had happened to her, becoming expert at dissimulating. There were things she did not talk about at all. Of course there were. For example her twice-weekly visit to the psychologist who during the First World War had worked with Rivers in Edinburgh. And her encounter – a car was sent for her – with the man she knew as Major Fawley.

FAWLEY

She always thought of Major Fawley as the priest. That was what she remembered of him from their previous meeting, in 1943 in rooms buried deep within an Oxford college: his quiet, priestly manner, the complex theology of his world. This time he received her, not in an Oxford college but in an apartment somewhere in Victoria, where a brass plaque at the street entrance listed *Excelsior Import-Export* and *The Wireless Network Company* as the commercial occupants of the building, and a certain Prof Meredith Jones, D.Sc., FRCPE as the single resident. But the actual incumbent was exactly the same as she remembered: the same innocent eyes, the neat nose set in a smooth, blank face, the sense of quiet coupled with a feeling of immanent threat, exactly like the priests of her schooldays. He evinced a faint expression of surprise at the sight of her standing there in the shadows of the landing when he opened the door, as though he had quite forgotten the appointment. 'Ah, Miss Sutro. How good to see you once again.'

There was that moment's awkwardness when

inviting guests into a flat, a shuffling around the narrow spaces available, an exchange of apologies, a desire to lead in conflict with a desire to allow the visitor to go first. But eventually they were seated, he at one end of a sofa and she in an armchair set at right angles to it. The room itself was as anonymous as if it had been part of a hotel suite, furnished following a single, cursory visit to Heal's and decorated entirely with prints of old London from a dealer somewhere in the Charing Cross Road. On the low table between two sofas and an armchair there were copies of *Tatler* and *Country Life*, the kind of thing you might find in a dentist's waiting room. A discreet young man brought two cups of coffee and a plate of biscuits and then quietly retired.

Fawley said, 'Goodness, it seems quite a time ago that we last met, doesn't it? Where was it exactly?'

'Oxford, Major Fawley.'

'Ah, yes. BNC, of course. My alma mater, as a matter of fact. A good, solid institution. Nothing spectacular like Magdalen or Balliol. Oarsmen, rugger players, lawyers . . .'

'And spies?'

He smiled a faint, enigmatic smile. 'Those as well. Perhaps it goes with the law.' He sipped coffee and offered cigarettes. As she took one he said, 'May I start by congratulating you on carrying out your mission with such flawless efficiency?'

She shrugged. 'It depends what you mean by

flawless. I was arrested and spent the next eighteen months in captivity.'

'It must have been a terrible experience. But you survived.'

'Pure chance.' She looked around the room, as though looking for distraction, or perhaps a means of escape. 'Anyway, I'm trying to leave that behind. To look to the future.'

'Quite so. At least now you are back with your family. It can't have been easy for your parents . . .'

'It wasn't. Nor for me.'

'Quite.' His bland façade seemed disturbed for a moment, as if perhaps he felt some blame. 'At least you can be assured that Clément Pelletier arrived in England safely and went on to contribute greatly to the war effort.'

'I'll have to take your word for it. Can you tell me where he is now?'

'I believe . . .' His tone suggested he was leaving himself room for later denial, 'I *believe* he is in Canada. Might you be making contact with him?'

'Of course I might. Is there any reason why I shouldn't? He was an old friend of the family – you know that.'

'Of course he was. And yours in particular.'

'Mine in particular.' She distracted herself from thoughts of Clément by taking notice of the perfect crease of his grey flannels, the polish of his shoes. Brown brogues. 'Major Fawley,' she asked, 'why have you asked to see me?'

He nodded, as though that was exactly the right question. 'I read your debriefing with Commander Senter. He is a clever man – a barrister by trade.'

'Another Brasenose man?'

Again that smile. 'I rather think, one of the universities north of the border. You manoeuvred your way around his questions like a true professional.'

'What exactly does that mean?'

'You never let him know why you went to Paris.'

'I assumed he knew already.'

Fawley shook his head. 'Not at all, not at all. And in that respect, I have a few questions to put to you that . . . ah, fall outside his remit.'

Outside his remit. She remembered the phrase from when this man had first intruded on her life, when he had hijacked her original mission and had her sent to Paris. The whole Paris business, the encounter with Clément, the Lysander flight out by the light of the silvery moon, all had been outside the remit of Buckmaster and Atkins and their entire organisation.

She waited. Lurking behind Fawley's affable manner and bland expression was, she knew, something to fear. Perhaps it lay in the manila folder that he was opening in front of her. He took from it a postcard-sized photograph and laid it on the table. 'Really all I wanted to do was tie up a few loose ends. For example, I wonder whether you recognise this man?'

She looked. A young man sitting alone at a table outdoors somewhere. His hair gleamed like patent leather. Over his left shoulder was the edge of a café window and part of an advertisement poster extolling the virtues of *Byrrh, Tonique Hygiénique*. The sun cast shadows across the man's face and he smiled at the photographer as though he was enjoying being snapped.

The image was a shock. Physical, mental, but she knew now how the two things could not be separated, how the mental intruded on the physical and the physical determined the mental. We are all one creature, the psychiatrist had told her. The mind/body distinction has no meaning. So the shock now was mind and body – a disturbance that was in her head and in the cage of her chest and in the pit of her stomach.

She said quietly, 'Yes, I do.'

'I thought perhaps you might. Can you enlighten me?'

'On the train to Paris,' she said quietly. 'When I travelled from Toulouse. He was in the same compartment. He followed me from the station. How do you know about him?'

'His name is Miessen. Is or was. We're not sure what happened to him.'

Miessen, nemesis. She knew all about names and non-names, pseudonyms, cover names, field names, codenames. She felt Fawley's eyes on her, touching her face like the fingers of a blind man. Did he read anything in her expression – a shiver of fear, perhaps? 'Julius Miessen, that's what he told me. He tried to pick me up.'

'Did he, indeed?'

'How do you know about him?' she asked again.

Fawley clasped his hands and made a little steeple of his forefingers. He rested the steeple against his chin and lowered his head, almost in a gesture of prayer. 'Miessen worked for us. We wanted him to keep an eye on you, try and keep you out of trouble—'

'Keep me out of trouble? He was a pimp. He offered me work if I wanted it. Escorting German officers. I was . . . embarrassed, suspicious.'

Nothing seemed to disturb the bland surface of Fawley's expression. 'When was this?'

'He followed me from the station. Austerlitz. My first visit to Paris. I went twice, you see. The first time to set the operation up, the second time to carry it out. This man met me on the train the first time, followed me out of the station and got talking to me . . .'

'Is that all?'

'The second time he also followed me from the station. He didn't intend to be spotted on that occasion but I picked him up coming out of the metro somewhere. I don't remember exactly. At first I had no idea who it was. I just thought I'd been burned. *Brûlé*. You know what I mean. I thought he was Gestapo and I'd been blown.'

'And what happened?'

'I threw him off in a church just by the Panthéon. The standard technique – in one door, out another, with a coat change on the way. If I'd known I was being tailed by someone from our side, I'd have done things differently.'

Fawley allowed himself a wry smile. What amused him? Her sudden enthusiasm for the tricks of tradecraft? Or the simple fact that she had got the better of one of his own agents? 'And is that it? Was that the sum total of your contact with him?'

She hesitated. She knew the danger of denial. They'd taught her all that at Beaulieu, and she'd learned more later, at Avenue Foch and at Fresnes. You mustn't deny what they already know. That gives them the lie, and they can break you on your lies. Quietly she said, 'Not quite.'

'Tell me.'

It was remembering that she hated. Memory was her enemy, undermining the fragile structure of recovery. And yet Miessen was one of Fawley's agents.

'When I was in Avenue Foch . . . they confronted me with him. They'd arrested him, and then brought him for me to see. He was . . .' She closed her eyes for a moment, seeing the figure once more, etched on the inside of her eyelids – the triad, the hybrid beast, the crucified man strung out between two thieves, his arms outstretched, his head hanging down.

'They'd beaten him badly.'

She remembered someone grabbing the crucified man's hair and pulling his head upright for her to see him and, presumably, him to see her. As far as he was able. Julius Miessen.

'They wanted to know if I knew him.'

'And you—?'

'Denied it. Of course I denied knowing him. And then they told me that he was a murderer.'

'A *murderer*?'

'They said he had killed two members of the security forces in Belleville, a week earlier. He'd shot them down in cold blood. And he would be executed for this crime unless new evidence came to light.'

'What had this got to do with you?'

'The shooting took place on the same day that they ambushed me at the Père Lachaise cemetery. I escaped by running into Belleville.'

'So Miessen was in Belleville at the same time on the same day that you were?'

'Yes.'

Fawley nodded thoughtfully. How much, she wondered, did he know about life in the field? How much did he understand the fear that undermined your very personality? 'So these security men were after you, is that right?'

'Yes, they were. And they were shot down in cold blood. Nine millimetre bullets, one through the left eye, one in the chest. The second man was dispatched with a bullet through the forehead. Expert shooting, that's what the Gestapo man told me.' She felt something tremble inside her, remembering Miessen's single eye watching her through its narrow slit. A soul gazing out at someone else in hell.

'And Miessen shot them and you got away?'

Miessen's single eye watched her, a small jewel of pale blue gleaming between the swollen lids. 'They asked him if he knew me. He denied it. And then they asked him why he killed two police officers.'

Fawley waited.

'He said it was an act of war.' She wanted to weep but she was determined not to. The tears stung, just there, behind her eyes. 'He could barely speak. They'd bashed him about and he could barely speak. But he said he killed the men as an act of war. So they took him out and shot him.'

Fawley watched her impassively. Then, like an undertaker packing things away after a cremation, he took the photograph of Julius Miessen and returned it to its manila folder. 'It sounds as though you owe him your escape from Belleville. And had you not escaped then, you would never have got Pelletier out of France. It looks as though we all owe him a great deal.'

She looked down at her hands lying in her lap. They'd always been strong. Not ugly, not masculine, but strong. 'I owe him more than that,' she said quietly, to her hands. 'Julius Miessen saved my life.'

Silence. A momentary frown creased Fawley's bland forehead. 'How did he do that?'

'The two men who were shot – Abwehr, Gestapo, I'm not sure what they were. The Gestapo assumed that Miessen killed them but they were wrong.'

'You mean, Miessen did *not* kill the men?'

For a moment something rose up inside her – panic, vomit, it was impossible to tell the physical from the mental. She breathed in deeply until whatever it was subsided. Looking him straight in the eye she said, 'No, Major Fawley, he did not kill them. I did.'

In the great stillness she felt the tears, bloody girlish tears welling up. The childish catharsis of confession. Bless me father, for I have sinned. Now I must do penance. But what penance should she do? What would he ask of her? 'They gave me a chance to say so, and perhaps save Miessen's life. And I looked at him, and I denied having ever seen him. I have the blood of three men on my hands, Major Fawley. The two I shot in Belleville that day, and the man whom I allowed to take the blame.'

Fawley nodded almost as though he understood. 'It's not as simple as that, is it? Morality is never simple. After all, Miessen backed you up. He accepted the sacrifice for the greater good.'

'Whose greater good? His or mine?'

'Who knows what his motives were? Perhaps surprisingly, they seem to have been rather noble. After all, you are alive and he, sadly, is dead. In our line of business that kind of thing happens.'

'But I'm not in your line of business, Major Fawley.'

His smile was sympathetic. 'Oh yes, you are, my dear. Yes, you are.'

And that was her only absolution. A sympathetic smile from Major Fawley. As he stood to see her out he asked, 'I presume that you haven't told Commander Senter about any of this?'

'I thought it fell outside his remit.'

He smiled at the irony. 'Quite so. Nor anyone else in the shortly to be disbanded Special Operations Executive, I imagine. Let's keep it that way, shall we?' He showed her out into the hallway. 'The car will be waiting for you outside. What are your plans?' Everyone seemed to ask that. As though she should have a whole life mapped out before her.

'This afternoon, d'you mean?'

'I meant, for the future.'

'Of course you did, and of course I don't know. Find a job of some kind, I suppose. I don't have any useful skills, except my languages. And an ability to kill people. Interesting qualifications for a girl who is not yet twenty-three.'

He looked pained. 'If anything crops up I'll get in touch.'

She considered him thoughtfully. 'Who exactly do you work for, Major Fawley?'

He smiled the patient, priestly smile. What would he have replied if he *had* been a priest? Much the same, really: 'I'm afraid I can't really tell you that. But, unlike your present employers, we operate in peacetime just as much as in war.'

113

ELECTION

Uncertain spring became summer. I remember the joy in our household when the election results were declared. Those were days when it was still believed that an election might change matters for the better or the worse. And we also believed that with the war finally over, the peace was about to be won by Mr Atlee's Labour Party. Industry would be nationalised, the means of production would be in the hands of the workers, the weak would be sustained by the strong, the poor by the rich, the stupid by the intelligent, and all would be well. It didn't quite work out like that but it's not my parents' fault for hoping.

Vera Atkins, on the other hand, saw things very differently. 'It's beyond my comprehension,' she said. When she said it was beyond her comprehension, she meant she considered it beyond anyone's comprehension – essentially incomprehensible. She drew on her cigarette and blew smoke into the air. 'It's the ingratitude that I find so painful. Churchill leads the country through the war to victory, and instead of thanking him

114

they spit in his face. It is, I feel, typical of the British people.'

What did Marian think? But Marian was far too used to dissembling to give anything away to Flight Officer – soon to be Squadron Officer – Vera Atkins. 'It's the same with all their heroes,' Atkins went on. 'First they put them on a pedestal and then they knock them down. Mark my words, once they get to know about us and what we did, they'll be trying to tear us apart too. That's why we must call the tune.'

'Call the tune?'

'We need to get our side of the story out to the public first.'

'I didn't realise there were different sides.'

'Of course there are. There are different sides to every story.'

'And what's ours?'

Atkins shrugged. 'That we did our best under the circumstances. Very trying circumstances at times. And sometimes we had to sup with the devil.'

Marian wondered at that. Which particular devil was Miss Atkins thinking of? The devil nowadays seemed to be the Soviet Union and yet Véronique had always extolled the virtues of Russia and its revolution. 'The Red Army will come to save us,' she used to say. A belief almost like a religion.

'So how are you bearing up?'

'I'm getting bored kicking around at home.'

'That sounds promising. As you know I've been

making some enquiries on your behalf, written some letters . . .'

'That's very kind.'

'It's the least I can do. It seems that there may be a place for you here.' She passed a letter across her desk. It was headed *The Franco-British Pacific Union*, and, underneath, *Union Pacifique Franco-Britannique*. 'That's pacific as in peace, not pacific as in ocean. Apparently they have a library that needs cataloguing . . .'

'But I'm not a librarian.'

'My dear, you can *read*, can't you? There can't be much more to it, can there? Are you going to turn it down?'

'Of course not. I'm happy with anything that'll get me . . .' Marian hesitated – 'away from my parents,' was what she wanted to say – '. . . a bit of independence,' was what she actually said. She picked up the letter and slipped it in her handbag. 'What are *you* going to do, Vera?'

'When they throw me on the scrap heap, you mean?' There was a glimmer of a smile, perhaps a smile of triumph. At Baker Street the organisation was being dismembered. Throughout the building offices were being emptied, files weeded and embarrassing items destroyed, furniture moved to other departments in other buildings where the more intractable problems of peacetime would have to be confronted. But Miss Atkins, Flight Officer, soon to be Squadron Officer Atkins, was going to Germany, to find out what had happened to her girls. That's

116

what she called them. My girls. She had her list there on her desk, with new notes against various names, but she didn't need to look down to read them out. She had them by heart: Andrée Borrel, Vera Leigh, Nora Baker, Yvonne Rudellat, Cecily Lefort, Diana Rowden, Eliane Plewman, Yolande Beekman, Madeleine Damerment, Denise Bloch, Lilian Rolfe, Violette Szabo. A roll call of the disappeared. 'We know now that Yvonne died at Belsen, shortly after the liberation. But that's the only definite news so far. Except for those of you who have come back.'

Marian contemplated the list in silence. Her own name might have been there among *les disparues*. She thought of annihilation, of being a name on that list and therefore of not being, not existing, surviving as no more than a few disparate memories in people's minds. The idea was thrilling, making the very core of her being tremble.

'Odette has been very helpful in trying to trace some of them. It seems a number of them passed through Karlsruhe prison.'

'I was at Karlsruhe.'

'Yes, my dear. But you don't seem to remember anyone.' There was a long pause, as though the reproach was being allowed to sink in. 'There is something I'd like you to do for me. What I was saying about getting our side of the story out.' She lit another cigarette. For a moment her face was wreathed in smoke. She might any moment disappear in a flash of light. Mephistopheles. 'I'd like you to do an interview for a newspaper. Would you do that for me? No names, of course, no breach of privacy. But these dreadful people are just hungry for news about what we did. Would you do that for me?'

Marian would like to have refused but she couldn't. Quid pro quo.

The interview, with a rather seedy journalist from the *News Chronicle*, took place in the lounge of a hotel in Portman Square, at tea time, amid tinkling teacups and ladies in fur coats complaining about rationing. The journalist promised to keep her anonymity by referring to her only as Miss Anne-Marie S. Miss Atkins was there like a referee, to see that the rules were obeyed and the conventions observed. She talked vaguely of days spent cycling round the country-side, of parachute drops and dead letter drops, of the police and the Milice.

'How do you spell that?'

'Malice with an "i".'

He liked the joke. He wrote it down earnestly in his little book, real letters among the shorthand hieroglyphics.

'You were captured, weren't you? By the Gestapo.'

'That was in Paris. I'd been sent to Paris—'

'Why was that?'

'To assist a fellow agent. And' – she glanced at Atkins – 'there was an important person who had to get to London. I had to arrange that.'

The man's eyes lit up. 'Important? Who was that, then?'

'I'm afraid Miss Sutro cannot tell you,' Atkins said. 'People frequently crossed between France and England, but—'

'I can't mention them by name.'

'Exactly.'

'So, why were you arrested?'

'I was betrayed.' The word 'betrayal' quivered in the air between them. For a few moments he nosed around it like a dog trying to identify a scent.

'Miss Sutro cannot go into operational details,' Atkins said.

The journalist looked resigned. 'Anyway, you were arrested. That must have been frightening. Were you tortured?'

'It depends what you mean by torture.'

'You tell me.'

'They hit me sometimes. And tried to drown me. The *baignoire*, they call it the *baignoire*.'

'But you didn't talk?'

'I didn't talk.'

And then the camp. He wanted to know about the camp. He'd seen the newsreels, of course, and interviewed someone who claimed to have been at the liberation of Belsen. What was her experience? 'My readers would love to know. We need to tell the public what it was like.'

'You can't.'

'You can't what?'

'Tell them. You cannot tell anyone what it was

like. It wasn't the stuff of words . . .' But she told him something anyway, or tried to, and at the end of the allotted hour they shook hands solemnly, as if it had been some kind of match and she had won on points. 'If I were you I'd write a book about your experiences,' he said.

'But you're not, are you? You're not me.' And she felt something strange, the sensation of uniqueness. It wasn't a good feeling, just one of separation, like being unable to speak the language that is common to all those around you.

ALAN

The letter came, quite innocently, through the post, when she had forgotten all about the correspondence. So it was only with vague curiosity that she opened it and saw unfamiliar handwriting and the address of the Officers' Mess, RAF Benson at the top. Who, outside the narrow purlieus of the Organisation, knew who she was and where she lived? But as she read it she felt sudden panic, as though someone had reached out and snatched at her wrist.

Dear Miss Sutro,

Thank you so much for your letter. It was very kind of you to reply so promptly. I'm sorry I've taken a while to reply but my parents had to forward the letter here and when it arrived I was away on detachment so I've only just seen it. Anyway, I must say I am delighted that you are back home safe and sound, but dreadfully sorry to hear about the death of Benoît Bérard. It is no surprise to discover he died in action – he struck me as being a most courageous, as well as carefree man. You must be very upset.

It is my intention, when I have the opportunity, to travel to France and thank all those who risked their lives for me and for others. There is talk of creating some kind of society of evaders to keep the remarkable spirit of those days alive, which would be wonderful. In the meantime, I wonder whether we might meet up? I'm based at Benson, so not far away from Oxford. I could always pop round and take you out for tea or something. It might be an opportunity for me to brush up my French – I learned quite a bit in the months I was there but not the kind that enables me to read Montaigne or discuss Voltaire.

Yours sincerely,

Alan Walcott (now at the dizzy heights of Flight Lieutenant)

Should she just end the correspondence there, with some brief answer saying that she was too busy these days? That would be the easy way out and the most comforting, closing the door in an instant and retreating to her room to live with herself and her memories. Thus she could become a recluse, dependent on her parents, avoiding her relatives, avoiding the outside world, wanting for nothing, chancing nothing, gaining nothing. She sat for a long while looking at the sheet of Basildon Bond before she picked up her pen and wrote a brief answer:

Perhaps we can meet up as you suggest. Is the Randolph a suitable venue, for tea some time? I am kicking my heels at home at the moment and am free most days – let me know when you can make it. You can always ring.

Yours sincerely,

Marian Sutro (Ensign, FANY but also, for reasons that escape me, an honorary Section Officer in the WAAF)

That little touch of irony at the end. Maybe he'd like that. She posted the letter and waited for a reply. There was the dentist to see – a molar and a premolar removed, a denture to fit, cavities to fill – and Dr Morgan to visit once again. There were shopping expeditions to Summertown and those walks with her father in the Parks. On Sunday she accompanied her mother to church, where the Catholic rituals of St Aloysius drifted over her like the smoke of incense, leaving behind a faint feeling of nausea. The mere act of leaving the house was becoming ever more difficult to achieve. Sometimes it brought panic, welling up inside her like a kind of vomit, an uncontrollable, visceral fear sweeping up through her heart and flooding into her head.

'It's like . . .' She had searched in her memory for something similar to explain it to Dr Morgan. 'Like suddenly finding yourself on the edge of a cliff, with nothing to stop you stepping over the edge. I used not to care about that kind of thing. I was a good skier. I've parachuted, for God's sake. And now . . . sometimes I find it hard to stand on the front doorstep.'

At Craiglockhart he had dealt with survivors of the trenches; now the problems were more varied and more diffuse: victims of the Blitz and the V weapons, men who had broken down in combat, aircrew from Bomber Command who had asked to be relieved from their duties and had the label LMF – lack of moral fibre – appended to their service records. And now the survivors of the camps, who had God alone knew what kind of hidden neuroses lurking in the depths of their minds. He assured her, in that faint Welsh accent that made him somehow more dependable, that talking about it would make things easier. 'And it'll get better with time, I can guarantee you that. But in the meantime if you really need to deal with such attacks I can prescribe something for you . . .'

They always sat in wingback armchairs – matching leather ones set at ninety degrees to one another so that, although he was not outside her angle of vision, he was at least outside her normal line of sight. She could look at him if she wished. Or she could look at the side of the club fender and the

124

arrangement of dried flowers in the corner of the room or the picture on the wall: a painting of mountains and crags and slate-grey cottages beneath a swirling sky that must be Wales but reminded her of Scotland and her training and those innocent days before the fall.

'I want to tell you about the camp,' she told him one day. 'About how we lived and how we died. People have the wrong idea – all the sensational news, the films of dead bodies, that kind of thing. It was different. Not worse, not better. Just different. Very drab, very monotonous. Defined by the colour grey. Our whole world was grey, our clothes were grey, our complexions were grey. Just shades of grey.'

There was a silence in the constrained space of the psychiatrist's consulting room. Was he waiting for her to say more? That's what they did, wasn't it? Let you lead yourself on into confessions you would not otherwise make. Like an interrogator. Like Fawley.

'And yet our lives were very complex. There were hierarchies, networks, friendship groups. All women, you see. I was part of a group of French girls. Just three of us and our Lagermutter, camp mother. We called her Mutti. We were a family but we were closer than a family, really. That was how things worked in the camp. You looked after each other. On your own you'd never survive; together, you had a chance. Above all, it was Mutti who mattered. She had been headmistress of a lycée

125

in Lyon so she knew about organising girls. Her name was Véronique Barthelemy . . .' She hesitated. She had never told anyone this, so why this particular man? Perhaps because he didn't matter. 'I want to talk about her.'

'Then do.'

She cast around for the right words. That was the problem with words – they nailed the thought down, made it explicit, fixed it, crucified it on the cross of exact meaning. But life has no exact meanings, only shades of meaning, hints, versions and contradictions, a confusion of loves and hates, of motives and desires. 'I have never felt like that for anyone else, nor ever will,' she said. 'For those few months she was the centre of my universe. Because of her I'm alive today.' She paused and thought for a moment. She had been trained to say nothing; nothing, more or less, was what she had said throughout her captivity. But having come this far with her confession she had to go on. And perhaps some kind of absolution lay ahead. 'I loved her in ways that I couldn't imagine loving someone. She was my whole life, my earth and my sky, my waking and my sleeping, my feeding and my shitting, my hope and my despair.'

She said that. Shitting. A word she'd never normally have used.

'I dream about her and I miss her.' She shrugged. 'That's all I wanted to say.'

*   *   *

126

Véronique Barthelemy. I looked her up. When she died in the winter of 1944 she was forty-one years old. On the internet you can find the occasional pre-war photograph of her, looking stern and slightly out of focus. She had been married, apparently, to a university lecturer who was part of the same resistance group and who was imprisoned and shot in 1943, the year she was sent to Ravensbrück. After the war Véronique was elevated to the pantheon of national heroes in that wonderful bureaucratic manner the French have, with posthumous awards of the Légion d'honneur and the Médaille de la Résistance. The lycée in Lyon where she taught now bears her name, along with a road nearby that skirts the banks of the River Saône. Lycée Véronique Barthelemy. Avenue Véronique Barthelemy. If I ever get to Lyon . . .

TROUT

One morning the phone rang just as she was coming down into the hall. She lifted the receiver to hear a strange voice on the line asking, 'Is that Miss Sutro? How about lunch next Wednesday, rather than tea? It's just that tea always gives me indigestion.'

It took her a minute to realise that it was the man called Alan Walcott talking. What was she to make of his words? Was she meant to laugh?

'Lunch is fine,' she said, cautiously, in case it might not be fine, in case the mere act of saying yes might commit herself to things she could not accomplish.

'At the Randolph? I'll meet you in the foyer at twelve-thirty. Is that OK? I'll be in uniform so you'll recognise me. The flight lieutenant.'

'There'll probably be a dozen flight lieutenants.'

'Only one will look as nervous as me.'

Wednesday was a day of sun. During the morning she spent an inordinate time in her room wondering how she looked, as though the thin, angular woman who looked back at her from the mirror was some kind of lie. She wore a tightly waisted, blue-and-white-striped dress that she had bought at Elliston and Cavell. She wondered whether she should wear a headscarf or a hat. And gloves, should she wear gloves? All these indecisions were ploys to put off the moment when she would have to go downstairs and open the front door and step outside into the world. Finally, she summoned up her courage and crept down, hoping to avoid her mother. Thankfully the sitting room was deserted. First she helped herself to a glass of sherry, then, hatless and gloveless but wearing a headscarf, she opened the front door, called out goodbye to her mother and set off to meet Flight Lieutenant Walcott.

The walk took her onto the Banbury Road and down towards the open boulevard of St Giles. She looked like a young woman out on a fine summer day, careless and fancy free; she felt like someone edging along the brink of a precipice. The space around her was enormous and threatening, like the Boulevard de Belleville as it had been on that day of her betrayal. Yet here there was no market, no army lorries, no soldiers lining up to sweep between the buildings in their search for her. Plane trees, yes, but the city was just Oxford on a placid midweek day in summer. Not Paris during the occupation, not the silver city tarnished to dull grey. No *barrages* and *rafles*, no grim-faced occupiers and glum Parisians, reduced to acquiescence and compliance, but a golden city of ancient stone and placid self-confidence, with birds singing and the occasional don cycling past, gown billowing.

She hurried into the gatehouse of St John's College for a moment and stood in the womb-like shadows while her fears subsided. The sherry was doing her good, relaxing her, bringing that small shift of indifference.

'Can I help you, miss?' one of the porters asked.

She tried a smile and wondered whether she should have worn a hat after all. Perhaps she'd have looked less like a miss, more like a madam. 'I'm fine,' she said. 'Just the sun.' As though sunshine were something to avoid.

'That's quite all right, miss. Anything you want, just say.'

Why had he even asked? Did she seem strange? 'Cultivate distraction,' the psychiatrist had told her. 'Try not to dwell on your anxieties. Train yourself to think of other things.'

She opened her handbag, took out a shining cylinder of lipstick. The pocket mirror showed no more than her mouth. She touched up her lips, feeling the soft, unctuous slide of one lip against the other, a sensuous gesture that was still unfamiliar. Two things sprung into memory: the gold powder compact that Vera had given her as they waited at the airfield for her flight to France; and the Swedish Red Cross workers dealing with newly liberated women from the camp – and discovering that what the women wanted as much as food and clothing was . . . lipstick.

And now she was going to meet someone who had known Benoît. A distraction there, sure enough, her mind's eye giving her a sudden glimpse of Benoît standing in the flat in Toulouse, outlined against the window, naked.

She adjusted her scarf, smoothed down her skirt and stepped out into the sunlight. Across the road was the Martyrs' Memorial where Hitler had burned only a couple of months ago and on whose spiked summit a ceramic chamberpot now hung lopsided, waiting for someone from the council to come and take it down. That gave her the blessed release of a moment's smile. She paused at the kerb for a bus to pass and gained the far pavement at the corner of the Randolph Hotel. A revolving door spun her into the hushed shadows of the foyer.

She stopped and looked, fear of outside being replaced by another anxiety, that of the gaze of strangers.

'Miss Sutro?'

There was only one flight lieutenant and he was standing directly in front of her. The same height as her. A square-cut sort of face and the solid build of a sportsman. She could, in that first moment of looking at him, imagine him playing rugby.

'Yes, I'm . . .'

'Alan,' he said, holding out a hand. 'Alan Walcott.'

There was a moment of awkward introduction, the usual platitudes, the normal manoeuvring round the curious fact of their meeting here in the formal environment of the Randolph with the staff in shabby uniforms and dust on the chandeliers. 'Is it too early for a drink?' he asked, ushering her through into the bar. It was only then, sitting by one of the ogive windows that he produced a fold of paper from the inside pocket of his jacket. 'Have you seen this? I expect you have . . .'

It was a cutting from the *News Chronicle*.

ENGLISH GIRL SURVIVED
S.S. TORTURE

News Chronicle Reporter

Some personal stories of the war may pass into history – and this may be one of them.

It is the story of Miss Anne-Marie S. a 24-year-old English girl, as she told it to me in a London tea room yesterday.

I cannot tell you her real name. It is still on the security list. This is her record:

In France she joined the resistance. Her job was carrying messages between different groups of resisters. But in the course of the work she was sent to Paris to arrange for an important person to be flown out to England. Of course, for security reasons I cannot mention that person by name. Although she was successful in this difficult task, she was betrayed by someone within the French underground and was arrested by Gestapo men at a railway station.

HIT IN THE FACE

They took her away and interrogated her. They hit her about the face. They plunged her into an ice-cold bath in which she nearly choked to death.

But not a word of her comrades or her work did she betray.

For months she was kept in solitary confinement in a Gestapo prison near Paris. Eventually, as Allied forces liberated the French capital, she was one of a batch of suspected English and French girls packed into a closed rail truck. For a week they travelled like this, with little food, drink or sleep, until they arrived at the notorious Ravensbrueck camp in North West Germany.

There, with the help of a nurse working in the 'hospital' she managed to change identity with a French prisoner who had died of disease. 'Probably,' Miss Anne-Marie says, with tears of gratitude in her eyes, 'this unknown victim saved my life because other English girls were murdered.'

GUARDS' WHIPS

Now masquerading as a French woman she was put to work in a factory. Guarded by S.S. men and women with whips and clubs, they toiled 12 hours each day.

The day came when, 17 months after her capture, she made her escape with two French companions. They hid for days in woods and later hitched a lift with a Red Cross ambulance that took them to the American lines. Only after weeks of medical treatment was she able to return to safety and the arms of her family in England.

'I don't consider myself a heroine,' Miss Anne-Marie says, shaking my hand and looking at me with fearless eyes. 'I just did my duty.'

'Remarkable story,' he said as she handed the piece of paper back to him.

She shrugged, not knowing what to say.

'Is it you?'

'Not really. It's a newspaper story *about* me. That's a different thing.'

'I suppose it is.'

A waiter came over. Did they have sherry? Sherry had become her saviour. The waiter smiled and inclined his head: for all the shortages, the Randolph could be relied on to satisfy that particular need.

'You can't imagine how I admire people like you,' Walcott told her as the waiter went off with their order.

'What on earth do you mean?'

'Acting beyond the call of duty.'

'I'm not sure what duty is. So I'm even less sure of what's beyond it.'

He replied quietly, in a matter-of-fact tone that carried with it a great conviction. 'Duty is what I did, and people like me. There's a lot of people did that – hundreds of thousands, I guess, maybe millions altogether. But I know it is a great deal less than what you and others like you did.'

In the event they decided against lunch at the hotel. 'Too stuffy,' was Walcott's verdict. 'Let's go for a drive instead and find somewhere out in the country. What do you think?'

'I think that would be fine. As long . . .'

'As long as I get you home in time for your tea?'

'I don't actually like tea . . .'

'We have a great deal in common.'

Laughter was a help. She felt better, light-headed now, her demons consigned to some backwater. The flight lieutenant was amusing and attentive and, as he had suggested on the phone, slightly nervous. It occurred to her that she was the source of this nervousness, that he saw her in a different light, that the person she was inside was very different from the person others perceived.

'Come and meet Gloria,' he said as he led the way outside. 'I hope you like her. She's not always very well-behaved but today seems a good day.' Gloria turned out to be his car, an MG sports car with its hood down and its green bodywork gleaming in the sunlight. He called it Gloria because, he explained, that was what it was – a glorious little lady. 'Is it OK? You'll have to hold your hair on. She's very windy.'

They drove up St Giles' and out along the Woodstock Road and into the country with Gloria's engine almost battering their conversation into submission. 'I managed to liberate some petrol,' he shouted above the noise, 'but if we run out we're stuck.'

'Where are we going?'

'A surprise.'

Marian didn't recognise the place until they'd parked the car in a country lane beside a pub. There was a narrow bridge over the river and steps leading down to a stone terrace beside a weir. The rush of water and a dash of spray filled the air. A wooden footbridge led across to an island where there were tables and chairs. You couldn't mistake it really but she had never seen it from this angle before, never approached it from the road. It was the same pub she and Benoît had reached on their walk up the river a few days before they left for France.

'How strange . . .' But the noise of the weir drowned whatever she might have said, while spray caught the sunlight and threw it carelessly about the place as though it were something harmless rather than the dangerous stuff that exposed and burned. Were there still fragments of light left over from that last visit, tossed about in the air, thrown back and forth between the river and the sky?

'You can't imagine . . .' she said as they carried sandwiches and drinks out onto the terrace.

'I can't imagine what?'

'What a joy it is to get out like this. I've been rather cooped up since I got back home.'

'Better confront the demons,' he said.

What did he mean by that? Did he somehow sense how she felt? Could he read her mind or had her behaviour given her away? She looked for distraction. 'Tell me how you got to meet Benoît,' she said. 'Were you shot down?'

He shook his head. 'You don't expect to get shot down in my line of business. We fly way up, above the flak and above the fighters.'

'What line of business is that?'

'PR.'

She knew PR. She cast her mind back to those days before her recruitment, when she had been a plotter in the Filter Room at Stanmore. It would be the day after a raid, or, if there was no wind, perhaps a day or two later to allow the smoke to clear. During the raid they would have been plotting hundreds and hundreds of aircraft rising like starlings into the air over East Anglia; but a day or two later a lone plot would materialise over Oxfordshire, a single aircraft climbing higher and higher and higher. Ten thousand, fifteen thousand, twenty thousand feet and still climbing as it headed out across the south-east and the Channel, over thirty thousand feet when it disappeared over the curvature of the Earth and the radar stations lost contact. 'PR,' the old hands would say knowledgeably.

A few hours later the solitary aircraft would be back, letting down to the heights of other aircraft before vanishing back into the Oxford countryside. A strange, ominous solitude. Photo Reconnaissance.

Alan Walcott was delighted that she knew. He talked almost ecstatically about it, of flying high above the weather and the war, floating in a Perspex bubble of blue and white. Slipping the surly bonds of earth, he said. Touching the face of God. Not that he was religious, but that was the kind of thing you felt. 'But if you get mechanical trouble you're stuffed. Which is what happened to me.' He laughed, as though it was a joke. 'Engine failure over the Ruhr. I was over thirty thousand feet when the damn thing cut out and I made it as far as Belgium before baling out. At which point I found myself swinging from a parachute over the Belgian countryside while watching my kite plummet into the Ardennes. Fortunately some farmers found me before Jerry did. They hid me in a barn for a couple of days then handed me over to one of the escape lines. Comet. Have you heard of it? Anyway, they got me and three others through Paris and down to Toulouse. Where we met up with Benoît. He was great. All the others were serious, business-like, telling you to do this, do that, not to talk, not to smile, play deaf or dumb or something; and then there was Benoît. And he just laughed.'

She put out a hand and touched his wrist. 'You know, I came here with him? To this pub, I mean. It was a few days before we dropped into France. We walked, all the way across Port Meadow.'

'I know.'

She felt a jolt of surprise. 'You *know*?'

'He told me. He said you walked him for miles along the river and then you came to a pub – a typical pub *de campagne*, he said. Warm beer and bad food but very pretty. Right by a *barrage*. That's what he said. It didn't take much to work it out once I found out what *barrage* was. Otherwise it might have been the Perch at Binsey. But once I knew it was a weir—'

'How strange. What else did he tell you?'

He looked at her, head on one side, eyebrow raised. 'Is there much else?'

'There's a bit.'

'Were you in love with him?'

So blunt. She felt herself blush. 'We were close. But the life we led didn't leave much opportunity for that kind of thing.' What kind of thing? She hadn't expected to be ambushed by embarrassment in this way.

'Because from what he said about you . . .'

'What did he say?'

'Nothing you couldn't tell your mother.'

'What do you mean by that?'

He laughed. 'There were four of us shacked up together in a farmhouse outside Toulouse, waiting for transport to take us south. He was meant to look after us. He kept complaining that it wasn't his job. His job was explosives and weapons training.'

'Just like Benoît—'

'But the two of us got talking. You know the kind of thing: a bottle of Armagnac and a log fire, the other three asleep in the next room. That's when he told me about you. He said you'd gone off to Paris and he'd considered going after you. Because you were a *casse-cou*. Is that the expression? Breakneck, reckless, something like that.'

She laughed. 'Probably *casse-cul*.'

'What's that?'

'A pain in the arse. What else did he say?'

Walcott drank some beer and put the glass down

139

with care. 'The point is, you don't say that kind of thing – even *casse-cul* – about a girl unless she means something to you. I think he was in love with you.'

There was a raucous noise in the background. She looked round to see a peacock on the terrace. How remarkable. A peacock looking for pickings among the tables. She hadn't remembered peacocks the last time. All she really remembered was what she had said to Benoît as they sat at a table in the garden just there over the footbridge: 'I'm a virgin,' she'd told him. 'I don't want to go to France a virgin.' And she'd waited for the laughter that never came.

'We were good friends,' she told Walcott. 'That's all. And now he's dead.' She emptied her glass and put it down alongside his as though to signal the end of the conversation. 'So what'll you do now it's all over?'

He looked thoughtful. 'I'll bet there are a few hundred thousand people asking the same question right now. I've no real idea. It's going to be dull, isn't it?'

Perhaps it already was. Her present life seemed episodic. She wanted it to have thrust and direction, as it had in the past, but now it just seemed stalled between one banal incident and another, between talking with the psychiatrist and going shopping with her mother, between walking in the Parks with her father and traipsing up to London for an appointment with the doctors.

She felt she was drifting through a neutral space, where there was neither love nor hate, neither danger nor safety, neither peace nor war; a place where crude, physical emotion – a raging heart, a sweating forehead, a rising panic – was triggered by stimuli she couldn't apprehend, and yet the feelings she ought to own, of contentment, of filial love, of sexual attraction even, were no more than vague memories.

'Perhaps dullness is what we need now.'

Walcott nodded, as though he understood. They didn't say much more, just agreed that the weather was fine, considering, and the pub was in a lovely setting, and they'd had a pleasant time. Then they climbed back into Gloria and he drove her home – 'in time for tea,' he said, but if that was a hint she didn't take it and didn't invite him in as he helped her out of the little sports car.

'That was fun,' he said.

'Yes.'

'Maybe I'll give you a ring some time.'

'Perhaps.'

They shook hands and he climbed back into Gloria. She stood watching as he drove off with a spray of gravel. What did his 'maybe' or her 'perhaps' mean? Was there an upward inflexion in his voice that made it a question? Or was it merely a statement of fact, indicating improbability? She didn't know. She felt like someone imprisoned behind a glass wall – able to see the people on the other side and perceive their muffled voices, but unable to hear them clearly or understand what they were saying.

Perhaps this encounter with Alan Walcott spurred her to write to Clément Pelletier. The right words didn't come easily but she persevered with the dogged determination that she applied to all her problems at that time.

How are you doing? she wrote. *I'm back in England now and wondering what on earth to do with myself. Perhaps you don't know that I spent a certain amount of time in a German concentration camp. You'll have seen the newsreels, I'm sure. Well, for me it wasn't as bad as the worst you'll have seen and now I'm fine and getting back my strength day by day. I can't say I have got over what happened to me because one always keeps things in memory, doesn't one? The trick is to look forwards rather than back, and get things into some kind of perspective.*

What perspective was that? On the cinema news-reels they continued to show film from the camps. One of them ambushed her when she went with my parents to see something with Rex Harrison and Constance Cummings, a Noël Coward film everyone was talking about. *Blithe Spirit.* Sharp, acerbic Coward dialogue. But the little trio of Gordon and Judith Wareham and Marian Sutro never got as far as the opening credits because before the feature there was a newsreel film with that bloody Pathé cock crowing triumphantly over the ruins of Germany followed by images of bulldozers shovelling skeletal corpses into pits, and the commentator's voice sounding throughout the cinema like a commentary to a sports event: 'While German civilians try to come to terms with what went on within the hell that was Adolf Hitler's Germany, prosecutors are preparing their case against the instigators of these bestial crimes . . .'

And quite suddenly Marian was weeping and gasping for air and vomiting in the aisle like a drunk. My parents managed to get her out into the foyer and calm her down a bit but there was no way they were going to return to watch the wit of *Blithe Spirit*. Instead they brought her home on the bus and fed her coffee and brandy while I eavesdropped the final scenes of the drama from the secrecy of my bedroom.

I imagine the psychiatrist had a field day with that one. 'Did you feel you were one of the corpses?' he would have asked at their next meeting.

'Certainly not,' would have been her sharp retort; but at the time she certainly looked like one because I caught a glimpse of her through an open doorway when I crept to the bathroom. She appeared haggard and grey and a scream away from madness. I'd never seen an adult in that state before. She slept the night on the sofa in the sitting room and by breakfast the next morning she had perked up a bit and was laughing and talking, but I imagine it was a frightening moment to feel that normality, the rational person called Marian Sutro,

143

could be so close to this weeping hysteric; that mere shadows on the wall could transform the one into the other.

She completed the letter and addressed it to Canada, where Ned said Clément was, at the University of Montreal; and Fawley had confirmed it, more or less. But perhaps he was already back in Paris after all. Perhaps he'd never get the letter; perhaps he'd never reply.

PART II

CARTWHEEL

I give you another memory. How this fits in, I don't quite know. Chronologically, I mean. I can see its significance, all right. So: the lawn in front of the block of flats in north Oxford where we lived. We are having a picnic. Other residents disapproved of our cluttering up the lawn like this but my parents took no notice of any complaints. Read that literally – they really wouldn't have noticed that there was any serious objection to their camping on the lawn with rugs and picnic baskets and all the paraphernalia. The sun was shining, the weather was warm enough, we'd have a picnic. As simple as that. And Marian is there, only this time she has brought a friend, an airman and therefore subject of admiration, a pilot who flies Spitfires and is therefore an object of veneration. Did he fly in the Battle of Britain? I asked.

He tousled my hair – I hated that – and laughed. 'It's a long time ago, old chap. I was still in shorts then. Far too young for the Battle of Britain.'

'So you flew Spitfires *after* the Battle of Britain?'

'That's right.'

'And did you shoot anyone down?'

147

There was adult laughter, although I couldn't see the joke. Spitfires were to shoot people down. What was he doing flying them if not that? 'I'm afraid the only things I shot were photographs,' he said.

'Photographs?' No doubt my tone was incredulous. What was the point of shooting photographs?

'It's called intelligence, old chap.'

My face was scorched with embarrassment. I was intelligent enough to grasp the play on the word intelligent, and my misery was exacerbated by the fact that another family had joined us, a couple with two daughters, prissy little things in bows and ruffles, who were laughing at my discomfiture. Later they insisted on doing hand-stands and cartwheels and generally showing off their athletic abilities and their underwear, while I glowered clumsily in the background.

Unexpectedly Marian got to her feet and kicked off her shoes. 'I can do that,' she said. There was laughter, and cries of delight from the girls. The men were lying on the ground, propped up on their elbows, drinking beer; my mother was kneeling at the picnic hamper and dealing out careful portions of homemade ice cream. Ice cream was a rarity in those days, to be talked of in hushed tones. So there was a sense of anticipation among the group, both for the imminent promise of ice cream and the challenge that Marian had set herself.

The man Marian had brought with her, the

Spitfire pilot who had never shot anyone down, watched thoughtfully. I hated him. I hated him for what I saw as possession. He owned some part of her. I wondered if he kissed her, did *things* with her. And all this time Marian stood, poised above everyone with one leg raised, looking, I suppose, statuesque. She wore the same green skirt as before, but now a red shirt. I remember that colour combination, complementary colours bold and decisive among the pastels of the other females. And the poise, pose, held for what seemed like an age.

And then she moved. It was sudden, brilliant and somehow unexpected, all over before I had drawn breath. She ran four rapid strides, skipped sideways and cartwheeled, Catherine-wheeled, whirled through the air with her skirt billowing and her legs describing a beautiful arc. There was a tantalising flash of stocking tops and suspenders, white thigh and whiter cotton, before she rotated onto her feet once more and turned for applause. Her face was flushed. Up to then her complexion had been pale, but now I saw blood in her cheeks. And there were other things I had seen – knickers and legs – that needed thought and contemplation; but there was noise all around me and I couldn't concentrate. 'Encore!' the Spitfire pilot was calling. 'Bravo!' cried another. And then I realised that among the laughter Marian was suggesting that *I* attempt the same feat.

Delighted to have been noticed by her, I was

mortified to be put on the spot. 'I can't,' I protested. Cannot. Am not able. Not, am shy, am bashful, am reluctant to show myself up, but rather *I cannot do a bloody cartwheel.*

Marian herself persuaded me to my feet and promised to show me how, holding out her hands for me to take and leading me, victim to the slaughter, to the centre of the lawn. Could I do a handstand at least? I attempted one, approximately. Behind us people cheered. I wanted to run away but was seduced by her proximity, the heady warmth of her presence. 'You just do a handstand sideways,' she said, 'leading with your stronger leg and going onto one hand then the other.' She stood behind me and held my arms, guiding me, laughing in my ear, enveloping me in her scent. I was, what, twelve years old? A child swept up in devotion to an adult. I raised my left leg, prancing like a horse, and launching myself forward as no horse has ever done. Then I planted my left hand in the grass and threw my rear parts upwards.

I never heard the snap. I believe there was one, but I never heard it. Inside the box of my head any sound was masked by pain and I heard the pain well enough, exploding through my shoulder and my brain like a great pulse of electrical charge. I crumpled into an ungainly heap. I remember the smell of grass in my nose. I remember trying not to cry but crying just the same – not tears but a scream, the dry scream of agony.

There was a moment of dramatic stasis. The

adults circled haphazardly, not wanting to touch the screaming creature lest they only made things worse. Marian cried, *'Oh mon Dieu!'* and ran to me. She felt she was to blame. I suppose that was the positive side of the whole affair. She touched my face, she supported my arm, held me carefully as I sat up, came with me to the hospital, insisting on coming, holding me as gently as any mother so that I seemed to have two mothers as I reached the casualty department, my own mother ordering doctors and nurses around – 'It's a fractured clavicle,' she told them. 'Nothing to get excited about' – while Marian stroked my cheek and explained to me how sorry she was, how very, very sorry. It was quite therapeutic for her, she told me long afterwards, to have someone to worry about other than herself. 'This'll help make it better,' she said. And she kissed me, a gentle touch of her lips on my cheek.

GUEST NIGHT

I can follow her through the alleyways of memory and recollection, tail her through the streets and the parks, through the obstacle course that those peacetime weeks and months had become. Much of my knowledge is second hand, gleaned from things overheard, or memories of moments captured and interpreted, or simply invented; but don't knock invention. Invention is what has got us human beings where we are. It helps us understand the workings of the universe. Maybe it can help me understand Marian. So I invent a telephone ringing in the hallway of the house on the Banbury Road and her lifting the receiver and saying, 'It's Marian Sutro here.'

Marian Sutro here. Not the hysterical young woman running out of the cinema, weeping and gasping, but the calm and collected one, the one who was trying to puzzle out who this man on the other end of the line might be.

'This is Alan.'

Try and observe your reactions objectively, the psychiatrist had advised her. Try and *objectify* yourself. So she did, and discovered a small grip of anticipation there inside her, like a hand tightening round her heart and throat. A strange sensation. 'Alan.'

'The very same. Look, we're having a ladies guest night at the Mess in two weeks' time. It's a bit of a formal thing but should be great fun as well. I was wondering whether you would do me the honour of being my guest.'

Do me the honour. Her mind stumbled over what he had said and what she might reply, over meanings and implications, all the hidden connotations in the code of ordinary language. 'Formal, you say?'

'Dressy. Mess kit, ladies in evening dress, speeches. Maybe it's not quite what you'd like . . .'

Confront your demons. Who had told her to do that? Both the psychiatrist and Alan Walcott himself. 'Will there be other guests? Women, I mean, other women.'

'Of course. Some wives, girlfriends.'

'Perhaps . . .'

'I'd quite understand if you didn't—'

'No, not at all.' Affirmatives tripped over negatives. 'Yes. Yes, I'd like to.'

'That's wonderful.' It was so difficult to read voices over the phone, so hard to make out emotion when you couldn't see the face, but it seemed to her, standing there in the hallway looking through a narrow window at the gravel drive, that there was real relief in his voice. He even admitted it. 'I had to summon up the courage to phone you,' he told her. 'You seemed rather offhand the last time. And then the business with that child, you rushing off to hospital . . .'

'Offhand?'

'I didn't really know if you wanted me to get in touch again . . .'

'I did,' she assured him. 'I did.'

'That's marvellous. Look, it'll be a pretty late do and everything, so I'll book a room for you at the George in Wallingford, if that's all right. I don't know if you know it. Old coaching inn, very quaint. You'd be my guest, of course. It means that we wouldn't have to drive all the way back to Oxford the same evening. Would that be OK?'

'Yes, yes, I suppose it would. Only . . .'

'Is it a problem? Please, if it's a problem . . .'

'No, no problem at all.' Only, I've not stayed in a hotel on my own since my training. Only, I'm afraid of the very idea.

'Then that's fine. I'll book a room right away.'

He collected Marian from home in the afternoon. It was easier to talk in the car, with the racket of the engine engulfing them and the countryside hammering past. 'How's the casualty?' he shouted over the noise.

She didn't understand at first. Was she the casualty?

'That little kid who had to be rushed to hospital. Your Florence Nightingale act.'

'Oh, Judith Wareham's boy. Florence Nightingale

154

didn't actually *cause* the injuries she dealt with, did she? Anyway, he's fine. Broken collarbone, strapped up a bit but he's fine.'

'You made a conquest there.'

'What do you mean?'

He changed gear with slick fluency, double-declutching, whipping the car through curves so that she instinctively put her hand to her head to keep her scarf from flying away in the wind. She fancied it was like being in an aircraft with him, tight beside him in the cockpit as he aimed the nose towards the oncoming tarmac. 'He couldn't take his eyes off you. Can't say I blame him.'

'Perhaps you'd be better off keeping your eyes on the road.'

He laughed.

'Have you told anyone about me?' she asked. 'In your squadron, I mean.'

'One or two. Do you mind?'

'It all depends what you said.'

'I said what's the truth, I'm afraid. That you are a damned remarkable girl.'

Girl. She liked that. Often she felt like an old woman, as old as the oldest woman, older than her mother, older than her French grandmother whom she hadn't seen since before the war, as ancient as any crone. But Alan Walcott called her a girl. 'I hope they don't make a fuss,' she said.

The hotel was an old, stooped building hunched around a cobbled courtyard. Inside there were low

155

beams and uneven floors and general shifting and creaking as you moved around. Alan quizzed her anxiously when she came down from her room. Was everything OK? Was she sure she was all right? As though she might be an invalid or some ancient, unwell maiden aunt. She didn't want that. She wanted to be normal, self-confident, that girl she had been when the whole damn thing had started, when fear was a rational emotion and new experiences were there to be confronted and conquered.

'Does it matter that I told people?' he asked, as if he was anxious not to have done wrong and the problem was nagging him.

Did it matter? That wasn't the only thing she didn't know. She didn't know what she was doing here with this unknown man either. Was she becoming his girlfriend? Was that what all this meant? 'I don't want to be the object of curiosity, that's all.'

'You won't be. They're good chaps. Everyone will be very friendly.' And then, quite startlingly, he put his hands on her shoulders and leaned forward and kissed her on the lips. And before she could decide what she felt about that he'd said, 'I'll pick you up at six-thirty,' and was outside, climbing into Gloria and roaring off.

Promptly at six-thirty he came to collect her. She'd had her hair permed. She was wearing more make-up than she had ever worn before and the dove grey Vionnet dress her mother had bought for her in Paris before the war began, the first real grownup dress she had owned. As she appeared at the top of the narrow staircase his expression was an untidy blend of shock and triumph. 'You look wonderful. I never realised . . .'

'What didn't you realise?'

'That you'd look so stunning.'

She was lit up by a forgotten glimmer of pride. 'I don't know whether that's a compliment or an insult.'

'It's a compliment. Clumsily expressed, but a compliment all the same.' He held out his arm for her to take. 'My lady's carriage awaits,' he said in an awkward attempt at humour.

'Let's have a drink first,' she suggested. 'Dutch courage.'

The Air Force station was only a few minutes away across the river. When they arrived, there were already cars outside the officers' mess, stewards at the door, a coming and going of men in uniform and women wearing what passed as evening dress in those days of austerity. The anteroom was crowded and awash with noise. She felt the panic crawl of insects beneath her skin as she came through the door. 'I don't think I can do this,' she whispered, grabbing Alan's hand for comfort.

He took glasses from a passing tray and handed her one. 'You're doing fine.' And it dawned on her that although she had not said anything about it, somehow he knew, somehow he understood the anxiety that eroded her fragile command of the moment.

Together they plunged into the crowd. A group of senior officers materialised before her, blue tunics and gold braid, medals glinting in the light – first the president of the Mess Committee, then Alan's squadron commander, then the station commander himself. Names and ranks she forgot instantly, eyes that looked her up and down, lingered over her bust and the line of her neck. 'Miss Sutro,' the station commander said. 'It's an honour to meet you.'

She didn't know how to reply. How could it be an honour? She attempted a smile while Alan said something on her behalf, something about his own experiences passing down the escape line through France.

'We always suspected Alan was having a holiday on the Riviera,' the station commander told her. 'Now I can see why.' People laughed. Alan steered her away through the crowd to find a group of pilots who were on his squadron. There were girls with them. One or two of the women tittered nervously when she was introduced, as though her presence was some kind of embarrassment. One of the men said, 'My brother served with 138 Squadron at Tempsford. Perhaps he dropped you. Jimmy Aldrich?'

Again she attempted a smile, recalling only young men grinning at her as they shook her hand beneath the overarching shadow of the aircraft's wing. 'I'm afraid I'm not very good at names.'

'Ginger-haired fellow. Looks like a blithering idiot.'

'Takes after his brother,' someone added. There was more laughter. Laughter seemed to be the universal panacea. There's a problem? Laugh. You feel nervous? Laugh. You feel frightened? Laugh.

'There I was, thirty-five thousand feet over the Ruhr and the bloody engine cuts out.' Laugh.

'Hanging from my bloody parachute and they're taking pot-shots at me.' Laugh.

'Tried to take off in coarse pitch and flew straight into the trees at the end of the runway.' Laugh.

Amid the laughter she drank gin and sensed the noise and the faces move away from her, as though they had stepped back behind a glass screen and could be heard only dimly. Alan was at her side, holding her arm. 'Gently,' he said. 'You're doing fine.' Somehow – she was unsure of the mechanism of this – he was inside the glass screen with her, just the two of them together with the others shuffling past beyond the pane, looking in.

Later – the minutes passed erratically – they all filed through into the dining room, junior officers and their guests first, senior officers at the door, laughter reduced to a buzz of conversation while they found their places at the long tables. Candlelight gleamed on silver. There were cups and tankards decorating the tables, and even a silver model of a camera. A model Spitfire angled across the top table where the senior officers and their guests sat. The three squadrons sat at three long tables arranged at right angles to the top table. Alan and Marian were on the borderline between the two, on the end of the high table, next to the squadron commander and his wife.

'An excellent flight commander,' the CO said of Alan, as though she might have an interest in his future. 'If he wants to stay on in the Air Force, he's got a good career ahead of him.'

The CO's wife was called Beryl. She was a blonde with the suggestion of good looks behind her prominent eyes and big teeth. 'My dear,' she whispered, leaning across her husband, 'never mind Alan's prospects – where *did* you get that divine dress?'

'Paris,' Marian said. She wished she could have said something different – Marshall and Snelgrove or Selfridges or somewhere. But Paris. 'It's Vionnet,' she added as if that might explain things.

'Vionnet? Goodness, how glamorous! It must be wonderful being French as well as English.'

'I'm afraid I've nothing to compare it with. It's just what I am.'

'So where's your family from exactly?'

People were listening, watching. She could feel eyes on her, the cold touch of curiosity. 'We lived in Geneva before the war. My father was with the League of Nations.'

'How very *international*. I must say, you don't look like someone who would do anything so extraordinary. But I suppose that's always the way.'

'I'm sorry? What d'you mean? There's nothing

much extraordinary about living in Geneva. A whole lot of *Genevois* do it.'

A shriek of laughter. 'No, I meant leaping out of an aircraft with a parachute. And then all the rest. Capture and everything. They say . . .'

'What do they say?'

'That you were most awfully badly treated.'

Under the tablecloth Alan's hand grabbed Marian's and held it tight for a moment. 'It was what we'd been trained to expect.'

The conversation stuttered. The stewards took the soup plates away and served something described as chicken supreme. Down the length of the tables glasses of wine gleamed garnet red, like jewels hanging from a necklace. The room hummed and roared around them and the subject slid away from Marian to other matters, to postings and possibilities, of what might happen to the squadron next. 'What are you going to do now it's all over?' the woman asked Marian.

'I've no idea.'

'No thought of settling down?'

'Perhaps I'll go back to France.'

'That'd be nice, wouldn't it? I'd love to go to France but Bill can't stand the food.'

They moved towards a kind of pudding, a blanc-mange the colour of lifebuoy soap. Then the table was cleared, port appeared and someone called for silence. Bill had been appointed to propose the Loyal Toast – Mr Vice he was called, which seemed bizarre, as though he might be about to

161

organise something disgraceful. He got to his feet and summoned the guests to stand. 'Ladies and gentlemen, the King!'

'The King!' they echoed, raising their glasses. As they resumed their seats and talk broke out once more, Mr Vice tapped a knife against his glass and brought the room back to silence again.

'There's just one further toast I'd like to propose,' he said. 'We have all of us done our bit over the last few years, but I'd like you all to raise your glasses to someone here who has done more than that. While we've been flying above it all – most of the time, anyway: I admit that Alan here did manage to get a rather lower level oblique than ops required.' There was laughter. Alan grinned and looked self-conscious. 'But Alan's continental holiday aside, while we've been flying as far above the action as we possibly could, this person was down there on the ground below us, living and working among the Krauts. And if we thought our work was a bit dicey at times, then hers was plain bloody dangerous.'

Marian saw faces turn towards her, ranks of pale moons.

'I believe I'm not even allowed to mention the name of her outfit because it remains secret, but Ronnie Aldrich tells me it used to masquerade as the Inter Services Research Bureau. So not all bureaucrats are what they seem to be. And I understand she is actually an honorary Flight Officer in the WAAF but she's here in civvies this evening and I must say her evening dress is a darn sight more stunning than mess kit. Anyway, it is a great honour to have her here as our guest – ladies and gentlemen, raise your glasses to Flight Officer Marian Sutro, latterly of the French resistance.'

Her heart convulsed. Gripped by something resembling fear she sat alone while the whole room rose, people looming over her, looking down on her, smiling and brandishing their glasses and their teeth.

'Marian Sutro!'

Her name echoed like a mantra round the dining room, the name that was hers and not hers, the name that had been covered by a whole panoply of other names – Alice, Anne-Marie Laroche, Laurence Follette, Geneviève Marchal – all hiding the one fragile fact of Marian Sutro, who sat alone at the table riven with fear.

It was Beryl who came to the rescue, grabbing her by the arm and ushering her out of the room to the sanctuary of the ladies. She sat Marian down and drew another chair close. 'I don't blame you,' she said. 'I'd have died a dozen deaths with all those people staring at me. But don't worry. Give them a few minutes and they'll have forgotten all about you.'

Other women followed them in. There were curious glances in her direction but the chatter was all about other things – men and boys, the awful pudding, the possibility of someone getting pie-eyed in the bar afterwards. Women leaned towards the mirrors to touch up their lipstick, speaking all the while. 'Did you see Sandra's dress? I thought her bosom was going to fall out all over the blancmange.'

'Who would have noticed the difference?'

Shrieks of laughter.

Somehow Beryl had conjured up two glasses of gin. She pushed one into Marian's hand. 'Here, take some medicine. Makes the wounded spirit whole and calms the troubled breast.' She offered cigarettes as well, Player's Airman.

Marian drew thankfully on the smoke. Smoke and gin seemed a good combination. 'Why didn't Alan warn me?' she asked.

'Oh, don't blame him, poor soul. He's floundering around not knowing what hit him.'

Behind Beryl the chatter went on: 'What about Raymond and Jenny? Is he going to pop the question?'

'He's already popped the cherry.'

Laughter.

'Did you see Brenda's shoes? How many coupons did they take?'

'Coupons, my backside. Her brother's in the business.'

Beryl leaned forward and took hold of Marian's hands. 'Look, darling, the problem is always that we don't know how others see us. We think one thing but half the time they see another. I'll be honest with you. When I first met Bill I was on the make, but he saw an innocent little girl with stars in her eyes. And when Alan looks at you he sees a woman who's way out of his class. Nothing like his usual girlfriends.'

'I'm not his girlfriend. We've only met up a couple of times – beer and sandwiches at the Trout and a picnic with friends.'

'Well, that's up to you. But ever since he's not stopped talking about you. The poor lad thought you weren't interested in him. He only plucked up courage to invite you this evening because I insisted. So he's frightened of you, and you're frightened of I don't know what. Memories, I suppose. Ghosts. Who can blame you? I've seen similar things with pilots – something happens and they lose their nerve and go to pieces. If it becomes official they get labelled LMF and demoted—'

'LMF?'

'Lack of Moral Fibre, darling. Unofficially, if their CO is in his right mind he doesn't report it and they get quietly posted away. People understand.' She squeezed Marian's hands. 'Believe me, darling, people *understand*. So don't go blaming them—'

'I'm not blaming anyone but myself.'

'Don't even do that. Try and see yourself as this lot see you. A stunning woman, dressed like a film star, who has done things no one here would dream of. Parachuted into occupied territory, lived a secret life, been captured and, I don't know, tortured probably. Then sent to a concentration

165

camp – we've all seen the films, for God's sake. And here she is, drifting into their mess like Greta bloody Garbo. They're bowled over, darling. All the women think you're gorgeous and all the men . . . well, I won't go into what the men think but it doesn't involve the Vionnet dress. So when you want to run away from people because you are frightened of them, just remember this: they are *terrified* of you.'

They went back into the fray. People had moved from the dining room to the bar. There was more laughter, the sound of the Englishman in drunken pursuit of fun. Women stood round the edges and watched as two junior officers played some silly game that involved sitting blindfolded on the floor and each trying to hit the other with a rolled-up newspaper. 'Are you there, Moriarty?' they called to each other.

Alan stood beside her and took her hand. 'Are you all right? Christ, you gave me a turn.'

'I'm quite all right, thank you.'

'I thought you were going to keel over.'

One of the younger officers came up and said, 'I saw your story in the paper. It was you, wasn't it? Anne-Marie S or something. I just want to say, how bloody thrilled I am to meet you.'

She smiled and didn't know how to answer. It was like being royalty, receiving congratulations for something that she didn't merit. They chatted for a while about nothing much. Music was coming from a gramophone in the anteroom – the strains of Artie Shaw playing 'Begin the Beguine'. Some people were dancing.

'Do you want to go back to the hotel?' Alan asked.

'I think I want to dance, although I'm not very good. The last time I danced was in 1943. It seems a long time ago.'

So he took her hand and led her out onto the floor. Dancing was a palliative. They shuffled around among the shifting couples, suddenly close together, their bodies touching for the first time. She felt calm and inconsiderable, no longer the object of curiosity but just someone there among others, doing what they did. It was during the dance that he kissed her. She had been expecting it of course, but still it was another small epiphany, a fractional release from things that bound her, the taste of someone else's cigarettes and wine, the hint of an intimacy that might be. They moved together so that he was pressed against her belly, a hard rib between them.

'Alan,' she said. Just his name.

His mouth was close to her ear, his voice very loud. 'Is that all right?'

'I think it's rather a surprise.'

She felt the breath of his laughter. 'Not entirely my fault. Yours as well.'

'I can't help it.'

'Neither can I. Maybe that covers quite a lot of things.'

It was after one o'clock that they finally left. Beryl gave her a kiss and told her she'd been the belle of the ball. Bill said well done, as though there had been something to do in the first place and, whatever it was, that something had been done successfully. She thought them all wonderfully friendly and slightly absurd. Drunk, probably. Was she drunk as well? The world seemed very easy at the moment, so perhaps she was. Even the rain that was falling as they went out to the car didn't matter. They crammed themselves into Gloria's narrow cockpit while drizzle rattled on the roof as though they were in a tent.

'They're nice,' she said. 'Bill and Beryl. *Très chouette.*'

'What's schwet?'

She laughed. 'An owl. *Sympathique.* I've no idea why an owl should be sympathetic.'

As they drove, the headlights carved an unsteady beam through the smudged, charcoal night. When they reached the hotel the place seemed shut up. They clambered unsteadily out onto the pavement, giggling and whispering in the rain, giving out a small cry of triumph when they discovered that the main door opened and there was a small light shining at the reception desk. But no night porter on duty. She retrieved the key to her room while Alan stood uncertainly in the shadows. 'Are you all right?'

She was all right. Better than expected. 'Do you want to come up?' she asked, wondering what her question signified, and what his response would mean. That was the trouble with questions and answers. You were never sure what either meant.

The stairs were uneven and full of insidious creaking. They tiptoed along a narrow corridor and when they came to the door to her room the key did not seem to fit.

'Are you sure it's the right one?' he whispered.

'Of course I'm sure.'

'I meant the room, are you sure this is the right room?'

That seemed most ridiculously funny. Fiddling with the lock, they stifled giggles. 'D'you know, they trained us in housebreaking?'

'You're joking.'

'Deadly serious. An ex-convict came and gave us lessons in how to pick locks.'

'And you can't even—'

'Open a damned door with the key.' There was a little explosion of laughter as the lock finally yielded. The room was damp and dusty, scented with her perfume, a kind of sanctuary. Scattered on the bed were the clothes she had changed out of earlier – stockings, underwear, her skirt on the floor, her jacket tossed across a chair. 'I didn't really expect this,' she said. But she felt quite determined, liberated by drink and by the tensions of the evening; and younger, much younger than she had been for months. There were other factors working within her as well: a reawakening of sexual attraction of course, the rhythms of her body re-emerging from dormancy; but also something else, the feeling that this might shake her out of the reserve in which she was trapped – that she might love him.

Alan frowned. 'Look, if you—'

She held up her hand. 'Don't. For years I haven't really been able to make decisions for myself. Now I can.' And then she kissed him, standing in the middle of the room among the litter of her things. His mouth tasted of cigarettes and whisky. There was something shockingly intimate about the contact, the sensation of his tongue, the feeling of his opening up to her and she to him.

He tried to pull away. 'Marian, I don't have, you know . . .'

'What?'

'A Johnny. French letter. Whatever you want to call it.'

She laughed. '*Capote anglaise*, that's what the French say . . .'

'It wouldn't be safe.'

'Safe? I haven't been safe for over two years.'

The aphrodisiac of laughter, the mingling of wine and whisky and cigarettes, the struggling with buttons and fasteners until they were more or less naked, clumsy together, falling onto the bed as though in some kind of conflict, all rules and constraints gone. She didn't care, that was the frightening thing. She didn't care that his chin was rough against her neck and her breasts. She didn't care when she felt his hands on her, opening her thighs, cupping her there, his finger inside, stroking. She didn't care what he was doing or might do. She reached down to take hold of his cock. She'd never done anything like that before, never with Benoît, never with Clément. The touch of it surprised her, the fluid mobility of the skin, the strange heaviness it possessed, as though weighted with some dense element as yet unknown. She drew him towards her. 'Marian,' he cried out. But she didn't want to say his name in return. That would change things, create out of this a moment of consummation, a declaration of intent, a bond of some kind. She knew what she was doing, how much this might mean, how dangerous it was. And she didn't care, because danger was something she had learned to survive.

'Come inside me,' she whispered and felt the thrill of saying it. 'Come inside me,' she repeated, pushing herself upwards against him. There was that sudden, shocking intrusion, a pushing and shoving, cries of 'Oh God' – appeals to a deity she didn't believe in except perhaps at this carnal moment, when all things seemed subsumed into one, the single fact of his presence there within her and her swollen self engulfing him and convulsions coursing through her, inundating her, leaving her exhausted on the bed, like a prisoner pulled from drowning and dumped unceremoniously on the floor to gasp for air.

*   *   *

171

Later, much later, he slipped from the bed and dressed. In the way that one is aware of things happening in a dream, she sensed his bending down to kiss her and then the door opening and closing so quietly that it might not have happened. Nine o'clock, she remembered before she drifted off to sleep: he said he'd come for her at nine o'clock.

When she awoke her watch said six-forty. Her head ached with memory and alcohol. Her mouth was dry. She crept to the bathroom and washed him from her, inside and out. She was a bit sore. What if she got pregnant? If she got pregnant she'd have a baby. It would give her something to do, someone to care about other than herself. But she wouldn't get pregnant. Her period was only a few days ago. These things didn't happen.

By quarter past seven she was in the dining room having breakfast before any other guests were up. Back in her room she packed her things and carried her case downstairs. According to the girl at the reception desk there was a bus for Oxford at eight o'clock. There was just time to pay the bill, scribble a message and seal it in an envelope. 'Flight Lieutenant Walcott will be coming at nine,' she told the girl. 'Make sure he gets it.'

She felt curiously free of all encumbrance. The outside world, Wallingford High Street, held no threat. It seemed absurd that it might ever have done so. Waiting for the bus was what she had done in Lussac, in Condom, in Toulouse, in a dozen other places in France when she was strong and composed and sure of herself. She felt like that now. She could do anything.

Dear Alan,
I'm sorry to leave like this. I thought it better that way instead of being rather awkward with each other. Thank you for everything, really. It was a lovely evening in every way. Please don't be upset.
Affectionately,
Marian

AFTERMATH

He rang. She knew who it would be, as one knows these things. A kind of sixth sense, although she didn't believe in such a power. 'Yes,' she said when he spoke his name. 'Of course.'

'Were you expecting me to ring?'

'Sort of.'

'Are you angry?'

'Certainly not.'

'Not ashamed, I hope.'

'No, not ashamed either. Ashamed is to do with religion, isn't it? I don't have any religion.'

'Look, can we meet? We can't discuss this on the phone. I want to see you, talk to you face to face—'

'Some kind of post-mortem?'

'Is it dead, then?'

There was a silence. 'I don't know, Alan.'

'Then let's talk about it.'

'I don't think so.'

He wrote her letters explaining how he felt for her. From the moment when he had first set eyes on her, when she had appeared in the foyer of the

Randolph Hotel, he had fallen in love with her. He'd never believed in love at first sight and yet it had happened. But he also understood. After all that had happened to her, he understood that she didn't want to be hurried into a relationship. Yet what had happened between them was not his fault alone, was it? They were both to blame and in retrospect it had been a stupid thing to do. But what had happened had happened. No use crying over spilt milk. Was that an unfortunate metaphor? he wondered.

She laughed at that.

And, he had to say it, that night had been the most wonderful of his life. Even though he couldn't recall much of it.

A later letter suggested that perhaps there was another possibility. The idea hadn't occurred to him earlier, but it was this: she had fallen pregnant and didn't want to burden him with the problem. But he would stand by her, of course he would. And acknowledge the child as his and give it – her, him – his name.

She liked that phrase: fallen pregnant. Falling out of grace, falling into pregnancy. She wouldn't mind being pregnant. It might give her something to live for. Might.

After reading it she tore up each letter and then, the careful training of the organisation being what it was, burned the pieces in an ashtray.

A BOMB

The news came one warm evening in August. She heard it while sitting in her bedroom, listening to the wireless. It was the usual newsreader's voice, high-pitched, eager, imbued with the sense that everything was for the best in the best of all possible worlds:

'President Truman has announced a tremendous achievement by the Allied scientists: they have produced an atomic bomb. One has already been dropped on a Japanese Army base. It alone contains as much explosive power as two thousand of our great ten-tonners. The President has also fore-shadowed the enormous peacetime value of harnessing atomic energy.'

She sat there as though slapped, while the disem-bodied voice maundered on about Bank Holiday thunderstorms and a record crowd at Lord's where Australia had made 265 for five wickets, as though nothing much else had happened. But she remem-bered. She remembered Clément explaining and Ned talking in the depressed, dispassionate tone of scientists, of what could be done and would be done. She remembered standing in the gardens outside Ned's flat with two flints in her hand and banging them together. The sulphurous smell of sparks. 'That's it,' Ned had said. 'You've just blown London off the map.'

That night she dreamed. The falling dream that she hadn't had for so long. Falling, falling into the darkness that became a flash of light. Clément was part of the dream, falling with her.

The next morning the main pages were covered in the story, a thin layer of triumphalism and evasion washing almost everything else onto lesser pages. An army base, the man on the radio had said; but it wasn't an army base. It was an entire city destroyed, a city she had never heard of. That was what Clément had explained, talking of Paris – how, if this kind of bomb exploded over the Île de la Cité, the destruction would reach south to Montparnasse and northwards all the way to the Butte de Montmartre. A city vaporised. And he was right. The sketch maps in the newspapers showed that it was so, with rings drawn around a simple cross in the middle of this Japanese city. The rings were labelled 'total destruction', 'severe structural damage', 'moderate structural damage', 'light damage'.

An entire city blown off the map.

She thought of the Japanese. She didn't quite know how to picture them. Images came to mind of submissive women, hands together, bowing like nuns. And savage, monkey soldiers being killed in their thousands on fragments of rock and spits of sand in the midst of the Pacific Ocean. What else was there? Samurai warriors. Geisha girls. Madame Butterfly. All reduced to charcoal one fine day.

The super bomb had happened.

At breakfast her father seemed bewildered. 'What have we come to?' he asked, of no one in particular, from behind his copy of *The Times*. 'Now it appears we can massacre tens of thousands of people without any risk to ourselves. It seems the very depths of barbarism.'

She tore a fragment of toast and buttered it with care. 'Do you know what, Father?'

He flipped the newspaper down and looked at her with a hopeless expression. 'Tell me, my dear.'

'If they had possessed a bomb like this when I was in the camp and they had dropped it on Berlin to end the war . . .'

'You would have cheered them on? Of course you would have, Squirrel. And, had I known the plight you were in, so would I. But it's a complex piece of mathematics, isn't it, balancing numbers of dead? I wonder how many deaths my daughter's life is worth?'

Why did that bleak little speech upset her so much? But the upset wasn't an overt one. There were no tears, no hysterics, just a profound misery eating away at the very foundations of her mind. She spoke quietly, almost as though she was only just understanding: 'That's what Clément was doing in Canada. That's why I got him out of Paris.'

The following silence was punctuated by the ritual sounds of breakfast, the buttering of toast, the pouring of tea, the stirring of sugar.

'Pelletier?'

'Clément Pelletier, yes. That's why they wanted him – to help build that bomb.' It seemed incredible, the implications unremitting and inexorable, spreading out like the shockwave of the bomb itself. From her small presence in Paris to this story on the news – another city on the other side of the world obliterated.

Her father looked at her over the top of his paper. 'Now how would you know a thing like that, Squirrel? It would all have been most secret. It says here in the paper, "complete secrecy guarded all these activities, and no single person was informed whose work was not indispensible to progress".'

She felt a sudden anger. 'Didn't you ever *listen* to what Ned used to say, Papa? Ned told me. For God's sake listen! Ned *told* me. He told you as well, although you wouldn't listen. This secret the papers talk about wasn't a secret at all. Ned said—'

'Oh, Ned always says—'

'—that everyone in science knew. It was obvious. Don't you remember that last Christmas in Geneva before the war, how he and Clément were talking about it all the time? Energy, vast amounts of energy liberated by the splitting up of atoms. And all you could say was it sounded like alchemy.'

He frowned, as if the mad ideas of his son

couldn't possibly have had an impact in the real world. 'The transmutation of the elements?'

'That was it, that's what Clément was working on in Paris with Frédéric Joliot. When I turned up in the city during the occupation, Clément knew very well why they'd sent me.' She looked around for something else to say. But there was nothing really, and nothing much to feel – just her own little fragment of guilt lodged like a sharp splinter in her sternum. Or worse, like a small nodule of uranium, apparently harmless but giving out radiation, a constant emission of radiation eating away at her tissues. 'It doesn't matter,' she said. 'It really doesn't matter.'

Three days later they dropped a second bomb on a second city no one had ever heard of; three days after that Japan surrendered and the war, the whole war, had finally come to an end.

FURZE

It was my mother who suggested we take Marian down to the cottage on the coast. It would do her good, Mother decided. The sea air would do her good. The sound of the sea and the cry of the gulls would all do her good. Ozone, no doubt she mentioned ozone; which everyone seemed to think would also do people good, although ozone is an allotrope of oxygen, and it's poisonous.

The cottage, Furze Cottage, belonged to my father's family. It was where he had spent most of his childhood holidays and where we had gone every summer until it disappeared inside the restricted coastal defence area in 1939. Clad in weatherboard, the building has something of the appearance of a houseboat about it – clinker-built and sturdy, capable of floating but marooned by a high tide on the side of a hill overlooking Pett Level, which is flatland trying not to be salt marsh and not always succeeding. In the distance is the low spit of Dungeness. At the back of the house the land climbs to the top of sandstone cliffs that, being dirty beige, are a marked contrast to the patriotic chalky white ones further along the coast in either direction.

181

The atmosphere of the house is of family intimacy of a faintly old-fashioned kind. At the seaward end there's a sitting room with sagging sofas, old leather armchairs and a log fire that smokes when the wind blows in the wrong direction; leading back from this is a corridor lined like a picture gallery with monochrome memories of past summers – my father as a young boy showing a fossil he had found in the cliffs; my parents on their honeymoon looking awkward and slightly surprised, as though whatever had happened in the privacy of their bedroom was not quite what they had expected; aunts and uncles disporting themselves in various clumsy swimming costumes; myself as a toddler with my mother almost smiling with delight. But for me it is different now because every time I go there I feel the presence of Marian. I barely even recall her parents, who were with us as well – it is just Marian. Marian sitting curled up in one of the armchairs; Marian in the kitchen, cooking brown crabs that we bought from a fisherman in Hastings; Marian down on the empty shingle beach where mines had only just been cleared, paddling in the water at low tide, her ivory limbs imbued with some kind of magic, as ethereal as any Pre-Raphaelite lady of the lake. She wore a navy swimming costume with a narrow pelmet across the bottom. I remember that, the scrupulous attempt to hide her crotch. I watched her closely, and tried not to; I hung around her whatever she was doing, and pretended to be about my own business. She must have seen through my subterfuges but I think she felt sorry for me, and apologetic for having been instrumental in my breaking my collarbone, which was still in the process of mending, although I was by then no longer forced to wear a sling. Perhaps that is why, while my sister made sandcastles under the careless eye of my mother, Marian was willing to join me in a search for fossils beneath the cliffs, or poke around among bits of wrack that lay about the place, wreckage from a recent storm. The rocks were encrusted with mussels which we broke open to reveal a slippery, viscid inner life. '*Moules*,' she told me. 'We French love *moules*.'

We French. *Nous autres Français. Moules.* I watched her mouth as she uttered the words. To speak French seemed to require a different movement of her lips, a plasticity, a mobility, a prehensile grasp of the sound. I shivered with repugnance and delight.

We returned to our towels and she lay down in the sun with her eyes shut. Lying a few feet away I could look at her more closely, at the angle of her neck, the soft hillocks of her bosom. Hiding beneath the pelmet of her costume was a sleek curved delta of cotton that concealed I knew not what: something marine, something molluscan of which I had only the vaguest idea. On the inside of her groin there was a scribble of hair like the byssus of the mussels we had gathered.

But such pleasures were as fleeting as the inadequate sunshine. Most days we went walking along the dunes or up on the cliff paths, talking of things that were centuries away from the war and its ghastly aftermath. In the evenings, in front of a fire of driftwood, while the others read, she and I attempted a jigsaw that we found in a wooden games chest. We knelt at the table and the picture gradually took shape beneath our fingers – Millais's painting of Ophelia drowning.

It was the first time I had been in such close and prolonged proximity to an adult who wasn't family. I was fascinated and thrilled by her physical closeness, by the brush of her hair against my cheek as she reached across to place a piece; by our sudden collision of hands as we each grabbed for the same piece and, laughing, wrestled with it for possession; by her scent which seemed to belong to her alone, as much her as the particular curve of her mouth or the strange gaze of her dark eyes. This sense of proximity to her was continued even when we all retired to bed because she occupied the room next to mine and the wall between us was mere plasterboard and I could hear her moving about, hear the flow of water in her washbasin, the creaking of the floorboards beneath her feet, the sound of bedsprings as she lay down. I followed her every move through the house, knew when she slept and when she rose, when she was in the kitchen making coffee or in the bathroom washing. One morning, as I hovered in the corridor, she opened the bathroom door and came out, pulling her dressing gown around her and giving me a glimpse, just a treasured glimpse, of one loose, lard-white breast with its surprising, roseate nipple. 'Whoops!' she exclaimed, and laughed, crossing the corridor and closing the door to her bedroom behind her and leaving my stunted twelve-year-old mind swollen with her presence, bloated with fantasy.

She, of course, saw things quite differently. Level-headed, she played the dutiful and attentive daughter and friend. She tolerated the boredom. She walked, went swimming, played with the little girl and the tiresome older brother who couldn't keep his eyes off her. Doubtless her parents found it all very touching and a confirmation of the idea they had, that the break would do her good, get her away from her nightmares, bring her gently down to earth. But Marian Sutro was practised in the arts of dissimulation. She knew when to laugh and when to argue – never too forcefully and always with a due concession at the end – when to show affection and when to show submission. She knew how to play the part, how to live her cover story as though it were her own.

'What a wonderful morning,' she would exclaim when she sat down at the breakfast table. 'What's the plan today?' As though a plan brought purpose to our stay. As though the future, either immediate or distant, might be given meaning. But

185

inside she knew the awful abyss of indifference, the great void left by what had happened to her and what had happened as a result of her. At night she lay awake and watched the sky through the window of her bedroom to witness the moon rise. *The sun shall not burn thee by day, neither the moon by night.* She felt burned by the moon, governed by the moon. It pulled at the tides of her body, touched her as Benoît had touched her, and Clément, and the Air Force pilot whose name she had almost forgotten. Walcott. Alan Walcott. And Véronique. She thought of Véronique dying on the sands of the Appellplatz while the other women watched. She thought of Benoît dead, and Yvette and Emile lost. And the dead darlings – Violette and Noor, Yvonne and Lilian and others, girls she had known only by reputation, or a glance across some briefing room, or a nodded acknowledgement as they passed each other in the corridor of Orchard Court. All dead. All dead, too, the tens of thousands in Hiroshima and Nagasaki, dead beneath the sun of Clément's super bomb.

And she, for reasons that were unclear to her, was alive. Beyond being touched, beyond emotion, beyond caring about anyone or anything. As cold and pale and desolate as the moon, planning things out with all the care she had shown when organising a *parachutage* or the pick-up with the Lysander; governed by the moon.

She waited until three o'clock in the morning, the time when, Napoleon himself said – and he should have known well enough – that you need real courage. She dressed, as silently as she could, in the slacks and an old sweater she used for walking, then moved silently through the house, carefully avoiding the particular floorboards that creaked – they'd even taught her how to do that at Beaulieu – to the front door. In the glass porch she laced up her walking boots and, once ready, made her way silently through the garden onto the cliff path. The moon was almost full, riding high over shards of cloud, beating the sea from pewter to silver. In its light she could see the path clearly enough and it took her ten minutes to reach the place she had chosen, where the path ran close to the edge and someone had erected an approximate fence.

It was easy enough to climb over the fence and walk over the uneven turf to the lip of the cliff. She stood there in the updraft of wind, looking out across the glittering sea towards France, with the wave noise coming up from below like the roar of a great engine. Before her lay the vacant space into which she might leap. Just a step.

How long she remained there without moving wasn't clear. Nothing was clear to her except the breeze and the sea stretching out across to the continent, and the moon. She thought of the impoverished space of her cell at Fresnes Prison where there had only been a narrow slot of blue or grey high up in the angle between wall and ceiling, where sometimes, if you got the right angle, you could see the moon; and the wide space of Ravensbrück where the moon was the only beautiful thing you ever saw. The sun was not beautiful; it was harsh and burning, the power of the atom made manifest, the strong nuclear force that had reduced two Japanese cities and their inhabitants to charcoal, unleashed. But the moon possessed almost no force, only the pull of gravity that Ned said was the weak force, the weakest force in nature, just enough strength to tug at the coat-tails of the earth and pull the ocean back and forth. Yet it would suffice to pull her down within seconds.

She stands, poised on the edge of the abyss. She jumps. There's a rush of wind. It's the falling dream, the flying dream, the dark hole down which she plunges or floats, watching the world go past, sometimes slowly, sometimes too fast to see clearly. This time it's cold and she gasps and cries out. This time it's fast and the world cartwheels round her, giving a glimpse of rock and a slanting, sly shine of water. This time there's the dull black of the cliff and the luminous black of the sky, and the moon swirling around her. Then the crack of her parachute overhead like the sound of a sail filling with sudden wind and the boat keeling over and somewhere someone laughing with the pure pleasure of it.

She sat down with a thump, her feet slithering from under her, bits skittering over the edge, her bottom settled on some lump of rock. And like a small child falling over she burst into tears, more from the shock and indignity of it all rather than any hurt. She had been fearless walking to the edge but now fear gripped her. Poised over the abyss, she moved and slithered. She remembered training in Scotland, splashing through the bogs, crawling through the wet grass and over the rocks, grabbing at heather, grabbing now at whatever her claws could find, pulling herself up the slope to the path and sitting there in the moonlight, weeping.

She hadn't bothered with her watch so how long she sat there she could only tell by the moon, which had shifted across the sky by the time she moved. How many degrees? Ned would have known. He'd probably have been able to convert it to minutes and hours. Twelve hours for one hundred and eighty degrees. Twelve goes into one hundred and eighty fifteen times. So fifteen degrees for each hour. Which left only the problem of how to measure degrees in the sky.

She got to her feet, shaking. She was not brave enough to die, ergo she had no choice but to live. There was some kind of logic to that, and some kind of obligation. She set off back along the cliff path, stumbling occasionally over a rock or a clump of turf, trying not to think too hard about anything. Life is an interlude between two deaths; there was no choice but to endure it. Eventually below her, lit by moonlight, drawn in chiaroscuro and cross-hatched with shadow, was the roof of the house. Furze Cottage. Silly name.

She walked down, opened the gate, went through the garden. In the porch she took off her boots and placed them on the little wooden rack where they had been before. Then she opened the front door and stepped silently into the living room, and gasped as she came in, because I was sitting on the sofa watching her.

'Christ alive!'

For a moment I thought she might be about to scream but she recovered her composure quickly enough. 'Sam. God, you gave me a fright.'

'I'm sorry,' I said. 'I didn't mean to frighten you. I was just . . . worried.'

'Worried about what?' Shaking – I assumed she was cold – she sat down on the sofa beside me, breathing out as though exhausted, folding her legs and clutching her knees to her. There was mud on her face and hands and the smell of crushed grass around her. She felt in her pocket and found a packet of cigarettes and lit one hungrily, pulling at the smoke and blowing it away. I noticed the dirt under her fingernails; and the trembling. On the table in front of us the jigsaw still lay, half completed: a frame of vegetation and Ophelia's face and disembodied hands. 'What the devil are you doing up at this hour?' she asked eventually.

It was a question that I could have put to her. 'I couldn't sleep.'

'Same as me. How long have you been up?'

'Dunno. Where d'you go?'

'I went for a walk along the cliffs.'

'In the dark?'

'It's practically daylight out there.'

I was incapable of discerning mood or motive in adults. Why wouldn't she go off for a moonlit walk? It didn't seem an unreasonable thing to do. And yet I knew other things about her, disturbing things I couldn't quite understand despite their being so obvious: her shaking, the hurried movements, the uncertainty. Nerves, I thought.

'Can I tell you something?' I asked.

'Of course you can.'

'You won't laugh at me?'

'That depends if it's funny or not.'

'No, seriously.'

'Seriously, no. I won't laugh. If it's serious.'

I nodded. For days I had been working out how to do this and now seemed as good a moment as I could have hoped for. In the half light of the sitting room I could face her without the awful handicap of blushing. 'I'm in love with you,' I said.

She didn't laugh. If she had laughed that might have been the end of it – cringing with embarrassment, I'd have slunk off to bed and never spoken to her, never even looked at her again. But she didn't laugh. I could see her face, brushed faintly by moonlight. She seemed to be considering my confession with great solemnity. 'Well, that's very flattering,' she said.

'I know you're much older. But I'll catch you up.'

That did bring a faint smile. 'Come here,' she

said, putting her arm around me and drawing me closer. We sat there for a moment while thoughts sacred and profane tumbled through my twelve-year-old mind. The shivering had stilled. Her body was warm again, alive, something I wanted to cling to.

'I really don't think I'm worth loving, Sam,' she said.

'That's for me to decide.'

'And I'm not sure you are quite old enough to love a woman. At your age you love your mother and your sister but that's a different thing. When you're older you'll fall in love with someone your own age and then you'll find out what it's all about.'

I was getting the sort of story that any adult would have told any lovestruck child in the same circumstances. I knew that. But in childhood it's easy to hold two contradictory thoughts at the same time, even easier than it is when you're an adult (and it's pretty easy then): so to me her words seemed imbued with wisdom and understanding.

'Is there someone *you* love?' I asked her.

She was silent for a moment, smoking and thinking. Then, 'There was,' she said. A boy, she told me, a French boy. Somehow I understood that by 'boy' she still meant a grown-up, someone of her own age, someone who did what she had done, which seemed impossibly brave and wonderful. I listened to her story with growing disappointment. Clearly I would never match up to this French boy, whoever he was. 'You did all that?' I asked. 'You really jumped out of an aircraft together in the middle of the night? Really?'

'Really,' she assured me. 'It was a night like this, with a big full moon.'

'What was it like?'

'Frightening. Exciting. A whole lot of things, all at once.'

I struggled to get my mind around the whole idea. This woman. A Halifax four-engined bomber. Night time, hundreds of miles away from home. The Gestapo waiting below. And a companion with her, a man, a boy, whom she wanted to talk about.

'He was much braver than me. Nothing seemed to worry him. Everything was a joke, everything could be shrugged off. D'you know what I mean?'

'Yes,' I agreed, as though my own life was populated by such people. Her arm was still round my shoulders. I lay with my face against her, feeling the warmth of her body and smelling her scent, mingled as it was with the smell of mud and grass. There was nothing that I could imagine more wonderful than this moment, except that she was talking about him.

'And yet, he was very tender. And thoughtful. I think . . . I don't know what I think, really. I think I was in love with him and didn't realise it at the time.'

'I know what you do when you're in love,' I told

her.

'I'm sure you do.'

'Did you do *that* with him?'

Looking up at her I saw what I supposed was a smile. 'It's what everyone does, Sam.'

'Were you married to him?'

'No.'

'But still you did it?'

She squeezed me against her. I could feel the soft mass of her breast against my cheek. 'It was wartime, Sam. You snatch what comfort you can in wartime.'

'Where is he now, this man?'

There was a moment of silence. The building creaked and shifted. Beyond the windows was the sound of the sea and the mutter of the wind. 'He's dead. He died in the fighting in France. So perhaps it's a good thing we did it when we did. And now I think it's time for both of us to get back to bed, don't you?'

I didn't but I would have agreed with her about almost anything. Holding hands we tiptoed back along the corridor. Outside my door she bent and kissed me. 'Sweet dreams,' she said.

In my room I waited breathlessly to hear her own door open and close. I knew she'd find nothing amiss. Everything in her room remained exactly as it was when she had left it earlier – her handbag on the chair, a pair of shoes lying on the floor, her nightdress thrown across the bed, even the note she had written to her parents and placed carefully on the pillow where they would have been certain to find it when they came looking for her in the morning.

She picked the piece of paper up and tore it across. Then, as she had been taught, she burned the pieces carefully in an ashtray and washed the ashes down the basin. I heard the sound of water running. Then she took off her clothes, put on her nightdress, climbed into bed – I heard the sound of the bedsprings – and began to face the remainder of her life.

Dear Maman and Papa,

By the time you read this you will already be worrying about where I am. I want to try and spare you any further doubt or anxiety – I have done away with myself. The coastguards will probably find my body at some time but don't let anyone put himself at risk on my behalf. They won't be able to save me. If you want to give them some indication of where I might be, tell them to try the beach below the cliffs, but it's high tide and my body may have been washed out to sea. Maybe I'll end up in France.

I'm sorry for all this. I can't say anything more than that – just sorry for the pain I will have inflicted on you both. Don't, whatever you do, blame yourselves – blame me. But try and understand that I cannot see any other way to go. Things that happened to me when I was in captivity seem to have taken something out of me. I can't put it back. Count me, I suppose, as one of the war dead.

Remember, please remember, that I loved you both, and Ned.

Squirrel.

You may wonder if I have made that up. In a sense, so many years after the event, I must have. But I've captured the gist of the note, the brevity, the concern about the pain and the coastguards, the curious use of the past tense of the final line, almost implying that, at the moment of writing, she no longer did. And the way she signed off. Squirrel. I know all this because I had been a spy as much as she. I had heard her moving about her room in the dead of night, heard her door opening and closing, listened to her feet moving along the corridor and into the sitting room. I had sensed, rather than heard, the front door open and close; and then I'd watched from the window as her dark shadow crossed the moonlit garden and disappeared up the cliff path.

I moved quietly, like a thief in the night. Moonlight gave her room a ghostly air. Her night-dress lay across the bed. I bent down and pressed my face into its folds and knew her smell. And then I saw the note. It had been placed on the pillow, in the shallow depression made by her head, a single fold of paper with her writing on it. I dared switch on the sidelight to see better.

Dear Maman et Papa . . .

. . . Count me, I suppose, as one of the war dead . . .
Squirrel.

I was suspended in one of those strange para-
doxes of childhood, where you know and don't
know, understand and yet remain bewildered.

My body . . .

I'd watched her body, sheathed in its swimming
costume, alive. And now would it be *dead*?

Don't let anyone put himself at risk on my behalf . . .

The words of someone who had risked
everything.

I loved you both, and Ned.

I replaced the note and slipped out of her room,
crept along to the sitting room and sat down on
the sofa. For a while I contemplated following her;
then thought better of it. She would wish to be
alone to complete whatever there was to complete.
Or maybe not. So I sat and waited, understanding
and not understanding; afraid and yet confident
that nothing would happen.

And then she came back.

PEACE UNION

In the first days of September Marian Sutro presented herself at the offices of the Franco-British Pacific Union. The Union may have sounded like a steamship company, but there the resemblance ended. It was a cultural organisation dedicated, so it claimed in a badly printed pamphlet, to promoting peace and understanding between two ancient enemies and present friends – Great Britain and France. It occupied a suite of ground-floor offices off High Holborn. The library was in the basement.

'We moved all the books out to Rickmansworth for the duration,' Miss Miller explained. 'And now we've got to move them back again.' She was a scrawny woman with an air of despair about her, as though she had been waiting too long for someone – Mr Right? – to rescue her from this place and had just recently given up. Her brother, she was quick to inform Marian, had been killed in Spain, fighting for the International Brigade, fighting the war, as she put it, long before the politicians in Britain woke up to it.

Her boss and the head of the Union was called

Mr Roper. He was middle-aged and portly with thin black hair that was dusted with dandruff. He had a penchant for bow ties and wore a green velvet waistcoat that he fancied gave him a literary appearance. Writing was his main occupation, short acerbic articles for poorly printed left wing publications. 'Our Soviet allies' was a phrase in frequent use, while 'capitalist warmongers' usually referred to the Americans. De Gaulle was frequently excoriated as a creature of the right wing; Jacques Duclos, *éminence grise* of the French Communist Party, seemed to be capable of doing little wrong. During the war, Roper had fulfilled some vague function within the Ministry of Information; now his main task seemed to be the persecution of his assistant Peter, a slender youth with a prominent Adam's apple and appallingly bad French. 'Pierre, *viens ici*!' would sound through the offices and, wherever he was, Peter was expected to drop his work and hurry to Mr Roper's side to receive praise and criticism in equal measure.

'This, Pierre, is Mademoiselle Sutro,' Mr Roper said when Marian presented herself. 'At least *she* can speak French, *n'est-ce pas*?'

Marian admitted that she could.

'We are given to understand that Mademoiselle – do you understand the term *mademoiselle*, Pierre? – Mademoiselle Sutro did something very *hush-hush* during the course of the recent hostilities. Whereas all you did was hide in a shelter while the Fascist buzz bombs struck down the dwellings of the workers.'

Peter grinned awkwardly.

'Pierre was a conscientious objector, you see,' Roper explained. 'He still is, I believe. I don't think it is something you can put on merely when the bullets begin to fly, is it? Once an *objecteur de conscience*, always an *objecteur de conscience*. *Même lorsque le paix éclate*. I don't expect you comprehend that, do you, Pierre? Even when peace breaks out.'

'Conscientious objection demands its own kind of courage, Mr Roper,' Peter said, blushing.

'It is, *mon cher*, the very antithesis of courage.'

Miss Miller whisked Marian away from this scene of conflict into the quiet shadows of the basement. She led the way round cardboard boxes of books and pointed out metal shelving with faded, peeling labels. 1 *Philosophie et psychologie*. 2 *Religion et Théologie*. Subsections descended to the floor: 21 *Religions préhistoriques et primitives*, 22 *Religions originaires d'Extrême Orient*, 23 *Religions originaire du sous-continent indien*, 24 *Hindouisme*, 25 *Bouddhisme*, isms, isms, going off into the dark. The musty smell of old paper and decaying bindings was like the smell of grave cloths in an ancient tomb.

'We use the *classification décimale universelle*,' the woman said. It was a surprise to discover that she pronounced the French with fluent perfection. 'I presume you're familiar with it?'

'Not really.'

'Oh well, you'll pick it up as you go along.' She

opened one of the boxes and took out a volume of Montaigne's *Essais*, a nineteenth-century paper-bound edition with the spine partly missing, and handed it to Marian. 'Many of the shelfmark labels have come off, which means you've got to go to the card index. That's over here at the desk.'

They traipsed round the nooks and crannies of the basement. In one corner there was a bed frame and, on the wall behind the shelving, pin-up photos of Danielle Darrieux and a bare-breasted Josephine Baker. Miss Miller tore them down. 'We had the Free French in here during the war. They used this as a dormitory. Poor lads, who knows what happened to them?'

'I expect they're at home with *Maman* now.'

Miller glanced at her with curiosity. 'What was it that you did during the war? If I may ask?'

The lies came easily. She was practised in lies, lies grown like rank weeds out of the ruins of her past. 'Mr Roper was exaggerating. I was with the FANY. First Aid Nursing Yeomanry. Driving senior officers around, mainly.'

'Must have been fun.'

'When they weren't pinching your bum.'

Miss Miller looked shocked. 'I'm sure they meant it in the nicest possible way,' she said without a glimmer of humour. They made their way back upstairs to the offices. 'When can you start? We need someone as soon as possible.'

'I've got to find somewhere to live first. At the

201

moment I'm sleeping on my brother's sofa. He's not far from here.'

Miss Miller smiled. She appeared to have more than the usual complement of teeth, a startling horse dentition that seemed suited to a snort and a whinny. 'I tell you what, until you do you can come and live with me. I always have a PG and my present one just told me she's leaving. How about that? It'll be fun, won't it? You can treat the flat as home. I don't, of course, allow male visitors after six o'clock, but then I'm sure you'll understand that. One has to keep standards up, nowadays more than ever.'

'What's different about nowadays?'

'The war, my dear. The complete breakdown in moral sensibilities. Where have you been for the last few years?'

'Abroad, as a matter of fact. North Africa.'

'Lucky you.'

'And thank you for your offer but I think I'm going to look for a place of my own. Perhaps buy a little flat.'

'*Buy?* You won't be able to afford anything on what they pay you here.'

Which was, of course, true. So it was that, at some time in my twelfth year, Marian Sutro moved away from Oxford, out of reach, beyond my immediate knowledge, to live with Miss Miller as her paying guest.

MBE

She is the withdrawn figure on the Tube, her face buried in a book. She is the narrow figure on the top deck of the bus, looking down on the street scene but not part of it. She is the woman in the queue who stands aside, the female at the cinema who sits alone. A quiet, sequestered life. When a letter comes from the French embassy informing her in the name of the French people and the French Republic that she has been awarded the Croix de Guerre *avec palme en vermeil*, with an invitation to attend an investiture ceremony at the embassy, she writes a polite letter of regret: while honoured to be thus decorated, she is unfortunately unable to attend the ceremony. She gives no reason, of course, but the reason is there plain enough: the desperate wish to be ordinary, not to stand out from the crowd, not to be seen but only to see.

That perhaps was the greatest legacy bestowed on Marian Sutro by her experiences during the war – the desire for camouflage, for mimesis. *Pour vivre heureux, vivons cachés*. To live happily, live hidden. She'd heard the proverb years ago during her training but she'd only recently found the source, when she was down in the library and leafing through a book of Florian's fables that needed to be put somewhere on the shelves. It comes in the Fable of the Cricket, who survives intact while the pretty butterfly dies at the hands of children. She was like the cricket – cryptic, camouflaged, concealed. A survivor.

The medal duly arrived at the library by recorded delivery. Not realising what it was, Marian opened the package and stood bewildered, confronting the bronze cross in its little presentation box. An ornate scroll announced *Liberté, Égalité, Fraternité* and addressed her in the name of the people of the Republic of France. *Magnifique exemple de courage et d'abnégation*, it said. *Une foi inébranlable* . . .

'I thought,' Miss Miller remarked, looking over her shoulder, 'that you spent the war driving officers around and trying to avoid having your bottom pinched.'

Marian closed the lid and stowed the box away in a drawer. 'It's nothing,' she said. 'What use do I have for it?'

The notification for her British award arrived at the house in Oxford with altogether different wording. His Majesty was pleased to confer on her Membership of the Order of the British Empire, Civil Division, for services during the recent hostilities.

Her father was furious. She had never seen him so angry before. 'An MBE?' he almost shouted. 'That's what they give school janitors and golf club secretaries.'

Quietly, not wanting to make a fuss, she put the letter away in a drawer in her bedroom and wrote a polite letter declining the invitation to attend the Palace for the investiture.

So, Marian Sutro, MBE, Croix de Guerre, travelling unknown on the Tube and the bus, her face bowed over a book that close inspection might show itself to be in French. Malraux, probably, or Céline. Slowly putting herself back together out of the component parts of memory and fear into which she has been splintered.

She saw the psychiatrist rarely now. Once a fortnight at most, a journey up to Oxford on the train, then a bus to the quiet, secluded house on the Woodstock Road, to the quiet of Dr Morgan's consulting room where she was meant to confront her demons. She told him nothing of what happened or didn't happen on the cliffs in Sussex. That was her secret; and mine.

CLÉMENT

One day in January Ned rang her at work to say he had a surprise for her and could she come round to his flat? He had something to show her.

'What?'

'That'd spoil the surprise, wouldn't it? You'll have to come round.'

She sighed. 'It'll only be something stupid.' But still she went. His flat was only a few minutes' walk away and sometime after six o'clock she climbed the familiar stairs, not expecting much of a surprise. Some idiocy. When he opened the door he seemed almost bursting with excitement, like a child at Christmas. 'Come on in, Squirrel. You'll never guess. Through in the sitting room. Go and have a look.'

'What on earth is this all about?'

'Just have a look.'

She opened the door cautiously. There was nothing exceptional about the room – the usual disorder of papers and cushions, the broken-backed sofa where she had slept when she had first started working, the table still half laid with whatever had been eaten at lunch – but what was not usual was the man getting up from the solitary armchair. It wasn't 'something' at all. It wasn't the inanimate object she had been expecting. It was Clément.

At the mere sight of him she found herself shaking, with fear or with happiness, she wasn't sure which. He had aged. Three years and he had aged. There was a hint of grey at his temples, lines on his forehead that she did not remember, a tiredness in the eyes. His hairline was receding. But on the other hand, what the hell did she look like? A haggard old crone, probably, her face scoured by incarceration, her body aged before its time. That was what she saw in the mirror; was that what he saw as she came in? There was a moment when she might have lost control altogether and burst into tears, but she managed to avoid that and instead just stood in front of him, shivering like a dog in the rain.

'Did you get my letter?' she asked. She wanted him to take her in his arms. She wanted all the comfort he could never bring her. But instead she stood there and let him hold her by the shoulders and plant a kiss on each cheek, as though she was a soldier being decorated with that bloody medal by some French general. And then he pulled her towards him and held her against his chest.

'Ned has told me,' he said.

His jacket was something smooth and expensive with a faint stripe within the dark blue. She spoke into the fabric. 'About what?'

'About what happened to you. I . . . never realised.'

'My letter, didn't you get my letter?'

She felt him shake his head. 'I never received any letter. Where did you send it?'

'Somewhere in Canada. The University of Montreal.'

'I've been in the States for the last six months. New York. So I guess it never caught up with me.'

'It doesn't matter now, does it?'

Ned was hovering beside them, anxious to see her reaction to his little surprise. He understood the collisions of subatomic particles but he did not comprehend the collision like this of persons, the damage it could do, the forces it could unleash. Slowly, carefully, Clément let her go, sat her down on the sofa, sat down beside her, held her hands as though otherwise she might slip away and be lost. She clung to the banal as the only way to keep afloat: 'When did you get here?'

'We docked yesterday, and I came up on the boat train this morning.'

'Was it on time?'

'Does it matter?'

She managed to laugh. 'Probably not, but I don't know what else to ask. How long are you going to be here? Why are you here? What are you doing?'

He smiled. She was a child again, and he her child-hood idol. But she noticed things: like the elements he toyed with, he had been transmuted into another species, harder, more decisive, something from the

New World; and his command of English had grown fluent, burnished to a transatlantic sheen. He lifted her hands and kissed them. 'Now what are you doing this evening?'

'Me? This evening? Nothing. I finish work, go home, have a bath if I've got a shilling for the meter. And then make myself some supper before going to bed. That's life over here. We're broke, Clément. The whole country's broke. I listen to the radio a bit, or read, and then . . .'

He stopped her with a finger to her lips. 'Tonight we're going to dinner at the Savoy. Isn't that the best place? That's where we're going, all three of us.'

'I can't afford the Savoy.'

'But I can.'

She had to change. She had to go back to the bedsit off Charlotte Street to have a bath and change. She found herself in a little flurry of panic, in case he might escape and not be seen again for years. It'd only take her twenty minutes to walk, she assured him. She did it virtually every day, there and back. Twenty minutes.

Again, the touch of his finger to her lips. They'd take a cab. He'd come with her. This time he wasn't going to let her go.

Not let her go. What did that mean?

In the cab they talked. There was so much to talk about it seemed an impossible task. Where he'd been, where she'd been, how their separate lives had got them to this particular place and time, in the back of a taxi driving up Charlotte Street towards the dreary little terrace house she shared unequally with Enid Miller. But not the war. Not what had happened to her then. She didn't want to talk about that. She had to keep hold of those memories, hold them tight and never let them go because once out in the open they would be transformed by words, a string of words, into something that would never match the reality. So she asked about him about Canada and the United States, places that seemed impossibly distant, impossibly wealthy, a world away from this Europe of ruin and deprivation. And then there was his marriage. She suddenly remembered his wife's name. Augustine. And the baby. Must be a toddler by now. More questions than answers. She felt that the journey should be prolonged, that they should drive round and round the city talking like this, trying to sort out all those things she had thought about, brooded over, longed for, loved and loathed. But all too soon they were turning in to Chitty Street, which she called Shitty Street because that's what it was, a short road to nowhere lined with old terrace houses which no one seemed to care for except Miss Miller. He'd not be able to come in, she explained, because there was that little house rule – no male visitors after six o'clock. Miss Miller had to keep up standards. 'She thinks the country's gone to the dogs.'

Clément thought that funny. 'What's special about six o'clock? What's to stop you having sex at three in the afternoon?'

She laughed, imagining it. Three in the afternoon.

But in the event Miss Miller was enchanted by the visitor. She deployed her French with simpering fluency. *Doctor* Pelletier, was it? Was that a medical doctor? Oh, a doctor of physics! Imagine! The idea seemed to send a shiver of delight through her. She was truly enchanted to make his acquaintance. *Vraiment enchantée.*

'Dr Pelletier is an old friend of my family, from before the war,' Marian explained.

'Indeed? Well, I'm sure that we can relax our rules this one time, can't we? If you show him into the sitting room, Marian . . .'

Thus Clément was established in an over-stuffed armchair beside the gas fire – 'Have you put a shilling in the meter, Marian?' – and given a sweet sherry and a copy of the *Manchester Guardian* while Marian went upstairs to her room to change. Her heart was racing. It seemed a ridiculous cliché but it was true – it seemed to be going at about a hundred and twenty beats a minute. Clément was there in the sitting room, displaying an Olympian calm, while she was up here feeling like a child again, reduced from her painfully acquired maturity to the condition of a puerile adolescent, complete with scurrying pulse and sweaty forehead. In the bathroom Miss Miller's carefully typed notice warned her: IN VIEW OF NATIONAL AUSTERITY MEASURES, PLEASE DO NOT DRAW BATHS MORE THAN FOUR INCHES IN DEPTH. But she drew one of at least six inches and lay in the warm water and tried to gather her thoughts. Once she had possessed a measured mind, one that could rationalise even at moments of stress; now her thoughts seemed in chaos once again, the random panic of a young girl. Downstairs was Clément, whom she had adored; Clément who was married with a child; Clément who had made love to her, once, in his own bed, in his apartment in Paris; Clément who had swept out of her life the next moonlit night on a field in the Cher Valley, leaving her bereft and alone in the cold. And now here he was, downstairs. Still married, so he said. Prepared to return to Paris in a few days and try to make a go of things. Dying to see his child – whose name she couldn't remember – once again.

This time he wasn't going to let her go. What had he meant by that?

She heard talking below. Perhaps it was Miss Miller quizzing him to find out more. The woman could have got a job as an interrogator.

What exactly is your relationship with Marian?

Exactly how long have you known her?

Did you have a sentimental relationship with her? Have you, perhaps, been *intimate*?

When the front door opened and closed Marian panicked. He'd left. He'd been forced to confess about their sleeping together – 'but those were exceptional times, in Paris during the war, and anyway it was only once' – and Miller had thrown him out. But then there were footsteps on the stairs – too heavy for Miss Miller – and a gentle tap on the door and his voice saying, 'Squirrel?'

Squirrel. The nickname that, outside of her family, he alone used. 'Yes?'

'She's gone.'

'Gone?'

'Yes, gone. Come out.'

'I'm in the bath.'

'Then finish and come out.'

I confess I've made this up. I know a great deal but I can't know everything. So, like me, you'll have to imagine her climbing out of the bath, her skin glistening like pearl, suds sliding off her pallid limbs and her loose breasts, the little forelock of hair between her legs tugged downwards by a rivulet of water. Imagine her haste as she dries herself. What, she wonders, is going to happen? She wraps the towel around herself with scant decency and opens the door. There's no one on the landing, but the door to her bedroom is ajar. 'Clément?'

When she pushes the door fully open, there he is, sitting in her single narrow armchair, waiting for her. 'What on earth are you doing? She'll go mad if she comes back and finds you here. I'll probably be thrown out on the street.'

He grinned. 'Penge.'

'What do you mean, Penge?'

'I don't mean anything. It's a place. Where in God's name *is* Penge?'

'I've no idea.'

'Well, that's where she's gone. To see her sister. Apparently her sister has fibroids—'

'Fibroids?'

'Whatever they may be. I insisted I wasn't a medical doctor but that didn't seem to stop her explaining in lurid detail. Fibroids give terrible trouble with bleeding and pain, she informed me. She speaks surprisingly good French, by the way. Anyway, this sister lives in Penge and I am reliably informed that Penge involves a train journey from London Bridge – are there trains at London Bridge? – and Miss Miller will not be back until late.' He held out his hands as though to demonstrate. 'So here I am, all because of fibroids in Penge.'

She laughed. Here he was. Clément, stepping out of her past, out of the nightmare of her final day of freedom in France in the autumn of 1943, out of the insane world of deceit and deception that had been Paris during the occupation. Clément, magically appearing in this strange new world of peace where whole cities could be obliterated in a flash. She stood for a moment, on the brink, watching him. Then she stepped forward and let her towel fall to the floor and said, 'I want you to fuck me.'

Actually, she said it in French. It was easier in French, a more or less innocent verb having long ago become indecent: '*Je veux que tu me baise*' – 'I want you to kiss me' – becoming, with use, 'I want you to fuck me.'

'*Je veux que tu me baise,*' she said, and then she began to weep. Clément got up from his chair and went to put his arms around her. Perhaps he understood something of the desolation she felt. He was, after all, a sensitive man as well as an intelligent one. The two don't always go together but in his case they did. He understood that the woman he had known since her childhood was, in some indefinable way, damaged, and although he couldn't know exactly where that damage lay, he guessed that somewhere in the gelatinous convolutions of her brain a small nexus of connections – synapses, maybe – had been broken. He was used to the complex machinations of mathematics – one of his achievements had been in the calculation of neutron emission by plutonium isotopes, work that led directly to the abandoning of the Thin Man design of atom bomb in favour of what became Fat Man which obliterated most of Nagasaki – but he would have been the first to admit his helplessness when confronted by the far more complex intricacies of the human brain. Yet any putative damage lay beside the fact that he had known this woman since she was fifteen, when she had been passionately in love with him in the way that only a fifteen-year-old can be and he himself had been more than a little in love with her; and beside the fact that their love had been consummated once, in his Paris apartment, on the night before she – this girl become woman – had spirited him out of occupied France; and beside

215

the fact that she was naked in his arms, and taking hold of his hand and putting it between her legs and rubbing herself against it while begging him through her tears to do what she wanted. *Baise-moi, baise-moi*, she begged him.

At the Savoy Grill waiters cruised round them while they talked of the future, little of which, she knew, would happen: how Clément would return to France where his wife and child were waiting for him, and how all of them might meet up again in Annecy at the Pelletier family home. They would love Augustine, of course they would, as much as they had loved Clément's sister Madeleine. They would make her one of theirs, the little quartet become a quintet, playing a childlike music with adult overtones. But that took them back to the days before the war and that was much easier, for the past had happened and so could not be gainsaid – the sailing on the lake had happened, the skiing at Megève, the playing silly games – pig-in-the-middle and *Kriegspiel*, that blind chess where she had adjudicated between Ned and Clément as each tried to work out the other's moves – all these things had happened. And so, for a couple of hours, it was as though nothing had changed, as though six years of wartime were hidden away in a chance fold of the fabric of time and Annecy in 1936 or 1938 joined seamlessly to London in the early days of 1946, with a cold rain outside and rationing still in force.

After the meal they went back to Ned's flat. Clément produced a bottle from his briefcase and announced, 'Bourbon,' as he poured them tumblers full. 'Terrible, flowery stuff but easy to drink. Typically American. Let's drink to something. World peace is too grand. Let's drink to us three.'

She smiled at the idea – the three of us! – and sipped whiskey and watched the two men talking and smoking. Ned was telling them about his new work. He would start shortly at some research centre that was opening near Oxford. He'd be on the government payroll, a civil servant with a government salary which was a change from the uncertainties of university research. Chadwick had recommended him and Cockcroft was the director so the job was a foregone conclusion really. He'd be working under Klaus Fuchs in the theoretical physics department.

Clément knew them all, of course. Cockcroft, Fuchs, Chadwick. It was incestuous, this world of atomic physics. He threw names around quite casually, like someone seeding fertile ground – Bohr, Lawrence, Fermi, people he had met in the States. They all seemed to be his friends. Soon he might go back to Canada. He saw himself as a channel of communication between the French programme, if there was to be a French programme, and the British and Canadian work in Montreal; perhaps even with the Americans, although that seemed unlikely. 'The Americans betrayed us,' he asserted. 'Fundamentally, they betrayed us.'

It seemed something of an outrage, that idea. They were our allies, weren't they?

'They took what we knew of the bomb and then kept us out of the development.'

'We?'

'The British and the French, especially we French. Oh, yes, Cockcroft and Peierls and Fuchs were there at Los Alamos, but only on sufferance. It should have been made by the Allies together but instead it's an American weapon, for their exclusive use.'

And so, inevitably, they were talking about the Bomb itself. The thing was always there really, skulking in the background of any conversation in those days, just as Hell had once skulked in the background of every conversation in the Middle Ages, or in her convent school. The vital thing, Clément said, was to think about it as something elemental, a force of nature like an earthquake rather than as a weapon. 'Weapons are designed to be used. The bomb must never be used.'

'But it already *has* been!' she cried. Blackened logs came before her eyes, figures carved in charred wood. They had shape but no form, arms but no fingers, teeth but no eyes. 'Two cities destroyed. Tens, maybe hundreds of thousands dead. People are still dying from radiation.'

Clément nodded, as though she had just learned the lesson he intended. It was like before the war, when sometimes he was so smug and self-confident about what he knew that she could have

218

hit him. 'That's exactly the point, Squirrel. Believe me, until Japan nobody really understood. When it was tested in the desert it had no context – the desert remained desert, however carefully they measured the blast.'

'Except the sand turned to glass,' said Ned.

Marian was stupefied. 'You mean it had to be used on *people* before they could understand what it could do?'

Clément lit another cigarette. His fingers were stained with nicotine, like Vera's. He blew smoke into the air. 'More or less. Working on something like that you get detached from reality, consumed by the problem. And in wartime you think of weapons, not victims. But now everyone understands – Oppenheimer more than anyone: this thing is so vast that nothing less than world government can contain it.'

'Who is Oppenheimer?'

They laughed at her ignorance. Robert Oppenheimer was the director of the project in New Mexico, surely she knew that. An exceptional man in a world where genius was almost commonplace.

She drank some more bourbon and looked from one to the other, from the pale, distracted face of her brother to Clément's world-weary expression. She remembered sitting at the table in his flat in Paris, eating by the light of a candle, surrounded by the funeral pall of the occupied city, arguing. The nature of a super bomb, something beyond the power of human imagination. And the possibilities of just such a German bomb, dreamed up by Otto Hahn and Werner Heisenberg, created with Czechoslovak uranium and Norwegian heavy water, conjured out of the arcane world of nuclear physics to become a nightmare that might end the war by being dropped on London. It had been a game once, that was the thing, a puzzle played by people like Clément and Ned at the level of the angstrom unit and the electron volt; and it had blossomed to become a weapon as powerful as the sun. She felt helpless anger.

'But it's *your* bloody bomb, isn't it?' she said. 'You talk as though it's someone else's problem.'

'It's hundreds of people's bomb. Thousands. Yours as well as mine. You helped, didn't you?'

'That's sophistry. *You* have to take responsibility. You knew exactly what the damn thing would do. You told me, that time in Paris. You explained exactly. And Ned did as well. You all *knew*. All you bloody scientists *knew*.'

'Does that mean it's all our fault?'

Anger. Impotence. The wine, the whiskey, perhaps it was those; or perhaps it was because of what had happened earlier in her cramped little bedroom in the house in Shitty Street. She felt him there still, alive inside her when so much was dead; and she wanted him again. A compulsion. 'It means you must take some of the responsibility.'

'Or blame?'

'If you like.'

He shrugged. 'Then so must you. If you hadn't got me out of Paris I would have spent the rest of the war there. And there would still have been the bomb. Perhaps even a German one.'

She felt stunned by anger and death and alcohol. In the camp there had been tens of thousands dead. But in those two cities that no one had heard of, tens of thousands died in a flash. And were dying still. Was it her own fault? In the myriad cogs of the world, the chain of cause and effect, was her own part significant?

She thought of a young woman examining a jar incised with beautiful figures, holding the thing in her hands and marvelling at the beauty of it. Then she takes off the lid and peers inside. And all the evils of the world fly out.

Pandora.

'So what hope is there?' she asked.

Clément smoked and pondered. He was still quite sober, barely sipping at the whiskey, maintaining that damned control, finding an answer for everything. 'Things are very dangerous at the moment because they're unbalanced. Only the Americans have the bomb – maybe we won't be safe until all the great powers possess the thing.'

'The Russians—?'

'Especially the Russians. I heard there was a straw poll at Los Alamos a few weeks before Hiroshima – almost fifty per cent of the scientists thought the information should be opened to the Russians.'

Ned leaned forward. 'Do you know that during the war Bohr came over to England to speak to Churchill? He'd already got Roosevelt's support and he wanted to plead the case with Churchill—'

'What case?'

'The case for bringing the Russians into the secret. That was last year, when work was still underway. A meeting was arranged with just the two of them. Churchill and Bohr alone—'

'How do you *know* this?'

He waved a vague hand. Typical Ned, always gesticulating. 'I know it, I know it. The meeting was a disaster. Came to nothing. Churchill thought Bohr was just a dangerous, naive fool poking his nose into things that didn't concern him. He even wanted him arrested. Arrested! Can you imagine arresting Niels Bohr?' There was a red spot in each of Ned's cheeks. Anger or alcohol? Maybe both those things, the one feeding the other. 'Keeping things secret won't stop the Russians. They've got the men to do it by themselves soon enough. But if we'd shared the information with them in the first place, we might have gained their confidence – as it is the Americans have forced them to find out for themselves. And to assume that the Americans have kept it secret because they want the option to use it again.'

'Use it *again*?'

Ned poured himself another whiskey 'It's what their military men want. Build a dozen more bombs and drop them on the Soviet Union.'

'But they're our allies!'

He laughed. 'That, Squirrel, was yesterday. Now, the Americans are terrified of them and they have the power to do something about it. A few atom bombs on the major Russian cities – Moscow, Leningrad, a couple of others – and the Soviet Union would be back in the Stone Age.'

There was a silence. Was it the silence of complicity? Clément stubbed out his last cigarette. 'I guess it's time for bed. I've got to be up bright and early tomorrow. I'll call a cab. I can drop you off on my way, if you like.'

She began to clear the debris away, the ashtrays, the glasses. Ned sat in the only armchair, holding onto his glass and watching. His mind had veered away from the subject in hand. Perhaps it was the drink. There was a sardonic smile on his lips as he watched Marian doing her little tasks. Suddenly he said to Clément, 'She told me about the two of you, you know that?'

Another bomb, this time small, personal, destructive but not deadly. Marian turned on him. 'Shut up, Ned.'

But Ned was beyond any sisterly stricture. 'You're lovers, aren't you?' he said to Clément. 'Were, are, who knows?'

'You've had too much to drink.'

He held up his glass, eyeing Clément through the amber liquid. 'I wonder when the first time was?'

She ignored him and walked out of the room

with the glasses. Clément followed her into the hallway. 'Why the hell did you tell him?'

'It was ages ago. We were talking about things . . .'

Ned called out from the sitting room: 'You know what? I'll bet it was at Annecy.'

'It was your fault bringing that bottle.'

'He's an adult. He can decide for himself how much to drink.'

'He's a child and you know it.'

Ned's voice came to them. 'You were just a little girl then, weren't you, Squirrel? What would the parents have said if they'd known? You can't have been more than fifteen. Is that legal? A fifteen-year-old?'

She busied herself in the kitchen leaving Clément to deal with her brother. She could hear Ned's voice raised in protest and Clément's quieter tones. 'Fuck you!' Ned shouted. 'Fuck both of you!'

She'd never heard such language from him, never heard such language at all since she left the WAAF. Not the girls, of course. But the airmen. Effing this and effing that. She couldn't even bring herself to think of the word despite the fact that she had done it, with Clément, just that evening. Fucked. She found her coat, vaguely aware of Clément persuading Ned to bed, vaguely aware of having drunk too much herself, and inhaled too much smoke, and wanting to be out in the cold, fresh air. 'Is he all right?' she asked when Clément appeared.

'He'll sleep like a baby.'

They crept out of the flat, closing the door behind them quietly like thieves escaping from the scene of a crime. Clinging together against the cold they walked as far as Cambridge Circus before they managed to find a taxi. Inside the cab he put his arm around her and drew her close. 'Why don't you come back to my hotel?'

'Don't be silly.' But she wanted to. The compulsion was there, like a predator lying in wait. 'Anyway, they wouldn't let me in.'

'I can slip the night porter a couple of dollars not to notice. They love dollars.'

'You'd make me feel like a tart.'

That amused him. 'How the hell would you know what a tart feels like?'

'Every woman knows,' she said.

He left the next day, taking the boat train to Newhaven to catch the overnight ferry to Dieppe. She went with him to the station to see him off. It was impossible not to recall that song they had played at the holding centre before she went to France: *Puisque vous partez en voyage*. A couple parting at a railway station. It seemed to be the only record in the place and they'd played it over and over again in the hours before her drop.

Puisque vous partez en voyage
Puisque nous nous quittons ce soir.

She bought a platform ticket and followed Clément through the barrier. Sounds echoed in the vast drum of the roof, the snort of steam, the slamming of doors, the rattle of people. They stood on the platform, talking about Paris, about his wife and child, about his sister Madeleine and his parents: the awkward, uncertain discourse of departure, enhanced by betrayal.

'You must come over and see us,' he said.

'Perhaps.' She felt impatient to be gone. Her feelings, whatever they had been, had shrunk in the bleak light of day. She tried to recall her emotions at their last parting, in the night time cold of a field by the Cher, with the Lysander roaring in the moonlight and Clément looking down at her from the cockpit. 'Maybe we're condemned to always be saying goodbye,' she said.

He turned her face towards him. 'Why didn't you come with me in that bloody aeroplane, Squirrel?'

She shrugged. 'People keep asking me that.'

'What people?'

'People. Just people.' She glanced round. Was someone watching them from the ticket barrier? She thought she'd seen the same figure earlier on when they arrived at the station, a bland, forgettable shape, immediately turning away. She had a sense for such things, the instinct for survival in a hostile world. 'What would have happened to me, anyway? You'd have gone off to Canada and I'd have been left behind in England, trying to persuade them to send me back to France.'

'At least you wouldn't have been captured. You wouldn't have been in that damned camp. You've not said anything about it.'

'And I'm not going to.' Doors were slamming up and down the length of the train. A whistle blew. 'You'd better go.'

He bent and kissed her, then turned and climbed aboard. For a moment he was visible behind the glass, like a faded photograph preserved from some half-forgotten past. Then the train began to edge forward, slowly but inexorably, like a glacier; then faster like a river, until finally it was streaming out of the station in a torrent, leaving her stranded on the bank.

ALAN

Clément Pelletier. It's easy enough to discover the bare bones of his life. Born in Paris in 1910, he attended the École Normale Supérieure and completed the *agrégation* in physics and mathematics in 1932. In 1938 he obtained a doctorate in mathematical science from the Faculty of Science of the University of Paris while working under Frédéric Joliot-Curie on the radioactive decay of uranium isotopes and their fission products. In 1940 he married Augustine Sousa and the next year the couple had a daughter. Mother and daughter left Paris in 1941 to take refuge in Annecy while Pelletier himself continued his research at the Collège de France and at Ivry until, in the autumn of 1943, he left France for England in a covert operation involving the British intelligence services. After a brief spell in Cambridge he travelled to Canada where he worked with Lew Kowarski and Bertrand Goldschmidt on the Anglo-Canadian nuclear programme. At the end of the war he spent time at Columbia University where his field of interest remained with uranium and the newly discovered transuranic elements. In 1946 he returned to his native country and recommenced work in Paris with Professor Joliot-Curie . . .

That's the kind of thing an encyclopedia says. Or Wikipedia, I suppose. What it doesn't mention is as significant as what it does. For example, the curious phenomenon of action at a distance, like the electromagnetic force or the force of gravity that physicists talk about – in this particular case his departing for Paris to attempt, among other things, the reconstruction of his marriage, which departure became a kind of gravity in reverse, repelling rather than attracting, flinging people this way and that, Clément back into the bosom of his incipient family, Marian back into the arms of Alan Walcott.

I remember my mother's shock as she put down the phone, the sudden change in expression from when she was talking to the person on the other end of the line. 'How wonderful,' she had been saying into the receiver. 'How marvellous. Are you happy? Of course you're happy. My goodness, it's a bit unexpected, but wonderful news. We'd love to, yes. Yes, we'd love to.'

But her expression changed to bewilderment when she finally laid the receiver to rest. 'That was Marian,' she told my father. 'You know that RAF pilot she was going out with for a while, the one whom she said wouldn't leave her alone? We met him once, didn't we? Well, they're getting married.'

★   ★   ★

229

It was, in the manner of those times, a small affair in a registry office in Chelsea. There's a photo taken on the steps outside – the happy couple in the centre with, on Marian's side, the thoughtful parents-in-law and on Walcott's the joyous Mrs Walcott senior (Alan's father had died of a perforated stomach ulcer in 1944). In the group there is also Marian's brother Ned and Alan's sister Morag. Outflanking them all is my father looking as tall and awkward as a wading bird among geese, and my mother laughing and putting her hand to her hair, thereby giving the impression that the wind has just blown her down the King's Road.

After the ceremony the disparate little party went for an awkward lunch at a restaurant nearby before the newlyweds drove off to Sussex to spend a week of nuptial bliss in – yes, you have guessed aright – Furze Cottage, the use of which, along with the gift of an entirely useless set of silver-plate fruit knives, was my parents' wedding present to the happy couple.

I tried – I still try – to imagine their stay on the Sussex coast. Parked outside the cottage, the little MG called Gloria; inside the cottage, the fetid reek of sexual discovery. Marian had to learn something new, the mechanics of a lasting sexual relationship, something that depends on seeing your partner all day, in all states, naked and clothed, clean and dirty, asleep and awake, fair and foul. Did she abandon herself to his embrace, lose herself in the heat of his love, find ecstasy in his arms? Subsequent events suggest not, but at the time, immersed in the stream of time and with no idea of the rocks and rapids that lay ahead, who knows? Perhaps, for that week of artificial bliss, she found Alan's particular attentions satisfying. Or perhaps the memories of Benoît Bérard and Clément Pelletier haunted the nuptial bedroom. Impossible to tell.

By the time of the marriage Alan Walcott had left the Air Force and found a job with a well-known tyre company for which his rudimentary French was apparently an asset. Although blessed with some exalted title – Regional Sales Co-ordinator, or something – I fear he was little more than a supervisor of travelling salesmen, frequently dispatched to Carlisle or Belfast in pursuit of improved sales, much of his salary being dependent on commission. All of this I gathered from overhearing my parents talk about them. Marian, so they said, was still working with her strange French organisation but surely that would come to an end quickly enough. Surely there would soon be an addition to their incipient family.

I hoped not. Whatever went on in the privacy of their bedroom, the thought of Marian rendered dull and distracted by motherhood, repelled me. I wanted to preserve the image I had of her cartwheeling across the lawn outside our block of flats or letting me cuddle up beside her on the sofa in Furze Cottage. Was she happy? I wondered. Content for the moment, perhaps. Alan was a considerate husband, probably as much in love with her as he had claimed in those letters and calls and occasional meetings when he laid siege to her spinsterhood. Whether she was in love with him is another question. She was *fond*, that weasel-word that hides so much. She appreciated his attentions but sometimes found them irksome. She understood his physical needs and sometimes shared them. She felt flattered by his affection and sometimes returned it. But she refused to give up her job when he suggested it, protesting that she could not hang about the flat all day – they had rented a place on the southern borderland of Kensington, near to Alan's place of work – and pretend to be a housewife. Of course when, if, she fell pregnant – that phrase again – she would hand in her notice and surrender to the world of mother-hood, but in the meantime she would damn well continue at the Franco-British Pacific Union, running the library under the auspices of Miss Miller – who quite liked Alan when she met him but did wonder whatever happened to that charming Dr Pelletier – and assisting in the Union's programme of visiting speakers and lectures.

And then the skeleton of Ravensbrück reached out its bony finger and tapped her on the shoulder. It came in the form of an official letter from the Judge Advocate General's office: would Marian Sutro, former Ensign of the FANY, former honorary Flight Officer WAAF, be prepared to appear as a witness for the prosecution at the trial of various members of the camp staff of the Ravensbrueck concentration camp, to take place in Hamburg in December of this year?

She thought about it for days before she told Alan, and when she did she knew exactly how he would respond. 'Why the hell should you put yourself through this?' he demanded. 'What's the point? All you can do is upset yourself when you are settling down to a normal life again.'

'I have a responsibility to people.'

'You have a responsibility to yourself! And, for God's sake, to me. I don't want you raking over all those memories. You've always told me you don't want to talk about it. And now you're proposing to do precisely that!'

All the obvious arguments were trotted out. It was the first real conflict of their marriage. But still she went, transported by the Royal Air Force, who flew her to Northern Germany in the cold of winter, into the frozen urban landscape that high explosive and incendiary bomb had sculpted out of the pre-war city of Hamburg – the place where that peculiar human meteorological invention, the firestorm, had first been conjured out of the elements.

Under the aegis of the ubiquitous Vera Atkins, Marian and some other women witnesses assembled in the only hotel left standing in the city, near the Hauptbahnhof. Vera had suggested she wear

233

FANY uniform but Marian demurred. She was not here as a FANY, nor as a WAAF, nor even as an agent of the now disbanded organisation that still baulked to name itself openly, the Special Operations Executive. She was here as a woman who had survived: Marian Sutro become Geneviève Marchal, the notable become nondescript. So she wore grey, a grey woollen dress, grey overcoat, grey stockings, grey hat. As grey as ashes. Each day she and the others were driven in Army transport through the frozen embers of the Altstadt to the court which sat in one of the few official buildings still intact, the curiously named Curio-Haus, where, in the main hall that had been transformed into a simulacrum of a courtroom, the accused sat like coconuts in a shy. Black number cards hung round their necks: 1 to 16, nine men and seven women. In the body of the court there were officers in uniform and barristers wearing gowns and wigs. Soldiers stood guard.

'It's a bloody miracle this trial is being held at all,' someone confided to her. He was a young Army officer in the Intelligence Corps, part of the war crimes investigation team. Apparently Ravensbrück camp itself was in the Soviet zone and so the Soviets had the right to hold any trial there might be; but because of the British interest – it was the SOE agents, really, the officer said – there was an agreement that it could take place in the British zone. One of the final acts of Allied cooperation. 'So you are particularly important to us,' the officer added, trying to reassure her, trying to still the subversive voice of panic that shouted within her. 'But don't worry. Just tell your own story. That will be enough.'

When her turn came she took the stand in front of the firing squad of a hundred sets of eyes. She told the court who she was and who she had been, and she swore to an almighty and omniscient God she did not believe in that she would tell the pure truth, although the truth appeared anything but pure. Then the prosecuting council, bewigged and begowned like a barrister but with the funereal manner of a doctor at a deathbed, began to ask her questions. When had she arrived at Ravensbrück? How had she come to be there? Which hut was she quartered in? What work had she done? Which work detail was she assigned to?

And the panic died. She spoke steadily and clearly. Stenographers recorded the words assiduously, while the accused stared glassily into space as though bored by the proceedings. Outside it snowed.

'One of the women in the hospital block saved my life,' she told them. 'She allowed me to exchange identity with a French woman who had died there. So I became Geneviève Marchal. It was Geneviève Marchal who survived, not Marian Sutro.'

'And yet you are here now. Marian Sutro is here.' The advocate glanced down at his notes. 'Or at least, Marian Walcott. I gather congratulations are due.' He attempted a smile although it was a poor jocularity, a stunted piece of banter in this place of grim recount. 'Now tell me, Mrs Walcott, are you able to identify this woman who saved your life by allowing you to change your identity? Is she perhaps in this courtroom?'

One of the women prisoners shouted out, in German, 'It was me! I did that!'

The presiding judge demanded silence.

Marian looked at the row of coconuts and shook her head. The advocate put his hands together almost as though beseeching his witness. 'Mrs Walcott, could you perhaps give your answer out loud? For the record. Is the woman who saved your life in this courtroom?'

Stenographers' hands were poised. The monotony of hate and depravity was like a drug, stunning mind and body, making memories unreal, turning persons recalled into figures in a dream.

'No,' she said. 'The woman is not here. I believe she died of typhus a few months later.'

'But there *is* a woman here whom you recognise?'

'Yes,' she said. 'Number five.'

'The witness has identified defendant number five, Dorothea Binz. Can you tell the court about the behaviour of Dorothea Binz?'

So she told them, a drab story of everyday violence, the pure truth: 'There was a morning *Appell*. At dawn. I think perhaps the court has been told about *Appell*. Every morning at dawn, whatever the weather. We were all lined up and this woman, number five, was inspecting our ranks because there had been some mix up over the count. And she said something to the woman standing next to me. This woman was . . .' Marian hesitated '. . . my friend. Véronique, she was called. Véronique Barthelemy. Binz hit her. Something Véronique said. I didn't hear it. Binz hit Véronique and knocked her to the ground. Véronique wasn't well. I went to protect her but the guards pushed me aside. Then the woman Binz stamped on Véronique's head. She stamped on her and killed her. As though she – Véronique, I mean – was just an insect or something. While all the others, me included, had to watch.'

She was shaking afterwards, shaking uncontrollably. Someone took her to a quiet room and gave her some tea to drink. She felt short of breath, as though she had just been held under water. When they drove her back to the hotel she was still shaking, still gasping. It was as if some piece of her internal machinery had broken, a stabiliser of some kind. She wandered into the hotel bar because she didn't want to go to her room and be on her own, but she didn't want to be with people either. 'Are you cold?' someone asked. 'It's bloody brass monkey weather, if you ask me.' A glass of brandy was pushed into her hand and it seemed to do the trick. Alcohol as therapy. She sat down on a banquette, pushing herself into one corner, cradling her brandy as though it were the elixir of life.

There was loud talk in the bar, perhaps an anti-dote to the quiet talk of the courtroom. Odette was there, the bright star surrounded by a little solar system of admirers. She'd got her George Cross just a few months earlier and people wanted to know about it. One of her admirers was a man with the unlikely name of Tickle who was, so he announced loudly to anyone who would listen, writing a book about her.

After a while a young Army captain came and sat beside Marian on the banquette. With him was a liaison officer from the Red Army, resplendent in tightly buttoned jacket with gold shoulder boards. Perhaps the captain was the one who had offered her brandy in the first place. Perhaps he was the one who had talked to her before she gave witness. He had Intelligence Corps shoulder flashes and a surprising fluency when calling the German waiter over to bring her another glass. 'Do you want to write my story?' Marian asked him, half in jest. The shaking had been replaced by a kind of euphoria.

The officer glanced at those near the bar. 'He does seem to tickle her fancy, doesn't he?'

The joke appeared outrageously funny. She laughed. It seemed some kind of blasphemy, to laugh. Like giggling in church. But laugh she did, at the man's silly jest, while he looked faintly embarrassed and his Russian companion entirely impassive.

'I'm Tony Bright,' the intelligence officer said

when the joke was finally exhausted. 'Known to my friends as Not-too. And my colleague here is . . .'

'Major Absolon,' the Russian announced. When she offered her hand he raised it to within a millimetre of his lips and breathed softly on it. 'A heroine for our times,' he said portentously. 'I am a great admirer of your war career.'

'You speak English very well.'

'Yes,' he replied and said no more, as though her remark had been a neutral one rather than an implied question, a straightforward observation with which he couldn't but agree. 'I must congratulate you on your recent marriage, I believe.'

'That's kind of you. Are you married, Major Absolon?'

He made a little helpless gesture. 'I had a wife. She was a nurse but she was killed in Leningrad during the siege.'

'How very sad.'

'There are many sad stories these days, aren't there? What is one more or less?'

'And why are you here? A Russian here in Hamburg, I mean.'

'To see how our allies manage this trial. I was also at Nuremberg, reporting for the Red Army newspaper.' He shrugged. 'Not a funny job. Funny is perhaps wrong. Amusing. Certainly not amusing. Here we have agreed that the British should do the trial. Ravensbrück is in the Soviet zone but the authorities agreed that Britain should do the trial.'

'How very friendly.'

He laughed. 'Friendly? I'm afraid it is just give and take. Is that what you say? The Soviet Union will want something in return.'

'I wonder what.'

'Who knows? Quid pro quo, isn't that the expression?'

It was the expression, exactly. Shortly afterwards the Russian excused himself and left her alone with Bright. 'Absolon's a fine chap,' he said. 'Seems a bit stiff but that's only shyness.'

'It was sad about his wife.'

'Yes, it was.' That might have killed the conversation but Bright seemed determined not to let that happen. He reminded her a bit of Benoît trying to chat her up in a bar in London all that time ago. So often people were at a loss for things to say but he seemed to have no difficulty, just like Benoît. They talked of music, films, a whole lot of nonsense, anything that could make her forget the courtroom and its monotonous record of evidence, or Odette's tinkling voice with its French accent thrilling the hangers-on.

'How do you find married life?' the captain asked.

'It's more or less what I expected,' she said, but she never explained what her expectations had been.

'I haven't got that far yet,' he replied, 'although I've been practising.'

'What on earth do you mean by that?' For some

reason she wondered whether he was about to make a pass at her. She shocked herself to discover that she rather hoped he would, and that, if he did, she wasn't sure how she would respond.

He smiled. 'Engaged. I met her in Belgium. I was billeted on her family . . .' His voice trailed away, as though leaving details of the billet to Marian's imagination. 'She promised to wait for me. We write most days, and once I hitched a ride and got back to see her. She's called Anna-Griet. Catholic, but that shouldn't matter, should it?'

'Not at all. I'm Catholic. At least I was.'

'There you are.' He looked at her thoughtfully, gazing right into her eyes and half smiling just as Benoît used to. Yes, she thought – and found herself blushing. 'I'm sure you'll be very happy together,' she said and to her surprise he laughed.

'How can you be sure? You can *hope*, but you can't be sure. We might make a colossal cock-up of the whole thing. If you'll forgive the expression.'

She matched his laughter. Cock-up. Really rather shocking. 'If you are really in love, then you won't.'

'I'm not even sure about that – my mother and father were very much in love when they got married, and two years after I was born she ran off with the lodger. Anyway, when I get demobbed I'm off to Belgium to find out.' He drank more brandy and thought for a moment. 'Do you ever regret it?'

'Regret what?'

'Getting married.'

'It's a bit soon for that, isn't it? Even by your mother's standards.'

Her reply struck them both as tremendously funny. Their laughter made people look round and they brought it under control, like naughty children. Later, when they were going in to dinner, their talk drifted on to other things, the kind of things people talked about at the moment, the chaos that was Germany, and the grim nature of post-war Britain, the possibilities and fears for the future. The waiter came and took their order, which, as Bright remarked, was a choice between not much and very little.

'What do you think about the Bomb?' he asked.

She produced a stock answer – terrible, frightening, something like that. When you've seen this city, how it has been destroyed, imagine an atom bomb. And the loss of innocence, she added, not quite knowing what she meant. Something to do with being able to kill at the press of a button. Imagine, she suggested, thinking of Ned, imagine a V2 with an atom bomb warhead.

Bright nodded thoughtfully. 'You know what I think?' He glanced round as though people might be eavesdropping on their conversation, but the people nearby were talking of something else, the black market, the problem of displaced persons, the difficulty of this, the impossibility of that. All his insouciance had vanished. Quietly, he said, 'I think the Yanks'll use it. Against the

Soviets.'

'The Russians? They're our allies.'

He leaned towards her. 'I read the signals. They talk about *when* the next war breaks out, not *if*. As though it's only a matter of time.'

'Another war? Haven't we had enough?'

'It wouldn't last long. All the Yanks have to do is bring a couple of those Superfortresses over here with a nice fat atom bomb in each belly. Drop one on Moscow and one on Leningrad and Bob's your uncle.'

Ned had said more or less the same thing. Bright's expression was hard to read, an amalgam of amusement and despair. 'It doesn't bear thinking about,' she said.

'These days there are lot of things that don't bear thinking about. Like what you were telling us in the courtroom. I saw it, you know that? I was with the 11th Armoured Division.' That meant nothing to her. Numbers, units, the whole world was under arms and everyone had a number. 'At the liberation of Belsen,' Bright explained. 'I was one of the first into the camp, with a medical team. On the 15th April. It was . . .' He shook his head. 'Words don't do it, do they?'

'No, they don't.'

'I was meant to find one of your lot.'

'One of *my* lot?'

'SOE. Perhaps you knew her. She was called Yvette. I don't remember her last name. But reports said she was using a cover. Marcelle Grenier. That's

243

who I was sent in to find. Marcelle Grenier.'

It was like a blow, precisely aimed, just below the sternum, knocking the wind out of her – the impact of a name, a mere breath on the air, become something physical. 'Yvette?'

'You knew her?'

She tried to breathe in, struggling against whatever had hit her in the stomach. 'Yvette Trocard. She was older than me. Married name Coombes.'

'Coombes, that's her. Yvette Coombes.' Tony Bright was watching her with concern. 'You all right?'

She breathed in deeply, tried to bring her mind back into some kind of balance. 'I trained with her. Then met up with her in Paris. I had no idea what happened to her, except that she was . . .' How to put it? What euphemism to use? '. . . held by the Germans. Did you find her?'

There was a silence around them. The noise of the bar seemed distant and irrelevant. She watched Bright for any sign. He drank some more brandy and replaced his glass with care. 'You've seen the newsreels. They were dying like flies, thousands a day – typhus, dysentery, starvation, everything. Some of them even died when we gave them food, *because* we gave them food . . .'

'And Yvette . . .?'

'According to a woman I interviewed, she died a week after we got there. A whole fucking week *after*. Sorry. My language. I shouldn't have said that . . .'

'It's all right.'

'We just didn't know where to look. There were simply too many of them. We tried, I promise you, but we never even found her body. It was one of those we had to bulldoze into a pit.' There was a glistening in his eyes. His mouth made a strange shape, almost as though he had lost control of his lips. 'I don't understand it,' he said, shaking his head as if thereby he might shake out any memories. 'Any of it.'

She reached out and took his hand. 'Don't try to,' she said. 'I've spent ages trying to understand everything and I can't. So don't try.'

They talked some more, the conversation jumping unsteadily to other things – his fiancée, Marian's own husband, the uncertainties of peacetime after the certainties of war. And they laughed a bit, which was dangerous but inevitable, and they drank a bit more and when it seemed that the bar was closing they found themselves climbing the stairs to the same floor. Their rooms were mere doors apart.

'A nightcap?' he suggested. And that was the excuse. A nightcap. He had a half bottle of whisky in his room and when it became rather more than a nightcap it didn't matter because Anna-Griet wouldn't mind because she wouldn't even know. The same went for Alan, didn't it? Deception brought its own rewards, its thrill of secret, arcane knowledge whose revelation could bring down plans and destroy lives, but like any such knowledge could be kept hidden and only used in some future moment when it might be necessary.

She left the next day. She hoped that Tony Bright wouldn't be around when she left the hotel but there he was in the lobby along with his Russian colleague, the man with the biblical name. Absolon. She and Bright shook hands as though they were mere acquaintances, as though they hadn't spent half the night together, naked in each other's arms. And she wondered what the Russian thought, or knew. He was impassive as he raised her hand to his lips. But he looked at her directly, with thoughtful, perhaps even sympathetic eyes.

'Have a good flight,' Bright told her as she climbed into the car. 'I'd come to see you off but I've got to—'

She put her hand out and touched his wrist. That unexpected contact seemed to shock him. 'It's quite all right,' she said. 'I'm fine.' Absurdly she added, 'If you're in London, look me up. Kensington 6877. We're in the directory.'

The car drove her through a bleak arctic landscape to the airfield where an Avro York was ready to fly people back to Abingdon. The noise, the hard unembellished interior of the aeroplane, the smell of engine oil and metal, all reminded her of the Halifax that had flown her to France. Alan was at the airfield to meet her when they landed. Through a friend in air movements he'd found out when and where she was due in. Good old Alan, as reliable as ever. They drove back to London and, compared with northern Germany, England seemed a small, fragile place, and London bright and fresh with bombsites few and far between.

The first Ravensbrück trial – later, there were others – lasted into the New Year. On the 3rd February 1947 fifteen of the original sixteen defendants were found guilty, one of them having died during the course of the proceedings. There was a Reuters report on the sentencing on page four of *The Times*, next to news about the fourth test match in Australia and below Winnipeg isolated by snowfalls. 'Eleven Death Sentences,' it announced, including five of the women, including Dorothea Binz. The hangings took place a month later, on the 2nd March, by that cheery cove Albert Pierrepoint who had been specially flown over from Britain for the purpose.

Marian's father sent her the newspaper cuttings, in case she'd missed them. Reading them she felt an overwhelming sense of horror, horror crawling like parasites all over her body, burrowing into her hair follicles, creeping into her sweat pores, tunnelling through her epidermis – this woman, Dorothea Binz, swinging over the pit, her vertebra snapped like a chicken's neck. Alan couldn't really understand her feeling. Good riddance, he thought. But he didn't say so. Instead he comforted her in that understanding manner of his that she found so aggravating because it was based on a complete failure to understand the substance of her emotion:

horror was the last refuge of her guilt – guilt merely by having survived when Véronique and so many others had died, a guilt that was compounded by the guilt of feeling absolutely no guilt at all about Tony Bright.

I'm trying to fit pieces together, build up a picture of her, like that jigsaw that we did at Furze Cottage but never finished. Ophelia drowning; Marian swimming to keep afloat. She could keep secrets but secrets weighed on her. Like the secret of what happened that night in Sussex, the secret that she shared, unbeknown to her, with me. Like the secret of Tony Bright. Like the secret Ned tells her one evening when he has had more than enough to drink.

Keep it secret, Squirrel, won't you?

I don't know what it is, yet.

Well, if you promise to keep it to yourself, I'll tell you. What we're working on now – it's worse, ten times worse, a hundred times worse, impossible to calculate. There's no critical mass, not like the atom bomb where you have to have so much of uranium or plutonium before the damn thing will detonate. But with this new thing there is no lower limit and no upper limit. You just feed it hydrogen – lithium hydride, that's what we reckon. A pretty simple compound, really. Almost nothing to it. Of course, you have to raise the temperature and pressure sufficiently to trigger the reaction . . .

How do you do that?

With an atomic explosion.

An *atom bomb* to start a—?

Hydrogen bomb. Hotter than the centre of the sun. Literally. Fusion, not fission. Infinitely more energy released. Truly the energy of the sun. Not a metaphor this time. The literal truth.

Will it never end? she wonders. All around her the world freezes as surely as the snow and ice of Hamburg; it is freezing into the Cold War.

COLD

The cold had something to do with it, that's what she claimed afterwards, although the psychiatrist insisted that the visit to Hamburg and the reawakening of old memories was to blame. But she felt it was the cold. It was cold and so she walked. It had been cold in Germany when she'd escaped from the camp, when she and two others had made a run for it. Then they'd walked to keep warm and to find someone who could help them and that was what she did now, she walked and walked to keep warm. And when it came to nightfall she knew that she must find somewhere to hole up for the night or else she would die, there on the pavement some-where in suburban London. In Germany the three of them had discovered an abandoned hut in the forest and they'd managed to survive, clinging to one another for warmth. But now there were no woods and no hut, just the road with buses and cars driving cautiously over the icy slush, and rows of semi-detached houses, and there at the crossroads a hotel with three stars to its name and an indifferent girl behind the reception desk who admitted that, yes, they did have a room but if she didn't have luggage she'd have to pay in advance. One pound five shillings for a single room, three and six extra for a private bathroom. Would she be wanting a bathroom?

'A bathroom? Yes, please.' She searched in her handbag for the money.

'You'll have to sign the register.'

'Of course.' The register was a large, official book with dark brown binding, the book of life inscribed with lives various and disparate to which she added, while the receptionist watched, Geneviève Marchal, and the address: 31 rue des Envierges, Paris.

'What's that?' the receptionist asked. 'You French or something?'

'Yes, I'm French.'

'You don't sound French.'

'I do when I speak it.' And she gave a little demonstration.

The girl sucked her teeth, understanding nothing. 'If you're foreign, you'll have to give us your passport.'

There was a moment's desperate search in her bag. 'I've lost it.'

'Then you can't have a room.'

'But I've nowhere else to go.' She felt panic, as though she was standing on the edge of something, perhaps tears or perhaps madness. 'Please. Just this once.' Pleading and at the same time knowing that she was making a spectacle of herself that the girl would remember, that when the police interviewed her she would be able to give them an exact description and Geneviève Marchal would be forever compromised – *brûlé*, burned, blown. 'I beg you.'

The girl considered her appeal. 'I'll have to call the manager. I can't just go breaking the rules.'

The idea of the manager sounded frightening, but when he came he was big and jovial and a friend to all. 'French, are you?' he said, looking her up and down. 'I was in France in the war. Catering Corps. *Voulez-vous promené avec moi, mademoiselle?*'

She tried a smile and suggested that maybe it was a bit cold for a walk. And besides, she'd already been walking for hours.

'Walking for hours, have you? Where from, may I ask?'

But she had no idea where from, and no idea where she was going. Just walking, that's what she was doing. Just walking.

'Question is,' the receptionist interrupted, 'can we give her a room if she hasn't got her passport? She's paid in advance, you see? But she's foreign, isn't she?'

The manager decided – 'Of course we can, my dear. Anything for our brave French allies' – and a key with a large, brass tag was produced. With that and the warning that the kitchens closed at nine o'clock, Geneviève was allowed upstairs into the dingy, ill-lit upper corridor of the hotel, to room number 15 with its battered wardrobe, narrow iron bed, cracked basin in the corner and picture on the wall showing horses galloping along a sandy beach.

She felt very tired. Outside, in the light of street lamps, she could see snow falling. The radiator was lukewarm and a cold draught leaked round the edges of the window frame but the room was warmer, much warmer than anything she might have hoped for. Still wearing her coat, she lay down on the bed and slept.

She dreamed the falling dream, the plunging, floating dream, the dream where she wandered without knowing where to go and awoke to no idea of where she was. It was dark outside, the view pooled by street lights. There was the throb of a nearby main road and the grime of dirty, urban snow. Where was this? A hot lava of panic bubbled up inside her. What the hell was she doing here? On the pavement below her window pedestrians breathed fog into the air. A double-decker bus passed by but she couldn't see the route number or the destination.

She sat on the bed for a moment and tried to gather her scattered thoughts. She knew *who* she was but not where she was, nor what she was doing here in this dull hotel room with the hard, narrow bed and the ghastly picture of galloping horses on the wall, and an unknown world outside.

London, of course. Presumably. Presumably London. But where and why? Questions crowded in on her, threatened to overturn her, like waves overturning a fragile rowing boat. Where was she?

A glance at her watch told her it was ten-thirty. The brass tag attached to a room key on the bedside table told her she was in the Old Oak Roadhouse, Edgware.

Dreams and memories chased themselves through her mind. Walking, she remembered walking. And cold. But not much else. After a while she got up, splashed icy water on her face and attempted to use the scarce resources of her handbag as make-up – some lipstick, a dab of powder, a comb though her untidy hair. Following the exit signs she made her way down to reception where a sallow girl looked up from painting her nails. 'Fraid you're too late if you're looking for dinner. Kitchen closed at nine. I did warn you.'

'Did you?'

The girl shrugged. 'Maybe you didn't understand my English. Being French yourself.'

'What do you mean? Of course I understand your English.'

A couple came in through the main door, stamping their feet free of snow and laughing together. A gust of cold air followed them like a blast of indifferent reality. They knew where they were and where they were going.

'I need to phone,' Marian said.

The receptionist sighed and pointed with one half-painted nail to a wooden booth in the corner.

'You'll need pennies. You got pennies or have you only got francs?'

'Francs? Why should I have francs? Of course I've got pennies.'

The interior of the booth smelled of stale clothes and damp. There was a notice explaining that this apparatus was for the convenience of guests of the hotel and was restricted to outgoing calls only. Users were asked not to take up too much time as others might be waiting.

She inserted her pennies and dialled, and Alan answered, a distraught, anxious Alan. She could tell that merely by the way he announced the number as he picked up the phone. She pressed button A and heard pennies fall inside the machine. 'It's Marian,' she said.

'Marian, where in God's name are you?'

'I don't really know, darling. And I don't know how I got here. In fact I'm not really sure what day it is. But could you be so sweet and come and rescue me? I think I must be somewhere in Edgware. Isn't that near Stanmore? I remember going to the cinema in Edgware when I was at Bentley Priory.'

'What the hell are you talking about?'

'I don't really know. Look, I'm a bit confused and a tiny bit frightened and I'd be grateful if you could come and get me. I'm at somewhere called the Old Oak Roadhouse.'

'I'll be there in half an hour.'

Then she put the phone down, went to the bar, ordered a gin and tonic, sat in a corner and waited.

FUGUE

Doctors, a hospital bed with nurses coming and going, starched figures with starched minds. They tested her blood pressure and her blood sugar and anything else they could find to test. Even her brain waves, with electrodes on her scalp and pens describing lines of activity on a moving strip of graph paper. There was no trace of anything materially wrong.

'We call it a fugue,' Dr Morgan said, meeting with them in his office in the hospital rather than his consulting room on the Woodstock Road.

Alan looked sceptical, but Marian liked fugue, with its musical connotations, its interwoven threads, its careful, artful complexity.

'Fugue involves dissociation and amnesia,' Morgan explained, 'both of which appear to be relevant here. The word means flight, of course. It affected you for only a few hours but people sometimes take off for days, assume a different name, live perfectly normally for a while as a different person and then have no coherent memory of what has happened. The Agatha Christie case, have you heard of that? She disappeared for ten days and when she reappeared she found herself somewhere in Yorkshire, living under an assumed name. It's thought to be a reaction to stress. Soldiers, for example, with shellshock . . .' His voice itself was a palliative, the gentle cadences of the Welsh hills somewhere behind his words. *Dissociative*, he said. *Amnesia. Depersonalisation.* Words that whispered through the consulting room long after they had been uttered.

'Does it mean I'm going mad?'

Dr Morgan smiled. 'Mad's not a word we use these days. And you're as sane as I am. We're talking about a neurosis, not a psychosis, and we can deal with it together. I suggest we meet up a little more frequently than we have been doing recently. Would twice a week be OK for the moment? Otherwise, just carry on as normal as long as you're not overdoing it. Work? Of course. Keeping yourself busy is usually a great help. Work isn't the prime cause, is it? Your trip to Hamburg, reliving your experiences, I'm sure that's the key.'

They took the train back to London, making plans about how they would deal with this problem. Alan was being understanding. He was always understanding. But why, he wanted to know, couldn't she just give up her work with that damn left wing lot and become a normal married woman?

She laughed, because she really would go mad if she was stuck at home with nothing to do. And the Peace Union were sure to agree to her having two afternoons a week off. She'd be able to stay

257

overnight with her parents when she had her appointments with Dr Morgan. That would be comforting for her, wouldn't it? Particularly when Alan was away on business. Everything, she assured him, would be all right. She reached out and took his hand, which was not the kind of thing she often did. 'Believe me, darling. Everything will be all right.' As though he were the one to be comforted.

FAWLEY

Marian Sutro, MBE, Croix de Guerre, travelling unknown on the Tube and the bus through the faint spring, trying to take inspiration from the season and think of the future, trying to forget about the past, trying to forget about her fugue, remembering it only as a dream, a wandering dream, a dream of person and impersonation. She is also trying to ignore the men following her, because they are not there. She knows that. The psychiatrist has assured her that these things – the fugue, the followers – are only illusions born of her experience. And, of course, she agrees – they *are* illusions, fantasies, products of her own, deranged mind; until the day that it is no illusion, the day when she's leaving work and she cannot dismiss the man watching her from across the road as a creature of her imagination. Perhaps he had been there on other occasions but then she had been able to dismiss him as a mere phantasm; on this occasion there could be no doubt. No dream, no demon, no phantom. As she emerges from the offices of the Franco-British Pacific Union one approximate spring afternoon,

259

there he is on the far side of the street, a man of medium build in a dark overcoat and bowler hat, with, by his side, a tightly furled umbrella. His face is partly concealed by a grey woollen scarf wrapped round his neck against the cold but he is watching her. As she turns to walk along High Holborn, he does precisely the same thing but on the other side of the road, keeping pace with her, walking briskly, his umbrella swinging in that unmistakable fashion that is the birthright of every English gentleman. At a zebra crossing he passes over to her side and walks just behind her. At the next side street there he is at her side.

'Marian Sutro,' he says, touching her elbow with a tightly gloved hand.

She felt fear, and that strange coldness that came to her with fear. The demons brought panic; true fear only brought this chilling calm. She stopped and turned.

'It *is* you,' he said, although he knew damn well it was her. 'Can I offer you a lift somewhere? I was about to get a cab.' As if by magic – something else that was the birthright of every such Englishman, perhaps – a free taxi materialised at the kerb beside them. He held the door open for her. 'Please.'

They sat back in the leather-bound interior. She pressed herself into the far corner, leaving as much distance as possible between his immaculately pressed trouser legs and her nylon-clad knees.

Despite the uniform of the city businessman there was still that bland, self-effacing quality about him that she had discerned when they had first met – reserved and thoughtful, like an Anglican divine who has all the arguments at his command but is reluctant to deploy them for fear of offending people. Major Fawley, smiling faintly and nodding as if in agreement with what he is saying: 'What a pleasant coincidence, bumping into each other like this.'

'Is it?'

'Perhaps not quite a coincidence. But pleasant, I can assure you. Now, where can I take you?'

'You can drop me in Piccadilly Circus. I can get the Tube from there.'

'Oh, please. At least let me deliver you to your doorstep.' He leaned forward to give instructions to the driver and with a little shock of understanding she heard him name the exact street. A tremor of anxiety and anticipation passed through her, a mirror image of what she had felt the first time they had encountered one another in rooms in an Oxford college, with the war going on around them and the prospect of a parachute drop to France lying before her. But when he sat back in the seat he was wearing that bland, clerical face that signified nothing. 'What a dreadful winter we've had, haven't we? How are things going? How is peace treating you?'

She told him, just the positive things – her marriage, her new job, her circumscribed life in

261

London – feeling all the time that he already knew most of it. Did he also know, she wondered, about her flight from reality, her fugue? 'Getting back to normal,' she said. 'Whatever normal means. I was lucky, I suppose, considering that I have no qualifications for anything. Miss Atkins found the job for me. Do you know Vera Atkins?'

Light from the window glinted on his owlish spectacles. 'I know *of* her. A singular woman, is she not?' There was a pause while she was allowed to wonder about the singularity of Vera Atkins. 'Incidentally, may I offer my congratulations on your witness at the Hamburg trial?'

'You know about that?'

'My dear, it was all over the papers. Even in *The Times*. It cannot have been easy for you but I understand you performed flawlessly.'

'I felt an obligation . . .'

'I'm sure you did. We all of us have accumulated obligations over the last few years, both personal and professional, haven't we? But tell me about Hamburg itself. I was there for some time before the war. I loved the city. How did you find it?'

'Like the surface of the moon.'

He shook his head disconsolately. 'How terribly sad. One wonders whether Germany will ever get back on its feet again. Or the rest of Europe, come to that.' The taxi veered round Eros and made its way down Piccadilly. Banal musings became a conversation: what did she think about all the countries of eastern Europe coming under Soviet rule? First Poland and Hungary, and now it looked as though Czechoslovakia was going the same way. Half the continent disappearing behind what they were calling the Iron Curtain.

Marian shrugged. 'It's hardly what we fought for, is it? But that's what imperial powers do.'

'I suppose it is.' He moved his lips into a thoughtful pout. 'Look, I'd like to talk over a few things with you if you're willing.'

'What kind of things?'

'Oh, this and that. What happened and what might happen next. What you might do for us. If you're interested.'

'*Do* for you?'

Fawley smiled. 'Let's talk about it later, shall we?'

They were in Knightsbridge by now, turning down the Brompton Road. A bus blocked their way. Behind them a car hooted with indignation as they sat there motionless and silent. When finally the traffic moved and the taxi turned into her street it was a great relief. From inside his glass box, the cabbie glanced round. 'What number, miss?'

'Just put me down on the next corner.'

The vehicle came to a halt and Fawley opened the door. 'It's been so nice talking to you, Marian. Do give me a ring. Any time.' He pressed a little fold of paper into her hand. 'There's my number. And by the way, it's *Mister* Fawley these days, rather than Major. Consider me demobbed, although the rank was really no more than a bit of flannel. Oh . . .' An afterthought. A silly point about nothing at all: 'Best not talk about this little encounter, eh? Not to anyone.' A brief smile, as though smiling itself were a secret. 'But do give me a ring. Any time.'

Groundbait, was that the word? Thrown on the surface of the water to get the fish to bite. But where was the hook? She attempted to bury the encounter in the morass of her daily life – shopping for the things she and Alan needed, getting to work in the morning, working late into the evening most days and getting back home no earlier than Alan. Feeling better, more confident, the fugue fleeing back into the realms of unimportant memory. Fawley could go hang. But the fact of his appearance was always there, worming its way into her subconscious, setting up memories and fears, and the strange thrill of anticipation; and the little fold of paper with its Victoria number remained in her handbag, anonymous, tantalising, echoing with the faint ring of danger.

RUSSELL

At the Peace Union she had her first triumph. It came about through the lectures programme. Usually the speakers were Mr Roper's responsibility but this time it was Marian who made the suggestion. Miss Miller was dismissive of the idea – 'Oh, we'd never get *him*' – but Marian felt differently. 'I think perhaps we might. I'm not promising anything but I think my father may be a help. You see, they were at Cambridge together. And imagine what a thing it would be if we could pull it off.'

A thing indeed, just the kind of thing she needed, to pull herself together, as her father put it. Pulling it off and herself together and through her recent turn and get her back on an even keel. All sorts of metaphors going round and round the family conversations. And her father did indeed pull it off, sending a letter to Trinity College in Cambridge to the great man himself – *My dear Bertrand*, it began – and receiving a most effusive and enthusiastic reply, so much that Mr Roper was persuaded to overcome his natural parsimony and consent to the hire of a nearby hall to accommodate the talk.

The event was announced in the press as an important initiative from that tireless worker for international peace, but despite Mr Roper's insistence that she should share in the triumph and take a place up on the stage, Marian hid at the back of the hall like one of the public. 'I don't want to be on display,' she explained to Mr Roper, but the real reason was that she feared the panic that might erupt inside her in the midst of all those people.

Alan had, of course, declined an invitation – 'To hear one of your socialist friends? You must be joking!' – but Ned was eager to attend. He had brought someone with him, a young man called Trevor. So the three of them sat together at the back of the hall while Mr Roper stood at the lectern to address the massed ranks of sympathisers and peace lovers. Behind him the guest speaker sat in a straight-backed chair looking for all the world like an ostrich who has determined not to bury its head in the sand.

'Lord Russell tells me,' Mr Roper said to the attentive faces, 'that the only reason why he uses his title is that it gets people to listen to him. But for us, deeds speak louder than titles. So, I'll present him to you as plain Bertrand Russell because it is through his deeds in the struggle for peace that he has *title* to our close attention.'

The pun brought polite laughter. Then the audience hushed and the great man rose to speak. It was what he said that was so disturbing. So much so that Marian, sitting right at the back, couldn't quite believe her ears as his bleating, exact voice drifted out over the audience like a chill breeze. He talked of the bomb, of the American monopoly that would soon be lost as Russia developed her own weapon, of new bombs which would soon be here, bigger and better bombs – by which he intended, with heavy irony, *worse* bombs. The hydrogen bomb, he explained, in that matter-of-fact manner of the scientist, that would unleash the whole energy of the sun upon the surface of the earth.

The auditorium was as silent as a cemetery, the listeners like so many headstones.

'Therefore there remains to us,' Russell asserted in the manner of one speaking incontrovertible truth, 'a short period during which the world might yet be saved from the indescribable fate of an atomic war which would in all probability exterminate the civilised portion of mankind.'

He thought perhaps that some men and women might survive such a conflict but they would be those fortunate – or perhaps *unfortunate* – few who may have been engaged in exploring the Antarctic Continent or investigating the theology of Tibetan Lamas. This was intended as a bitter little joke although no one laughed. Such survivors, the man went on, would surely be too few to re-establish civilised communities even should they wish to repeat such a grim experiment. And even if mankind, in the course of a millennium or two,

267

were slowly to climb back to its present intellectual level, it was to be presumed that it would again inflict a similar catastrophe upon itself. To this end the good Lord saw some kind of world government as the only possible solution.

There was a stir of approval at this benevolent idea. After all, that was the title of his talk: World Government and the Road to World Peace. The audience warmed up, expecting further comforting platitudes. 'However,' the great man said, 'the Russians have shown themselves opposed to any such overarching world body unless it is to be run by them. We see at this very moment how they are acting towards the besieged city of Berlin and how they have swallowed up the two countries whose earlier fates were inextricably bound up in the start of the last war.'

Now there was a certain amount of unease among the listeners. Russian motives were not to be impugned so easily. And against this unease, Russell moved on to consider how the West might react to such aggression. There were, he decided, three possible courses of action for the Western world to take, none of which could be described as easy.

The audience waited, hoping for some kind of palliative. The white-haired sage, philosopher and mathematician, observed them with his customary look of innate superiority. Philosopher or mathematician, the calculations were the same: the first course of action was an immediate attack on

Russia, which the United States and her allies would surely win quickly and decisively.

There was a collective intake of breath in the crowded hall.

The second course of action was to wait until Russia acquired her own atom bomb, in which case there would almost certainly be a large war between two evenly matched belligerents. This might also end in Western victory but only after frightful carnage, destruction, and suffering.

People in the audience began to mutter among themselves.

The third possible course of action, the speaker decided, was inaction – out of pure fear, to fail to do anything at all. This last possibility would result in the West bowing to Russian domination of the whole of Europe. It would mean the end of European civilisation.

'I consider,' Russell said, his fluting voice rising high above the murmurings of the audience, 'each consequence to be more catastrophic than the one that precedes it.'

There was a gasp of horror as people understood what he had just said. Three possibilities and the least catastrophic was immediate war against the Soviet Union. Journalists scribbled on their pads. Someone called out, 'Better red than dead!'

Russell observed the people before him with an imperious expression. 'Was that a question or a statement?'

Marian stood up. People nearby turned to see her. She felt the weight of their regard, and a rising tide of panic. 'Lord Russell!' she cried out, and waited while the noise of the audience subsided. 'I came this evening to hear words of peace. And all I have heard is a call to war. I think what you say is wrong, profoundly wrong, because it fails to address the one factor that I would expect you to consider – the goodwill of the men and women of our former allies, the Soviet Union!'

There was applause, some cries of hear! hear!

'My dear madam—' Lord Russell began.

'I'm not!'

The good Lord looked confused. 'I'm sorry?'

She felt panic no longer, just a keen and calm sense of outrage. 'I'm not your dear madam. I'm a woman who took up arms against the Nazis, which is more than you did. And I do not wish to be forced to do the same against the Russians!'

There was tumultuous applause all around her. Up on the stage a hasty exchange took place between Mr Roper and the guest speaker. Marian turned and picked up her coat. 'Come on,' she said to Ned, 'we're going.'

They shuffled along the line. People around them stood to applaud. Up on the stage Lord Russell was burbling something but she took no notice. As she left the hall with Ned and his friend in her wake, she could only hear the man's voice calling out in the background. 'My good lady,' he was saying. 'My good lady!' He sounded like a sheep bleating.

They retreated to a pub just round the corner. She was shaking, a mixture of fright and elation. Ned was laughing. 'Little sister bearding the great philosopher. The poor man will scurry back to Cambridge with his tail between his legs.'

'Did I make a fool of myself? But I couldn't believe some of the things he said, could you? Doesn't he understand the horrors? I mean . . .'

What did she mean? Perhaps she meant that anything was better than what she had witnessed during her captivity. But more than that, she had an idea for the future, perhaps an absurd one, but nevertheless a possibility. Maybe the only hope. 'Like poison gas,' she suggested to Ned. 'Think how poison gas was so awful and so indiscriminate that no one used it in the last war. Mightn't atomic weapons be like that? As long as both sides were equal in some way, neither would employ them because the other would. And any idiot could see that if that were to happen everyone would be destroyed. Russell hadn't thought of that, had he? The great mathematical philosopher hadn't thought of that possibility.'

'Meanwhile,' Ned said, 'we've got to survive five, maybe ten years while the Russians catch up.'

'Is that the difference?'

He shrugged. 'That's what people say.'

The pub was filling up, men jostling at the bar.

271

Trevor had been dispatched to get drinks. He came back with two pints of bitter and a half of mild for Marian. 'I thought you did all right,' he said. 'Gave Lord Bertrand a real earful.' He was a rather handsome young man, with a mocking expression. He referred to Ned as 'Teddy' and there was something vulgar about his accent. She couldn't place it precisely. She still wasn't used to English accents, couldn't tell Yorkshire from Lancashire, or Birmingham from Liverpool. This, she rather thought, was Liverpool. It suggested lack of education, yet it transpired that he had read Russell's *History of Western Philosophy* and admired the man greatly, despite what he'd heard that evening. 'Trouble is,' Trevor said, 'Russell could argue the hind legs off a donkey and donkeys can't always argue back.'

She laughed. 'Are you calling me a donkey?'

He seemed a bit put out. 'That's not quite what I meant. And you're certainly not an ass. Not like Teddy here.'

There was more laughter. Ned the donkey. She watched the two of them together, their bantering, the tension between them that seemed at the same time to push them apart and yet draw them together, as though there were a force between them, one of Ned's mysterious forces of electromagnetism or gravity or something. He had explained to her once how objects cause gravity by distorting space, bending it, giving it curve and flex. Here, in the narrow confines of the pub, space had indeed been distorted, the distance between two men warped by their own presence, their bodies distorting the space separating them so that even when they were apart it seemed that they were together.

Trevor glanced at his watch. 'Look, I've got to be going.' He gave Ned an affectionate punch on the arm. 'If I don't get my beauty sleep the sergeant will be cross.'

'The sergeant?'

'Trevor's doing his National Service,' Ned explained.

The young man stood up and held out his hand to Marian. 'Nice meeting you, miss. And thanks for the invite. You did marvellous.' He smiled knowingly and was gone.

Ned picked up his glass of beer and drank. People were pressing round them. She slipped into French so that others wouldn't understand. 'How long have you known Trevor, Ned?'

'Not long. A month or two.'

'You seem very close.'

'What's wrong with that, Squirrel?'

'He just doesn't seem your type.'

'Oh, he's exactly my type, dear sister. Exactly what I'm looking for.'

She considered him, her brother whom she had worshipped and loved, both at the same time. And she thought of Véronique. 'Is he . . .?' She couldn't bring herself to utter the word. But he supplied it himself, almost eagerly:

'Is he what? Queer? Yes, he's queer, I'm queer. There, I've said it. Are you appalled, Squirrel?' His voice was taunting, like it had been in childhood when she was attempting something that he could do but which was beyond her. She searched around for a reply, some way of expressing her thoughts, and found none.

'How long has this been going on?'

'It's been *going on*, as you put it, ever since I first thought of people as male and female.' And then he looked worried, as if he had spoken too much. 'Squirrel, for God's sake don't say anything about this to the parents. You must promise me.'

'Of course I won't say anything. But . . .'

'But what? There aren't any buts. They'd never understand.'

She shook her head. 'But in Geneva, I thought you and Madeleine . . . You seemed so close.'

'Madeleine?' His tone was incredulous.

'Clément's sister.'

'I know perfectly well who Madeleine is. She was a good friend that's all. She knew everything about me, you see. She knew how I felt and she accepted it.' He hesitated. 'She even knew that I was in love with her brother.'

The bar was crowded now, the noise level rising. She finished the last of her beer and put the glass down, wanting to be out of the place. But his words stopped her. 'You were *in love* with Clément?'

'Does it surprise you?'

'Of course it does.' She cast around for something further to say, something that would ground all this in the normal and the quotidian. Her brother queer, the lover of some skinny, common youth. And in love with Clément. She thought of Clément, the smooth, dark shock of his body, his hard flesh where hers was softest and most fragile, the naked shamelessness of it all. 'Are you still in love with him?' she asked. 'Clément, I mean. Are you still in love with Clément?'

There was a bitter taste to his laughter. 'Always will be, I guess.'

'And does he know?'

He shrugged. 'There was an awkward moment in Paris before the war. Too much to drink one evening and a confession that I'd rather not have made. It was all a bit embarrassing. That's why I left and went to Cambridge.'

She attempted a smile, some semblance of sympathy. 'Poor Ned. I never realised . . .'

'Of course you didn't. No one realised, except Madeleine. Certainly not the parents, certainly not Clément, until that disastrous evening. And then you told me that you two had slept together. I think I came near to hating you then. That you should have him when I couldn't.'

She tried to deflect the conversation onto easier ground. 'What about Trevor? How did you meet?'

He shrugged. 'We know the places to go.'

'But it's dangerous, isn't it? Illegal.'

'Of course it is. We have to behave like spies.

Signs, passwords, keeping it all secret. But you know all about that, don't you, Squirrel?'

She smiled with him. Bitter, like the beer. 'Look, I think I'd better be getting home. I'll have to get a cab.' She picked up her coat, looked round for her handbag. 'Talking of spies, I bumped into Major Fawley the other day. Remember him? Are you still in contact? Do you know what he's up to?'

He followed her out of the bar. It had come on to rain. The pavements glistened. 'No idea, I'm afraid. I've not seen him since the end of the war. They picked up a number of German scientists and he wanted my help. But that was a couple of years ago now.'

'It doesn't matter.' She went up on tiptoe to kiss him. 'And don't worry about your little secret, it's safe with me. Now you'd better hurry if you don't want to get soaked. And thanks for introducing me to Trevor. I liked him.'

She walked towards Shaftesbury Avenue. The walk did her good. It made her think, about Ned and his secrets, about Clément and his; and about hers – a small nexus of deceptions and lies covering people and things. Perhaps she would tell it all to the psychiatrist just as once she would have told such things to a priest.

At Cambridge Circus she managed to flag down a cab. 'Where we going then, love?' the cabbie asked as she climbed in. 'Bloody evening, in't it? 'Scuse my French. Warm enough back there for you?'

276

'It's fine, thank you.'

And she thought of Véronique, wondering whether that was of the same species of emotion. Could love for a man be of the same nature as love for a woman? Did the love lie in the mind of the lover or in the nature of the loved one? What would have happened had Véronique survived? Would they have lived together in Lyon, in happy companionship, their private lives the subject of idle speculation among the students of whatever institution Véronique came to head? Or perhaps everything would have been different, the intimacies of the camp diminished to vague and awkward memories, whatever had once drawn them together transmuted into a friendship that survived only through an occasional encounter and the exchange of affectionate letters.

The taxi drove her through the heart of the West End. Bright lights now, Piccadilly Circus a maelstrom of neon. She wondered what to do. In the war it had been easy. The moral boundaries were two dimensional, drawn in black and white. But now things seemed complex and diffuse, lines cross-hatched and overlapping, shapes irregular and enigmatic, drawn in shades of grey as though with a piece of charcoal. *Clair-obscur.*

The next day the papers were full of Bertrand Russell's speech at the Conway Hall. The *Manchester Guardian* and the *Daily Telegraph* covered it in detail. 'Earl Russell Calls for Atom War' was the headline of the *Daily Worker*. The telephones at the Peace Union were ringing without interruption.

'What in heaven's name were you thinking of?' Mr Roper demanded when Marian got to the office. 'I had to make apologies on your behalf.'

'Apologies? What did you tell him? That I was a bit unstable? That I'd been through a great deal in the war? That the dear woman was a little weak in the head?'

He reddened. 'Nothing of the sort—'

'Well, I'm afraid I couldn't have faced him after what he said. In the current climate I believe in peace at any price, Mr Roper. Not what Lord Russell seems to believe in, which seems to be war at any cost.'

KRIEGSPIEL

Two days later she dialled the number Fawley had given her. A breezy voice answered – 'Wireless Network Company, how may I help you?' – and for a moment she wondered if she had made a mistake. But then she recalled the brass plaque outside the flat in Victoria where she had met him after her return from Germany. Her memory for this kind of thing still worked well enough: *The Wireless Network Company* and *Excelsior Import-Export*. And the singular Professor Jones.

'I'd like to speak to Mr Fawley.'

'Who is this speaking, please?'

She gave her name and waited while the telephone network coughed and whirred; then a neutral voice was talking in her ear and explaining how good it was to hear her again and did she want to arrange a meeting?

A taxi came to pick her up. Was it the same taxi as before, with the same driver? She rather thought it was. But the address to which it took her was not the one he had used for her debriefing. It wasn't in Victoria at all but somewhere behind Sussex Gardens, in an anonymous terrace house next door to a doctor's surgery and a small hotel.

Fawley himself answered the door, ushering her in almost as though he were an estate agent and she a client come to inspect the place. She glanced round the sitting room as if looking for distraction, or perhaps a means of escape. But there was neither – no pictures on the walls, no view out of the window, just a large wall mirror in which her reflection seemed to float like a fish in an aquarium. She'd heard of one-way glass – perhaps someone was sitting behind the mirror watching her; perhaps Fawley himself was observing her.

Moments later he reappeared, full of apologies. 'Can I offer you anything? A cup of tea, perhaps? Or would you rather coffee?' There was a kitchenette in one corner of the room where he busied himself with a tin of instant coffee and an electric kettle. It was a strangely domestic scene that betrayed something of his hidden, private life. He'd have a wife, presumably, and possibly children. She imagined them living out in the suburbs – Kew or Chiswick or somewhere. What did they think the paterfamilias did with his life as he went off to work every day wearing a bowler hat and carrying a tightly furled umbrella? Perhaps they assumed he worked in some ministry or other – Supply or Works or the Board of Trade – a civil servant doing his duty as he had always done.

They sat in uncomfortable armchairs on either side of a dead gas fire, he with his comforting cup of tea, she with her dreadful coffee.

'So how are you? You've been through a great deal. How are you bearing up?'

Bearing up. She liked the phrase. Standing straight and bearing a great weight on her shoulders without giving any hint that it was so. 'I'm fine,' she said, and she was fine. It was true. Her panics, her fugue, seemed behind her now. Surely she was developing a carapace, like a crab, born soft-shelled and vulnerable but with an outer integument that hardened with time. She could think about Benoît and remain indifferent, about Veronique and not care, about Tony Bright and shrug. There had been others and there would be others still; to bring with them the paltry comfort of physical intimacy but nothing more. And she would not run away from anything.

'And how's Edward?'

A chill filled her heart. Ned was still the soft-shelled crab, helpless in the face of prejudice. 'He's well.'

'You know I hold him in great regard? We worked together excellently during the war. His enthusiasms against my . . . balance. And of course it was through him that we—'

'Hijacked my mission to France.'

The man looked pained. 'Hijack is a rather racy term, isn't it? American, I believe. But it was indeed through him we realised that, with your

281

assistance, we might be able to snatch Professor Pelletier from the jaws of the lion.'

'Anyway, Ned's fine . . .'

'I gather he is involved in work of national importance.'

'Something near Oxford, I believe. He never discusses it with me.'

'I'm sure he doesn't.'

'Mr Fawley,' she said, 'why did you ask me to ring? Surely it wasn't to have a chat over a cup of coffee about the Sutro family.'

He seemed to taste her question, roll it between his lips, test it with his tongue. 'You're quite right, of course. But I could put a counter question. I could ask you why you rang.'

Kriegspiel, she thought – that blind chess that Ned and Clément used to play in the Annecy days. You knew your own moves but not your opponent's so you moved in the dark, probing, waiting, trying to work out what lay in the shadows. The game needed a third person to adjudicate, someone who could see both boards. Then it had been fifteen-year-old Marian Sutro; but now there was no adjudicator and she was one of the players. 'And what might I answer?'

'Because you are intrigued. Because you wonder why I should emerge from the shadows and make contact with you. Because you think I might enliven your – let's face it – somewhat humdrum post-war life.'

There was the stillness about him of the father

confessor, waiting to hear how she might respond. 'It's not humdrum at all. I enjoy my work.'

Again that thoughtful, prayerful pose, fingertips touching like gothic spires. He had noticed, of course, that she hadn't mentioned her marriage. 'I saw reports on the papers the other day about Lord Russell making his opinions felt. Quite a stir, he created.'

'He said things many people didn't want to hear. Including me.'

There was a faint smile on the Fawley face, as though he knew all about her outburst. 'So, the organisation you work for, the Franco-British Pacific Union. Tell me about it.'

Why on earth should he be interested? But she told him anyway, about the library, the meetings they held in the room on the first floor, earnest, serious lectures on the theme of world peace and disarmament. The Russell lecture was very much the exception. Most were worthy and rather dull. But all that was going to change. They were going to organise their first conference. It was even now being prepared – Scientists and Artists for Peace, it would be called. She was probably going to Paris to see Professor Joliot-Curie who was most enthusiastic about the project. They also wanted a major artist. There was talk about Picasso himself. What could possibly be offensive about all that? It was naive, idealistic, sometimes absurd; but what was wrong with it?

Fawley smiled. No doubt Picasso was for him a

charlatan of some kind, a Spaniard throwing pots of paint in the public face. 'Nothing. There is nothing wrong in the slightest with that kind of thing. But we are constrained to keep an eye on things, aren't we? These days the battle lines are no longer as clearly drawn as they were during the war. These days we never know where our enemy may be hiding.'

'I don't think he's hiding in the Union Pacifique.'

'Possibly not. But answer me this? Where does the Franco-British Peace Union get its money?'

'Money? I haven't really thought about it. There's a membership fee for the library. That's half a crown for a week or six pounds for a full year. Non-members pay to attend lectures. One shilling usually. As I said, the talk by Lord Russell was a bit of an exception. I think we made a profit on that. And we do collections, of course. And people donate. For God's sake, it's for a good enough cause, isn't it? We don't want another damn war, and with the new weapons that Dr Pelletier helped build . . .'

'Of course we don't want another war, Marian.'

Was it the first time he'd used her Christian name? There was a sudden shock of familiarity. What was he called? Cedric, she fancied, and had to keep herself from laughing. 'So what's the problem with the Peace Union's money?'

'Nothing, except that those charges barely even cover running costs. Who pays your wages, do you think? And who pays the rent for the desirable office space in High Holborn?'

'As I said, I've not thought about it much . . .'

'Well, give it some consideration. In my line of business we spend a great deal of our time tracking money. Money leaves a scent behind it, a trail that the bloodhounds can follow. The fact is that your organisation is largely funded through a merchant bank called the Co-operative Eastern Trading Bank, which receives monies from what appears to be your parent organisation in Paris called the Union Française Pacifique. This in turn is financed by the Banque Commerciale pour l'Europe du Nord, which is also based in Paris.' His French accent was quite good. It reminded her of how Buckmaster spoke, the careful enunciation, the orotund vowels. 'Now, the Banque Commerciale pour l'Europe du Nord, which sounds so worthy and so innocent, happens to be entirely owned by Gosbank in Moscow. Gosbank is the central bank of the USSR. Effectively, Marian, you are working for the Soviet Union.'

There was a silence. The Soviet Union. Once the brave ally sacrificing millions of men and women in the bloodiest battles against Nazi Germany, now, according to Bertrand Russell and many others, an ill-defined menace threatening the very peace of the world. She thought of Véronique extolling the virtues of Communism and placing all her hope in the coming of the Red Army. She thought of the Russian she met in Hamburg – what was his name? Absolon. A quiet man, marked by personal tragedy.

'And this leads to a difficulty, regarding you and Edward. You see, in the days when you were put through the cards – I believe that was the phrase, wasn't it? – we only carried out negative vetting. "Nothing against", and that was good enough. But now, what with a few scares we've had, positive vetting has become the rage. Now we're looking for reasons why we *should* give someone clearance, not reasons why we shouldn't. We are going into life histories, family background, bank accounts, who you see on Saturday night and – I don't want to embarrass you – who you wake up in bed with on Sunday morning. And having a sister who works for a Soviet-financed organisation . . .'

She felt a sudden surge of anger. 'So you're suggesting I resign my job for the sake of Ned's career?'

He allowed himself a reassuring smile. 'I don't think that will be necessary . . .' His tone left something hanging in the air, a condition, a sine qua non, a stipulation, a whole thesaurus of strings attached. 'But things might be easier if . . .'

'If?'

'If I had a word in the right quarter and pointed out that you were actually one of us. You are, you see, a natural. I thought that from the moment we first met in Oxford.'

Was this blackmail, glossed over with a thin varnish of flattery? He watched her, looking to see which way she might move. And she remembered unarmed combat training, all those years ago in

286

Scotland. They taught you that the first move was always to draw your opponent towards you. It brings him off balance, gives him a false sense of security, gets you in there where you can jab your fingers into the eyes, or slam the heel of your hand up under his jaw, or your knee into his groin. It was always a 'he'.

'What do you want me to do?' she asked eventually.

EEL

So Marian slid, as smooth as an eel, into that shadow world she had known during the war. She worked assiduously in the library of the Franco-British Pacific Union, she attended meetings, introduced lecturers, and, following her heady but equivocal success with Bertrand Russell, helped to arrange speakers on subjects that ranged from *The French Revolution – From Terroir to Terror* all the way to *Can The Atom Bomb Ever Be A Force For Peace?* And once every few weeks she would phone a number and the taxi would duly pick her up as she walked along some agreed street and sweep her away to a rendezvous with Fawley. SWALLOW was the codename by which she was known, swallow, with its implications of flight, of speed, of swoop, but also with hints of gullibility. There were times when she felt embarrassed by the poverty of the information she brought. 'My colleagues are just so ineffectual,' she would complain. 'I can't believe they are anything other than what they say they are – idealists trying to do their bit for the peace of the world. I know it sounds rather naive put like that, but . . .'

Fawley would nod seriously and note what she said, and repeat his mantra: all we need is information. Information and analysis equals intelligence. You provide the information, we'll do the analysis.

'I'm off to Paris in a few weeks,' she told him, 'to liaise with people there.'

'Paris rather falls outside our remit but I'm sure that others will be interested in anything you can glean.'

Others. Shadowy figures hung around the edges of her imagination, agencies whose very names were secret. It had been like that with SOE itself. The firm. The organisation. The Inter Services Research Bureau. What was the point of having a real name if no one knew it? It was like that Eliot poem, 'The Naming of Cats'.

What, she wondered, was her own real name?

PARIS

Her first visit to the city since the war. Paris with a superficial gloss to it, like a piece of silver plate that has been polished up but is still worn away in places to show the base metal beneath: the drab buildings in need of cleaning, the broken pavements, the impoverished shops. But Paris with a strange, febrile vitality, Paris that was home to the theatre of the absurd and was itself a kind of theatre with people performing on its various stages, writers in the cafés of the Left Bank, politicians treading the boards of the National Assembly or berating crowds in place de la Bastille, black jazzmen from America sounding off in basements and cellars, models strutting on catwalks wearing clothes that outraged the poor of Saint-Denis and Belleville, tarts and pimps on the pavements of Pigalle. Paris canaille. She had a row with Alan when she told him she was going on her own. 'I'll be all right. I was all right in Hamburg and this is nothing like that—'

'You were *not* all right in Hamburg. You came back from Hamburg a wreck. And then that turn you had, losing your memory—'

'And losing my mind? You know what the doctor said. A one-off event. Nothing to get obsessed about. I've been fine since then and I've got to keep looking to the future. This is Paris. This is now.'

This was Paris now. She could feel it as she got down from the train – the smell, the sound, the sense of place. And memory, of course, of Paris before the war, travelling with her parents and meeting up with Ned and Clément, her eyes wide, her senses alert to every gleam and glimmer of the city. And then Paris during the war when she'd been alone and frightened, hurrying through the tunnels of the métro pursued by demons.

But this was Paris now, with Clément himself waiting for her, standing on the platform in the Gare du Nord amid the flow of passengers from the Calais train and taking her in his arms while people looked on and smiled. There was no question what would happen this time. He would take her to the hotel that had been booked for her near the Panthéon and see that she was settled in. The next day he would come for her and take her to the Collège de France to meet with his boss, the aquiline Frédéric Joliot-Curie, the man who, together with his wife Irène, had won a Nobel Prize before the war, the man who cracked open the secrets of the universe with the precise hammer of his cyclotron. She would talk with him about the Scientists for Peace congress, about what he might do and what the effects might be, about the mechanics of the thing, about where he would stay and how he would be transported from hotel to venue, about speeches and interpreters, about colleagues and acquaintances. After that she would have meetings with the director of the Paris section of the Union Internationale Pacifique and with a serious young man who was a cultural attaché at the Soviet embassy in rue de Grenelle. There was the possibility, only the possibility, of a Russian scientist taking part in the conference. The name of the great agronomist Trofim Denisovich Lysenko was being mentioned.

But none of this really mattered. During her stay in Paris, what mattered was what happened in the hot and cramped interstices of her programme. The grappling with Clément on the hotel bed on the afternoon of her arrival; the awkward dinner with him and his wife Augustine at some over-priced restaurant overlooking Notre Dame; and the other encounter that came as a coda to her meeting with the Soviet cultural attaché – the sudden shock when the office door was opened and a figure stood there in the doorway, a tall, bony man with slightly receding hair and a focused, aquiline face that she thought of as Jewish. Maybe that explained his unusual, biblical name: Absolon.

'Mrs Marian Walcott,' he said. 'Or should I say Sutro? I could not let you go without seeing you.'

They shook hands warily, each trying to gauge the other, looking for subtle signs and significances. He was, apparently, working for the TASS news agency. No longer a soldier but a journalist. 'Can we meet up?' he asked when they had exchanged the expected platitudes. 'Can we do that? Would you be kind enough to grant me audience? I am most busy at the moment but perhaps dinner tomorrow? Are you free? At your hotel at eight o'clock?'

She didn't know. She really didn't know.

'The Hôtel Lyonnais, isn't it?' he said. 'I'll be there even if you are not.'

Marian Sutro travelling on the métro once again, rattling through the tunnels, emerging at the surface in a nondescript part of the city that the tourist never visits. Marian Sutro for the moment free of attachments, free of followers, still full of the memories of Clément while trying to dismiss memories of Absolon whose very presence here in the city seems something like a threat.

The Hôtel Lyonnais. How did he know that?

People pushed past her on the pavement. Cars, almost vanished during the occupation, now created a minor traffic jam round a section of roadworks. On the corner of rue des Couronnes a young man was selling copies of *L'Humanité* and shouting at passers-by not to believe what the government told them, not to believe the lies and the half-truths. Believe *L'Humanité*.

In a run-down café she ordered a pastis and took stock. Two men were sitting at a table playing cards and drinking. At another table outside on the pavement a young couple was deep in some intense argument, he holding her hand and shaking it, as though somehow this might stir his point of view into her head.

'Where are you from, then?' the barman asked.

No stranger ever asked a question like that the last time she was in the city. Questions drew you in to other people's stories, got you involved, got you into trouble. Now no one cared. She watched water drop into the pastis and turn the clear liquid into a dense cloud. The lie came readily to her, clouding the truth just as the water clouded the pastis. 'Grenoble.' A cover story invented on the fly. 'Just got in on the train.'

'What are you doing here?'

'Just looking round.'

The taste of the drink was like aniseed balls, evoking memories of midnight feasts at school, an innocence it seemed almost impossible to imagine. As the drink went down she felt that small blur of indifference that came with alcohol, the heightened sense of detachment, the feeling of carelessness. She had drunk pastis with Benoît that evening in Toulouse, the last evening in Toulouse – an evening when innocence was erased for ever, leaving behind no more than a residual aftertaste of guilt.

The barman wiped a couple of glasses and looked her over. What did he see? *Une gonzesse, une poule de luxe*, a posh bird slumming it? 'First time in Paris? This isn't the pretty part. Belleville's not so *belle*.'

'I was here during the war.'

'Were you, indeed? Things aren't much better now, I tell you. You still want to be careful. There are people here who'd skin you alive. Only the other day one of the fashion houses tried to take photos here. Models in fancy dresses, a photographer, lights, the whole lot. Local women attacked them. Tore the dresses off of the models. Left them in their knickers.' The barman grinned. 'True story.'

She paid and went outside. The market in the middle of the boulevard was as it had been during the war, stalls selling second-hand clothing, people picking through the coats and jackets just as they did in the days of the occupation. But now there were food stalls as well – dirty vegetables piled high, cheeses stacked like building blocks, scrawny chickens hanging by their necks, even a butchered lamb. 'At your fucking prices we might as well still be under the *frisés*,' a woman was shouting at one of the stallholders. There was derisive laughter from her audience.

Marian turned off the boulevard into the narrow streets at the foot of the *butte* where an old woman tried to sell her a sprig of lilac. 'It'll bring you luck, dearie.'

She began to climb. The street rose steeply between rotting tenements. Washing hung like bunting over the smell of ordure, of drains, of cooking. Was this the street down which she had run five years ago? Houses were boarded up, windows broken. Buildings leaned drunkenly towards each other. Struts of creosoted wood held a side alley open like someone separating a pair of punch-drunk prizefighters. Notices announced that the buildings had been condemned as uninhabitable by the Ville de Paris and that *rénovation urbaine* was in progress, but you couldn't see it. In a narrow, weed-infested space a group of kids kicked a ball made of rags bound up with string. They shouted *con*! and *merde*! and other words she couldn't comprehend. From the shadows of a doorway a woman watched her progress. 'Nothing for tourists here,' she called out. 'This isn't fucking Montmartre.'

Marian went on upwards. The climb became steeper until finally there was a flight of stairs leading up to the crest of the hill. She stopped and looked around, recalling no stairs in the desperate rush of her flight, just the steep descent down uneven cobbles, and the view across the whole of the city, the Tour Eiffel rearing up like a stiletto from a muddled sea of roofs. Spring sunshine brushed uneven strokes of light and dark across the city; when she was here before it had been a leaden day of unremitting gloom. She remembered only because it was impossible to forget. But did she run over *these* broken paving stones and uneven setts? Was *that* the drain where she threw her pistol? She cast around helplessly, fancying she might go down on her knees and reach her arm into the dark hole to find the weapon still lying there, the 9mm Browning whose heft she could still feel in her hand.

An old man approached her, drunk or mad, mumbling incoherent words. She shook her head at whatever he was offering or asking, and walked on, following the road from the edge of the hill, following the thread of memory back to the intersection at the end where six streets converged onto a narrow square. A single recollection stood out from the mess of memory like a fractured bone from an open wound – high up on a wall the street sign saying *Rue de Envierges* with below it a hammer and sickle in dripping red paint. The sign was still there but the hammer and sickle had gone, painted over with a mask of grimy white so that all that remained was a shadow, a vague crescent cut through by a diagonal, like a fog-obscured moon pierced with a lance.

She looked round the little square. Posters. Red posters announcing a meeting of the Parti Communiste Français where Jacques Duclos would address the faithful; multicoloured posters advertising some event or other – a circus, a play, a film at the Belleville-Pathé. Official posters in small print over the seal of the Mairie de Paris. From a bakery on one corner a woman emerged with two baguettes tucked under her arm. At another corner there was some kind of repair shop where two youths were doing things to the intestines of a motorbike. On a third corner there was a café and directly opposite was the impasse, the cul-de-sac, the blind alley, the dead end where the dead met their end.

She crossed the square and peered in: a street going nowhere except to a flight of stairs. This was where. She had run into this dank, cobbled place, then stopped at the foot of the steps to turn and see the Gestapo men, the SD men, whatever men they were, filling the entrance behind her. A rat in a trap.

Cautiously she stepped forward into the shadows, into the embrace of rotten plasterwork and grimy windows and memory. Drainpipes crawled downwards like veins through ulcerated flesh. There was the smell of piss, of cat and man. A torn poster advertised a tonic wine that would make you beam with delight. Beneath it Armand had chalked eternal love to Agnes.

And then there was the plaque. It was a plain thing, a rectangle of white stone high up one wall bearing the title *Front National, Comité du Quartier*.

En cet endroit, it declared, *en Novembre 1943 deux agents de nazi-fascisme ont été exécutés par Julius Miessen, martyr pour la cause de la liberté.*

In this place, in November 1943, two agents of Nazi-Fascism were executed by Julius Miessen, martyr for the cause of freedom.

She felt strange, as thin and feeble as tissue paper, as though the light was passing through her and the slightest breeze might blow her away. There at the top of the steps, for a fleeting moment, is the figure of Julius Miessen; and, when she turns, there are the two men silhouetted at the entrance to the impasse, sealing off the way back. She is at the axis of her memory. The world, the walls and the stones wheel round. Panic threatens to overwhelm her.

'You, come here!' one of the men shouts.

She looks back again, up the cliff of steps. Miessen, if it was Miessen, has vanished. Cautiously, feeling her way, she turns and goes back towards the two men at the entrance. She can feel the hard grip of wood and steel in her pocket, the weight of the Browning semi-automatic pistol. It is almost an extension of her arm, a prosthesis implanted there by hours of training. You don't aim the bloody thing. You're not at a shooting gallery. You cover the target with your weapon, holding it with two hands, the body square on, the feet apart, knees flexed. Double tap. Bang! Bang!

How is it that some memories are fragmented, broken and disjointed, whereas others remain whole and complete? This memory is complete. She looks up to the top of the steps and there he is: the man who calls himself Julius Miessen, who met her on the Toulouse train, who followed her from the station, who haunted her like a ghost through the streets of the city. She looks back and there they are, lying in pools of blood on the damp stone setts, one of them still moving, trying to raise himself up, trying to pull something from his pocket as she covers the few yards towards him.

From three feet away, she shoots him through the eye.

★   ★   ★

Someone was coming down the steps. At the sound of his footsteps she spun round, thinking, for an absurd moment, that it must be Miessen. But it was only a middle-aged man, his face rough with stubble, his eyes shaded with a peaked cap. He barely seemed to notice her as he walked past. Perhaps he didn't see her. Perhaps she had become entirely transparent, no more than an insubstantial memory trembling on the cool early summer air. No more substantial than the memory of the two men lying dead on the cobbles in their puddles of blood.

The man went on out into the bright light of the square while she stood there in the shadows for a long time, looking, thinking about time and place. It was here; it was not here. Ned would have talked about the spacetime continuum or something, explaining that everything had moved on so that all that remained for her to see was a mere husk, distant not only in time but also in space.

Where, she wondered, do memories lie? How do memories lie?

She turned and went back into the square and across to the café. Inside, behind the dull gleam of a zinc counter, a woman watched with narrow, suspicious eyes.

'I noticed the plaque in the impasse.'

The woman shrugged. 'What of it?' She wiped a table for Marian to sit, but it wasn't clear which of the two benefited more from the operation, the grimy table or the equally grimy rag that she used.

'Were you here then?'

'Been here thirty years. What do you want?'

What did she want? An interesting question without a ready answer. 'A pastis, please.'

The drink came, with its little jug of water. 'So what happened? In the impasse, I mean.'

Another shrug. The woman was pale and desiccated, as though she had been hidden in the shadows for too long, and starved for most of the time. 'Nothing much. A shooting. Kind of thing happened in those days, didn't it? You're not too young to remember.'

'Tell me about it.'

'I didn't see it myself.' She returned to the domain that was exclusively hers, behind the zinc counter, and called, 'Georges! Come here a minute, will you?' Then to Marian, 'He'll tell you. He saw it all.'

Peremptorily summoned, Georges came in from the back, smoking a *caporal* and scratching himself.

'She wants to know about the shooting.'

Georges eyed Marian suspiciously. 'Why's that?'

Never hesitate, a voice said inside her head. Never go anywhere or do anything without having a plausible reason. Never be caught out. 'I'm a journalist. Doing a piece on incidents in the *quartiers*. Local colour kind of stuff. For *L'Humanité*, *Combat*, anyone who'll take it.' It was a cover story made up on the fly and she knew she had nothing to support it, no notebook, no pencil even. But he didn't seem to care.

301

Perhaps the idea of being quoted in the press was enough.

'Gestapo,' he told her. 'They were chasing this girl, see. Got her trapped in the impasse, like a rat in a cellar. And just as they were going to arrest her this guy comes along and shoots the buggers. Bang, bang, straight through the heart, each one. Cool as you like. Maybe he was her lover or something. That's what I reckon.'

'Her *lover*?'

'Got to be some reason, hasn't there?'

'Why were they after her?'

'A Jew, wasn't she?'

'A Jew?'

'They were always after Jews, weren't they? Where were you at the time, for fuck's sake?'

'Geneva.'

He laughed. 'Well out of it, I'd say.' His laugh turned into a raucous cough. He took a drag on his cigarette to calm things down. 'Anyway, as far as I could see, she got away. Ran off down there—' He pointed vaguely beyond the windows of the café. 'Don't know if they caught her. They were all over the place, looking for her.'

'And the man? This Miessen . . . Doesn't sound French.'

'Dutch, so they say. French mother. They got him shortly after. Dragged him through here so everyone could see, poor bastard. Real mess, he was. Blood all over. A few days later they shot him, that's the story. In Fresnes Prison. D'you know Fresnes?'

'I know Fresnes.'

There was something in her tone that gave her away. He drew on his cigarette again, looking at her shrewdly. 'How come?'

'I did a piece about it. Fresnes then and now, it was called. For *Combat*.'

'Is that right?' He licked his lips, as though tasting the texture of her answer. Maybe he read *Combat*. Maybe he was trying to recall the article. 'Anyway, whatever happened to him, now he's a hero and they put up a plaque to his memory and claim him for their own. And journalists who were safe and sound in Geneva at the time write stories about him.' A laugh, full of phlegm. 'Fat lot of good any of it'll do him, that's for sure.'

She counted out the money for her drink. Still he was watching her. Something in her manner had awoken his curiosity, some little hint she had given, perhaps some mistake she had made. 'She was about your age, the girl was. Younger. Looked a bit like you. Almost be your sister. I saw her, you see. I was standing right here and I saw her as she came out of the impasse. Running like hell, she was. Wearing a black and white coat, I remember that. Classy, it looked. Not the kind of thing you see round here.' He looked her over now, at her own clothes which were not the kind of thing you saw round there, either. 'What *do* you know about it all?'

She got up from the table. The door was open and outside there was the refuge of bright sunshine.

She thought of Miessen's battered face, hiding behind it the only other brain that stored the truth. The other two witnesses both had bullets through theirs. How insignificant and ephemeral the act of remembering. 'I know she wasn't Jewish,' she said. 'Nor was she his lover. And she wasn't my sister.'

ABSOLON

On the way back in the métro she thought about it, about the impasse and the plaque, about memory and record. Miessen, not her. Absolution of a kind. Back at the hotel she found a message waiting for her at the reception desk. Absolution become Absolon. He assumed that everything was still all right for dinner that evening and would come round at eight o'clock.

Memories and half-memories. What happened in the impasse in Belleville, and what happened that night in Hamburg after the Ravensbrück trial, that single night with Tony Bright that she had clutched to herself and imagined as something without significance and devoid of consequence. Did this Russian know anything about it? Had he and Bright talked it over the next day, perhaps over a few vodkas – dreadful male banter she could only imagine? Would Bright have told Absolon, nudging him in the ribs and laughing over his little triumph? She's a good lay. Something like that. Screw, she's a good screw.

When she came down into the narrow reception hall with its two dusty armchairs and its painting of the cathedral of Saint-Jean in Lyon, there he was, wearing a well-cut grey suit, his hair thinner than she remembered, his face narrower, leaner, more lined, but Major Absolon nevertheless. She couldn't even recall his first name.

'Marian Sutro,' he said, bowing over her hand. 'How good to encounter you again.'

'How did you know?' she asked. 'How did you know which hotel?'

He laughed. 'Are you being suspicious of me? We journalists keep ourselves informed. So how are you? You look well, much better than when we met in Hamburg. Tell me, do you have news of Tony? Tony Bright? I regret it has not been possible to keep in touch. Our two worlds are so far apart these days.'

'No, I don't. I expect he's happily married and living in Belgium. What was her name? Anne?'

'Anne-Griet. He never stopped talking about her. Look, I am so glad you did not reject my invitation. Will you have dinner? Is that all right?'

She felt lightened by her strange absolution, intrigued by the possibilities of this meeting. Careless, all of a sudden. 'Why not?'

He took her to a small bistro nearby where he seemed to be well known. They sat at a table in a far corner and talked a bit about each other, what had happened since their first encounter. He'd moved into journalism at the end of the war. From writing accounts of the fall of Berlin and the

306

liberation of the camps for *Krasnaya Zvezda*, the Red Army newspaper, it was a natural move to TASS, the Soviet news agency. He smiled wryly. 'It means I can travel abroad. We are trying to create a workers' paradise but the decadent West has its attractions. Vienna for three years and now I've got Paris.'

'You're lucky. I've only got grey London.'

It was easy, this chatting. She'd forgotten how easy, how one subject led smoothly to another, from what she was doing in London to politics; from politics to philosophy, from philosophy to art and science. She found herself agreeing with him, and he with her. They wanted the best for mankind, of course they did. And the Russian people were attempting a great social experiment, possibly the greatest such experiment in human history, didn't she agree?

'Are you trying to recruit me?' she asked.

He looked at her with that mock-serious expression that seemed so much part of him. 'Actually, I'm trying to seduce you. But it seems I am a bit out of practice.'

She allowed him a laugh. The wine was working its clever deceptions. She felt light-headed and happy, the visit to Belleville pushed to the back of her mind, other things pushed to the back of her mind as well, Clément for example, along with the great load of emotional history that they carried between them; and the burden of Alan's affections that weighed her down so. But not the pure lightness of what happened in Hamburg between her and Tony Bright. Why couldn't she conjure up any shame? And why did she feel that it all might happen again, with this man who was at this very moment trying to decide whether to have a glass of Sauternes with the dessert. 'A half bottle between us, how about that?' he suggested. 'A Barsac, perhaps. Slightly less sugar.'

The waiter brought a bottle and poured. She raised her glass and looked at Absolon through the golden lens. His head was small and inverted and moving in the opposite direction to the way she moved, which seemed impossibly funny. A real image. Parallax or something. Dangerous laughter flowed between them. After the meal they stood hesitantly on the pavement outside. 'What do you want to do now?' he asked. 'There's a *boîte* I know. It's not far.'

'Why not?' she said.

The *boîte* was little more than a basement cellar that had once been an air raid shelter and was now, by virtue of being painted black, a nightclub. At one end of the tunnel a jazz quartet played, led by a Negro trumpeter whose eyes gleamed like pearls in the shadows. His trumpet threw careless notes and brilliant reflections around the place while the audience listened with rapt attention. One or two got up to dance but that seemed a distraction from the focus of the evening which was the Negro and his wandering, echoic music that talked of pain and anguish and some kind of peace.

'Bourgeois decadence,' Absolon said. 'And think,' he added, indicating the audience, 'they're almost all Communists. It makes writing articles about them very difficult. In Russia good Communists are not meant to behave like this.'

Soft laughter, their heads close together. She felt the breath of his amusement. And at that moment, quite unconsciously and without any exchange of words, agreement was reached. They left the place soon after, drifting on alcohol and a memory of the music that seemed to follow them through the streets. A threnody, she thought, uncertain what the word meant. Occasional couples passed by. She wondered whether they were being followed. She always wondered whether she was being followed; usually she felt she was but knew she wasn't. Now, she just didn't care. They walked because it was a fine night and because she enjoyed walking and anyway it wasn't far, just across the boulevard Raspail towards Les Invalides, and she didn't care if they *were* being followed all the way to the narrow town house near the Soviet embassy where Absolon had his flat. She was transparent, as light and translucent as tissue paper, climbing the narrow stairs with Absolon behind her to catch her if she fell.

The next day Clément and Augustine came to see her off at the station. Augustine embraced her warmly. She was so delighted finally to have met up with Marian. 'Now we know each other, you must come and see us again. You mustn't hide away in grey and foggy London.'

Augustine's perfume was floral and bright, Marian's dark and musky – the scents clashed even as they embraced. 'I look upon you as a true friend,' she whispered in Marian's ear, whispered so that her husband wouldn't hear, as though the two women shared a secret that he was not party to. 'And I don't mind that you fuck him.'

HAPPY CHRISTMAS

That Christmas she persuaded Ned to spend the day with their parents in Oxford. It would be the whole family together for the first time since before the war, with Alan as the only outsider.

It was not a successful time. Ned argued both with their father and with Alan. He always argued. The debates with her father were low key, under-pinned by a whole childhood and youth of conflict; those with Alan were more outspoken, culminating in a row about nothing. They'd listened to the King's Christmas broadcast on the wireless – the hesitant, fluting voice – and it was something Alan said, about the King and patriotism among the British public, that awoke Ned's scorn. 'Patriotism? Isn't patriotism dead?' You could see the anger in his expression, and his contempt for Alan's plodding certainties.

'It got the country through the war, didn't it? Won it for us, in fact.'

'That was brutal necessity. Drowning people clinging to a rock and singing patriotic songs to keep their spirits up, while waiting for the Soviet Union to rescue us.'

311

'You're just being offensive. And anyway, it was the Americans who rescued us.'

'That's the American story. But it was the Russians who lost over twenty million men and women.'

Alan should have left it there. With no one to stoke the fires the argument would have died. But he circled back to the theme of patriotism – the British had patriotism, the Russians just had fear – and then he delivered what he thought would be a decisive blow. 'And what about Marian? Didn't she parachute into France out of patriotism?'

Ned snorted. 'Is that what she's told you?'

'Do you know any better?'

Marian tried to intervene – 'Why I volunteered is my own business' – but the two men were well into the argument and beyond caring what she said. 'She went, dear brother-in-law, because she was little more than a besotted child who thought that she would be able to meet up with the love of her life in Paris. In fact you could say she went to France in order to lose her virginity.'

'Ned!'

'Which is precisely what happened.'

She shouldn't have risen to the bait. She should have walked out of the room and left the two men to their idiotic argument as her parents had already done. But she didn't. Instead she turned on her brother and used the one weapon she had against him. 'And when are you going to lose *your* virginity, Ned?' she asked.

He smiled. She hated that smile. It was the

expression he had always turned on her when she was young, a look of pure contempt. 'As a matter of fact, I have, Squirrel. With the very same man as you did. But perhaps he never told you that.'

She stared at him. Once she'd have been surprised; but now she understood that anything was possible, even this. 'Ned!'

He was appalled. She saw it in his expression, in the moment before he left the room – the horror of what he had just admitted. She followed him into the dining room which was still redolent of the unhappy lunch that had been eaten there. Their mother was putting the final things in order, the last pieces of cutlery from the canteen, the unconsumed candles back in their box. 'Are you still arguing?' she asked. 'Surely not at Christmas time.'

They waited until she had gone before saying anything and then it was Ned who spoke first. 'I didn't want to tell you like that,' he said. He flapped his hands helplessly. 'It just came out. I'm sorry, Squirrel, I'm sorry. It was . . . unforgivable.'

'But is it true?'

He shrugged. 'More or less. That evening I told you about. Too much to drink. He had anyway. I was stone cold sober. We just . . . messed around. Embarrassing really.' And then suddenly he was crying, actual tears running down his face, his features crumpled into something resembling the angry little boy he had been. She went and put her arms around him and he let her comfort him.

'I want to go home,' he said quietly. 'Will you drive me to the station? I want to go home.'

'We'll drive you home.'

'I don't want to go with that husband of yours, Squirrel. An hour in the car with him? I couldn't bear it.'

On the way to the station she asked about Trevor. How was he? Where was he? Ned shrugged. 'He was posted, somewhere in Yorkshire. I don't really know.'

'You're not in contact?'

'I told you, Squirrel.' That bitter little smile. Ned's other mood. 'We're like spies. We work in secret and we don't ask questions if we don't need to know.'

'Is it true?' Alan asked as they drove back to London that evening.

'Is what true?'

'About that French fellow and your brother.'

'I don't expect so. Ned's just jealous. He probably made it up.'

'But is he a queer? Your brother, I mean. Is he really a queer?'

They drove in silence for a while, the question hanging in the air between them. She tried to bring some order to her thoughts, tried to quell her prejudices and reinforce her beliefs. 'He's homosexual, Alan, if that's what you mean. He can't help it, any more than you can help liking women.'

'Can't he see a psychiatrist or something? Can't something be done these days?'

'Could you be cured of liking women?'

He laughed humourlessly. 'Not unless they cut my balls off. Anyway, it's not only disgusting, it's illegal. Imagine what might happen if he got caught soliciting in a public lavatory.'

'I don't imagine Ned does that kind of thing.'

'They all do, Marian, they all do. We had an aircraftman on the squadron. Used to go up to London whenever he had leave, and they caught him in Piccadilly Underground station trying to pick up someone in the gents. Unfortunately he chose a policeman. Got two years in detention and a dishonourable discharge.'

She thought of the possibilities, the scandal, the shock to her parents.

'And what about you?' he asked after a while.

'What about me? Do you mean, do I pick people up in public lavatories?'

At least he laughed, but there was little humour in it. 'I mean, did you really lose your virginity to that French fellow?'

'Not to Clément, no. Yes, we were lovers if you must know, but I actually lost my virginity to Benoît.'

'So I'm third in line, am I? Or were there others?'

'No others before you, no.' Would he notice the careful use of words? 'Since my sexual history is a subject for general enquiry, what about yours? Who did you lose your virginity to, Alan?'

He was silent, staring ahead through the windscreen, his hands gripping the steering wheel as though clinging to a life belt. 'To you,' he said.

315

FUCHS

The news broke in February, a cold, damp February, the very depths of winter.

'Do you know what's happening?' Ned demanded. 'Do you know what the hell's happening?' He'd phoned her at work and when she got to him he seemed helpless, almost hysterical, casting around as though a solution might be found somewhere in the chaos of his flat in Bloomsbury.

'What's going on? For Christ's sake, Ned, what's the matter?'

'They've arrested him.'

'Arrested? Who?' She thought perhaps, Trevor. Or some other friend. Maybe Ned himself was under threat.

'Klaus Fuchs, of course. Who else? Under the Official Secrets Act. Flat-footed policemen blundering their way in and taking him away in handcuffs.' He grabbed something from the table and flung it down on the sofa. It was nothing, just a journal of some kind. The gesture seemed to sum up his sense of futility. 'He was at Chalk River, he was at Los Alamos, he's one of the leading theoreticians . . .'

'What's he's accused of?'

Ned shrugged. 'Klaus is an idealist. If they paint him as a monster and a traitor, don't believe it.'

'That's not answering the question, is it? What did he do? Did he pass information to the Russians?'

'He always believed that we should. Many others agreed, as I've told you. Oppenheimer believes it – and look how they're treating him now. Shunning him, threatening to drag him in front of one of their bloody Senate committees.' Now Ned's voice trembled with fury. He understood the illogical behaviour of sub-atomic particles but not the illogical motions of politics and politicians. 'The Russians were our allies, weren't they? Our saviours, maybe. And now they are being made our enemies. That fool Russell. You heard him.'

She thought of Véronique, of how she used to extol the virtues of the Russians, of how she insisted that the Red Army would come to their rescue. Which, eventually, it did, but too late for her and tens of thousands, hundreds of thousands, of others. And Absolon, she thought of Absolon, who carried a belief in Communism within him like a religious faith.

Within a day it was in most of the papers: Klaus Fuchs had appeared at Bow Street Magistrates Court, charged with two acts of communicating secret information to a foreign power.

'Whatever they say about him,' Ned told her

when they met up again, 'you must remember that he is an honourable man.' Honourable sounded strange in his mouth. He was not given to delivering encomia. 'He was trying to balance things out, Squirrel. Don't you see that? What we've talked about. Look at the way the Americans have behaved. They closed us out of the atom bomb project and now they're in England, they're in Germany, they're in Italy, they're crawling all over Europe. They've got big bombers and over a hundred atom bombs and every one of them is aimed at Russia. Do you know, they have a new bomber so big there's a gallery inside the wings so that a crewman can walk inside to service the engines?'

'Don't be ridiculous.'

'I'm not being ridiculous. I'm telling you the truth. It can carry an atom bomb on a round trip of nine thousand miles and more. They can wipe all the major Russian cities off the face of the earth in a matter of hours . . . and their bloody generals *want* them to do it. Only the president himself – the man who gave the order for Hiroshima and Nagasaki, for God's sake – has been able to stop them. What happens when he goes? What lunatic might come in his place?'

They contemplated the idea of a lunatic in charge of the bomb.

'They've been to see me, do you know that?'

'Who have?'

'The flat-footed men from the Special Branch.

They're interviewing anyone connected with Klaus. They've seen Peierls and his wife because Fuchs used to stay with them in Birmingham. They've interviewed half a dozen others, too. Cockcroft knows all about it, of course.'

'And what did you tell them?'

'What should I have told them? That I agree with everything he did? That I think he's some kind of hero? I told them that I like and respect the man but I'm not a close friend. That I had no idea of anything he may have done in the privacy of his own life. And that as far as I'm concerned Klaus Fuchs is a brilliant scientist and a decent man.'

'So why don't you resign?'

He frowned. 'You think I ought to? It did occur to me. Hand in my notice and at the same time release my story to the press. I can just see the headlines. Fellow Scientist Stands Behind Red Master-Spy.'

'Boffin Backs Betrayer. That'd be the *Daily Mirror*.'

'Nest of Traitors in Our Midst. The *Express*.'

For a moment they laughed together, children again. Then he fell silent and serious. 'I hate them, do you know that? I thought having a socialist government in power might change things—'

'It has—'

'No, it hasn't. The same grey men are in charge. The same narrow view of the world – us against them, and if there's a dispute then we'll fight over it. Except that now one side has got atom bombs.'

'The Russians have theirs. They tested one last year.'

'And you know why? Because of people like Fuchs. But still they're years behind the Americans . . . and they'll be further behind still when the Super happens.'

The Super. It was no secret. The good Lord Russell himself had even mentioned it in his lecture. But the project itself had been announced to the world just three days after Klaus Fuchs's arrest, when the US president Harry S. Truman declared that his country would actively pursue research into the possibility of constructing a thermonuclear device – a hydrogen bomb.

'For the planners it's just a bit of simple maths,' Ned insisted. 'When should we launch an attack that guarantees the largest number of Soviet dead against the least number of dead Americans? It was that kind of calculation Bertrand Russell was making, don't you remember? When a bloody pacifist starts talking like that we really are in the shit.'

'Ned!'

'*Merde*, then. Does it sound nicer in French? Fuchs sees this. He's just a decent man acting according to his conscience. How can that be wicked or evil?'

She let him go on like this for a bit before she spoke again, quietly, feeling the thrill of incipient confession. Because what was about to be said could never be unsaid. 'Maybe you ought to, Ned.'

'Ought to what?'

'Once the whole Fuchs thing has died down, of course. Once they've put him in prison or whatever they are planning to do.'

'What are you talking about, Squirrel?'

'Maybe you ought to get in touch with the Russians.'

Ned laughed, that braying laugh. 'You're mad.' But she could see the look of complicity in his eyes. She knew it well, throughout their childhood. A glimmer of anger, a glimmer of pride, a small flare of impulse. The possibility lay between them like a sexual proposition, almost too dangerous to explore.

She lay awake at night. Faces passed before her eyes – the dead of Ravensbrück wasted by disease and starvation, the dead of Auschwitz gassed and Hiroshima charred to cinders. How to stop it all? She saw death around the corner, smelled it on her skin, felt it deep in the core of her being. Hers had been a bitter, personal war and now it had become a bitter, personal peace.

Sleep was no relief because when she slept she dreamed. She dreamed of horror, of desolation, of a great light in the sky, brighter than a thousand suns, of a great darkness where shades lived out their days devoid of food, devoid of love, devoid of hope. During the days she watched the world teeter on the brink and wondered when it would step over.

But nothing happened. Life continued. She went about her business as the ever more important co-ordinator of events at the Peace Union. She listened to earnest talks by serious people who advocated everything from world government to subsistence farming, and then went home in the evening to hear Alan talk about his work and his plans for the future. She became practised in the art of dissimulation. She found that she could keep her life divided like the watertight compartments of a submarine, her work at the Peace Union sealed off from her marriage; occasional visits to Oxford sealed off from the world that Ned inhabited; her meetings with Fawley sealed off from everything.

'They may approach you,' Fawley warned her. 'If they do, let me know immediately.'

'Who may approach me? About what?'

There was something unusually ill-kempt about him, as though he had spent the night sitting up watching someone through binoculars from an observation post. Was that the kind of thing he did? Surely not. 'You're just what they're after, aren't you? Not a card-carrying member of the party. A fellow traveller. They like fellow travellers. So they may make a move. It may be a legal – someone from the embassy – or may be an illegal – someone operating under deep cover as an ordinary civilian. You'll know when it happens.'

'But how can *I* be of interest to anyone?'

He smiled patronisingly, as though he were used

to dealing with people who didn't really understand the world he moved in. 'Not you, Marian.
Your brother.'

'*Ned?*'

'Of course. Now Fuchs has been arrested, they'll
be looking for a replacement.'

'And you're suggesting Ned might—'

'I'm just pointing out that having a fellow traveller as a sister might seem to open up possibilities
to them. And if they do contact you, you'll let me
know straight away, won't you?'

'Certainly, I will.' She paused to consider what he
had said. 'Is this why you recruited me, Mr Fawley?'

He gave off a faint air of self-satisfaction. 'Irons
in the fire, Marian. In this business you always
have to keep irons in the fire.'

'Is that what I am, an iron in the fire?'

'Forged steel, my dear,' he said.

ODETTE

Of course I knew none of this at the time. At the time I knew only about Marian, my mother's friend whose past life seemed illuminated by strange lights – the brilliant chiaroscuro of adventure and derring-do, the pale fluorescent glare of despair, the shadowy mysteries of sex. Her visits punctuated my adolescence, bringing with them embarrassment and excitement in equal measure. I remember cycling round the driveway in front of the flats where we lived, with her on the crossbar of the bike. I remember the wrath of neighbours at the noise we made. I remember walking in the Parks when she challenged me to a running race, which she won with ease; and punting on the Cherwell when she collided our punt with a group of American tourists who received a blast of French invective for getting in the way. Rarely did her husband seem to be with her. Indeed often she complained of his absences, such as on the occasion when we went to watch, in a West End cinema, the film *Odette*. Apparently Marian had been invited to the premiere but had turned the offer down.

'All those bloody journalists wagging their tails around Odette Sansom? No thanks. Anyway, if it's half as bad as the book it'll be a disaster.' Nevertheless she wanted to see the film and her husband was away on some business trip or other – bouncing up the pyramid of his wretched tyre company, she said – so a few days after the premier my mother and I travelled up to London to join her, and sat through a showing of the clumsy farrago in which Anna Neagle and Trevor Howard attempt to impersonate Odette Sansom and Peter Churchill. It was, is, a sorry affair, symbolic of those post-war films when the brave Brits can do no wrong and the wicked Hun no right. Marius Goring gave his impression of how a clever German might look: all dark glasses and a sinister cigarette holder and even – does memory serve me right? – black leather gloves; while, on the other side of the great divide, Maurice Buckmaster 'played himself on screen almost as badly as he played himself in real life'. Marian's own words. At her former boss's appearance her laughter rang through the auditorium, attracting furious looks from the rest of the audience and a demand for quiet from the usherette. But she didn't laugh when they half drowned Anna Neagle in the *baignoire*, or tore her toenails out with pliers. Instead Marian sat staring straight ahead, gripping the arms of her seat like someone preparing herself for the electric chair. At that point I wondered if I would witness a repeat of her breakdown in the Oxford cinema five

325

years earlier. Would I be called upon to comfort the hysterical woman, to put my arms around her and stroke her palsied cheek? But this time there was no drama. The ten months of Odette's time in Ravensbrück were translated into a few minutes on the screen and Marian sat through it all without movement or sound. At the end, when Anna Neagle, in tears and without make-up, falls into the arms of Trevor Howard, who has shaved and changed and generally spruced himself up – and wasn't weeping, of course – we made a dive for the exit.

It was early evening and raining. Despite the bright lights, Piccadilly looked inconsolably drab. A queue was forming up for the next showing. 'I need a drink,' Marian decided as we stood on the pavement debating what to do.

'But Sam . . .' My mother said.

'Oh, Sam's fine.'

I remember a taxi but not where it took us. I recall the interior but not the outside of some plush place that might have been a hotel, might have been a club, where the staff seemed to know her and there was, surprisingly, I thought, a certain amount of bowing and scraping before we were installed in leather armchairs in the corner of a bar. She drank gin and French, while I was limited to mere ginger beer. 'Sam can have a sip,' she said, offering me her glass over my mother's protestations. There was a smudge of lipstick on the rim. I raised the glass to my mouth, wanting to turn it so that my own lips would meet the imprint of hers but not daring such boldness. The drink brought that little shock of alcohol, that seductive bitterness, volatiles hitting the nose, hints of possibilities.

'You'll give him bad habits,' Mother said.

'How do you like it?' Marian asked of me.

'It's good.' I returned her glass reluctantly and looked with new satisfaction round this exotic den, scented with cigarettes and alcohol, into which I had been smuggled. On the wall nearby was a framed photograph of a woman in uniform. A heart-shaped face and a delicate little mouth. A studied innocence about her expression. Hair permed to give her a girlish look.

'That's her,' Marian said.

'Who?' Anna Neagle was the first name that sprang to mind. The resemblance was there but the suggestion only brought a little twist of irony to Marian's expression.

'Maybe the casting wasn't so bad after all. That's Odette. Sansom as she was, Churchill as she is now. That's her.'

There were other portrait photographs on the walls, of other men and women, some of them also in uniform. This place was, I understood vaguely, some kind of mausoleum for those people, the agents, the spies, whatever they were called. Was her own likeness there? I seized the moment, emboldened by my first sip of gin, and asked her.

She shrugged indifferently. 'Somewhere, I expect.'

'Did you do what Odette did?'

Marian gave a bitter laugh. 'Do you mean, did I climb into bed with my circuit leader? Not quite.'

'Marian!' My mother appeared shocked on my behalf. She seemed to be doing everything on my behalf that evening.

'Oh, he's grown up enough, aren't you, Sam? He and I understand each other, don't we?'

'Yes,' I said uncertainly. I wasn't, of course, and I didn't. I knew that climbing into bed signified having sex and I had grasped as much about reproduction as I could glean from the encyclopedia, but I understood nothing about the compulsions of love and lust, nothing about the currency of sex, the deals that are done between adults, the bargaining and the horse-trading. Nothing about the agony or the ecstasy.

'There you are, Judith. You underestimate your offspring. He's old enough to drink gin, he's old enough to understand that people climb into bed with each other when they shouldn't. The truth is, that's how they arrested Odette – in bed with Peter Churchill. Not exactly how they showed it in the film, was it? Or in Jerrold Tickell's book. And it was only the purest luck it wasn't someone else – she went through men like a warm knife through butter.'

'Marian, really!'

I was hot with embarrassment but I persisted, an awkward child determined not to be put off. 'I meant the spying, going to France, all that. Is *that* what you did?'

Again the idea seemed to amuse her. 'It was a long time ago, Sam. Water under the bridge.'

But it wasn't really a long time ago. The film came out in 1950. So the events it portrayed took place just seven years earlier. I calculated the thing as I sat there between my mother and this woman of my dreams: when I was five years old and just starting to understand that there was some kind of war under way, Marian Sutro would have been having her toenails torn out like Odette Sansom.

Of course she didn't have her toenails torn out. Her feet were slender, the toes long and straight, the nails unblemished, although sometimes crimson. But not with blood; with nail varnish. I can assure you of that.

'Dear Marian,' my mother said after that expedition to the cinema. 'She's so much happier than she used to be. I suppose time heals. And finding Alan seems to have done her the world of good, whatever we thought of him at the time.'

'Don't know how they stick together,' my father said. They were talking in the sitting room. I was down the corridor in my bedroom, doing my homework. 'He thinks Churchill is God and she's somewhere to the left of Lenin.'

'Not everything is about politics,' mother answered.

'You mean they enjoy the sex—'

Which was the moment when the door slammed, shutting me out of their conversation and leaving me only with the indistinct sound of my mother's protests and my own fantasies.

Thus Marian would occasionally swim into my world, a bright, sometimes laughing presence who made me blush when she insisted that *nous faisons la bise*, whose politics were just this side of outrageous, who might, to the embarrassment of adults and adolescent boys, enjoy sex. In the meantime I got on with the business of growing up, acquiring all those attributes that render young boys disgusting, to themselves as much as to others. I smelled if I didn't wash more frequently than I would have wished. Hair grew in predictable places. Limbs lengthened and puppy fat seemed to convert, by some alchemy that my physiologist father could probably have explained (but I wouldn't have listened to), into sinew and muscle. I heard of her more than I saw her: she was doing this and that, working for some left-wing organisation or other in London; she was off to Paris, off to Geneva, places that seemed exotic to me, who had never stepped outside the borders of England. I knew nothing of the secrets that she carried with her, the drug that lifted her up and brought her down.

PART III

ABSOLON

On the Korean peninsula East and West were locked in a struggle to the death. On Trimouille Island in the Monte Bello group off Western Australia the United Kingdom set off its first atomic bomb. On Eniwetok Atoll in the Pacific engineers began to assemble a complex device called Ivy Mike. And in London the Peace Union in conjunction with the Embassy of the Soviet Union organised an exhibition of Socialist-Realist Art.

Marian had done most of the work. She'd found a gallery in Duke Street, co-ordinated with the cultural attaché at the Soviet embassy, booked caterers for the opening reception, phoned round the newspapers and magazines, even overseen the unpacking and display of the artworks themselves. Now the space, previously used to house pallid imitations of Picasso or approximate representations of Cornish fishing villages, was hung about with smiling couples shovelling coal, and strapping blondes striding into a sunlit future. Among the guests were critics from the *New Statesman* and the *Manchester Guardian*. The journalist from

333

Tribune was deep in argument with a colleague from the *Evening Standard*. A man who wrote for *Horizon* was peering at the paintings and making copious notes on his copy of the catalogue. And the Surveyor of the King's Pictures and Director of the Courtauld Institute – a man of impeccable sensitivity and, the public learned two decades later, a Soviet agent – was pontificating to a group of disciples about the influence of Picasso on Socialist Realism.

'Quite a triumph, Mrs Walcott,' Mr Roper told her. He was careful always to use her married name, ever since an embarrassing moment among the library shelves when, for a few fetid seconds, putty-like fingers had kneaded her breasts and 'Marian' had overtaken 'Mrs Walcott'. On that occasion she had kneed him in the groin with sudden and startling efficiency, thus putting to an end any suggestion of breast-kneading or the use of first names. Now they were standing in front of *Girls Working on the Collective Farm II* by Aleksandr Deyneka and eyeing muscular femininity like visitors at a zoo examining a new species of primate. 'A daunting prospect for Russian manhood,' Roper decided.

It was then, just as he went off in search of important guests, that someone immediately behind her spoke her name. Not her married name, but her maiden name: 'Marian Sutro.'

She turned.

A shock, followed immediately by a great

imprecision of emotion: thrill mixed with disquiet; excitement mingled with something akin to fear; suspicion blended clumsily with the desire to laugh out loud. 'Gosh,' she said. 'This is a bit awkward, isn't it?'

'Only as awkward as you want to make it.' Absolon took two glasses of wine from the tray of a passing waiter and handed one to her.

'I don't really *know* what to make of it,' she said. 'That's the problem. What on earth are you doing here?'

'A posting.' He held out both arms as if about to bow. 'Behold, the new Press Officer at the Soviet embassy. Who is, at this moment, looking for a quote from Miss Sutro – or does he call her Mrs Walcott? – about her view of the success of this exhibition. Not whether it *is* a success. Success is guaranteed in the Soviet world. But what Miss Sutro *thinks* of the success.'

She considered his question. 'What do you want me to say? The English intelligentsia demonstrates the same aesthetic interests as the peace-loving Russian peoples?'

'That'll do as a start.'

'While decadent abstraction is consigned to the scrap heap of history.'

He laughed. 'Excellent.'

He seemed older than before, and tougher. Or maybe her memory of Paris was corrupted. But there was the same irony gliding beneath the surface of his words, the same sense that he knew

335

better than anyone what was going on, how every-thing was some kind of superficial game that hid powerful currents beneath. He laughed when she asked whether he was still single, as though she might be spying out the ground ahead. The life of a diplomat wasn't really suited to domesticity, he told her. You met women all the time, but none you could marry.

Someone called her: 'Mrs Walcott, if you have a moment . . .'

As she turned he touched her wrist. 'Can we meet?' Even among the crowd his closeness awoke in her that familiar compulsion, part cerebral, part organic: disturbing, as though she wasn't entirely in control. 'In private, I mean.'

'Is that a good idea?'

'I can give you my address.'

'What are you suggesting? That we pick up where we left off?'

He ignored her question but gave her his card. The address was in Bayswater, in a street just off Moscow Road. 'How's that for irony?'

'Mrs Walcott . . .?' A volunteer was hovering. Some domestic disaster to report.

Absolon held her arm 'Give me a ring and let me know when you can come round.'

GRU

O n its coral island the device known as Ivy Mike steamed in the tropic sun. It steamed because it was a cryogenic system, the deuterium fuel for the fusion stage being supplied in liquid form at -249.5°C. The steam was water vapour condensed by cold out of the damp tropic air. To achieve such frigid cold, the whole assembly had been set up within a vast vacuum flask, with compressors working all the time, struggling like Sisyphus against the forces of nature that forever attempted to warm the flask up to the ambient temperature of the central Pacific.

Twelve thousand miles away, in London, Fawley watched Marian Sutro with an expression that mingled anticipation with satisfaction, like a child promised sweets. 'David Trofimovich Absolon,' he told her. 'Newly accredited press officer at the Soviet embassy. We have, over the years, been watching this man. He started his career in the Red Army, writing for *Red Star*, the Soviet Army newspaper. After the war he appeared to move into full-time journalism with the TASS news agency. His writing appeared in *Izvestia, Pravda,*

337

that kind of thing. Various foreign postings – Berlin, Vienna, Paris. And now he turns up as press officer at the embassy here. We think he is probably rather more than that.'

'More?'

'He is almost certainly an officer in the GRU.' Marian looked blank.

'*Glavnoye Razvedyvatel'noye Upravleniye*. The Main Intelligence Directorate,' Fawley was warming to his theme, almost, but not quite, rubbing his hands in delight. 'It's possible, but unlikely, that he's part of the MGB, *Ministerstvo Gosudarstvennoi Bezopasnosti*, the Ministry of State Security. That's a rival organisation. You know the kind of thing from the war – the Abwehr and the Sicherheitsdienst. One watches the other and they both watch us and neither is really sure who the true enemy is.'

'You mean Absolon's a *spy*?'

He pondered the matter, like a cleric ruminating about the distinction between priests and deacons. 'I suppose one should call him an intelligence officer. He'd be responsible to the London GRU *rezident*, who himself reports directly to Moscow Centre. The ambassador doesn't come into it. Indeed, for most purposes the London *rezident* outranks the ambassador.' There followed a pause, one of Fawley's pauses when you knew that the question was already formulated and he was letting the silence expand sufficiently to allow it appropriate space. 'How exactly did you come to know this man, Marian?'

'I told you, I met him in Paris a little while ago.'

'Met him?'

'At the Soviet embassy. I had a meeting, and there was Absolon. We had dinner together . . .'

Another pause. 'In a group?'

'The two of us.'

'Just the two of you? You never mentioned this before.'

'I didn't think it mattered. It was a personal thing.' She felt angry. What had it got to do with Fawley or anyone else? 'Look, I knew him already. We met in Hamburg during the Ravensbrück trial where he was a liaison officer with the Red Army. Someone introduced us and we got on quite well. His English is excellent.'

'So I believe. It seems he spent a large part of his childhood in England. His parents were academics.' There was another pause. You could measure conversations with Fawley by the silences. The longer the silences the more there was to say. 'You say you had dinner together. Do you mind telling me the exact nature of your relationship with this man?'

'My relationship?'

'How well did you get to know him?' He looked at her impassively, the priestly face, waiting. In all her dealings with him, she had never shocked him. But now she wanted to see it in his eyes – puritanical disapproval.

'It was largely sexual, if you want to know, Mr Fawley. We became lovers. Just one occasion so far but I daresay there will be others. Does that make me an unacceptable security risk?'

He considered her for a moment. What was he trying to assess? Was he endeavouring to work out the motions of her mind, understand how she might sleep with someone quite casually, as she pleased? Was he measuring her against his own tidy suburban standards? He shook his head. 'Not at all, Marian. It suggests that, with your expert help, we may be able to turn him.'

'*Turn* him?'

'If you have no moral scruples about it, of course. I would hate to cajole you into anything that you were unhappy with.'

Unhappy. She considered *unhappy*, watching Fawley with curiosity, as though he were a specimen in the zoo, some nocturnal primate behind a glass wall.

'There is a term for it,' he added. 'Most eloquent, really. Honey trap.' And then, quite easily, as if it were the most normal thing in the world, they were planning what might be done and exactly how, the minutiae of an operation that she recognised from those days in the war, planning her own mission to France. 'You'll have to tread carefully,' Fawley said. 'Can you manage it?'

Something lit inside her, some little flame of elation. 'Can I manage it?' she repeated. 'Of course I can.' And she thought, because she was no fool, because she understood how they worked, because she was, in Fawley's own words, 'one of us', she thought, They've been waiting for this to happen.

PHOTOS

She felt a sense of exhilaration, as though she'd taken a drug of some kind that lightened her mood and stripped away her fears. As she walked through the narrow streets of Soho she watched for watchers on her tail, half hoping that she might find them so that she could throw them off with the carelessness of someone tossing aside a scarf. But to her disappointment there was nobody following her, no one interested in this woman catching a bus on Oxford Street to go down the Bayswater Road. She got off the bus two stops too far and watched to see whether anyone got off with her but there was no one trailing her as she left the main road and made her way back through the side streets towards the absurdly named Moscow Road.

The address Absolon had given was not far from where the Security Directorate used to be, not far from where she had been interrogated by Senter in those days when she was a nervous wreck just returned from Germany. That irony struck her. Perhaps it would amuse Absolon too.

The house was one end of a terrace, set back from the street by a small garden that had been paved over to allow a car, a black Austin saloon, to be parked off the road. She walked a little way past, glancing up at the windows of the terrace opposite. Lace curtains. Blank reflections of the sky. A residential street in the silence of mid-morning with nothing unusual about it. She turned left and left again, circled round a block and came back to the house. This time she went straight up to the front door and rang the bell. Immediately the latch released, as though someone inside had been waiting and knew that she was there. The door opened onto shadows and multi-coloured brush marks of light from a fanlight above the lintel. And Absolon waiting in the narrow hallway.

There was an awkward moment of greeting, each nodding forward to kiss, both going the same way for an instant, the confusion resolved with an embarrassed laugh as they sorted out the double kiss, left cheek to left cheek, right cheek to right. He hung her coat and ushered her through into the sitting room with a certain formality, as though she were being interviewed for a job or something. 'You found the place,' he said, which was obvious really, because here she was, wasn't she? 'It's good to see you again,' he added.

'Yes, it is. To see *you* again, I mean.' She laughed to cover her confusion.

'Were you followed?'

'How do I know if I was followed? Why should I be?'

'You never know.' He fussed around her. Would she like to sit here? Or over there? Was that quite comfortable for her? A cushion, perhaps? She looked round, trying to get the measure of things. The plain furnishings must have come with the house – a three-piece suite of pre-war ugliness and a coffee table with copies of the *Illustrated London News* and *Punch*, the kind of things you might find in a dentist's waiting room. Over the dead fireplace was a painting of an English pastoral scene. Only the desk was clearly his – a chaos of papers and books around an old Remington typewriter: handwritten notes, a copy of *The Times*, an ashtray full of cigarette ends; and a framed photograph of a plain-looking woman wearing a padded jacket and a beret. The camera was angled upwards to look at her and she was smiling, as one does when confronted by a lens. Was that his wife?

He nodded. 'Yelena. Taken in 1943, just before she was killed.'

There was a moment's silence, as if the dead were being acknowledged in some way – he, his wife Yelena; she, Benoît, or perhaps Véronique. Had she told him about Véronique? She couldn't quite remember. He walked over to the window and looked out. Lace curtains added a haze to the view. Outside, a couple walked past, heels clipping the pavement out of synchrony with each other, a stuttering syncopated sound like something you might hear in a jazz band. On the other side of the street a car drew up and a woman got out with a bag of shopping and a terrier dog on a lead. Mundane events in mundane lives.

'Do you want something?' Absolon asked. 'A drink, perhaps? Or coffee?'

'No thanks.'

He was standing there looking out of the window as though uncertain how to proceed. But wasn't it plain enough? She'd come here for one thing only, hadn't she? Wasn't that understood?

'This isn't easy,' he said in the portentous tone of someone carrying bad news.

'What isn't easy?'

'May I speak to you honestly?'

'Is there another way? What's this all about?'

Absolon coughed. He didn't turn to look at her. Was he embarrassed about what was happening? Confronted by the photograph of his wife, was he feeling some kind of guilt? She didn't know. That was the confusion of casual intimacy: you know so much and so little about the other. She had opened her body to him and yet he remained as foreign as another country, apprehended only in the way that a casual visitor recalls such a place, by a glimpse, a smell, a taste.

'Apparently there was a visit by two dancers from the Kirov State Ballet,' he said. 'A couple of months ago, before I arrived.'

'We helped arrange it.'

'I believe so. And it was, in many ways, immensely successful. So I am told.'

'So what's that got to do with us now?'

Again, a little cough. 'I am going to put my cards on the table.' He enjoyed his English idioms, she remembered that from the first time they'd met. Sometimes he got them slightly wrong – something a little anachronistic perhaps, or the precise context incorrect – but more often than not he was dead right. And in this case the turn of phrase seemed even more appropriate because he left the window and went over to the desk, took a card from a drawer and laid it carefully on the table in front of her. Except that it wasn't a card, it was a photograph.

He turned it round for her to see.

The print was grainy but the scene was plain enough: a narrow room illuminated by the stark light of bare bulbs. Two men were sitting on a sofa directly across the room from the camera. There were glasses, an open bottle, cigarettes in ashtrays. The younger of the two men had his feet up on a low table. He had a wide, Slavic face with a hint of Asia in his high cheek bones and slanted eyes. His elaborate lips held a cigarette that he was just about to take between two fingers of his left hand. He was entirely naked. The man next to him was wearing underpants and a vest. Also smoking. She recognised the naked youth as one of the ballet dancers, a young man called Ilya. The other man, the one in underpants and vest, was Ned.

345

'Oh, Christ.' She felt ill. Vomit crouched behind her breastbone, poised to leap upwards. She managed a few incoherent phrases. 'Where . . .?' 'Oh my God . . .' That kind of thing. And part of her thought, this is the axe falling, and it has come from an entirely unexpected direction. She had been waiting for the solemn officers of the law to tramp into Ned's life with a summons to the nearest police station. She had feared exposure, scandal, shame, the tearing apart of lives. And instead she got this man from the Russian embassy, in an agony of concern and embarrassment.

Absolon produced a silver cigarette case and offered her a cigarette. There was a moment's business with a lighter before she could draw smoke in and settle her stomach.

'Where did this come from?' she said finally, knowing the answer even as she asked the question. The embassy had rented a flat to house their precious dancers and keep them out of harm's way. Keep them from the temptations of London life. And here was one of them, stark naked with her brother. 'You set him up, didn't you? You put temptation in his way and you deliberately set him up.' But she knew there was another part of the truth. It was she who had invited Ned to the performance at Sadler's Wells, and afterwards it was she who had taken him backstage to introduce him to the performers. She recalled Ilya, a strange, self-regarding youth who kept flexing his muscles as they spoke, as

346

though if he stood still his joints might seize. At the time he had made her think of a racehorse, something animal and highly trained and mindless. She recalled his shaking Ned's hand, and then later, seeing the two of them in a corner of the dressing room, laughing together, each trying to understand what the other was saying and neither really caring.

'There are . . .' Absolon hesitated . . . 'other shots. Not the kind of thing I can show you.'

'What the hell do you mean by that? I'm not a child. If you are about to blackmail Ned I may as well see all the evidence.'

He snapped angrily. 'I'm not trying to blackmail anyone. If I were, I wouldn't be showing this to you. I'd be presenting it directly to your brother.'

There was silence. Outside a car drove by. Somewhere a door slammed and someone called out. But the words were indistinct and irrelevant because what mattered, all that mattered, was the photograph on the table of her brother, and the second one that Absolon retrieved from the same drawer and laid on the table beside the first. This one was different. Ned was naked now, kneeling before the equally naked Russian dancer like a suppliant before a religious statue. Ned's mouth was full.

For a moment she toyed with the idea of grabbing the beastly things and tearing them up. But that was absurd. There'd be copies. These probably *were* copies. She would just look like a hysterical fool.

'Let me explain,' said Absolon.

'I don't want to hear.'

'But I think you have to. For my sake as well as for yours; and your brother's. I have managed to take charge of this case—'

'It's a *case*?'

'Of course it's a case.'

'And you're not just a humble press officer to His Excellency the Soviet Ambassador, are you? You're a spy, an agent, an intelligence officer, whatever euphemism you care to use. You probably always were, even when we met in Hamburg, certainly when you fucked me in Paris—'

The word *fucked* stuck in her mind. The rasp of it. The violent fricative and harsh plosive. He had done that to her, spread-eagled her and fucked her. Anger bubbled to the surface of her distress. She looked at him with something close to hatred. 'You targeted me, Absolon. I believed in the things you said – that your country was trying the greatest social experiment ever and rubbish like that. And all the time you were laughing at me. We shared our ideas as well as our bodies and you didn't give a damn. Fucking me and laughing at me, that's what you're doing. Weeping over your dead wife and telling me how lonely you were and all the time you were just doing the bidding of your masters. Go after her, they told you. Win her over. A honey trap, isn't that what they call it? You win over a gullible woman and you get to stick your cock inside her as well.' She slithered to a halt, on the edge of tears.

'None of that's true,' he said.

She fumbled with her cigarette, drew on it, felt the acrid smoke inside her. 'You would say that, wouldn't you?'

He waited. That was the gift of an intelligence officer – to wait. Even through a mist of tears she understood that well enough.

'So what *is* true?'

He gave a sour laugh. 'Isn't that what joking Pilate asked?'

'*Jesting* Pilate. And he asked, what is *truth*? Which is rather different. And he wouldn't stay for an answer. But I'm staying. And waiting.'

There was a silence. Thoughts scrambled through her mind. Fawley, what Fawley would think of this. And Ned. His stupidity. Cupidity, perhaps. And hers as well, coming here on this nondescript afternoon to a nondescript corner of London expecting to have sex with a near stranger. *We may be able to turn him.* Clément would laugh if he knew. And what would Benoît have said? Suddenly, inconsequentially, she realised that she didn't know Benoît, had never really known Benoît any more than she knew this tall thin man with the ascetic, angular look of a Jew. A man to whom she had offered her body with barely a thought about the implications. She was no better than Ned with his priapic dancer.

'The truth is,' Absolon was saying, 'in my world there's no difference between ordinary work and intelligence. The overlap is complete. I'm a

349

diplomat, with diplomatic status and within my work I have . . . various responsibilities.'

'You mean, you're a spy.'

'And when I get posted to London, I find this case dropped in my lap. Is that what you say? Dropped in my lap?'

'It fits.'

'It was started by my predecessor, but he has been unexpectedly recalled. So I've inherited it. With clear instructions from Moscow.'

'From *Moscow*?'

'Unfortunately it has gone that high. We in the field are just dancing to their tune. No different from what you were doing ten years ago.'

'There was a war on then.'

'There's a war on now, except that this one doesn't yet involve killing people. We hope to keep it that way but I doubt that the Americans do—'

'You targeted him. Maybe not you personally but the system. The bloody system.'

He came and sat down near her, not touching her but close. 'Of course he was targeted. What do you expect? We look at anyone who may help our cause in any way. Do you think the British and the Americans don't do the same? And now with Professor Fuchs out of the picture we obviously considered the new possibilities and how we might approach a likely informant. I'm afraid my predecessor came up with this particular idea. I can't pretend it's very pleasant and I'm not even sure if it would have been effective, but that's what he did.'

'And what would *you* have done in his place?'

Absolon shrugged. 'How do you recruit an agent? The three Vs – *vzyatochnichestvo*, *vymogatel'stvo*, *vera*. It works just as well in English: bribery, blackmail, belief. Tell me, why did you go to France during the war?'

She shook her head. 'I can barely remember now. Anyway, I was a different person then. A girl who believed in things like honour and freedom. And I was angry as well, angry at the way the Germans had walked in.'

'So, belief of some kind. The believers make the best agents. Knowing what I know about your brother, I certainly wouldn't have attempted bribery and I'd probably have ruled out blackmail. Neither produce good agents. I might have approached him directly. Or perhaps . . .' He glanced at her with a faint smile. 'I'd have approached his sister. Whom I know to be sympathetic to our cause.'

'You think *I* might have persuaded him to betray his country?'

'Could you?'

The offer was there. The blackmail was there and the offer was there, one in each hand. He dared to reach out and touch her. 'I remember what you said to me in Paris.'

'I said a whole lot of things in Paris. If I were you I wouldn't believe all of them.'

'You said your brother hated working with the bomb. Like so many others he thought the thing should never have been used on Japan . . .'

'I told you that?'

'Yes, you did. You told me he agreed with Oppenheimer, who was himself in favour of sharing the science with other nations. Just like Fuchs, and Professor Pontecorvo and many others.'

She shifted away from him, as though taking back something less material, her confidence, her trust. 'So what are you suggesting?'

'This is my idea: that we keep all knowledge of these photographs to ourselves. Pretend they don't exist. But you have to approach your brother with the suggestion that he might continue where Professor Fuchs left off. I am sure you can convince him that would be the right thing to do.' He opened his hands as if to show that there were no other options available. 'All he has to do is follow what he believes. And he'll never have to deal with us directly. That will be your job.'

Something lurched beneath her, as though her whole world had shifted.

'We would have to set things up, of course,' Absolon was saying. 'It'd take time. And we'd have to establish a protocol for meetings. What do you think?'

'What do *I* think?'

'We'd have to do this together. You'd have to be in agreement.'

'Or else you use those photographs?'

352

He shrugged. 'I don't have control over every-thing. People above me only want results . . .'

'So I don't have much choice, do I?'

She waited a moment, looking at him. And then she made her move. It felt like walking a tightrope, feeling the balance, knowing that a slight shift either side might be fatal. She reached her foot forward and poised to transfer her weight onto it, feeling the rope wobbling. No safety net. 'There's just one thing,' she said.

'What's that?'

She slid her weight forward – 'There must be a quid pro quo. To keep my side quiet' – and stood carefully in balance, watching bewilderment register in his expression as though he was a spec-tator looking up from the ground at what she was doing up there above him. Astonishment at what was going on overhead. The sheer audacity of it.

'Your *side*?'

'I'll need something from you in return. They think . . .' and she hesitated for a moment, trem-bling in balance, leaving him time to wonder who her side might be and what exactly they might think. 'They want me to turn you.'

She saw it in his face: pure, unadulterated shock. 'Who do?'

'You can imagine who.'

'You're telling me you are working for the *British*?'

'Is that any surprise? Look, Absolon, we can take our time.' *We*. Him and her. Together. 'I warned them it would take time to gain your confidence.

353

And even then it only need be low-grade stuff, but it'll have to be something. And it'll keep them off our backs.'

He began to laugh. It was a delight to see him laugh. It was genuine laughter, a real amusement at what she was doing. 'Are you serious?'

'Oh, I'm deadly serious, Absolon. If you don't play, I don't play. It's in both our interests.'

'You mean, all the time you have been working for—'

'Not all the time, no. Not in Paris. That was me, entirely me.'

His laughter subsided like a tide, leaving only a thin flotsam of amusement behind. 'But now?'

She shrugged, eyeing him thoughtfully. 'They're no different from your lot, are they? They look for weaknesses, they examine the opposition just as you do.'

'And they decided you were my weakness? How did they know about our little fling?'

Fling. She liked that. His colloquialisms that somehow seemed practised, as though he kept up to date using a dictionary of slang. 'They know what I do with the Peace Union. They called me in for a chat.'

'And you told them?'

'It's not *them*, it's one. He was my handler during the war.'

'I should have guessed at something like that. And now you're proposing that we play one off against the other?'

'I don't see any alternative, do you?'

'Do you have any idea of the danger? Moscow Centre wants total loyalty or nothing. They don't think like you and I do. They're paranoid. Is that the right word?'

'It sounds right to me.'

'And paranoids are dangerous. They're dangerous for you and they're dangerous for me.'

'But they don't need to know, do they? If you really think that's a problem, they don't need to know. You feed me small stuff – what's the word for it? Chicken feed, is that it? – you give me chicken feed and I give you gold in return.'

He watched her thoughtfully. 'The question is, can I trust you?'

She put her head on one side, as if to consider him better. 'My dear Absolon, can *I* trust *you*?'

Could she? It is so very difficult to unpick the spider's web of intrigue and betrayal, isn't it? Some threads are irrevocably knotted together, others snap at the merest breath of enquiry. Later, much later, I asked her about Absolon, but she only laughed. 'My dear, you make the most of what you can get, don't you? And Absolon was *very* attractive.' I remember the accent on the word 'very', a hint of rolled French r.

H BOMB

On its desert island, the device called Ivy Mike detonated. A double flash, the flash of the primary followed microseconds later by the flash of the secondary. The primary was a plutonium bomb of the Nagasaki type, releasing a storm of X-rays that flowed down into the secondary and impacted upon the hydrogen atoms in the vacuum flask so fiercely that they fused into helium and, for a fragment of time, into all the atoms of creation and a few more besides. In that process – although 'process' implies time and this occurred in the infinitesimal space between the units of time – temperatures were created that were greater than the centre of the sun. Within a second the fireball erupted to over three miles in diameter. Within one minute the cloud had risen to over one hundred thousand feet and spread out to cover eight thousand square miles of the surface of the Pacific Ocean. The island on which the device had been constructed vanished entirely. The thermonuclear age had begun.

'They've done it, haven't they?' she said. She held the morning newspaper in her hands, with the headlines in grimy newsprint: US Explodes H-bomb.

Ned looked helpless. 'What did you expect?' He had rented a cottage on the edge of a village near Harwell. It was a place of low ceilings and small windows but without the corresponding attraction of ancient wooden beams. The only heating was provided by a coal fire in the sitting room and a paraffin stove that Marian kept upstairs to warm the spare room, where she slept when she came to visit. Now she sat in front of the fire while he paced up and down between the wingback armchairs and the windows, opening and closing his hands as though trying to rid himself of something adhering to his fingers.

'It's probably not a useable weapon yet. Probably they used liquid hydrogen, that's what fellows are saying. You couldn't use that in a weapon. The next step is lithium hydride. That's obvious. And once they move on to that . . .'

'The papers say it was huge.'

He shrugged helplessly. 'Eight, ten, megatons. Twenty, thirty times the size of the Hiroshima bomb. Something like that would obliterate the whole of London.'

'And the Russians?'

'The Russians, the Russians. They're blundering along way behind.'

'What Lord Russell said that time—'

'Lord Russell's a fool.'

'So what can we do?'

He stopped in his pacing. 'What can *we* do? Nothing.'

'What can *you* do, then?'

The question lay there between them. He laughed. 'I used to think that the best thing to do would be go and live on a Pacific island, as far away from the mess as possible. But now they're blowing the Pacific islands to dust. Did you read the story? The island where they assembled the bomb entirely vanished—'

'An exaggeration—'

'Probably not.'

She felt anger, the sheer, blind anger of the helpless. No metaphors were good enough. 'What can we do?' she repeated.

He resumed his pacing. 'It's trying to predict the future, isn't it? What might happen if . . . The war in Korea, for example. They say that MacArthur wants to use atom bombs. Can you imagine that, Squirrel? Atom bombs against Korea, atom bombs against China, atom bombs against Russia. Can you imagine? And the next excuse might be in Europe. Berlin, maybe. Or Poland. Who knows?'

She looked at her brother, daring him to understand what she meant. 'Or could it be like I said – like poison gas, each side too frightened to use it. And that can only happen if there's some kind of balance.'

'So what are you trying to say?'

'You cannot leave this in the hands of the

politicians and the military, Ned. You can do something, *we* can do something together.'

'What? Arrange a public meeting where Lord Russell can tell us all to go and attack Russia?'

She shook her head. 'We can help the Russians. Like Fuchs did, like Alan Nunn May, like Bruno Pontecorvo. All men who acted out of their beliefs. What motivates the others – Chadwick, Cockcroft, William Penney, all those others you talk about? Self-interest and fear. Nothing more. You said it yourself. And in the meantime, the Americans build up an arsenal big enough to end human life on the entire planet.'

'It's too dangerous,' Ned protested. 'It's too difficult.'

'No, it's not. I told you I can make contact for you. Just trust me, Ned.'

'Are you *serious*, Squirrel?'

'Of course I'm serious. I'll mention to the right person that my dear older brother wishes to get in touch with someone from the Soviet scientific establishment in order to exchange views. That'd be a start, wouldn't it? It's what you want to do, isn't it?'

There it was, out in the open, the taboo broken. He'd stopped at the window, looking away from her out of the window at the abandoned strip of grass that constituted the garden. At the far end was a wooden hut that the estate agent had optimistically called a summer house. 'Do you think it's possible?'

'I'll see what they say.'

'Just ideas, nothing more.'

'Don't worry,' she insisted. 'It'll be all right.'

Of course, she didn't mention the photographs. Little sister protecting big brother, old roles neatly reversed. And she didn't mention Fawley's proposal to her, that she attempt to turn Absolon. In the past it had been the other way round – Ned would persuade her about what was right and what was wrong. Now it was different: while he had somehow remained a child, she had grown into something else – an adult, with an adult's ability to manipulate, to persuade, to convince that black was white, that evil was good. He came and sat down beside her, letting her take his hand for a while: brother and sister united by bonds that were too convoluted to untangle.

'Who is this person that you know, Squirrel?'

'An old friend. I don't think you ought to know his name.'

He looked at her with a childish cunning. 'Do you sleep with him?'

'Sometimes.'

That amused him. A braying laugh. He held her hand open almost as though he was reading her future there in the palm. And then he kissed it. 'You're no better than me, are you?'

GENEVA

Things moved with molluscan slowness. Marian could imagine enciphered messages going back and forth between the Soviet embassy in Kensington Palace Gardens and some glum, anonymous fortress in Moscow. 'They want to go carefully,' Absolon explained. 'All the dust thrown up by the Fuchs case. And Pontecorvo. And Burgess and Maclean. They want everything to settle down. Is that what you say? Let the dust settle?'

It was what you said. But there was more to the waiting than a mere desire for the dust to settle. 'And they're frightened of *dezinformatsiya*,' he added. 'Disinformation. They have a morbid fear of being sold counterfeit goods. I'm afraid nothing I say will convince them – they want to meet him.'

'*Meet* him? Who wants to meet him?'

'They'll send someone who knows the subject. A fellow physicist.'

'Here?'

He opened his hands helplessly. 'It's difficult in Britain . . .'

'Then where?' She was suddenly angry, protective

361

of her brother. 'I'm not having him travel to anywhere in the Soviet Bloc. Who knows what might happen? Anyway, the British authorities wouldn't allow it. And not to somewhere like Finland, either.'

But Absolon had all the answers ready. 'There's a physics conference of some kind coming up in Geneva. The International Union of Pure and Applied Physics. He can get a place on that easily enough . . .'

According to Absolon there would be a little rigmarole to establish contact, one of those exchanges she recalled from the war. Ned would have to learn the words exactly: 'Remarkable how the politicians fight while we get on with one another without any problem.'

'Apart from language difficulties.'

'Those can always be overcome.'

It was their first visit to Geneva since before the war, brother and sister travelling together for old times' sake. Their father told them how much he wished he could go with them but things kept him in Oxford – business at his college, correcting proofs of the book he was writing, the need to look after their mother who was having such trouble with her hip. So they went on their own, just the two of them taking the train to Paris and the overnight sleeper to Geneva. They stayed in a *pension* near the railway station and took a bus to the conference. The city was the same but the people they had known had been scattered by the war and the demise of the League of Nations. Perhaps there were still some she had been at school with before she was packed off to the convent in England but how could she relate to anyone she had last known when she was a mere fourteen? All that remained were the ghosts of memory, of sailing on the lake, of walking with Clément in the Jardin Anglais, of being young and having a whole world ahead of her.

The conference of the International Union of Pure and Applied Physics was held in one of the university buildings on the edge of the Parc des Bastions, an edifice that might as well have been a bank as a place of learning. Each morning, like a mother taking her child to school, she ushered Ned in, hopeful that he would be happy, that he would be safe, that he would not be bullied. And dutifully she met him at the end of each day with anxious questions – how did it go? did you make any nice new friends? what did you learn?

'Don't fuss, Squirrel,' he complained.

The contact was made on the last day. It was a seemingly innocuous encounter among hundreds of others, a nondescript man called Chernikov who came up to him during a coffee break and introduced himself with the bland assertion that, 'I believe we're interested in much the same field.' And then: 'Remarkable how the politicians fight but we get on with one another without any problem.'

'Apart from language difficulties.'

'Those can always be overcome.'

'He was a bit shy at first,' Ned told his sister. 'Then bolder and bolder once we both knew what we were about. We went for a little walk together and he asked me lots of questions and I gave him a little envelope with some stuff about the decay products of lithium deuteride and he gave me a collection of dross in return. And we went on our different ways contented. Altogether it was smooth as a pick-up in Regent's Park public lavatory.'

'Ned!'

He raised his eyebrows. 'You're not going to take the moral high ground with me, are you, Squirrel? Not when you're being fucked by your Russian. You know what I said – you're no better than me.'

They caught the Paris train that evening and were back in London the next day. The world seemed unchanged.

STALKER

A moment of the purest coincidence. There I am, going through the cheap books on the pavement outside Marks & Co in the Charing Cross Road, when I look round and spot her. Marian Sutro. She's crossing the road towards Shaftesbury Avenue. For a second, putting a book down, I am about to call out to her; but then something else takes over, a desire to know more than ever I can gain by a casual and short-lived encounter on a street corner in the middle of London.

So instead I followed her, tailed her, did the spy thing. I did it expertly, make no mistake, keeping to the opposite side of the street, keeping well behind her, stopping when she stopped and turning to the nearest shop window to watch her in reflection. In this manner we made our way towards Piccadilly. She was wearing a spring dress with blue polka dots on a white ground so she was pretty conspicuous even with the traffic that passed between us and the maze of people through which she had to thread her way. And her walk . . . I recalled her walk from that summer in Sussex and watched now with a little thrill of admiration and lust: long-limbed, long-striding, her skirt swaying with the movement of her backside. You want a cliché? Coltish. She was what? Twenty-nine, thirty, something like that, but to me she seemed rather older. This was the woman who had done the impossible, who still did things that were beyond my capabilities – travelled to Paris, travelled to Geneva, turned cartwheels. I hurried after her, following the uncertain and narrow line between adolescent prank and adult obsession, while the colt strode steadfastly towards Piccadilly Circus with, so I fancied, the press of people parting to let her through. And then she vanished.

I hesitated uncertainly, wondering if my silly game were over. Where had she gone? Into some shop, or one of the cinemas that lined the street? I'd not seen the moment of disappearance. It had happened as a double-decker bus passed between us. Perhaps she had even climbed aboard and been swept away towards Piccadilly while I was stranded on the far bank.

Dodging through the traffic, I gained the other side. I may have lost her but now I knew something about her, that she might on another occasion appear at Cambridge Circus coming from, where? Holborn, probably. And that if I lay in wait at one of the bookshops I might be able to run her to ground. I peered into the foyer of a theatre, wondering whether she might have gone in to buy tickets.

And then, from immediately behind me, she said my name. 'Sam?'

I don't know whether to mark it as a question or as a statement because she didn't phrase it as either one or the other but rather an amalgam of the two, giving a faint upward intonation of uncertainty at the end. 'It *is* you,' she said. 'I wasn't sure.' She stood there on the pavement jostled by the crowd but quite indifferent to it. There was a pallor to her face, and a hint of relief.

'I wasn't sure it was you either,' I said, mendaciously.

'But now you know.'

'It's good to see you.'

She didn't quite accede to that. 'I thought you might be stalking me,' she said. 'It's quite frightening, having a stalker follow you, d'you know that? A relief to discover it's Sam.'

'I'm sorry. I wouldn't have wanted to frighten you.'

'I'm sure you wouldn't. But what on earth are you doing in London? Goodness, how you've grown up. You must be—'

'Nearly twenty.'

'Nearly twenty. And doing . . .?'

'National Service at the moment. I'm . . .' I hesitated. We never really knew how to refer to it. Was it meant to be some kind of secret? But there was no hint of secrecy about the Joint Services School for Linguists where I was enrolled as an officer cadet. We always assumed that we were

367

doing what it said on the box – an official interpreters' course. 'I'm learning Russian, as a matter
of fact.'

'Russian? How remarkable.' She considered me
for a moment, head slightly on one side, almost
as though she was measuring me up. 'Look, I'm
meeting someone for lunch—'

'Oh, please . . .' I moved away.

'No, don't go.' She put her hand out and touched
my arm. 'Perhaps you'd like to join us? You see,
the man I'm meeting *is* a Russian.'

'A *Russian*?'

'Yes, a real, live Russian. So you'll be able to
practise on him. And I'll . . . well, I think a chap-
erone might be useful. Gorshkov – that's his name,
Comrade Gorshkov to those who know him well
– is something at the embassy. We've worked
together, visits of orchestras to London, that kind
of thing; but I think this lunch may be intended
to mix business with pleasure.'

Did I look blank?

'I think he might want to get into bed with me,'
she explained blithely, pushing the door open and
leading the way into the restaurant. 'Oh, do I call
you Sam or do you want to be Samuel these days?'

I hurried to catch up with her. 'Some people call
me Samuel but I don't like it.'

'Then "Sam" it will be.'

The restaurant was a palace of faded, baroque
elegance attempting to imitate a Parisian restaurant
of the belle époque period. Now it's a multimedia

entertainment centre, whatever that means, but then it was all wall mirrors and plush banquettes and marble-topped tables. We found the Russian already installed at a corner seat, examining the room from the perspective of a dry martini. He was a stout man with sly eyes and a domed forehead that shone in the light from the chandeliers. There was something lizard-like about his look, as though he was suspicious of everything about this strange country. At Marian's appearance he leaped up and greeted her effusively; but his face fell when he understood that I was to join them.

'Sam is an old family friend,' Marian explained, as if that justified everything. 'And he speaks Russian.'

The man frowned. *'Russian?'*

'I'm learning the language,' I said, in Russian. 'But I can only manage simple conversations at the moment.'

Suspicion hung around Comrade Gorshkov like a dirty smell. 'Are you a spy, then?' He laughed but it wasn't really a joke. He really wondered whether it might be true. As the waitress came and took our order he even looked round to see if anonymous men in raincoats and trilby hats might be watching from nearby tables. But there was nothing in the London lunchtime crowd that attracted his suspicion. We talked a bit, about Pushkin, about Gogol. Dead Souls. When I expressed admiration for the poet Anna Akhmatova he smiled uncertainly. I loved Akhmatova, for her aristocratic looks, for her irregular lifestyle (would I ever dare to behave like that?), and for that bitter-sweet early poetry that I could grasp even with my stunted Russian. But this was in that awkward period after Stalin's death but long before Khrushchev's speech at the 1956 Party conference. Apparatchiks like Gorshkov didn't know what to think about either her or Pasternak, the last two pillars still standing amid the wreckage of Russian literature. 'She is being allowed to publish again, I believe,' I told him in case he hadn't heard. 'Maybe you could invite her over here.' For a few ridiculous seconds I saw a possible coup – Anna Akhmatova brought out from obscurity, brought to London and shown to the West for what she was, one of the poetic wonders of the world. And I might get the opportunity to fall at her feet.

Gorshkov made a small gesture of helplessness. Musicians were easy because musical notes were devoid of political import. So Marian's organisation could bring over any number of orchestras and dance troupes but the idea of Akhmatova being shipped over to meet the poets of the West – Eliot, say, or Auden – was, for the moment, still beyond consideration.

The talk shifted away from such awkward matters to the conference that Marian was organising. Scientists for Peace, it was to be entitled. She would have J. D. Bernal and J. B. S. Haldane from Britain, and Joliot-Curie and Pelletier from France, assuming that Joliot's visa application wasn't refused as it had been previously. The Soviet Union would supply some suitable stooges. He didn't use the word stooge – I did.

'You are not being helpful,' he said reproachfully.

'Well, Haldane and Bernal are hardly representative of the British scientific world. Both of them are card-carrying members of the Communist Party.'

Marian smiled. I remember that smile with fondness. The smile of collusion.

'Does that make them any less great scientists?'

Well, no, it didn't. I had to admit as much.

'So there you are,' he said triumphantly.

Eventually the ordeal was over and the Russian – cultural attaché, Marian had called him – signalled for the bill. To my relief she chipped in on my behalf while he paid for the two of them with the ill grace that came from having to make an investment that had clearly not paid off.

'I think you saved my life,' Marian said as we watched the man depart. 'What do you think? Would he have invited me back to view his Socialist-Realist etchings if you hadn't been here?' She lit a cigarette and blew smoke towards the ceiling as though blowing the man away. 'So tell me about your language school. It sounds like one of those places we trained at during the war. *Are you going to become a spy?*'

I laughed at the idea. 'You sound like your

371

Russian friend. It's only language training. No one in Britain speaks Russian, that's the problem. Not like French or German. So they need to train people up.'

'For when we go to war.'

'The Cold War is hot enough for me.'

'And do you enjoy the course?'

'It rescued me from square-bashing. In fact, it's rather like university. Lots of learning but lots of laughs as well.'

She nodded thoughtfully, smoking and watching me. 'Are you being honest with me, Sam?'

'Honest?'

'You were following me, weren't you?'

I felt awkward under her gaze. 'I happened to see you.'

'And no one put you up to it?'

'What on earth do you mean?'

But she didn't say. There was just that gaze, the level regard of her dark eyes. I remembered something I'd overheard my mother say to my father: 'You know what Marian told me?'

My father's reply had that tone of faint weariness that he adopted whenever Marian's name came up. 'What did she tell you?'

'She told me that she had once killed two men. Shot them. Can you believe it?'

'No,' he'd replied.

Somehow, subject to her steady gaze, I believed it with all my heart. Only gradually did she lower the twin weapons of her eyes and allow the conversation to move to other things. We talked of my parents – 'I must get in touch with Judith. We haven't met up for ages' – of what she was doing that involved meeting with Russian functionaries. Some charity that wants to bring peace to the world, was how she described it. 'We all want to bring peace to the world, don't we? Some of us with doves and olive branches, others with missiles and bombs. Which one will work? I wonder.'

I glanced at my watch. 'Look, I really must be going. I've got a train to catch.'

'I've got to take a cab. I'll drop you off.'

So we climbed into the back of a taxi together. It was curiously intimate, to be closeted with her in the back of the cab, enveloped by her scent. She looked at me with that direct gaze again. 'You've changed, Sam. The boy has become a man.'

I felt myself blushing. 'It happens.'

'When was the last time I saw you?'

'I don't remember,' I said; but I remembered exactly. She'd been in Oxford visiting her parents and had come round for supper one evening. I'd been a tongue-tied sixteen-year-old with ambitions to go to Cambridge to read history. She had exhorted me not to do what everyone else did but to find my own path, as though going to Cambridge might be something not altogether admirable.

'It must be a couple of years ago now,' she said. 'These days I just don't get to Oxford as much as I'd like . . .'

We were stuck in traffic on the Tottenham Court Road. Muttering something about it being worse than the bloody blitz, the driver turned off into backstreets. Marian peered out of the window. 'I used to live round here. Awful digs in Chitty Street. I called it shitty and it was.' She turned to me. 'Perhaps we should do this again. What do you think?'

'What, exactly . . .?'

'Meet up for lunch. It was fun, despite Comrade Gorshkov. I mean, he won't be there the next time, I promise you that. How often do you come up to town?'

'Some weekends I'm free . . .'

'I can't do next. But after that . . . What do you enjoy doing? A gallery, how about that? Alan loathes galleries. The National. We could do the National.' She seemed excited at the idea.

'The Tate,' I suggested. 'There's an exhibition opening next month. Modigliani . . .'

She looked at me reproachfully. 'All those elongated nudes showing their pubic hair?'

I tried not to be fazed by her outspokenness. I'd hardly ever uttered the phrase 'pubic hair' and certainly never in polite company. The very word pubic seemed freighted with too many hidden meanings and implications. Marian was sitting there in her blue summer frock as light as gossamer and she had pubic hair, just down there, between her thighs. The thought made me shift with discomfort. 'I think it's mainly drawings, and some sculpture.'

'Very well, the Tate it is.' She took out a pocket diary and wrote my address and phone number. I felt youth sloughing off me like a skin being shed.

The taxi emerged from the side streets onto the Euston Road and drew to a halt outside the station. She looked at me with an expression of faint amusement. 'We go back a long way, don't we, Sam?'

'I suppose we do,' I replied.

'From a little boy spying on me in Sussex . . .'

'Before that, even.'

'Broken collarbones. The wounded cartwheeler.'

Behind us someone hooted. The cabbie called over his shoulder, 'You getting out? I can't stay here all day.' As I opened the door Marian leaned across and kissed me, those two kisses, *deux bisous*, one on each hot cheek. I climbed down reluctantly, the last vestiges of adolescence still clinging to my coattails. 'I'll be in touch,' she called.

I got back to Cambridge to a cold and narrow bed filled with fantasies. In the successive days Marian occupied my mind in both fact and fiction, as well as in those carefully wrought fantasies of possibility that occupy the spaces in between. It seemed weeks later, so many that I had almost abandoned hope, when a card came through the post. In a rather childish, rounded script it said no more than, *Strange meeting. Sorry for the delay. What about the 15th? The Tate? 12.30?* She'd signed off with a little pair of kisses, those *bisous* that seemed to carry her accent and her scent; and her initials *MW*. A neat inverted symmetry.

Странная Встреча, *Strannaya Vstrecha, Strange meeting* is, of course, the title of a well-known poem by Anna Akhmatova. *Strange meeting by the Neva's banks*, it begins, and tells of someone – although it isn't clear who; the poet's hopes, perhaps – drowning among the creaking and cracking ice floes of the winter river. I wondered at the time whether Marian knew that. When I turned the card over I found myself looking at the Millais painting of Ophelia drowning.

NORTON

arian and David Absolon met. I can't fit the precise dates of reports in her file into the approximate calendar of my memory, but during that time, in those days, they met. They met in various places: in a pub in Richmond, at the botanical gardens in Kew, sometimes in a café in Charlotte Street not far from her old digs. 'Shitty Street,' she told him and he laughed.

By now the source had a codename. NORTON. The motorbike or the Eliot poem? She didn't know. A name plucked out of the air by a faceless bureaucrat in the intestines of the Soviet security world. NORTON, not yet burnt. At one of the first meetings Absolon handed her a tiny camera, a Minox the size of a PEZ mint dispenser. 'What the hell do I do with this?' Ned demanded when she showed it to him. But once they'd got onto technicalities, talk of focal length and aperture number – terms Absolon had made her learn over a pint of beer and a flabby steak and kidney pie in a pub in Kilburn – Ned's interest was awoken. 'It's much safer than carrying papers around,' she explained. 'All they need is the film cartridge. They'll see to the rest.'

Thus she was the go-between, the link, the person walking the tightrope between Ned's cottage in the Berkshire countryside and the terrace house in Bayswater where Absolon lived. She moved along, keeping balance, with no safety net beneath her. At a meeting with Fawley in a safe house in Pimlico she explained her progress. 'Absolon has fallen into the honey trap and he's feeding greedily,' she told him. Her words seemed to have some kind of effect. She saw his eyes widen slightly, his pupils dilate. Was he imagining greedy feeding – her legs open and Absolon at the trough? 'Does that satisfy you or do you want more details?'

But the remainder of his bland face, the confessor's face, remained impassive. 'It cannot be easy for you,' he said.

'Oh, it's easy enough, believe me. What's not easy is moving from having an affair with him to suggesting he might betray his country. He believes in the Communist system, whatever its shortcomings. It's never easy to overcome belief, is it?'

He gave that little pinched smile she had come to know so well. What, she wondered, did he believe in? King and Country? Or the wife and children in the little house in Surbiton? Or perhaps the ineffable God of Anglicanism, pavilioned in splendour, girded with praise and voting Conservative? She could only guess about him and yet he knew almost as much about her as would a father confessor. He knew her present and her past, the schoolgirl she had once been and the adulterous woman she was now, her life and her loves. 'You must show extreme caution, Marian,' he warned. 'They will be suspicious. They'll watch you both like jackals. And be careful of your own emotions. The dangers aren't only from outside.'

But what did he know of emotions? What did he know of the breathless anticipation, the awful compulsion that was like a burgeoning disease, assuaged only by Absolon's presence, the pivotal moment about which her whole world spun, memory and anticipation all focused onto the one moment of union? No amount of watching could understand that; and anyway, there were no watchers, no one across the street or among the bushes or in a parked car down the road. 'With Absolon I want to be left alone,' she had insisted. 'I know what I'm doing and I'm not in any danger. And don't forget, he's a professional. Any hint that either of us is under surveillance and he'll be out of here in an instant.'

On two occasions they went away for the night, to a small hotel on the Thames at Marlow. She always chose a time when Alan was away on business and she told him she was going to Oxford to see her parents. But still they were careful, booking in as Mr and Mrs Laroche and as part of their cover speaking French to one another. Spying was so like adultery, she thought. The secrecy, the deception, the constant betrayal, in heart as much as in action.

It was on the second of those occasions that she warned Absolon about his side of the agreement. They were lying in bed in the morning, with a thin grey light leaking out of the clouds outside the hotel and the chambermaid keen to get in to do their room. 'My side are becoming impatient,' she told him. 'They want something more substantial from you.'

He lay there in the warmth of their bedclothes. Dark hair against the almost luminous white of his skin. She knew him better than she knew Alan, knew the creases and corners of his body, his smell and his taste. 'It's not easy,' he said. 'It's a balancing act.'

'I know all about balancing acts. But you've got to start giving me something concrete.'

'You don't understand the level of suspicion I have to deal with. Everyone watches everyone else. Even the scientists, so I've heard. You know who's in charge of the atom bomb project in the Soviet Union?' He turned his head to look at her. 'I shouldn't be telling you this, and it's only a rumour. But do you know who?'

She didn't. She lay amid the pillows and felt his hand between her thighs and didn't give a damn about who was in charge of anything.

'Lavrenty Beria.'

But she had no idea who Beria was. She waited a bit, feeling his hand moving. 'Absolon, I think they'd be willing to make a deal,' she said. 'If you were to come over I think they'd give you the whole lot – a new identity, a new life in Canada or Australia or anywhere you want.'

The hand was stilled. 'In return for what?'

'A full debrief. Everything you know. Your whole life, really.'

'And what about you?'

She lay motionless in case her slightest movement might shift the pattern of the moment. The plain room, lit by a weak morning sun. Bare, hotel furniture. Her clothes lying on the floor. 'I'd come with you,' she said quietly. 'Canada, anywhere.'

She also spent the occasional weekend at Ned's cottage. 'You can come with me, if you want,' she'd assured her husband, but he didn't want any contact with her queer brother. She could see that, even if he didn't say it directly. 'I've got better things to do,' he might say. Or, 'I wouldn't feel comfortable,' as though Ned might try and seduce him. So for those two days it would just be the two of them, brother and sister shut away in their little conspiracy. Ned was nervous, more nervous than usual, jumping when the phone rang at the cottage, glancing over his shoulder to see if anyone was following when they went shopping in Reading or Newbury. He would smuggle material from work to photograph over the weekend. Security was a chimeric beast, at times overweening in its attentions but in other ways careless – the guards gave a cursory glance in his briefcase when he left the laboratory but they never thought, or dared, to search his pockets. Perhaps it wasn't considered a gentlemanly thing to do. 'So I don't have to take that bloody camera in to work,' he explained to Marian. 'Can you imagine if security found that on me?'

In the shed at the end of the garden he had made a makeshift copy stand out of pieces of doweling and strips of plywood. The thing could be disassembled and the component parts looked like nothing at all – offcuts, leftovers – but once put together the contraption would hold the camera at the correct height above any document to be photographed. Two Anglepoise lamps, one on each side, gave clear illumination. He clicked the release cable and the little camera snatched the image and secreted it away within its tiny cartridge. On the very first occasion Marian watched, looking over his shoulder to see how things were going. The document he was photographing was an academic paper of some kind, each page stamped across the top with the rubric TOP SECRET. She felt as though she was peering through a keyhole into a locked room and watching something indecent taking place. Thereafter she stayed in the cottage whenever he worked away in the garden shed.

TATE

It is the simultaneity of events that intrigues me, their strange synchronicity. While Marian was conspiring with her brother I was cycling between my digs and the Victorian villa that housed the Joint Services School for Linguists. While she was spread-eagled beneath her Russian lover I was struggling with Russian conversation and anticipating, in an agony of expectation, our forthcoming appointment at the Tate Gallery. If you had asked me what I was expecting I would have been hard put to find an answer. Perhaps nothing more than the thrill of being in the company of someone who was in so many ways an exotic stranger – the Frenchness, the war record, the almost suicide, all those things I didn't comprehend. And, I suppose, the undercurrent of sexuality that I detected in her. But I was naive in those days. We were all naive, virgins almost all of us – virgin soldiers playing at academics. We might talk about women but rarely encountered any and I could barely recognise sexuality in an encounter.

On the Saturday in question I had some kind of

commitment that I had to get out of, one of those absurd playlets we used to put on, written by a student whose later works graced the West End stage. With some difficulty I extricated myself from a sketch that I had been rehearsing. Family reasons, I explained mendaciously. My aunt is ill. Something like that. I even talked about the John Radcliffe Hospital in order to give my lies verisimilitude, and worried, as I did, about the difficulties of creating a cover story on the fly, of compounding lie with lie, detail with detail, to create a complex fabric of deception that could all be undone with one twitch on a loose thread. Occam's razor applies to deception as much as it does to any argument: don't go multiplying your entities without good reason. Further, the excuse brought to my blushing mind the rather ridiculous fact that Marian was certainly old enough to be my aunt; indeed almost – but not quite – old enough to be my mother.

'Woodhouse aunt or Saki aunt?' the author of the sketch asked.

I fudged an answer – 'Sherry aunt, in fact' – which seemed to amuse him and earned me my release. So it was that on Saturday morning I travelled up to town in an orgy of anticipation and a nagging concern that my dwindling financial resources might not be up to the adventure. And, of course, an even more acute worry that she wouldn't make the rendezvous. I imagined her in her Paris days, meeting agents beneath the eye of the Gestapo, exchanging passwords and code phrases. How would meeting with a callow youth match up to that? But when I walked along the pavement from the Millbank bus stop, there she was, standing at the top of the gallery steps looking like Lady Tate herself welcoming visitors to her domain.

I didn't know quite what to make of that morning. I didn't even know how to go round an art gallery in someone's company. Do you look at the pieces together and exchange whispered ideas or do you go your separate ways? Is there an etiquette? I examined her examining the Turners, concentrating on them as though this was the most important thing in the world, and I assumed that she knew something about them that I didn't. Once or twice she caught my eye and smiled across the gleaming expanse of stone floor. She seemed to match the austere classicism of the galleries – a coldness, a monochrome exactness that stirred me to paroxysms of barely contained delight. What was running through her mind as she gazed on *The Lake, Petworth: Sunset, Stag Drinking* or *Tivoli: Tobias and the Angel*? I wanted to understand, wanted to occupy the space behind those shadowed eyes, eyes that had seen things I could not imagine.

And then we found ourselves standing in front of the Millais of Ophelia Drowning – the brilliant, luminous, captivating original of the image we had toyed with all those years ago in the cottage in

385

Sussex. For a long while she drowned before our eyes. Then quite softly Marian took my hand. The contact was like an electric shock. 'It was a very unhappy time for me, you know that?' she said.

'I know.'

'I could never tell how much you understood.'

My breath was held. 'Perhaps more than you think.'

'You were all very kind to me at a time when I didn't really appreciate it. Your mother was very kind.'

'She tries to be kind to everyone, but she doesn't always succeed.'

Very gently she shook my hand as though shaking it free. 'Let's go and see your Modiglianis.'

And then there was the moment – we were crossing the great space of the Octagon – when she was distracted by something. It seemed nothing much at the time. 'Do you mind waiting here a moment?' she asked, and left me standing by one of the pillars while she went off to talk to someone. A tall man in a rather crumpled dark suit. I thought perhaps, an official of the gallery. I noticed brilliantly polished shoes and a receding hairline, before he turned away and moved with her behind a pillar. They talked for a while – I fancied it was an animated conversation – and then he disappeared into one of the neighbouring galleries while she came back across the Octagon towards me.

'A friend,' she said, trying, and failing, to sound dismissive. 'Acquaintance, more like.' But I saw

386

the light in her eyes plain enough. My imagination blossomed into a fantasy about secret assignations and adulterous encounters. 'It's not what you're thinking,' she added.

How, I wondered, did she know what I was thinking? Could she read my mind or did my expression give me away? And if that was so, what other secrets might she descry? The unknown man dismissed, we continued on our way into the special exhibition. Its title was 'Modi or maudit? Modigliani in Paris'. We laughed together at the pun despite the fact that I didn't quite understand it. There were sculptures, of course, those blank, Cycladic faces that Modigliani favoured; and there were the nudes, nudes elongated and languid that lay around the gallery like women in a harem. Tufts of dark hair smirked from pubis and axilla. I tried to avoid Marian's glance, and blushed when I failed.

Respite was offered by the smaller gallery where the drawings were hung, where there were blessed shadows in which I could hide. Each drawing – mere strokes of pencil or charcoal – stood in its own pool of thoughtful light. And there she was: Anna Akhmatova. Until that moment I had no idea that the two of them, Akhmatova and Modigliani, the poet and the painter, had had an intense, pre-revolutionary affair in Paris. The only evidence was a card on the wall – *Anna Akhmatova, 1911. Black crayon on paper. Alexandre collection* – and the drawing itself, a spare sketch of curves, mere suggestions of limb and torso, lines of beauty and lineaments of desire. The breasts were tipped with a pencil point, the head was in profile with the famous Akhmatova nose as blunt as a Roman senator's and her hair gathered and fringed like a Roman matron.

Difficult to describe my emotions. This image was an epiphany, proof of the fell hand of coincidence at work in our sublunary world. You speak of the devil and there he is beside you; you dream of an angel and there she is before you.

'Dreams come true,' Marian said, at my shoulder.

We had lunch in the café. This was long before art exhibitions became a focus of pilgrimage, so the place was almost deserted. There were sandwiches made with counterfeit ham and others with something that resembled cheese. And Marian sitting opposite me watching with curiosity as I told her the story of the First Secretary from the British embassy in Moscow visiting Akhmatova in Leningrad in 1946, and how the two – the visitor from the West, a young Russian specialist at the embassy, and the great poetess – had spent a night together.

'A *night* together?'

'Talking,' I insisted. 'He was a philosophy don, for God's sake!'

'Don't philosophers do sex?'

'They spent the whole night *talking*,' I insisted.

'How extraordinarily unimaginative.'

'About poetry and culture, about the Russians in exile and the ones who stayed behind, about the whole disaster of Russian literature.'

She laughed at my blushes. I talked passionately, I suppose, and it's a short step from passion to embarrassment. When we came to leave she refused to let me pay. 'My treat,' she said. 'If you can call spam sandwich a treat.'

So I let her pay and followed her out of the gallery in a confusion of thanks and protestations: 'If you pay for everything, it'll make it difficult the next time. If there is going to be a next time. I mean, if you want to do something else, not necessarily the Tate. Perhaps a cinema or something . . .'

I must have sounded a complete fool but she did me the honour of not pointing it out. 'Why not?' she said. 'I've had a lovely time.'

I agreed. Lovely it had been. And more than lovely, although I didn't tell her that: thrilling, exciting. She summoned a cab – 'Isn't your train at three-thirty? We'd better hurry' – and then, as we sat in the taxi heading up Whitehall, she asked, 'Why . . .?'

'Why what?'

'Do you have to get back this afternoon?'

There was no reason in the world.

'So why not come and stay? Come for supper and stay the night. I'll be able to repay some of Judith's hospitality and Alan will enjoy the company. Someone who can talk cricket with him. You can talk cricket, I take it?'

'I hate cricket.'

'Well, make it up. Men can do that kind of thing. Women can't. A woman sounds daft talking about bowling maidens over but it seems a natural thing for a man to do.'

'To bowl maidens over?'

'To talk about it. They rarely manage actually to do it.' She caught my hand again, this time to press her point home. 'What do you say?'

'I haven't even got a toothbrush.'

'I'm sure we can manage something. And you can borrow a fresh shirt from Alan. You look about his size. Go on, be brave and unconventional.'

Of course I said yes. It seemed a spontaneous idea on her part, that was the thing. Beautifully judged, because she was a natural at the subtle arts of deception. I remember her leaning forward to talk to the driver, the curve of her back, one arm stretched out to open the little hatch in the partition. 'Forget King's Cross. Take us to South Kensington.'

The flat in South Kensington was in a red-brick block dating from the 1930s. As she let us in I remember my feeling of curiosity at seeing how someone else lived. My own family home was a clutter of things – papers and books piled on the floor, bikes in the hallway, manifestoes of whatever cause my mother had espoused at the time on the kitchen table – but the Walcotts's flat was plain and spare, barely touched by the accumulation of stuff

390

that you get when somewhere is lived in for years. They might have rented it just the other day, or been about to sell up and move out. Not a thing out of place and barely any place taken by something trivial or decorative. The sitting room occupied the corner of the block and had curved windows that made me think of the waiting room in an airport – a pre-war airport with languid women drinking cocktails and smoking cigarettes in long holders and waiting for a DC3 on the tarmac outside to be fuelled up. A chrome model of a Spitfire on a side table heightened the illusion, but the famous pilot was conspicuous by his absence.

'I'd quite forgotten,' she said as she searched the refrigerator for ice. 'Alan had to go down to Portsmouth to see his mother. The poor dear's twisted her ankle or something. So I'm afraid it's just you and me until he gets back.' She glanced at me with a faint smile. 'Is that all right?'

It was. It was beyond my dreams, but I didn't tell her that. What we actually talked about I can't recall but I do remember the ease with which we chatted, the amusement and the laughter. Our conversation was like a dance. We knew the steps instinctively and laughed at the small triumphs of understanding that we achieved. I thought to myself that there had been nothing like this before, that this woman with her austere face, was closer and warmer to me that anyone else I had encountered. Do I sound absurd? The truth was, I was falling – if I had not already fallen – in love.

We were interrupted by the sound of a key in the front door. 'That must be him.' And, to my disappointment, it was indeed Him, the Spitfire Pilot himself, back from strapping his mother's ankle, huffing and puffing and complaining about the traffic on the A5. He looked askance when he saw me.

'It's Sam. You remember Sam Wareham, don't you? Of course you do. I told you we'd bumped into each other the other day. Judith's son.'

We shook hands. Despite having been out of the Air Force for a few years now, Alan Walcott still looked every inch the model of a modern fighter pilot. Not tall – you couldn't be too tall, he explained, or you wouldn't fit into the Spit's cockpit – but somehow giving the impression of height. At ease with himself. Good looking in the manner of the times: Brylcreemed hair, square-jawed, firm of gaze. He clenched a pipe in his hand as though it were a joystick and looked me over as if I was on parade. Did he remember me? For a moment he thought not, and then connections were made and understanding dawned. 'Do you mean the cartwheel king? Goodness gracious, all that time ago. And you thought I was ever such a miserable chap for not having shot down any Germans. You've grown a bit, haven't you?'

'And my collarbone's healed,' I said.

He laughed. 'I remember a sound like a pistol shot. Echoed round the Close, it did. Well, I never – when I came in I thought you must be another of Marian's left wing lot. You're not a lefty, are you?'

I wasn't sure how to answer that. Marian's politics had never occurred to me. But she came to my rescue. 'Sam's at Cambridge at the moment. Doing a Russian course.'

'Russian? Why Russian?'

'He's doing National Service. They need Russian translators.'

'Going to be a spy, are you?'

'Why must you see spies everywhere, Alan?'

'Because they *are* everywhere, aren't they? Look at that Cambridge couple, Burgess and Maclean. Rotten apples infect all the rest. And those damn scientists, friends of your brother's every one.'

'Well, Sam's not a Russian spy, are you, Sam? And he's not going to infect anyone.'

Her husband looked at me through narrowed eyes, as though searching for Huns in the sun. 'But you are at Cambridge, aren't you?'

'Not the university—'

'Maybe it's something in the air there. The Fens. Damp and deception.'

'I've got a place at Oxford, actually.'

'No better. Look at Marian and her family. Left wing lunatics, the lot of them.' He laughed. It was a joke and we laughed with him. He went on to talk about his mother, how her ankle was, all that kind of thing. And work. And even cricket. I watched the two of them together, how they reacted to each other, how their glances went. From that

393

very first conversation, I saw the gulf. Alan seemed a two-dimensional sort of chap, with sharply defined views, even on things he knew nothing about; Marian was different. She was complex, full of fears and full of courage, possessed of the third dimension of unknowability. I knew that she'd been stalked through the streets of Paris by the Gestapo yet kept her cool. I knew that she'd been interrogated – I presumed hideous physical torture – yet revealed nothing. I knew all that, or as much as my mother knew about it, but I sensed much more. She loved peace and hated it; adored freedom yet hankered after the constrictions of wartime. She was fond of Alan, and yet often expressed her impatience with him, sometimes even her dislike. She loved life and loathed it. I knew that. What I didn't know was what was going on behind the scenes of her life at that time. Each person presents only a two-dimensional façade to the observer and the façade she presented allowed me no glance round the edges. At least, not then. So I had no idea about Absolon, no inkling of Fawley, no hint of the careful leak of documents that had passed through the conduit of Edward Sutro and Marian Walcott into the hands of Moscow Centre.

I returned to Cambridge the next day feeling, in some ill-defined way, let down. 'Come again,' she'd said as I left their flat to walk to the Tube station. 'Whenever you like. We enjoy company.' But there was no arranged date, no promise to call, nothing to suggest that those words had been anything but an empty valediction. So I immersed myself in the intricacies of Russian grammar and the exquisite cadences of Akhmatova's poetry, and tried to pretend I was not thinking of Marian Sutro all the time.

CHILTERNS

O ne day she and Absolon had a picnic in the Chiltern hills. It was a cool day, the air bright with the memory of a night-time shower. They took with them a Thermos flask of coffee and some sandwiches and climbed up through beech trees to a monument overlooking the Vale of Aylesbury. Rabbits scuttered out of the way as they walked up the slope. The grass was cropped close around the monument, almost as though it were mown. Above them white clouds bloomed in a blue enamel sky while away in the distance a giant cumulonimbus grew and blossomed like a cauliflower over Oxford.

In Absolon's presence she no longer thought of Benoît, or Clément, or Véronique, or Alan. They all seemed irrelevant. And she no longer contemplated death and betrayal but speculated instead on the possibility of staying with this man, Absolon, for the rest of her life, in Canada maybe, under an assumed name. Absurd, of course; but she had these thoughts.

'Have you considered their offer?' she asked him.

'I've thought about it. It's not easy.'

'Of course it's not easy.'

'A lifetime of work. And belief. A lifetime of belief.'

'People change their beliefs.'

'I'd need to talk with somebody.'

'I can arrange that.'

The cloud had spread across the sky like a great anvil as she gathered up their things. At its heart there was a lightning flash. 'Perhaps we'll have a storm,' she said.

Was that an omen? They held hands like children as they walked down through the woods and there was a moment among the trees when her fear was overcome by a sudden, insistent shock of desire. A strange thing, like a charge of static electricity. An explosion of lust there among the beech trees. She wanted him. She wanted to lay down among the beech mast and pull her skirt up for him. Perhaps this very thought struck a reaction in his mind – some kind of action at a distance – for he turned to her and pushed her against a trunk and pressed his mouth on hers and scrabbled with his right hand among her clothes. But then there were sounds below them, children calling, an adult voice trying to bring order, dead branches breaking underfoot. They separated, composed themselves and walked quietly down the slope past the upcoming troop of boy scouts who giggled as they went by, knowing, as kids know, what was happening.

'Nearly caught,' Absolon said.

She laughed with delight. 'Would it have been a great scandal?'

'A diplomatic incident. Soviet journalist caught with his pants down. War heroine exposed for a strumpet. Is that the word? Strumpet?'

'It was, about two hundred years ago.' And she felt it again, that shock of lust that she loved and hated – the kick that was like a drug, a surge of delight and liberation sweeping her up to the summit of sensation; and on the other side of the peak, the slope down which she slid into something resembling the shame. Bless me, Father, for I have sinned. But there was no Father. There was no one. Just the echoing spaces inside. Ned had long ago explained to her that the atom itself is mainly empty space, all its mass concentrated into the tiny core of the nucleus. The rest of the atom is nothing at all. Matter itself is almost nothing at all. The material world is little more than an illusion – yet this desire was not an illusion.

Down at the car park families were milling around getting out picnics. Two boys were assembling a kite out of bamboo struts and tissue paper. 'That car,' she said, not pointing or even looking in any particular direction. 'The black Ford. Haven't we seen it before?'

Absolon shrugged. 'It's nothing.'

But as they drove away the Ford pulled out behind them. It followed them for fifteen minutes as they made their way back to London in the sudden rain, and then it was no longer there.

Absolon appeared unconcerned. She glanced back through the rear window to see if she could spot a different vehicle doing the same thing as the black Ford. That motorcycle, maybe, trailing a plume of spray? Or the van that stuttered through the traffic lights behind them as they drove along Western Avenue. Or the family saloon – a Morris – that seemed to stick on their tail for a few minutes before they reached Shepherd's Bush. But she couldn't be sure. Within a few minutes they were at his house, safe behind the net curtains, with the rain coming down and the radio playing to confuse any microphones.

Later, when they were lying in bed in the reluctant moment before she had to get up and wash and get dressed, she whispered, her mouth close to his ear: 'You know those photos . . .?'

'Which photos?'

'The ones of Ned.'

'What about them?'

'I want you to get them for me. The negatives. He's earned them, hasn't he? It's wrong to have them hanging over him, even if he doesn't know they're there. A Sword of Damocles even if he can't see it.'

'We've all got one of those hanging over us.'

'Anyway, I want them.'

'Is that why you're doing this?'

She pulled away from him to see his expression. 'Are you serious? You know very well.'

'No, I don't.'

She lay down beside him again, her mouth close to his ear once more. 'I'm doing it,' she whispered, 'so that I can keep fucking you.' The word she would never have used now thrilled her, the raw, splintered sound of it almost conjuring up the act, almost onomatopoeic. Alan and she had sex. With Absolon, she fucked. It was the difference between swimming in a pool and plunging into the ocean.

'Can you get them for me?'

'I'll see,' he said.

An hour later she was making her way to the nearest Tube station, sure that she was not being followed, convinced that all was well, secure in her ability to look after herself in the ambiguous world of betrayal and deception, and confident above all that Absolon was willing to come over. Defect seemed the wrong word, having at its heart a deficiency, an insufficiency. Whereas for her, at that moment, he seemed complete.

TIGHTROPE

It is difficult now to understand what the NORTON source really involved. Most of the immediate witnesses are dead – Edward Sutro of a brain tumour at the disturbingly young age of fifty-six – and all the relevant files on the Russian side are locked away in the registry of the GRU, which is still thriving and living on in Ulitsa Grizodubovoy in Moscow. We are not going to know their side of things until someone opens up the archives and who knows when that might be? So all I have before me are what I have gleaned from the main registry at Millbank.

One of the registry clerks tracked everything down for me. She's an enthusiastic woman – little more than a girl, really – who wears tight skirts and has a disarming sway of her hips when she walks. 'Here you are, sir,' she said, handing me the file with a little smile of triumph. 'A bit dusty, but then it's been hanging around for ages without anyone taking any notice of it.' She might have been talking about me.

The file is headed 'Tightrope', which gives a nice impression of the game that Marian Sutro was playing. It was the usual thing, dog-eared, battered, decorated with various labels like a well-travelled suitcase from the thirties. Inside were various bits and pieces – surveillance reports, interview summaries, some internal memos, a missive or two from Broadway which was where Six was quartered in those now distant days, and a partial account of an interview with Absolon himself.

There's an archaeology of old files. You scrape away at them as an archaeologist might scrape away at the earth of a dig. You peer at artefacts – the marginal notes, the initials, the redactions – and you try and work out what was going on all those years ago when the events they shadow possessed emotional impact. Alan Nunn May and Klaus Fuchs were once vicious, evil traitors. Now they just seem rather naive but essentially honourable, decent men trying to do what they saw as the best for the future of mankind. Perhaps that goes for Edward Sutro and his sister Marian. And maybe even David Absolon. They'd given him the codename OXLIP. *Treat with utmost caution*, one of the marginalia warned. It was signed Hollis.

I interviewed OXLIP over a period of two and a half hours. During this time he appeared rather anxious but no more than might be expected under such circumstances. He frequently laughed, but without much humour, which I took to be a sign of nerves, and was often inclined to make somewhat exaggerated hand gestures to emphasise the point he was making. Our conversation initially centred on his personal history, which is covered elsewhere in this file and therefore which I will not repeat here. Suffice it to say that what he said appears to be entirely consistent with what we know of him from other sources.

One point should be emphasised: he appeared somewhat upset when talking about his late wife (killed during the siege of Leningrad). This I take to be an indication of his continuing feelings for her, which may have bearing on his current situation viz a viz SWALLOW.

Once we had dealt with that side of things we moved on to the current situation. Here he was very much vaguer, both about what he wanted and what he might provide us. Yes, he has been an active GRU officer for decades and is willing to confide in us about GRU practice throughout those parts of European operations he is familiar with but he is altogether unclear about how much of current operations he knows. Furthermore he is unclear about what he wants personally. Clearly he is not interested in money. Clearly he is interested in SWALLOW. He talked about a new life in Canada or something but whether he expects SWALLOW to be part of this is not clear. (N.B. she is married, and happily so as far as I am aware.) However, what OXLIP's real motivation is remains obscure, possibly to himself as much as to us. When I suggested that he might continue as he has been in recent months, i.e. as an agent in place providing us with useful intelligence, he havered. And when I suggested the quality of his information might be improved, he became almost indignant. Did I realise the danger he was in, the risks he was taking? Questions like that. I informed him that I have been in this game since long before the war and don't need lectures on the dangers involved.

He also asked how could he trust us. I told him, as one intelligence officer to another, that he couldn't. All he could rely on was the fact that we would work in our own best interests and it was not in our interests to endanger him in any way.

We agreed to meet again in a fortnight. I didn't want to push him any further than that and certainly didn't want to go into specifics. It is my opinion that he is not yet ready to come over but is warming to the idea. In the meantime, SWALLOW can definitely act to bring him closer to our way of thinking.

Swallow. Why do I find something faintly obscene about that codename? I'm afraid I can imagine her swallowing Absolon, hook, line and sinker.

CINEMA

Nothing among the brittle bits of paper hidden away in those old and dusty manila folders gives any hint of what was to happen. Only imagination can fill the gaps. In the Peace Union office in Holborn Marian went about the ordinary things of life. Filing and phoning, that was what Miss Miller called it. The tedium of the quotidian that underpinned any anxiety that Marian felt. At home Alan was distant. He had his life, she hers. They were civil to one another but there was a divide between them, with politeness the currency of exchange across the border, and the apartment in South Kensington a neutral territory on which these careful transactions could be made.

'Have you ever been unfaithful to me?' he asked her once.

She smiled and touched his face. 'My darling Alan, if I had been, would I tell you?' Then her smile became a laugh. 'But of course I haven't,' she assured him.

Was he gullible enough to accept this piece of sophistry? Who knows?

★　　★　　★

The blow came in the form of a phone call to the office, passed on to Marian by a faintly curious Miss Miller, who mouthed 'It's a man' as she handed the receiver over. On the other end of the line was Absolon's neutral voice telling her to meet at the usual place at half past one.

Marian felt a small tide of nausea swell up inside her. 'All right,' she said, and put the receiver down. There was no 'usual place'. The 'usual place' was where they had agreed to rendezvous in an emergency. The time quoted would always be one hour after the time intended. She glanced at the wall clock and saw the minute hand approaching midday. 'I'm going to take an early lunch,' she told Miss Miller. 'I'll do this stuff later.'

'Who was on the phone?'

'Oh, that. Someone cancelling a meeting. He'll ring me back.'

She took the Tube. The Tube was the best way to throw off a follower, the place you could deploy the tricks of the trade with ease. Stepping onto the train shortly before the doors closed, then immediately off at the very last moment, was effective. Whoever was following was left behind, stuck among the commuters in the steel and glass worm as it disappeared down the sinkhole of the tunnel. But she could see no one behind her as she went down to the platform, no one trailing her as she emerged into the maze of Piccadilly Underground station. Up at the surface were the

406

usual crowds, the traffic swirling round Eros, the lights – Wrigley's gum, Wills's Gold Flake cigarettes, Lemon Heart rum – sparking and flashing even in the middle of the day. She bought a ticket for the circle in the Pavilion cinema and felt her way through curtains into the clotted darkness. An usherette with a dimmed torch showed her to a seat. It was like finding your way through the city in the blackout, fearful of tripping, fearful of bumping into someone or something, fearful of what was just around the corner. As she took her place the main feature was already running, a film called *The Thief* according to the posters outside, with Ray Milland looking unshaven and desperate. For a while, letting her eyes accommodate to the dark, she watched the screen and tried to decipher what was happening. There was no dialogue, which seemed strange. Milland paced, stared at the wall of his room as though it was a prison cell, moved a chair, glanced at a newspaper. You could hear these things – the scrape of chair legs, the rustle of newsprint, the actor's breathing – but nothing else except the music score that told you the emotion to feel, the rising desperation as he looked around his drab little cell, the climax as he slammed out of the room. Next he was running in a park somewhere. New York. There were skyscrapers in the background. New York, where she had never been but Clément had. Columbia was in New York, wasn't it? Ray Milland ran as though trying to escape something, but there was nothing behind him, only passers-by glancing at him with curiosity. Walk, don't run, she thought, trying to will him. Never look in a hurry, never show indecision. And then she remembered how she had run from Père Lachaise that time, run like the wind, run as though she had the hounds of hell on her tail.

'They've recalled me.'

Absolon's whispered voice was directly behind her. She half turned and felt his face against her cheek. He was in the seat behind, leaning forward towards her.

'Keep still and listen. I'm being posted. Immediately.'

'Immediately? Where to?'

'Back home.'

'Are you in trouble?'

He gave a little laugh. 'You never know. Most likely to be jealousy. Anyway, someone will contact you. They'll want to keep things going, keep Norton going.'

She felt the panic bubble up inside her. 'But you're my contact. It's your thing.'

'Not any longer, I'm afraid. Maybe we haven't been as clever as we thought. Unless . . .'

'Unless?'

'Nothing. Anyway, it's too late now. I must go.'

'No, don't.' She half turned and clutched at his arm. 'Come with me. Now. I can contact someone immediately.' The urgency in her voice. The sensation of grabbing at ideas like a drowning person clutching at bits of flotsam. Someone in the shadows nearby hushed her to silence. Absolon's face came closer. 'I can't do that. I've got to go. They want me on a plane this afternoon.'

'To where?'

'I told you. Home. Moscow.' He reached over her shoulder and dropped something into her lap – an envelope, just an envelope. 'I can't explain now.'

'What do you mean, you can't explain now?'

'Maybe some time. We'll see.'

Then he kissed her on the cheek and was gone. She slipped the envelope into her handbag and turned back to the screen where Ray Milland's whole world seemed to be collapsing around him.

Ten minutes later she left the cinema by an emergency exit just beside the ladies. Out in the glaring daylight there was the usual lunchtime crowd that might have concealed a dozen watchers, but what did it matter who was watching her? They knew where she worked and where she lived. Both sides did. Absolon had gone and she was on her own, burned and useless. Perhaps there was a kind of comfort in that. Back in the office she attempted to do some work but she couldn't concentrate. She felt sick, physically sick, and had to run to the bathroom to vomit. Once her stomach had settled a bit she summoned up the courage to open the envelope that he had passed to her. Inside were a dozen strips of 35-millimetre film negative. No note, nothing else. As she was about to examine them there was a tentative knock on the door and Miss Miller's voice asking if she was all right.

'I'm fine,' she called, stuffing the negatives back into the envelope and the envelope back into her handbag. When she opened the bathroom door there was Miss Miller waiting. She could see what the woman was thinking. 'No, I'm not pregnant,' she snapped. 'It must have been something I ate.'

That evening she worked late and waited until everyone had gone, Miss Miller with a baleful glance and a knowing 'you need to take care of yourself'. Only then did she dare open the envelope again. She held the strips of celluloid up to the light to try and make out the images. There were harlequin figures shaped in black and grey patches, performing against a white backdrop, difficult to decipher but easy enough if you knew what they were. Figures wrapped in each other's limbs. Figures filled with each other's parts.

She took the negatives to the bathroom and tried to burn them in the basin. During her training there had been an explosives lecture in which the instructor had shown how you could make a bomb using old film stock. 'It's nitrocellulose,' he'd explained. 'Better known as guncotton.' But this was safety film and it burned poorly, with much black smoke and lots of melting. She cut up the charred remnants with scissors, wrapped them in lavatory paper and flushed them away. Then, like a child, like a bloody silly little girl, she broke down in tears. Tears for Ned, tears for Absolon, tears for herself. There was the ache of absence like a physical void inside her, physical as much as emotional. Where had Absolon gone? What had happened to him? And why, for Christ's sake, did she care?

HOUSEBREAK

Her world trembled. She sensed cracks beneath the surface, as though something had broken inside, some fissure opened up in the fragile construct that was her life. She rang the number that she knew and arranged a meeting with Fawley but he could offer no comfort.

'They've taken him away,' she insisted, her voice on the edge of dissolution 'They've dragged him back to Moscow and I've no idea what has happened to him. You've got to do something.'

But what could Fawley do? He looked at her with solemn concern, his fingers steepled together and gently bouncing against each other. 'It seems likely,' he said, and he couldn't keep a hint of reproach from his tone, 'that they got wind about the two of you. Possibly that he was passing you information but more likely that you were having an affair.'

'It can't be that,' she cried.

'Why can't it?'

She paused, trying to see the way ahead, trying to measure the implications and the consequences. 'Because he was running me as an agent.'

For the first time, the very first time, she saw

412

shock in Fawley's expression. Nothing overdone, nothing exaggerated. Just a widening of the eyes and a slight opening of the mouth, immediately closed, immediately brought back under control. When finally he spoke, his voice was soft, lenitive, like the soft caress of a confessor. 'An *agent*? What in heaven's name are you talking about, Marian?'

She almost told him. She almost laid out all her sins before the priest. But instead she shrugged. 'Nothing. I wasn't giving him anything significant. What's the expression? Chicken feed. Just information about the Peace Union, about our contacts – trades unionists, journalists, academics, people who might be sympathetic.'

'Is that so?'

'You have to cover your back, don't you? You taught me that.'

'Don't you think you should have told me?'

'I'm telling you now because it no longer matters. It's one of the basic rules, isn't it? You're safe as long as you're useful. So we were both safe because we were useful. Safe from them and safe from you. But then something happened to change all that, didn't it? They must have discovered that Major Absolon of the GRU was planning to defect. How did they get to know that?'

His mask was back in place now, bland and smooth. 'These things happen, Marian. They happen. Perhaps he himself made a mistake. Took his eye off the ball.' The cricket metaphor, the bane of an English gentleman's conversation.

'But he wouldn't have, would he? He's a professional. He knows what to do.'

'Was he in love with you?'

That stalled her. She didn't know, she just didn't know the answer. 'That's not the point. The point is, they must have known he was about to come over. How did they *know*? Somehow they knew what he was going to do. And you've got to do something about it.'

'My dear Marian, you know perfectly well that there is nothing in the world I *can* do.'

She went home, like a refugee having nowhere else to go. Alan offered no comfort. How could she explain to him that she felt bereft, as though someone had died? How could she explain anything to him? They ate a desultory meal together, talking about the ordinary matters of life, the cost of things, the end of rationing, a film they might go and see, an art exhibition that she wanted to visit but he didn't. And all the time she thought about Absolon, where he might be and what might be happening to him. Russia had absorbed him, Mother Russia that seemed so vast and so amorphous. Thousands and thousands of square miles. Mountains, rivers, the vastness of the steppe scattered with cities one had never seen, never imagined, knew only from reports during the war. Stalingrad. Perm. Kursk. Kiev. All enveloped in a kind of fog. And Absolon was somewhere there, dispersed among the mists.

Later she lay in bed while Alan made love to her in that stolid, insistent way of his that seemed as much a social convention as an act of affection. When it was over she rolled onto her side and tried to sleep, with his sperm inside her doing what it had done ever since they had got married – nothing. Perhaps if she had got pregnant all things would be changed. Perhaps the yearning for Absolon, the fear and the anger would be gone for ever with a child growing within her. But she didn't get pregnant. She never had and she knew she never would. There is no objective reason, her doctor had assured her, no damage that we can see. But still nothing happened, and she lay like this in bed, sensing her own sterility, afraid for and longing for Absolon.

The next day she came back early from work. It seemed an early evening like any other, the city living beneath its skin of grime, the Tube over-crowded, people complaining. She reached their block of flats and climbed the stairs to the first floor, to the door that said *Walcott* on a little brass plaque. For a moment, as she searched inside her handbag for the keys, everything seemed normal – the quiet anonymity of the landing and the mechanical beat of the descending lift gave nothing away. But when she opened the door she knew immediately that something was different. Something had shifted in the order of her private universe. The disposition of magazines beside the

415

telephone in the hallway. Something. She went to the sitting room. She felt it here as well, the recent presence of other people, like a smell on the air – cushions slightly displaced, things on the desk not quite in their usual order, not how she had left them that morning. Fear crawled out from its lair and took hold of her.

'Alan?' she called, but there was no reply. Cautiously she pushed open the door to the main bedroom. The room was empty, but things were subtly different, a hairbrush sitting in a way she hadn't left it, her make-up moved, the placing of things in her drawers altered. In the spare bedroom she fancied it was the same, and in the room that Alan used as an office. Things had been shifted, drawers opened but not closed precisely, papers shuffled, pens misplaced.

And then revulsion at the thought of the intrusion was replaced by understanding, because nothing was missing. Not a single item of her possessions or Alan's had been taken. Back in the bedroom she scrabbled through the drawers to check. His gold cufflinks were there in their little box. Her jewellery was untouched. Money in the top drawer of the desk remained where it was. Every drawer, every box, every file in the study had been opened; but nothing had been taken. They'd been looking for something – anything – and of course they hadn't found it because there was nothing to be found. No secrets, no evidence. Not even a phone number.

Slowly – a stiff gin and French helped – the grip

of fear slackened. Lessons at Beaulieu had taught her that you have to make a choice between a hidden search and an open search, the latter disguised as an ordinary burglary. Whoever it was had chosen the former and they hadn't done it well. But she knew that they were still watching her, that they'd followed her from work, that in all probability they were watching the flat even now. She went to the window to glance casually out. There was nothing obvious, just the street and the parked cars and pedestrians walking. What, she wondered, were they after?

When Alan came home she told him nothing.

The next day Ned rang. His cottage near Harwell had been broken into. He'd walked into the village to phone her and his voice was shaking with emotion as he spoke. 'Someone's ransacked the place,' he told her. His voice was the voice of a child, almost blubbing. 'They've turned everything upside down.'

'Did they take anything?'

'Take anything? Yes, of course they did. That's what burglars do, isn't it?'

She took time off work and went down to help. She found him pacing up and down in the sitting room, opening and closing his fists as though there might be something comforting to grasp if only he could lay hold of it. Around him was the litter of his impoverished life – drawers had been opened and their contents tossed onto a heap in the middle of the room, wardrobes and cupboards emptied. Apparently the kitchen window at the back had been broken in order to get in and what little he had of any value had been taken – little more than a radio and a record player and ten shillings in cash. The records themselves – some Bach, some Vivaldi – had been smashed.

'Presumably not to their taste,' he said gloomily. 'But I don't see why they have to punish me by breaking them.'

The police had already been round, and someone from the security section at Harwell. Kids from the local council houses, the police constable had suggested. They'd asked for a list of missing items and Ned managed a smile when he explained to Marian how clever he'd been: 'They also stole the camera, but I didn't mention that. I thought it better not to.'

'They took the *camera*?'

'Yes. They went through the summerhouse as well and found it there. Don't worry though, there was nothing on the film.'

'That's not the point, is it, Ned? The point is, what happens if the thieves are caught and the damn thing is found?'

The smile slid untidily from his face. 'It's nothing, Squirrel. Just a gadget.'

Impatiently she set to tidying the place up. It was only when a semblance of order had been restored and they were sitting down with a drink that she broke the news about Absolon. She tried to make it sound like nothing much, a mere hiccup in the plans, her contact recalled to Moscow. 'So for the moment we'll just have to lie low.'

But Ned looked uncomfortable. 'I'm having second thoughts about the whole business, Squirrel. I don't think I want to continue, really.'

'Second thoughts? It's a bit late for second thoughts.'

'They've got enough information, haven't they? What more do they want?'

'It's no good asking me that, is it? I don't know anything about it. All I know is my contact has been recalled.'

'That's the man you were fucking, isn't it?'

Anger flared inside her. 'Don't use that disgusting language!'

He laughed. 'You're such a prig, Squirrel. I'll bet you use it all the time when you're with him. That's the way, isn't it? The disgusting becomes sublime. It all depends on the context.'

She thought of Absolon, what she did with him and could now no longer do. 'Anyway, it's none of your business.'

'But it is my business, isn't it? What we've done is because of what you've done. It's betrayal whichever way you look at it. And I want to get things stopped. Having that security man round today was the last straw. Wing Commander someone or other. He sniffed around the place as though it were I who'd done something wrong.'

'It's just your imagination. I expect he was concerned about whether there'd been a security breach.'

'There's been that all right, hasn't there? And I want it to stop.'

She travelled back to London. Fear, like a caustic fluid, seeped into her mind. She sensed them watching her with wide eyes, like predators in the night. What had they been searching for, in Ned's cottage, in her flat? Traces of Absolon, perhaps. Evidence of his deception, clues to his threatened defection. She imagined him in some cell beneath the Lubyanka, like a rat in a cage, helpless. She knew. She could share everything with him, even this. Memories of Fresnes Prison emerged from the stew of memory like monsters from the deep: a few feet of concrete; a faucet in the wall and a cracked earthenware water closet in the corner; a bed and a table, both hinged to the wall; a stool chained to the table; a thin blanket and a palliasse. Nothing else. The rattle of a trolley outside in the corridor brought thin soup and a piece of bread. There were cries in the night and, sometimes, the careful tapping of Morse code on the pipes. But always some thin thread of hope, that the Allies would come, that the war would be over, that all would be resolved.

Did Absolon have as much as that?

AMBASSADOR

At the Joint Services School for Linguists in Cambridge, I struggled with Russian irregular verbs and unstressed vowel reduction; in London, Marian Sutro battled with her demons. Work brought some kind of distraction – a lecture series by the anfractuous Dr Eric Hobsbawm on European revolutionary movements; a talk by Professor Blackett of Manchester University on How the Atom May Work for Peace; an essay competition among schoolchildren entitled 'What World Peace Means to Me'. I remember an article in the *Guardian* – the principal source of news for us students, and still published from Manchester in those days – about a conference she had organised. There was even a photograph of the principal protagonists delivering a petition to Number 10 Downing Street. An aging French poet and a young, long-haired film director were there, and the suave figure of the French atom scientist Clément Pelletier.

'French Intellectuals Anti-Atom Bomb Letter To PM', was the headline. Needless to say, the Prime Minister did not receive the missive in person.

And then another postcard came to my digs, bearing another picture from the Tate Gallery, only this time a Modigliani portrait of a girl. I examined the image for clues, but clues to what, I couldn't say. It was a rather sentimentalised face, all doe eyes and rosebud mouth and a skin colour that suggested an excessive consumption of carrots; but at least Marian had spared my blushes and avoided one of the nudes. On the other side was her now familiar writing and a suggestion for another meeting. 'Formal invitation on the way,' she wrote. The invitation came some days later, accompanied by a ticket to a concert at the Wigmore Hall. After the concert there would be a reception for the performers, a string quartet from the Soviet Union. It was to this reception, in the presence of His Excellency the Ambassador of the Soviet Union, that I was cordially invited. There was also a scribbled note from Marian. *This time bring a toothbrush.*

I recall little of that concert. I just remember dark suits and long dresses and the shuffling movement of people, the gleam and shine of two worlds that were quite foreign to me and were both presented here in uneasy juxtaposition – the world of diplomacy and the world of the arts. The quartet – three swarthy men and a woman violinist of ethereal beauty – swayed and pulsated beneath the sunburst cupola of the auditorium like animated figures in a Fabergé jewel box. I forget what they played. It would have been all Russian, of course: Shostakovich, probably, something by Khachaturian, something else by Prokofiev.

But I remember Marian well enough. She was wearing a black evening gown and a short bolero jacket and she had her hair piled up. I had never seen her like that, never seen her doing what she called 'my Parisian thing'. I remember the slender nakedness of her neck and a skein of silken hairs that drifted round her pale skin like cigarette smoke. She took me to the reception afterwards where there was a press of people and much fawning around the musicians. Holding my arm she steered me through the throng. 'You must show them that even Englishmen can speak their language,' she said.

The musicians frowned and nodded when I congratulated them in my tortuously improving Russian.

'How are you finding it in England?' I asked the female violinist.

A faint scent of onions hung around her. Was this the smell of fear? She looked terrified at having to admit that she was enjoying her visit very much. 'We cannot see as much of London as we would like because we have work to do. Always practising, always practising.' The ghost of a smile lit up her face when she thought of something safe to say: 'We are very honoured to represent our country in this manner.'

Someone took her arm and led her away, perhaps

towards people who did not speak Russian. An official of the embassy appeared by my side and asked where I had learned the language. 'You speak very well,' he said, in English, and a moment later I was being introduced to the ambassador himself.

'*Vashye Pryevoshodityel'stvo*,' I said. 'Your Excellency, it is a great honour to meet you. And to hear your wonderful musicians.'

He was a shrewd-looking man, small and desiccated. His lips moved thoughtfully as he considered my little speech. 'In the Soviet Union we do not have Excellencies,' he said. 'There we are all comrades.'

I think it might have been intended as a pleasantry but before I had time to respond the lackey had ushered me away and the hangers-on had closed round the great man again like pilot fish around a shark. At the same time I noticed Marian making her way through the crowd. And then there was the incident. I didn't hear much, just her voice raised above the general noise, and a throb of shock that reverberated through the onlookers. She'd asked a question, that much I heard. But exactly what she'd asked and what the answer might have been there was no way of knowing. In a moment she was out of the press and being escorted away by two men wearing ill-fitting black suits. She shook their hands off like someone getting rid of dust or dirt. Astonishment encircled her. What had happened? Nothing much to disturb the even tenor of the evening – a moment of embarrassment, a flurry of outrage, hastily constructed conversations to cover the incident. A few minutes later the ambassador left and the reception more or less came to an end.

In the taxi afterwards Marian laughed it off. 'I asked the old trout a question, that was all.'

I imagined political protest, something awkward about the Korean war or the arms race, but I was wrong. 'About a friend of mine who used to work at the embassy,' she explained. 'They posted him away suddenly and I've not really heard from him since. I just want to know, that's all.' There was a light in her eyes, an expansiveness in her gestures, which suggested rather too much to drink. 'What about you? You got to talk to His Excellency as well . . .'

'Not Excellency. "In Soviet Union we are all comrades," that's what he told me.'

'What a sour old puss. Did he at least smile? Perhaps he was making a joke.'

'In Soviet Union, there we are all comedians,' I said, with an exaggerated Russian accent. Laughter, displaced by alcohol, rose and overflowed. Incontinently we leaned against each other while the cab wound its way through the London streets towards South Kensington. It wasn't late when we reached our destination but we treated it as such, giggling like children returning after hours and frightened of waking the adults. We crept up the staircase to the front door of her flat and she

425

hushed me to silence as she turned the key in the lock. 'He's asleep,' she whispered, closing the door silently behind us. With a hand on my shoulder to balance, she slipped her shoes off. 'Better not wake him.' She padded across the hallway, then stopped and turned back and looked at me shame-faced, her voice suddenly normal.

'How could I be so stupid?'

'Stupid?'

'I forgot. He was going tomorrow but he brought the flight forward to this afternoon. To the United States. Most important for his career.' Her mouth turned down at the mention of the word career. 'He wasn't coming to the concert anyway – can't bear the things. But . . .'

Was she explaining too much? Was I victim of some silly subterfuge? I knew only the implications of what she was saying, implications that plunged me into a state of anticipation that I had never known before. I could see it in her eyes, or thought I could. Something passed between us that I didn't understand then and don't understand now: action at a distance, a little radiant burst of enigmatic energy. 'What about a nightcap?' she suggested. And then, almost as though she didn't understand what might be happening either, she asked, 'Is that what we should do?'

'I'm sure it is,' I answered. So we had a whisky each, in the sitting room, with something on the record player – Edmundo Ros? – and something else in the air. She sat on the sofa much as I remembered from that terrible night at Furze Cottage, with her legs drawn up under her and her feet bare. She'd slipped off her jacket. Her shoulders were white and almost luminous, like alabaster. I remember a vaccination scar the size of a small coin pressed into the skin of her upper arm, as though she had been branded with a medallion.

'So, what is it they say?' she asked, raising her glass. '*Za vashe zdorovye!*'

'Something like that.'

She laughed and downed the whisky in one gulp. 'There: true Russian style. Now tell me how you enjoyed the concert.'

So I told her. Very much indeed, I said, and thanked her for inviting me.

And the little violinist? Would I have enjoyed her?

What, I asked primly, did she mean by that?

She laughed. 'If you had the opportunity, would you sleep with her?'

I contemplated this question with a degree of uncertainty. Yes or no? Yes might make me seem some kind of immoral degenerate. No might make me appear a prude. 'She had a curious smell,' I said. 'A hint of onions.'

'How very earthy. But you haven't answered my question.'

'Yes, then.'

She laughed delightedly, holding her hand to her mouth. 'Did you fancy her more than your poet? More than Akhmatova?'

427

'Akhmatova is rather old now. But neither are on offer.'

'No, they're not.'

We watched one another. I was confused, wondering what exactly was happening.

'Do you remember that time at Furze Cottage?' she asked. 'When we sat up half the night talking?'

'Of course I do.' For her it would only have seemed a short while ago; but for me it lay on the far side of the boundary between adulthood and childhood, as far away as another continent and another century. I recalled it and didn't recall it, saw the two figures sitting there on the sofa in the sitting room in the cottage as though I was neither of them, as though I had conjured them out of my imagination.

'What did you think at the time?'

'About what?'

'Me. About me going for midnight walks. What did you think?'

'Something vaguely Brontë-esque, I suppose. Striding over the cliffs through the wind and the rain—'

'It was bright moonlight.'

'I wondered if you'd come back.'

'Really?' She looked at me, head on one side. 'Where did you imagine I'd gone?'

I hesitated, but alcohol had done its job, stripped away any reticence. 'I knew, Marian. I knew where you'd gone, more or less. I mean, I knew what you were intending to do.'

Her expression didn't change. Even when full of alcohol she still had that ability to hide what she was thinking or feeling, to dissimulate. 'You knew? How did you know?'

I shrugged. 'I was a child, more than a little in love. I followed you everywhere, don't you remember?'

'My little spy. Did you follow me that night?'

'Not exactly. I heard you leave and then' – I tried to laugh it off – 'I went snooping.'

Her brown eyes had that luminous quality about them, as though they were giving out rays rather than taking them in. Was that how she had looked at her captors all those years ago? Eyes of anger, eyes of hate, was that it?

'Snooping?'

'In your room. I was only a child, for Christ's sake . . .'

'You read the note I left?'

I nodded.

'And you kept my secret?'

'Never told anyone. Until now.'

She pondered this. 'So it's *our* secret, then. All these years I thought it was only mine but all the time I shared it with Sam the Spy.' There was a fragment of a smile. 'Strange to share secrets.'

'You must have many.'

'More than you can imagine.'

There was a pause. I thought she might tell me something more but she only swung her feet off the sofa and stood up. 'I think it's time for bed, don't you? Can you undo my buttons? I had to get Alan to do me up and now, thank God, there's you to undo me.'

She turned her back on me and stood there while I did as I was commanded, my fingers stumbling with the buttons, a dozen and more of them down the length of her back as far as the concavity at the base of her spine. As the buttons came undone the material opened up like a wound, to expose white flesh and the supple snake-like corrugations of her spine. Her shoulder blades resembled vestigial wings folded awkwardly below the skin. I wondered if there might be scars, if she might have been whipped or branded or whatever they had done to Odette, but there was nothing to disturb the even fabric of her flesh except a few small moles, scattered at random across the undulating skin. As she turned, holding the dress against her chest to prevent it falling, we were standing very close. I could smell her, that same smell I remembered from so long ago. Something raw about it.

'Sam,' she said. 'Would you like to sleep with me?'

There was a hiatus, a stillness, a caesura. More than that – a yawning chasm between the world now and the world of a moment ago. This was the woman whom I had known for much of my life – since before the time when I possessed clear and consistent memories. This was Marian Sutro whom, for all that time, I had worshipped and adored. She was to me the paragon of all female virtues: courageous, independent, slightly bloody-minded, more than a little amused by the idiocies of others, disturbingly attractive. A fruit that was both acerbic and sweet, bitter and emollient. And she had suggested that I might sleep with her.

Or had she? Perhaps she had merely asked the question hypothetically – did I *fantasise* about sleeping with her? Just as earlier she had asked about the Russian violinist. In which case the honest answer was, again, yes.

Thoughts twisted and coiled round on themselves, like snakes that might have dropped out of the trees into Eve's lap: how much I knew about this woman, and how little. Had I even heard her right? Had she really said 'with me'? There seemed, to my virginal mind, a dozen innocent possibilities.

'Well?' She was smiling faintly, almost mockingly, looking up at me from under strongly drawn eyebrows.

Something was stuck in my throat. I tried to swallow, trying to rid myself of the obstruction. 'But what about Alan?'

'Alan has his own life; don't you worry about him.' And abruptly there was a change in her demeanour, a hardening, a snap. 'Look, my naive little spy, I've made you an offer. It won't stay on the table indefinitely.'

'And if I say yes, we sleep together. Just like that?'

'How else should it be?'

I wonder how many lovers she had had by then. Can I count them? Benoît Bérard, the first. Then Clément Pelletier. Véronique Barthelemy, camp mother and comforter, must, I suppose, be included. And then Marian's husband, of course. But the intelligence officer called Tony Bright as well, and also, I believe, a brief and unsuccessful affair with a fellow SOE officer whom she encountered after the war – two lost souls, trying desperately to recapture things that were forever lost to them. And there was Absolon, David Trofimovich Absolon. Doubtless there were others. Where, I wonder now, did I come in the register of Marian Sutro's lovers?

'Yes,' I said. 'Of course.'

We used the guest room. I would have liked to use her own bedroom, where she habitually lay with the Spitfire pilot who had never shot down an enemy aircraft, but perhaps that was one step too far. So we found ourselves in the narrower confines of the spare bed, clinging to one another as though to save ourselves from drowning. I remember each moment in the smallest and most particular detail, the smell of her, the exact touch of her cool skin, the taste of whisky and cigarettes in her mouth, the loose texture of her breasts as I nuzzled my face against them, the rough hair where she guided my hand and the slippery oyster I discovered embedded there – an encounter never again so shocking and so delightful. And then her hands were on my head, pushing me down beyond the point where my imagination faltered. I hadn't conceived that such a thing was possible. Believe me. Those were different times from nowadays, times when such acts had to be discovered for yourself or learned from someone else. You wouldn't find them in a glossy, illustrated book or on a website that anyone can access – it was knowledge to be imparted by adept to neophyte as one might pass on the rituals of a secret society, with all the magic and mystery and misunderstanding that that entails. I remember not knowing what was happening and being fearful; and then finding myself amazed at the pure wonder of it, the strange embrace, the sensation of drowning within her, of floundering in her heat and her delicate, elusive flavour. And her breathless explosions of pleasure, which in her case were uttered in French – *oui, oui, oui!* – and the coincident marvel of discovering that she could find such delight in what I could do to her. It was sexual love of an intensity I have never experienced since.

'Don't be silly, Sam,' she said when, in the subsequent post-coital diminuendo, I made an affirmation of my love. 'One day you'll find someone perfect to love.' Which was almost exactly what she had said when we sat together on the sofa in Furze Cottage a decade earlier. And it was not true. I never did find anyone perfect to love – does anyone? – and I truly loved her then and

I truly love the memory of her still, despite all that happened later.

Afterwards she slipped out of the bed and went to her own room. I felt bereft.

BREAKFAST

Marian Sutro (I still cannot bring myself to think of the surname Walcott) in her kitchen in the bright, cool light of a Sunday morning, making toast. She is barefoot, barelegged, wearing a plain grey skirt and white blouse. Her hair is loose, her face without make-up and touchingly vulnerable. She looks older than her years. I remember her feet, their bony whiteness, the way they flexed as she moved around the room. Long toes, nails painted blood red. I never imagined that you might be fascinated by your lover's feet but now I discovered that you can be – you can be fascinated by any part of her, and bewildered by the beauty.

'I'm sorry about last night,' she said, not looking at me. 'I think I had a bit too much to drink.'

'There's nothing to apologise for.'

'Isn't there?' She glanced round and made a little self-deprecating face. 'What would your mother say? Dirty old Marian seducing her little boy. I should be ashamed.'

'But you're not?'

'I gave up shame a long time ago.'

'And I gave up being her little boy a long time ago. Anyway, I wanted to be seduced.'

'Were you expecting it? Am I that bloody obvious?'

'I was pleasantly startled.'

That amused her, which I took as a positive sign, although, God knows, laughter can signify many things and only a few are benign. For a few minutes she busied herself with breakfast. Every movement she made fascinated me, even the manner in which she tore off a corner of toast and applied butter and marmalade to that piece alone, then popped it in her mouth. I'd not seen someone eat toast like that. In our house we spread the butter and marmalade over the whole slice, like a navvy at his tea break. Her method seemed cautious and refined. Perhaps it was French.

'*Alors*, Monsieur Wareham,' she said, looking at me thoughtfully. Coming under her gaze was a disturbing experience. I knew her and didn't know her. Knew more about her body than I ever imagined even in my most fervid fantasies; and knew so little of the mind that was part of that body. 'When we've finished breakfast, I think you'd better go.'

'Go?' I was dumbfounded.

'I think so, yes.'

'That's it? I mean, it's over as soon as it's begun?'

'Perhaps we went a bit far. I think I need some time. To reflect.'

'So when will I see you again?'

She shrugged. Gallic indifference. 'We'll see. But for the moment, let's just be the best of friends, shall we? I don't want it all to end in tears, Sam.'

So I finished my frugal meal in bitter disappointment and afterwards she walked with me to the Tube station. A chaste kiss on each cheek at the barrier and a final breath of that perfume I now knew so well. Something sweet, something sour. My sister had hated it.

GORSHKOV

On the Monday there was consternation at the Peace Union. Mr Roper was beside himself with fury. 'All that work we put into gaining the confidence of our Soviet brothers and it's all destroyed in a moment with an outburst by that stupid woman!'

That stupid woman was standing in front of him, as contrite as a schoolgirl.

'What was it all about, anyway?' Roper demanded.

'A *friend*,' said Miss Miller primly.

'The press officer at the embassy,' Marian explained. 'He was doing a story on the Peace Union and then suddenly he was recalled.'

'Which upset *Mrs* Walcott no end.' Miss Miller looked tight-mouthed and indignant. 'One really ought to learn to keep one's private life separate from one's work.' She turned on her heel and flounced out of the meeting.

'And now I've got to go back to building bridges,' Roper said gloomily. It was unclear whether he mean with the Russians or with Miss Miller.

★   ★   ★

A few days later Gorshkov, the man from the embassy cultural department, phoned. He wanted Mrs Walcott, no one else. 'To discuss,' he said when she had finally been brought to the phone.

'To discuss what?'

'Something.'

'Am I in trouble?'

'We don't talk on telephone.'

So they arranged to have coffee in the rather dreary café in Holborn that they had made their meeting place ever since the failure of their lunch encounter in Piccadilly. The bell on the door made a peremptory ping as she went in, and the Russian looked up from his corner table with an uneasy smile. He half rose from his seat to greet her. 'Sit,' he said, pointing to the empty chair in front of him. 'Sit.'

The waitress brought her coffee.

'So what is this all about?' Marian asked. 'Is it about Major Absolon? Is that it?'

'Your intervention with ambassador was not considered appropriate.'

'All I asked for was some information about one of your colleagues. Why is that a problem?'

Gorshkov had the manner of someone struggling with a foreign language, unsure whether he was being understood, unsure whether he had got the words right or was committing the kind of solecism that brought either laughter or dumb incomprehension. 'It was not appropriate to ask Comrade Ambassador in that fashion.'

'So do I have to say I'm sorry?'

'That is not necessary. Comrade Ambassador is very understanding.' He glanced round, as if someone might be listening but there was no one near enough to be interested in what he was saying. 'But he wonders why should you be so concerned about Comrade Absolon.' There was anger in the man's eyes. And something else – a thin, insidious worm of jealousy.

'Because his departure seemed so sudden. He was doing a story about the Peace Union for us. And then he wasn't here any more. I thought perhaps he'd done something wrong. I don't even know where he has gone.' She paused, and gave him a smile. 'Could you find out for me, perhaps? Where he is, what he is doing? Would that be possible?'

He sniffed. 'I have to tell you something.'

'What?'

The door pinged again. People came in and out. 'I have spoken with David Trofimovich.' Gorshkov tried to look modestly triumphant. It was not a success.

'You've *spoken* with him?'

'Why not? We have the telephones in the Soviet Union, don't we? It is not only the capitalist world that has these things. Soviet science—'

'Of course you do . . . My brother is a great admirer of Soviet science.' A trick of dissimulation. The apparent indifference, the carelessness. 'So tell me, how is Absolon?'

'He is well. What do you say? In good spirits. He sends his regards.'

'And *where* is he?'

He raised his coffee cup to his mouth, as if it might hide him from lip-readers. 'In Moscow.'

'In Moscow. Where in Moscow?'

'He has been posted to his headquarters. Of course I cannot say where that is. These matters are state secrets.'

She sipped coffee. He was not telling the truth, she could see that. The pat answers, as though rehearsed. The expression that was unconvincing and unconvinced. 'Is that all you have to tell me?'

He looked relieved, as though she was conforming to the conversation he had been told to expect. 'There is someone from Comrade Absolon's department who wishes to speak with you.'

'Where?'

'At the embassy.'

'I presumed I was no longer welcome.'

'You will be invited to the embassy. There you will meet this man.'

'What's his name?'

'His name? I cannot tell you his name. Just that you will meet. I am not authorised to say any more.' He got up from his chair and counted out the exact change for two coffees.

She reached out and took hold of his wrist. 'Wait.'

He froze.

'Tell them that I want to hear directly from Absolon. A letter, a proper letter, so that I know he is all right.'

He looked down at her hand in horror, as though by grabbing him she had transgressed all boundaries of decency. 'Please—'

'And a return address where I can write to him. Tell them that. I won't do anything without that. You tell them that.'

'I am not authorised to say any more,' he repeated. 'Now please, I must go.'

She knew the date, clearly enough. A reception in honour of the British-Soviet Friendship Society to which Mr Roper had already been invited as representative of the Peace Union. Now, unexpectedly, a second invitation arrived, for Mrs Marian Walcott, MBE.

Roper evinced surprise. He called her into his office like a head teacher upbraiding a promising but insolent pupil. 'After your last performance I imagined you were *persona non grata*,' he said.

She delivered a thin smile. 'I expect they value my independence of mind.'

'Are you being sarcastic?'

'I'm being ironical.'

'Well, I hope we don't have any repetition of last time. That might finish us with our Soviet friends.' Then he relented a moment and his tone became almost sympathetic. 'You haven't heard anything about this man?'

Absolon, she thought. Not *this man*. David Absolon. Where might he be? What might be happening to him? She knew, that was the thing. Deep in her own memory, from her own experience, she knew every horror that might befall him. 'Nothing,' she told Roper. 'Nothing whatever.'

The postcard came a few days later. It arrived by way of her father. She was in the habit of phoning home once a week and he mentioned it almost in passing. Apparently it had been there among all his other post in college, in an envelope addressed to Professor Frank Sutro, which seemed strange. 'I'm not a professor,' he pointed out to her indignantly, as though it were a great solecism. 'I'm just a boring old doctor.'

'What did it *say*, Papa? Who was it *from*?' But he'd torn the envelope up and thrown it away, keeping only the card which he handed to her when she next went down to Oxford. The picture showed an innocuous view of a lake with a sailing boat in the foreground and wooded hills behind. *Grüße vom Bodensee, Greetings from Lake Constance* was inscribed across the bottom of the image. The message on the back was cursory. *Happy days*, it said in handwriting she didn't recognise. It was signed '*A*'. There was her own name in the addressee section and a poste restante address in the name of Anton Albrecht at the post office in the German city of Konstanz. 'I don't know anyone by that name,' she said. But she wondered, of course she wondered. And when she was back in London she wrote a letter to Herr Albrecht asking if, perhaps, there had been some mistake.

EMBASSY

The Soviet embassy occupied a number of neo-classical villas in Kensington Palace Gardens. Carved out of white stucco and couched amid trees and bushes, they looked like the homes of Tsarist plutocrats. Inside, past the uniformly unsmiling guards, there were chandeliers and velvet drapes and rococo furniture and the faint sense that the servants had taken over the mansion and hadn't quite got things right. Service was offered with a scowl. Drink and food were too much or too little. Conversation between embassy officials and the guests was stilted and awkward, the stuff of amateur dramatics. The guests included a posse of Labour MPs and carefully selected representatives of the arts and sciences, people who might, in theory at least, be sympathetic to the Soviet cause. They applauded politely when the ambassador delivered a glum panegyric to the British-Soviet Friendship Society. It was then that Gorshkov emerged from the throng to take Marian's arm and lead her away from Mr Roper and his gaggle of fellow writers.

'Now you come with me,' he said. He drew a

curtain aside, opened a concealed door and quite suddenly they were in a corridor, with the noise of the reception shut away behind them as though the lid of a box had been closed. There was a moment of uncertainty, anxiety even. 'Where are you taking me?'

'You ask about Major Absolon.'

'You have some news?'

'I told you, someone who must speak with you.'

For a ridiculous moment she imagined that it might be Absolon himself, brought back from Moscow to reassure her. With Gorshkov still holding her elbow, they went down a corridor where windows overlooked the shadowy gardens at the back of the villa. There was a turn, a short flight of stairs, a second corridor. Memories of 84 Avenue Foch began to intrude, the movement from room to room, from floor to floor, the fear and the relief, her interrogator reassuring her in dulcet tones while the threat of the *baignoire* lay there before her. At last they stopped before an anonymous door. Gorshkov knocked, opened the door and ushered her into a large office.

A man looked up from his desk. He was silver-haired and blue-eyed, the kind of blue you see in the heart of a glacier. His skin seemed polished by winter days on the Russian steppe. Although he was wearing a grey suit, somehow it was easy to imagine him buttoned into a military uniform, his chest emblazoned with medals. On the wall above his head was a photograph, framed in black crêpe, of the late Joseph Stalin. To one side, in an alcove, was a bust of Lenin.

The man indicated the solitary chair in front of his desk. 'Mrs Walcott, please sit down.'

Marian composed herself as best she could, back straight, knees together, hands folded in her lap. Gorshkov had slipped quietly out of the room, closing the door behind him. She felt a small tremor of disquiet at his departure. 'What am I doing here?' she demanded. 'What is this all about?'

The man behind the desk looked at her through rimless glasses, as though she were a specimen brought to him from a distant and only half understood continent. He attempted a smile. 'May I start by thanking you for work you have done in name of world peace? Of course I do not talk about' – he gestured dismissively in the vague direction of the reception that was going on elsewhere in the building – 'all *this*. I talk of what you and your brother have done.'

'Are you in a position to talk on behalf of world peace? I don't even know who you are.'

'My name is of no matter. Call me Kuznetsov. Colonel Kuznetsov. Do you know meaning of kuznets? It means "smith" in your language. There are many, many Kuznets in Russia. As many as Smiths in England. So, although sadly I do not speak for the world, I can speak for much of Soviet Union. We are pleased with what you have done. We thank you. Perhaps you deserve medal.'

'I'm not interested in medals.'

He glanced down at a paper on his desk. 'Apparently not. I see your people only made you MBE. Member of Order of the British Empire. That is not worth very much, is it? I think we would give you a medal that is worth more, perhaps Order of Lenin. What do you think of that?'

'I don't think anything of it. I did what I did – what *we* did – because we believe that the secrets of nuclear weapons should not be the possession of one country. It's as simple as that.'

Kuznetsov nodded, tapping a pencil thoughtfully on his desk. 'But it seems that you allowed personal matters to get in the way.'

'I don't understand.'

'I am talking about Comrade Absolon.'

She shrugged. 'I want to know what has happened to him, that is all. I was working with him and suddenly he disappears. What am I to make of that?'

'That he was moved away.'

'Why? Where to? He seemed frightened the last time we met. I want assurance from him that he has come to no harm.'

'Why should he have come to harm? He is official of Soviet Union and so he is under orders. I cannot tell you where because that information is confidential, but I can assure you he has not come to harm.'

'I want to know that from him.'

Kuznetsov looked at her with those bleak blue eyes. 'Tell me about Comrade Absolon,' he said. 'Tell me about your relationship with him.'

A chill seemed to have descended, conjuring up the cold fog of espionage. She tried to peer into the murk, remembering Fawley's words: GRU and MGB – the Main Intelligence Directorate and the Ministry of State Security. *Like the Abwehr and SD. One watches the other and they both watch us.* Was this man from the rival organisation? Was she treading even now into the mire of an internecine war? 'Absolon was my contact. What more do you want to know?'

'How often did you and he meet?'

'Eight or nine times. I can't be sure. Once a month, roughly. He must have logged the meetings.' Kuznetsov was still watching her intently. She remembered the instructor in unarmed combat, the one who had taught them how to use the fighting knife. His eyes had been like that: a clear blue, like a doll's. 'What has happened to him?' she demanded. 'He was recalled suddenly. Something has happened to him, hasn't it?'

Kuznetsov ignored her. His face seemed curiously devoid of real expression, as though it had been carefully modelled to give a representation of a human face but without any kind of emotion, like an illustration for a medical textbook. 'When did you first meet him?'

'In 1946, at the Ravensbrück trial in Hamburg. Look, what has happened—'

'Please answer my questions, Mrs Walcott. Tell me about that first meeting.'

So she told him, trying all the time to think how the smallest thing, the least hint, might inculpate him or her. She told him about the trial and about her role as witness, and her encounter with Absolon in the bar of the hotel afterwards. 'I saw him later on at dinner, and that was all.'

'And this man Bright. He was intelligence agent?'

'He was in the Intelligence Corps, as far as I remember. That makes him a soldier, not an agent.'

'And you did not see Comrade Absolon again?'

'I think he was there the next day when I left the hotel but I didn't speak to him. Or maybe I said goodbye. I can't really remember. Then I ran into him in Paris a few years later—'

A frown. 'You *ran into* him?'

She gave what she hoped was a sympathetic smile. 'A figure of speech. I met him by pure chance in Paris, at the cultural department.'

'It was not planned, you mean?'

'No, it was not planned.'

'And what happened on this occasion, after this *collision*?'

A voice came out of the past to help her, the voice of an instructor at Beaulieu. 'Stick as close to the truth as you can,' it whispered. 'Lies are your most precious resource: use them sparingly.'

'We talked a bit and agreed to meet up the next day.'

'When?'

'In the evening. We had dinner together.'

'And then?'

'And then . . .' She frowned, as though trying to remember. 'We went to some kind of jazz club. The kind of thing Paris is famous for. The Left Bank, you know the kind of thing.'

'And afterwards?'

'Oh, goodness. Afterwards, I suppose I went back to my hotel. Look—' she glanced round, as if looking for escape of some kind, 'I really ought to be getting back to the reception. People will miss me . . .'

'I think it is quite all right. Your associate, Mr Roper, has been told that we are taking care of you.'

'And if I insist on going back?'

'Then you will not be able to help us . . . or Comrade Absolon.'

'So is he under some kind of investigation?'

Kuznetsov ignored her question. Another trick of interrogators: to be able to ignore what they please and pursue what they want. 'Can you tell me the purpose of this meeting that you had in Paris?'

'Purpose? There was no purpose. I told you, it was a chance thing. We were acquaintances. We got on together. Of course, he knew something about my war career from the trial in Hamburg. Perhaps that interested him.'

'And that is all? He was interested in your career in war?'

'Well, I must admit that afterwards, I did wonder . . .'

'What did you wonder, Mrs Walcott?'

'I wondered whether he might have been trying to recruit me.'

'And was he?'

'In Paris? Apparently not. We talked politics only in the most general terms. He knew my views, I knew his. Which were, I can assure you, very orthodox.'

'And then you met again in London.'

'Yes, we did.'

'Tell me about that.'

Kriegspiel, the war game, the blind chess that Clément and Ned used to play with her as adjudicator. But she was not adjudicator now; she was a player. She moved forward into the darkness, not knowing where Kuznetsov's pieces lay, not knowing which squares were empty and which occupied. She told him of the chance encounter at the art exhibition and then the subsequent meeting in his house. 'That was when I told him about my brother.'

'What about your brother?'

She hesitated. 'That he wished to meet up with someone from the Soviet scientific community for an exchange of information. That he was unhappy with the way that nuclear research was going in the West and he felt these matters were too dangerous to be the property of one nation or group of nations only. We'd been talking it over

451

for some time, my brother and I. We believe that with the hydrogen bomb the world is facing its greatest threat ever, far worse than anything that happened in the last war. It's obvious, really, isn't it? Hiroshima and Nagasaki multiplied a hundred times, right across the Soviet Union. We wanted to do something to stop that happening.'

Kuznetsov appeared unmoved. 'What next?'

'He – Absolon, I mean – arranged a meeting in Geneva between my brother and a Soviet scientist. I think the name was Chernikov. Is that right? Academician Chernikov?'

Kuznetsov said nothing.

'And then there were meetings in various places. In a pub somewhere, then in Kew Gardens. Gardens and parks are good places to meet, but I expect you know that. The usual business of running an agent. It must be on your files. There must be records somewhere in your registry.'

'Describe to me what happened at these meetings.'

'I'm sure Absolon kept a log—'

'Please do as I ask, Mrs Walcott.'

'I was just a courier between my brother and Absolon.'

'What exactly did you give him?'

'Film cassettes. Small ones, from a Minox camera. I had no idea what the film contained. And he gave me a new one in return. Sometimes there was nothing, of course. Look, Absolon can tell you all this. Have you asked him?'

He ignored her question. 'What else did he give you?'

She hesitated. What else did he know? What had Absolon told them? She tried to feel the possibilities. 'Nothing else.'

'Nothing?'

She filled the silence. 'We talked. General things often. We enjoyed each other's company.'

'Did you make sex with him?'

Something sour rose in her throat. Kuznetsov's eyes seemed to see through her dress to the bare flesh beneath. She felt violated, as naked as she had been before her interrogators in Paris, stripped of clothes, stripped of protection, stripped of artifice. She swallowed and breathed in deeply, trying to keep the emotions at bay, trying to let the vomit subside. What more did he know? What had Absolon told them? That was the danger of interrogation – you never knew what other people had already said. 'We were lovers,' she admitted. 'Is that a crime?'

'Perhaps in this case it is. Comrade Absolon is charged with taking part in a sexual relationship with an agent of the British Security Service—'

'I'm *not* a member of the Security Service.'

'And in the course of this relationship, betraying secrets to the enemies of the Soviet people.'

'That's not true. I'm not a member of the Security Service and he gave me nothing.'

One of the more abstruse effects of adrenalin is to slow the passage of time down but not the workings of the mind. Her mind worked quickly now, skating over the facts and the suppositions, the little hints, the suggestions and suspicions. What did Kuznetsov know, and what did he not know? *Kriegspiel* again. You grope in the dark. You make your moves not knowing whether they'll work or not. You probe and you try to sense – something insect-like, something bat-like about it – where your opponents pieces lie. Where is the fragile barricade of prawns, where the rooks, where the knights and bishops, and where, above all, is the queen?

Absolon's voice still whispered in the ear of her memory. 'Maybe we haven't been as clever as we thought. Unless . . .'

What was the 'unless'?

And then she understood: unless there were a leak from within Fawley's own organisation. Unless there were a Soviet agent deep inside the Security Service, burrowing away within the bowels of the organisation like a parasitic worm, feeding on snippets of information vital to the Russians, betraying any agent who might be inclined to betray.

She drew a careful breath and moved forward into the darkness, not knowing what lay ahead, whether any step might incriminate him or her. 'I'm not a member of the Security Service,' she repeated. 'Someone approached me, that's all. Someone I knew during the war. Do you know what I did in the war, Mr Kuznetsov?' She looked at him, insisting on an answer.

Eventually he said, 'I believe you were an agent of British Special Operations.'

'Exactly. We fought on the same side, didn't we, you and I, the British and the Russians? The Great Patriotic War, isn't that what you call it? So, the person who recruited me then got in touch a little while ago. I presume you all know about each other—'

'What is this man's name?'

'Fawley,' she said. 'That's the name I have always known him by. He suggested that Absolon might be willing to give information. He had no idea about what was happening with my brother but he knew that I was friendly with David Absolon—'

'How did he know this?'

'I presume we were seen together. Anyway, he asked me to make an approach to Absolon and I saw that it might be a good idea if Absolon gave me small stuff to pass back to Fawley. Chicken feed, isn't that what you call it? I thought that would keep the Security Service off our backs.' She smiled, perhaps with relief at having made this move without any obvious disaster. 'Keep us safe from the British intelligence,' she explained, thinking perhaps that 'off our backs' might be too much for the man's English. 'Why don't you ask Absolon? Ask him. I'm sure he'll confirm what I say. We used my contact with Fawley to protect what we were really doing, which was to pass information from my brother to you. Ask him.'

There was something in his expression, a small

455

fracture in the mask, a shift of uncertainty in the pale blue eyes. She insisted, sensing the weakness but not yet fully understanding it, trying to lever it open, trying for all she was worth to open up the hairline crack into a fissure. 'Why don't you ask Absolon yourself? He betrayed no secrets. I promise you that. I gave him valuable information, and in return he passed me small stuff, intelligence of no real value. As simple as that. He'll confirm everything I say. Ask him.'

And then she understood. She sat there before the man called Kuznetsov and everything resolved itself into one simple fact – *he couldn't ask Absolon*. Absolon was not in their hands. They'd lost him. He was not in Moscow, not in some dreadful KGB gaol below the Lubyanka, not in a camp somewhere in Siberia. He'd escaped them and gone to ground, like a fox, a bright fox who leaves nothing to chance, not even breathing a word about it to her in the darkness of the cinema, not daring to drop so much as a hint.

Her mind scurried over the possibilities. She wondered what resources he had. Money, you always needed money. Probably illicit funds quietly stashed away in some Swiss bank account during years of working in Europe, money stashed away for just such an eventuality as this. She knew how loose intelligence agencies could be with funds. She herself had carried hundreds of thousands of francs in a money belt, all of it unaccounted and untraceable. And he'd need a false identity, of course, at least one. Passport, visas, residence permits, bank details, all that kind of thing. One of them in the name of Herr Anton Albrecht.

The postcard was the one chink of light in the opaque curtain he had drawn around himself.

Kuznetsov asked, 'How do you know this? That it was information of no importance?'

'Because that is what Absolon told me.'

'So you only have his word for it?'

'Of course. I was just a courier. A postman doesn't read the mail, does he? And anyway, if I had done so, I wouldn't have known its value. I'm not an intelligence analyst. But I'm sure Absolon will confirm everything I have said. I would hate to think he is in any kind of trouble.'

She glanced at her wristwatch. A present from Alan, a lovely, elegant little golden thing with 21 JEWELS SWISS MADE in minute letters that you could barely read without a magnifying glass. 'Look, Mr Kuznetsov, I really must be getting home. It's almost ten o'clock and you really cannot keep me here any longer.' She smiled. 'I have been very sympathetic to your cause, I have helped pass invaluable information to one of your agents, but that doesn't give you the right to detain me against my will. I'll need a taxi, if you don't mind, unless you have some other means of spiriting people out of the embassy. I'm sure all comings and goings are carefully monitored by the British Security Service.'

He attempted one little riposte – 'You forget,

Mrs Walcott, that here you are on Soviet soil; here it is we who decide what happens' – but she could tell he had no confidence in it.

'Mr Kuznetsov, I hardly think you'll risk a diplomatic incident for someone like me.'

FAWLEY

An embassy car delivered her home. There was no subterfuge and no pretence. She had been a guest at an official reception and she had felt unwell. Perhaps a little too much fine Russian champagne. The embassy medical staff had dealt with her in the smooth and efficient manner of Soviet medicine – a rest, some aspirin, nothing more was needed – and here she was, being taken back home in complete security. There was even a nurse to accompany her, just in case.

She let herself into the flat. Alan was already fast asleep. She undressed and washed and slipped into bed beside him, drawing comfort from his presence. She felt an inordinate happiness that she wanted to share with him, but couldn't. He mumbled and turned and accepted a kiss without waking; but she wanted more than that. She wanted to tell him that Absolon was free. An absurd joy.

The next day she arranged a meeting with Fawley. The usual way, the usual phone call, the usual taxi taking her to a safe house somewhere in the inner suburbs, Chalk Farm on this occasion. And he was his usual, thoughtful, attentive self, sitting in the bare sitting room with a cup of tea and a plate of digestive biscuits, like a maiden aunt receiving a visit from a favoured niece.

'He called himself Kuznetsov,' she said.

Fawley made a wry face. 'Half of Russia is called—'

'Yes, I know. It means Smith. He told me.'

'But I can get you to look at some photos and identify him, see who he really is. It sounds as though it may even have been the station chief, the *rezident*. In which case you were mightily honoured.'

'That's not really the point. The point is, he matters. He's important, I could tell that. And he said something that worried me.'

'Worried you?'

She'd considered her options, shuffled them in her mind, dealt them like cards, read them and then dealt them again. How much to tell? What exactly to tell? How to tiptoe through the minefield of truth, half-truth and lies? 'Kuznetsov made it clear that he knew Absolon had been passing us information.'

Fawley seemed to think for a moment. 'How can that be a surprise? They are holding him, aren't they? He has probably confessed. I regret to tell you that their methods are little different from the Nazis, except that nowadays it is the fashion to use drugs as well as beatings. As you may imagine, it is an exceptional man who stands out against that.'

'But they're not. Holding him, I mean. They've lost him. He's given them the slip, gone to ground.'

Was there surprise in Fawley's expression? Perhaps just the faint curiosity of a man who has seen and heard everything. 'They've *lost* him? How do you know this?'

'I sensed it from the way Kuznetsov spoke. And it was there in his eyes. Shifty.'

A small, sceptical smile. 'Shifty is stock-in-trade, my dear.'

'And Absolon has contacted me.'

The smile faded. There was a silence in the dull room. Traffic noise could be heard from outside, vehicles on the main road, the bell of an ambulance or a police car going to some emergency. But the real emergency was here, in the narrow confines of this safe house with its drab brown furniture and the reproduction of *The Hay Wain* on the wall. 'He has contacted you?'

She considered her knowledge, parsing it, trying to assess its importance. 'I received a postcard. I'm sure it's from him, although he's using an assumed name. Posted it from somewhere in Germany. And I think he'll get in touch again.'

'Are you certain it's from him?'

She shrugged. 'As sure as I can be.'

'What did it say?'

'Nothing much. "Happy days", that's all. It was signed "A".'

461

'That could be anything. How do you know it's from him? Did you recognise the handwriting?'

'I've never seen his handwriting. But I just know, that's all.'

He repeated her words, like a barrister repeating a witness statement to demonstrate the paucity of it: 'You just know. But how do you even know that "A" is a he? It could be Anne, couldn't it? Or Annabel. Or Araminta.'

'Anton, the name was Anton.'

'Someone who remembers you from school in Geneva. Someone you knew in France during the war. Any number of possibilities.'

'Who else would send a card like that?'

'Like what?'

'Enclosed in an envelope. He's trying to establish a line of communication, don't you see?' She leaned towards him eagerly. 'The point is, if he has gone to ground somewhere in Europe, if they haven't got hold of him, then how do they know about the information he gave me to pass on to you?'

Fawley's fingers, slightly feminine, soft and white, were now tip to tip, bouncing gently. 'What are you suggesting?'

'Who *knew*?' she asked. 'That's the question, isn't it? Who knew that David Absolon was an informant? Me, you . . . Anyone else? You tell me.'

A little stiffening of shock. Perhaps outrage. Was heresy being implied? Was sacrilege being committed? 'My dear Marian—'

'It's not impossible, is it? Look at those cases

that have hit the headlines. Look at Burgess and Maclean. Who tipped them off? The newspapers are saying all sorts of things about a Third Man.'

Fawley's smile was forced now, a little rictus of discomfiture. 'Idle speculation, my dear. I can hardly imagine that any one of my colleagues would be the source of leaked information, if that is what you are implying. And I can assure you that I—'

'That's not what I mean.'

'Well, my dear, I wonder what you *do* mean?' *My dear.* He was angry, petulant, like a schoolmaster let down by a favourite pupil. 'I'm sure there are other possibilities, within the GRU, for example.'

'But why would he have told anyone on his own side? He would have been betraying himself.'

'Perhaps everything that he gave us was disinformation. The opposition enjoy that kind of thing, playing games, trying to toy with us. Maybe they had it all planned out. Maybe your friend Absolon was not quite the man you took him for. Look, my dear, I think you had better let me have the postcard in question. We can submit it to scientific examination, establish its true provenance. Where did you say it was posted?'

Something in the narrow interstices of the conversation disturbed her, some fractional imperfection in the bland smoothness of his words. 'I didn't. It was posted in southern Germany. Munich. But I don't have it any longer. I destroyed it.'

'What a pity. And the return address?'

'Poste restante at the central post office.'

'And how did it reach you?'

She lied. It was easy to lie. You keep something in reserve, always something in reserve. It's like having money in the bank – you never know when you might need it. 'At the Peace Union. The only address he knew, I suppose.'

'Did you reply?'

'I sent a note suggesting he might be mistaken.'

A comforting smile. 'Let's see if he sends another missive, shall we? In our world it's always better to wait and see. *Festina lente*, that's the watchword. If it turns out you are right, then we'll see what to do. Maybe we can bring him in from the cold, offer him warmth, safety, a new life, a new identity in Canada or wherever he pleases. In return for what he knows.'

Festina lente. He sounded like her father.

In the taxi she lit a cigarette and drew in calming smoke. She was no stranger to fear. She knew the whole spectrum, from anxiety to terror. Fear had been her bedfellow for years, fear and memory of fear, the one playing on the other, impregnating it and engendering panic. 'Fear is useful,' the psychiatrist had explained. 'Fear keeps us out of harm's way. But panic is useless.'

She wouldn't panic. She'd allow fear to determine what she would do but she'd not let panic in, not panic with its surge of irrationality, its upswell of unreason. In that direction chaos lay. She smoked and watch the houses pass by outside the cab. London enveloped her, a place of fog and rain where the outlines were blurred and the shapes of buildings blended back into the cloud. Bombsites were like the ruins of some ancient civilisation, conjuring up mythic memories in the minds of the survivors squatting in the ruins. Lights glistened in the tarmac even at noon, even as she made her way to Ned's flat or to the Underground or to the cinema where she watched films alone during her lunch break and wondered about Absolon. She wouldn't panic but she began to understand what she might do.

MUSEUM

Ordinary days, waiting. Humdrum work at the office, evenings spent at home watching, for the first time, television. One evening there was a dinner party for some of Alan's business colleagues during which she played the dutiful wife; on another, an evening lecture to attend, and a piano recital at the Wigmore Hall. And during these days, she began to notice them. They weren't there all the time, just at crucial moments of her day. Men in fawn raincoats and trilby hats, men in dark coats and bowler hats, men in overalls carrying bags of plumbing gear, men in vans and cars parked on the opposite side of the street, always men. Watching. They knew where she worked and they knew where she lived. They were watching her.

She told no one. Fear crept up on her and condemned her to silence. But then, she told herself, this wasn't Paris during the occupation, was it? It was London in peacetime. So when she saw them watching, from across the street from the Peace Union offices, in a black Ford V8 car she crossed the road and tapped on the window.

The man inside looked startled but wound the window down. He had a sallow, impoverished face.

'I'm sorry to disturb you, but you don't happen to have a light, do you?'

'What?'

She held up a cigarette. 'A light.'

'Oh, yeah. A light.' The tones of the East End. A quick fumble in his pocket and there was a lighter, the little flame flickering in the breeze. She leaned forward into the warm fug within the car and drew the flame into her cigarette. 'Thank you.' She blew smoke away, her hand on the window frame. 'You waiting for someone?'

'Yeah, that's right. Waiting.'

'Because this is a no parking zone.'

He looked round anxiously. 'Right. Thanks for the information.'

In a few minutes he drove away. It was a triumph of a kind. Small, but distinct. They wouldn't be able to use him again. Or the car.

Back in the Peace Union all was as normal: Mr Roper in his office, arguing on the phone with someone, Peter working downstairs in the library, Miss Miller going through the mail. 'They're doing it again, damn them,' Miss Miller said, more to herself than to anyone else. It was the 'damn them' that awoke Marian's interest. 'Damn' explored the limits of Miss Miller's expletives. Sometimes she said 'blast'. 'Damn' was extreme.

'Doing what?' Marian asked.

'Opening our mail.'

'Who's opening our mail?'

Miss Miller gave her pinched lip expression. She was a curious mixture of arch conservative and determined socialist. She adored the new Queen and yet applauded the more extreme pronouncements of Aneurin Bevan; she loved Mr Churchill the war leader and hated Sir Winston the newly-knighted peacetime prime minister. And now she said, as though uttering obscenities, 'The Special Branch. Or MI5. Or someone.'

'How on earth do you know?'

'Oh, you can tell easily enough. They think they're so clever but when they steam the flap open the paper becomes crinkly and it doesn't always fit properly when they stick it back.' She waved an envelope, like Chamberlain waving 'peace in our time'. 'You notice it if there are lots of them.'

'They've done this before?'

'Sometimes. I always report it to Mr Roper but he just shrugs his shoulders. I think we should make a formal complaint.' She indicated the neatly piled envelopes on her desk. 'They've only bothered with the foreign ones this time.'

Marian went over to have a look. Three letters, two from France and one from Germany. She felt uneasy, like the onset of travel sickness. 'When did this start?'

'Only noticed it a few days ago. I daresay they have the same problem at Labour Party headquarters. They're a law unto themselves, these security people.'

Kriegspiel, Marian thought. She was playing it now, with Fawley; and he didn't know she had just got him in check. During her lunch break she went round the corner to the nearest phone booth and rang her parents. Her father answered, his familiar voice trembling slightly on the line.

'Just a small thing, Papa,' she said. 'You remember that postcard, don't you? If anything else comes for me like that, don't tell me about it over the phone, all right?'

His voice was puzzled. 'Why on earth not, Squirrel?'

'It doesn't matter why not, Papa. Just don't. Just say this: Aunt Philippa called the other day.'

'What on earth are you talking about? And what if Aunt Philippa does call?'

'You know perfectly well she won't. And if she did, I wouldn't want to know.'

She replaced the receiver on its cradle and pressed the B button as one did, just to see if the machine would give any of your money back. Outside, across the street, one of the watchers pretended not to notice her.

Nothing to do but wait. You must be prepared to wait, one of the Beaulieu instructors had said. Just wait. Sometimes she went to the British Museum, for distraction. At other times she'd take a bus down to the National Gallery, or go just round the corner to Sir John Soane's Museum. There was any number of places she could choose but

469

the British Museum was a favourite. It was a mere stroll through Bloomsbury, and it was one day like any other when she went up the steps and through the great classical portico into the marble halls. There was the usual shifting crowd of visitors: tourists, of course, and secretaries on their lunch breaks and disconsolate school groups. She walked more or less aimlessly, past sculptures and carvings, trinkets in gold, pots and pans, the treasures and the detritus of civilisations long gone and found herself quite by chance in one of the rooms on the first floor. A small crowd of children had gathered around the glass box where Ginger crouched among his dusty grave goods. His skin was burnished to autumnal russet, a thin straggle of hair sprouted from his cranium like rusty wires.

'Cor,' people murmured, clustering round like passers-by at the scene of a traffic accident. 'Blimey.'

For a moment, remembering the bodies she had seen in the camp, she felt the rising tide of panic that used to beset her. Here was someone, baked by the crematorium of the Egyptian desert sands more than five thousand years ago and now held up for general curiosity. Would they do this with the victims of the camps, turn them into exhibits in some unimaginable museum of the future?

'Is he real, miss?' a child's voice asked.

'Of course he's real. Everything in the British Museum is real.'

'So what happened to him? Did someone kill him?'

'I expect he died of natural causes.'

They seemed disappointed by that. Eventually, reluctantly, the children moved on to find another mummy, leaving just Marian and one other visitor looking down on the desiccated form of *Gebelein man, predynastic period, c. 3500 BC.*

The other visitor looked round at her, and, with a shared start of surprise, they recognised each other. He was that bit older, of course. There might even have been a brushstroke of grey over his temples. But it was Tony Bright just the same.

There was a stumbled moment of exclamation – 'Good Lord!' 'What on earth are you doing here?' – the two of them talking over each other and Marian feeling a little tremor of mingled fear and excitement, like an earthquake far away just making the cups rattle and the windows shake. 'How extraordinary, bumping into each other like this,' she said. 'Aren't you supposed to be in Belgium, married to, what was her name? Anne-Griet, wasn't it?' And then, when she saw his expression, 'Oh, God, have I been tactless?'

He laughed. That easy laugh she remembered, when there seemed so little to laugh at. 'Not really. It never really happened.'

'God, I hope that wasn't my fault.'

He grinned. 'Not really, but I have to say you did awaken me to other possibilities. No, after Hamburg I got back to Belgium and discovered her in the arms of someone else. Figuratively, I hasten to add.'

'How unfortunate. And now what are you doing?'

He waved a careless hand, as though to show how unimportant such things were. 'Lecturing here at UCL. Trying to bolster the German department. It's not the most fashionable subject at the moment, although things are getting better.'

'Married?'

'No, not married.'

He paused as more tourists approached. 'Perhaps we've had enough of Ginger,' he suggested. 'Let's see about the box of bones over here.'

Together they moved across the room and looked into the collection of bones that might have been excavated from a disused cemetery only a few months ago but were, so the label said, from Tarkhan, Egypt, c. 3000 BC. 'Not very encouraging, is it?' Bright said. 'Look, why don't we go and have a bite to eat or something? Or are you pushed for time?'

'No, that'd be lovely.'

So he took her arm and guided her towards the exit, talking all the time in that way she remembered from Hamburg. A confusing few days that had been, didn't she agree? What with dealing with the Russians and then meeting her. He didn't know whether he was coming or going. 'Sorry, unfortunate turn of phrase. But it was a huge conflict of emotions, I can tell you.'

'And for me.'

'I'm sure it was. And now?'

'Things are better, much better.'

In the pub across the road from the museum they found a secluded corner table where, over a reheated pie and a glass of shandy, she told him about Absolon. Just the meeting in Paris and then his reappearance in London. 'We've seen a bit of one another,' she said.

He laughed. 'Lucky fellow. Hamburg didn't mean nothing to me, you know. It wasn't just one of those wartime flings. In fact, it was lovely. I think of it often.'

'Do you?' She was embarrassed about his thinking of it being lovely. Loveliness was not a word she would have used. She glanced at her watch. 'Oh, goodness, it's getting late. I really must go—'

He put out a hand to stop her. 'Must you? It seems so short. And it's Friday. Almost the weekend.'

She smiled, wanting to laugh but not daring to. There was that same attraction, still there after so many years. 'I'd have to phone work.'

'Why don't you? What could we do? Go for a walk in the park. Something . . .'

There was a public call box in the corridor outside the toilets. 'Something's come up,' she told Miss Miller. 'I'm afraid I won't be able to come in this afternoon. I'll make it up with overtime.' She came back to their table feeling light-headed and happy. 'There,' she said, 'I've done it. As free as a bird.'

Bright had bought her another drink, a gin and tonic this time. 'To us,' he said, raising his own

473

glass. 'We could always go back to my flat. Not far from here.'

She sipped the gin and watched him. 'What are you suggesting?' But she knew exactly what he was suggesting and the shock was that the idea did not shock her. She remembered him well, the smooth benison of his presence inside her.

'It's astonishing, isn't it?' he said. 'Here we are, together again. Out of the blue.'

'Yes, here we are.' She looked round to see exactly where. Her vision seemed to lag behind the movement, as though the pub, with its wooden panelling, its mirrors and its gleaming bottles were only obeying the laws of physics with reluctance. 'How strange it is. As though it was meant to be. As though it's fate. What do you think?' She was feeling peculiar, as if she had already drunk too much. Her words echoed inside her head. Tony was looking at her with concern.

'Are you feeling all right?'

'I'm just tired. It's been a difficult time recently.' This time the pub moved of its own accord without her doing anything to help it along. She stood up, putting out her hand to steady herself. 'I think I need the bathroom.'

Tony Bright was standing as well, concern pasted across his face. 'The lady's not well,' he said to the barman. 'A bit of fresh air, perhaps.'

He grasped her round the waist, solicitously, like a husband or a boyfriend. He had been her boyfriend, hadn't he? For eight hours. Her paramour. The door swung open and they were outside on the pavement without her knowing exactly how they'd got there. The bulk of the museum across the road was possessed of its own animated life, moving this way and that like a great beast breathing. Tony's arm was round her and his face was close to hers. 'You'll be all right,' he said. 'I'll get you home and you'll be all right.' Almost magically there was a cab there at the kerbside, the door open onto a dark and welcoming cave with the smell of cigarettes and old leather inside just like the car that she remembered when she didn't want to remember, the one with the two men crowded in on either side of her, their hands gripping her, their breath on her face. Somewhere far away a door slammed and the world began to move and Tony Bright was reassuring her – 'you'll be all right,' he was saying – and his hands were on her thigh, pulling up her skirt. She saw the top of her stocking and the whiteness of her bare flesh and wondered what he was going to do. She opened her legs, wanting to feel his touch. And then there was a needle, she could see that. A needle and a syringe. 'You just need to relax,' he whispered.

Nothing. Then dreams – the falling dream, the flying dream, dreams peopled by those she knew and by strangers. She heard herself speaking as though far away while their voices were close to – Véronique's, Benoît's, Clément's. There was a taste, a smell, the flavour of garlic. Alan was there as well, wreathed in disapproval, as though the smell offended him. But she didn't care what she did or what she said. He could watch if he wanted to, or not. It didn't matter. Véronique stroked her body, from top to toe, every part of it, and then others did the same, and then no one at all and she was just there by herself with only strangers talking at her. And she was talking back at them, telling them things they didn't want to hear, until the others came back, Benoît and Clément and even the young boy called Sam who was so clumsy and so devoted, spying on her all the time, watching whatever she did. And Tony Bright with his hand between her legs. But never Absolon. Where is Absolon? Her dream was without Absolon and she heard herself asking them, shouting at them – WHERE THE HELL IS ABSOLON? – and getting no answer.

Sometimes the various dreams coalesced into a single thing, a gathering of doctors muttering at her side. One of the doctors was Tony Bright, she knew that. White-gowned and rubber-gloved, they inserted tubes into her body. Perhaps they fed her through tubes. Perhaps they emptied her body and her mind through tubes. Tubes and needles. And all the while they asked her questions that she had no answers to, the same questions she asked them which all come down to a single question: *where is Absolon?* And she didn't know what to answer them because she didn't know, she just didn't know.

476

When the doctors went away others crowded in. Her parents looking concerned, her mother stroking her brow. Ned was there laughing at her, and Fawley playing *Kriegspiel*, his brows knitted with concentration, his hand reaching out to move one of his pieces, and the piece he picked up was her. He held her carefully, between thumb and forefinger, her own naked self, wriggling like a worm between his fingers.

Where is Absolon?

Time passed. How much, she couldn't say. Time is a relative thing. Ned taught her that. It may be stretched and squashed like chewing gum, like space itself, like truth and lies, like fear. Fear spread out thin like the grey sand between the huts and the ranks of ragged women stretching out across the Appellplatz, or fear compressed into a moment of existence like the moment when the woman called Binz stamped on Véronique's head, or that moment in the impasse, with two men standing there before her and the weapon in her hand. Shots rang out in her mind, echoing from the walls. For a moment one of them looked up at her, before she shot him once more, a single shot straight into his eye.

How much fear can you compress into one moment?

Then the fear had gone and she was turning cartwheels and laughing and people were telling her how amazing she was, until she was poised like a gymnast on the lip of the cliff preparing to jump, and when she jumped the world spun round her, turning over and over while the roar of engines sounded in her ears and she drifted down to the rocks below and hit grass with a thump and stood, wondering where she was, where everyone else was, what has happened or was still happening.

WHITE

She woke to whiteness. Slowly her world assembled itself out of bits and pieces: a bare light bulb floating beneath a white ceiling. Walls of the same, even whiteness. A window, bright with light, but opaque. The mattress beneath her. The thin pillow beneath her head.

A cell.

She remembered Fresnes Prison, the grey of concrete.

She tried to remember other things, her dreams, how she had happened here; but the memories, vivid memories, darted away out of her mind's grasp like coloured fish darting away from her hand at the very moment she tried to grasp them. Her head ached. Thirst, like fear, gripped her by the throat. Cautiously she sat up.

In the far corner of the room there was a basin. There were other things – a wooden wardrobe, a chest of drawers, a picture on the wall – but the basin was what she wanted. Carefully she moved her legs off the bed. She was wearing some kind of surgical gown, with short, loose sleeves. Looking down she noticed a sticking plaster across the

479

crook of her arm, where the flesh was sore and slightly bruised. Beyond the foot of the bed was an aluminium drip stand and a metal cabinet. These clues assembled themselves into something other than a prison cell.

A hospital room.

Very slowly she stood up. The world wobbled and swayed for a few seconds but once it had settled down she crossed the room to the basin with the utmost care, turned the cold tap and bent to drink. Water was what she needed. Other things could wait; for the moment her thirst was the only thing that mattered.

When she had finished drinking she called out.

'Hello?'

There was no response. Her voice sounded loud in the white room but there was no sound beyond the walls.

'Hello!'

Louder this time, but still no movement, no sound beyond the walls of her cell.

She went back to the bed and sat for a while, letting her mind settle, letting the fear subside. Was she ill? Where were the doctors or the nurses? She tried to gather her thoughts, scattered as they were to the distant corners of her mind. She remembered the museum. She remembered a pub. And meeting . . . Tony Bright. And then . . . not much else, except the dreams, confused dreams, people doing things, asking questions. Had she suffered some kind of crisis, a nervous breakdown, perhaps? Was that it? Another attack, like the one she had had before. A cerebral event, that was what the doctor had called it. A fugue.

'Hello?'

Nothing.

Cautiously, she went to the door, took hold of the handle and turned it. The door opened. She stepped back, fear pumping behind her breast-bone. Outside was nothing. Just an empty corridor. She left the door open, retreated to the bed and sat there, fearfully watching the gaping door and the segment of corridor – grey linoleum on the floor, white wall, a skirting board in which there was a single electric plug. No one came.

She scratched herself, scratched her head, picked at her nails.

No one came.

After a while she got up from the bed, went to the door and quietly closed it.

She felt safer like that, with the door closed. This room she knew, more or less. The world outside was a raging, fearful place. She went back to the basin where there was a mirror in which she could examine the pallid, dishevelled face of Marian Walcott, née Sutro. There were other possibilities – Anne-Marie Laroche, also Laurence Follette and Geneviève Marchal – but it was comforting to know that she was Marian Walcott, born Marian Sutro, married to Alan Walcott. As though she might have forgotten. She plucked at her hair to try and bring some kind of order to it. 'Marian,' she said out loud to herself. And then, to the rest of the room: 'Hello?' Louder this time but still no response.

Was there no one around, no nurse, no doctor, no attendant to come running?

Cautiously, she opened the wardrobe. Clothes, *her* clothes, hung there in the shadows like her own flayed skin; below them her shoes, with her handbag beside them; on the shelf above were her underclothes, carefully folded. She grabbed up the handbag, scrabbled through the chaos of things inside and picked out her watch. It signalled twenty-five past eleven. But which eleven?

Where was she?

When was she?

Again she opened the door but this time she summoned enough courage to peer out into the corridor. 'Hello? Is anyone there?'

Her words fell on deaf walls.

Her head still ached, her mouth was still dry and now she felt the familiar gnaw of hunger. She drank more water, then sat on the bed and went back to her memories, more calmly now, trying to unpick the clues from the dross. Tony Bright in a pub. Her parents looking at her with concern. Alan there as well at times. But also Clément and Benoît and Véronique, which was impossible. And then the whole jumble of words and images, faces she knew and faces she didn't, as in a dream. She peeled off the plaster in the crook of her elbow and examined the smudged bruise beneath the skin and the bleak red point at its centre. There was another puncture point on her left thigh, which brought back a memory of the inside of a taxi and Tony Bright pulling at her skirt and petticoat and telling her that it would be all right, just to relax, that she would be all right.

Tony Bright.

Quietly, not wanting to awaken the ghosts of the building, she took her clothes from the wardrobe and laid them out on the bed. Then she removed the surgical gown and dressed. Lipstick from her handbag brought some colour to her deadened lips and pallid cheeks. Powder from the silver compact Alan had given her made it something like the face of Marian Walcott that she wanted the world to see.

It was ten to twelve.

One of the instructors spoke to her from a decade ago. *Always try and improvise a weapon of some kind. A gun gives you advantage over someone with a knife; a knife gives you an advantage over someone with a stick; a stick gives you an advantage over someone unarmed.* She felt an absurd, childish snatch of excitement as she took the wooden coat hanger from the wardrobe, broke out the cross piece, pulled off the hook and created a weapon of a kind.

You get inside someone's guard and you can kill him with a stick, the voice said. *Even you lovely ladies.*

She slung her handbag over her shoulder and

opened the door. There was no one. Cautiously, she went down the corridor. At the far end was a window framing the brilliant green of trees. Stairs went down to a hallway. There was no stair carpet, just the bare, unpainted wood where a carpet might once have been. Holding the banister and treading softly she went down. No carpet downstairs, no furniture even, just the bleak look of emptiness. No pictures on the walls, bare light bulbs from the ceiling, a few panes of stained glass in the front door creating the only decoration – some kind of fleur-de-lis design throwing splashes of red and blue and green across the walls.

She peered into empty rooms and smelled dust and paint. A kitchen at the back gave some evidence of recent occupation, the vague hint of food on the air, like an imperfect memory. She went back to the hall and tried the front door. It was unlocked. She sat on the bottom stair while fear wormed its way into her bowels like a parasite. Here was safe. Crouching here inside, was safe. Outside the demons waited.

She breathed deeply as Dr Morgan had told her. But Dr Morgan had helped her against irrational fear – the fear she had now was entirely rational. Were they waiting for her outside?

At half past twelve she opened the front door and looked out onto a gravel driveway. It curved away from the house between ill-kempt, herbaceous borders towards a gate.

She was somewhere in the country, but *where* was she?

It was half past twelve, but *when* was she?

Softly she stepped out onto the gravel. It was impossible to keep her footsteps quiet but no one seemed to notice as she ran across to the bushes at the side of the drive. Behind her the house – a mock Tudor mansion – looked out on the world with blank eyes. Keeping to the shadows, she made her way down the drive towards the gate and the road beyond. There were fields and trees and bird-song all around her. There were cows in a meadow across the road and a distant view of a wooded hill and a church tower.

Turn left or right?

She dropped her improvised weapon and turned left. A ten-minute walk brought her to a village – a small collection of houses round a green; a pub called the Chancellor's Arms; a church dedicated to Saint Michael the Archangel. There was a village shop with a telephone kiosk beside it. Covenham, the name sign said.

She remembered her first outing in France immediately after the parachute drop, how she'd walked into the town of Lussac trying to look as though she belonged while feeling every eye on her. Now she felt the same, walking into an unknown village somewhere in England, attempting to look as if she knew where she was and what day it was.

A bell tinkled as she opened the door into the

485

village shop. A man came out from the back and looked suspiciously at her, sucking his teeth as though he had just put them in. 'Sorry to disturb you,' she said. 'I just wanted a paper.'

'Which one?'

'The *Guardian*?'

'We don't have the *Guardian*.'

'The *Daily Mail*, then.'

He handed over the paper. There was the date across the top. Monday. Three days. And there, at the bottom left of the front page, was her photograph. It was an old image, the one used for her identity card during the war. Her hair was permed and made a halo round her face, and the face had that look of unsmiling insouciance that she remembered. 'War Heroine Vanishes', was the headline.

She kept her head down as she searched for change in her purse. 'Can you tell me exactly where I am? I've been walking and I'm rather lost. Well, walking – my car had a puncture, actually.'

He sniffed and manoeuvred his teeth. Was he recognising her? 'Centre of the universe, we are. Covenham.'

'Yes, I saw the sign . . .'

No further information seemed to be forthcoming. She found the right coins and handed them over. 'I'll have to phone. Is the phone outside all right?'

'Right enough. Push button B when you're done. Phone works but something's broke inside and you'll get your money back even after the call.'

She paused at the door, trying to keep her face turned away from him. 'The house along the road. I passed it a while back. Mock Tudor.'

'The Vale? Been unoccupied for a year or more. There was a bit of coming and going there over the weekend. Estate agents, probably, with clients. Why d'you ask?'

'I just wondered. Thought it looked nice.'

She rang Alan's work number and waited while a secretary put her through. There was a silence on the other end of the line when she spoke her name. She had to imagine his expression and discovered that she couldn't. Was he angry, was he relieved, was he bewildered? She just couldn't tell. All he said, after a long pause, was, 'Jesus Christ, Marian, where the hell have you been?' And now she could sense fear even over the telephone line. He'd contacted her parents and Ned, of course. He'd been ringing round the hospitals and then he'd called the police out. It had even been in some of the papers.

'I've just seen,' she said.

'I didn't know if it was another turn, you know. That fugue business again. Or whether you might have walked out on me, or had an accident. I had no idea.' And she couldn't explain to him, not over the phone, perhaps not even face to face. A kidnap, some kind of clinic, visions, hallucinations, dreams, unconsciousness, and waking to an empty house. The whole story seemed ridiculous.

'Please come and get me, Alan,' was most of what she said.

'Where are you?'

'A place called Covenham.'

'Where's that?'

'I've no idea. I can't ask them what county I'm in, can I? I'll sound mad.'

But maybe she was mad. Maybe this whole affair was somehow her fault, a product of her own, deranged mind. A fugue state. Frantically she looked round the telephone booth. 'Wait. There's the directory. It's Surrey. I must be in Surrey.'

'I'll find it on the map,' he said. 'Give me the number of the telephone, stay right there and I'll ring you back.'

So she waited in the confines of the telephone booth, feeling vulnerable, feeling trapped, feeling the rough tides of panic ebbing and flowing inside her. Five minutes later the phone rang and it was Alan's voice telling her that if the traffic was all right, he'd be with her in an hour.

She replaced the receiver and thought for a moment. Then she picked up the phone once more, dialled directory enquiries and got the number for University College London.

The university switchboard knew no one by the name of Tony Bright, and certainly not in the German department. Nor Anthony Bright. There was an Andrew Briggs in Zoology, did she mean him?

She didn't.

She left the phone booth and took refuge in the saloon bar of the pub, beneath the lowering black beams and the horse brasses and the sulphurous smell of yesterday's fire. The place was almost deserted. A couple of farm labourers were in the public bar next door laughing over something or other but the saloon bar was empty. 'We can run you up some sandwiches,' the man behind the bar told her. 'Cheese and pickle all right?'

'Cheese and pickle would be lovely. And I'd like a beer, please.'

'Would that be bitter or mild?'

Mild, she decided. Mild sounded wonderful. Lenitive and soothing.

'You been in before?' he asked.

'No.'

''Cos I thought I recognised you.'

She smiled and averted her head and took her pint of mild over to a dark corner. After a while two young men came in. They glanced at her crouching in the corner but all they saw was a rather ill-kempt woman with evasive eyes. More interesting were sports cars and tractors and government subsidies.

Bright, she thought. Tony Bright, the lecturer who didn't exist.

Fifty minutes later she saw Alan's Riley draw up beside the phone booth and she went out to meet him.

HOME

'I just don't know,' she said shaking her head and fighting tears. 'I just don't know.' They were closed in the car, on the way back home. She felt violated, as though she had been tied down ankle and wrist and they had queued up to abuse her.

'How could you not know?' Alan protested. 'For God's sake, you've spent two days out of contact with anyone and you don't *know*?'

'I'm sorry, darling, I just don't.' She so rarely called him darling. Darling seemed like a confession of something she hadn't previously been able to own up to. Here she was, in the passenger's seat beside him, trying not to cry and calling him darling. Was it that which convinced him? He remembered her strange fugue, those few hours out of touch with the world. He wasn't a fool. He knew it was easy enough to throw accusations around, but he was intelligent enough to see there was once again something disturbing in her manner – a sense of distraction, a bewilderment about the missing days. 'My mind's a blank. Like that other time. You remember – the Old Oak Roadhouse, wasn't it?'

He glanced across at her, seeing her vulnerable and distraught as she had been when they'd first met. Someone struggling with demons. 'Another of your turns? We must get you to hospital.'

'I want to go home.'

'You're ill.'

'I feel all right. Tired but all right. A bit headachy.'

'And I've got to deal with the police and the newspapers—'

'Why were the newspapers involved?'

'Because I wanted to find you, for Christ's sake. How else was I going to get your face seen all over the country?'

They reached the flat in sullen silence. Were there people watching? As they turned in at the entrance and went down into the basement car park she tried to see. Was there anyone waiting for her return? She glimpsed the occasional pedestrian walking past, a customer coming out of the furniture shop across the road, a parked car with a man sitting in the driver's seat. It could be anything.

Down in the basement was only bare concrete and the smell of oil.

HOSPITAL

They admitted her to hospital for observation, that euphemism for medical ignorance. Once again, X-rays and electroencephalographs told them nothing. Physical examination told them nothing. A doctor made her touch her nose and walk in straight lines, one foot in front of the other, and stand with her arms out straight in front, and that told them nothing. The doctor talked with her in that oblique, evasive manner characteristic of his kind, asking her questions a young child might struggle with – what was the date? what was her date of birth? what was the Prime Minister's name? where, in all the possibilities in the world, did she live? – and receiving the correct answers with something like disappointment. There was an awkward moment as he examined her when he took hold of her left arm and held it straight to display the needle mark in the crook of the elbow. 'What's this?'

She shrugged. 'I gave blood last week.'

He palpated the puncture with its little halo of inflamed flesh. 'It looks recent.'

'I bruise easily.'

He considered the wound for a moment and then moved on to other things, tapping, peering, prodding, finding nothing wrong, nothing to account for the fact that of the last three days she remembered almost nothing. It seemed, he decided, she had suffered a fugue, something deep inside the brain where the subjective elements of experience and personality merge intangibly with the physical world of neurones and synapses. He leafed through her papers. 'I see that this has happened before,' he said, as though that explained everything.

The next day her parents came to visit, bringing flowers and biscuits and grapes. Arrangements had been made for Dr Morgan to see her once she had been discharged. That was the best thing, wasn't it? And she could stay with them when she came to see him.

Couched in the world of nursing and doctors, of people making decisions on her behalf, she felt lulled by a spurious security. But she knew she was not secure. Outside they were waiting for her to make a move.

CONVALESCENCE

I heard about Marian's disappearance through a phone call to my digs from my mother.

'Have you seen?' her voice asked, in that particular pitch which told me that even if I had, she was going to tell me all over again. But I hadn't, I really hadn't.

'Well, apparently she's vanished. It's all over the papers. The police are dealing with it but I think she may have run off. You saw her not long ago, didn't you? How did she seem?'

'It was a couple of months.' It was also a delicate matter and I was relieved that we were speaking on the phone so my mother couldn't see my blushes. 'She seemed fine. Fun, funny, you know how she can be.'

'She's deeply disturbed, Sam. She might seem fine but she's deeply disturbed.'

'How on earth do you know that?'

'I know, darling, I know. Look, I must dash now but I'll keep you posted.'

Two days later she phoned again to report that Marian had been found safe and sound. 'What on earth happened?' she wondered aloud.

I had no idea.

'I think I'll give her a ring and find out.'

'It's none of your business,' I told her.

'What use is a friend if not in a moment of crisis?' But moments of crisis had nothing to do with it – Mother was just desperate to get the inside story. A few days later another call brought the news that Marian had had some kind of nervous breakdown, wandered off on her own with no idea where she was or even who she was. 'You know, like Agatha Christie,' mother said.

'What the hell's Agatha Christie got to do with it?'

'It happened to her. I remember it in the papers, years ago before the war. My parents were agog but I thought it sounded quite good fun. Becoming someone else for a few days, taking a new name. Anyway, now it's happened to Marian, poor thing. And apparently it's not the first time.'

'How do you know all this? Have you been talking to Hercule Poirot?'

'Don't be facetious. I spoke to Marian herself yesterday. I must say she sounded pretty good, said it was all over and she was none the worse. Incidentally, she sent her love. She's very fond of you, you know that?'

'She's felt guilty ever since she broke my collarbone.'

'That's being unfair. Look, why not give her a ring? She'd love to hear from you.'

But I didn't, for a long time I didn't. I contemplated the idea but my courage failed. Had things been different, had there not been that single occasion when the barriers between us had come down, I might have dared. But I could only see her through the distorting prism of that night, and the subsequent bathos of the morning after. And courage failed me.

ACROSTIC

Marian Sutro travelling to Oxford for her weekly appointment with the psychiatrist. She watches for watchers and knows she is jumping at shadows, yet still she jumps. At her parents' house she indulges in those little internecine skirmishes that go on within families. They fuss over her as though she is an invalid; she protests that she is an adult and does not need their tiresome attentions. 'We're only trying to help, Squirrel,' her father says. But it was only when she asked him directly that he admitted he had received a second envelope, just like the first, addressed to her.

'You were going to keep it from me!'

'Of course I wasn't, Squirrel. I just think, perhaps—'

She demanded that he give it to her – 'It's outrageous to keep something from me like that. Anyone would have thought I was a stupid teenager' – and reluctantly he handed it over.

It was a full letter this time, sealed in an envelope with only her name on the outside – Mrs Marian Walcott – but this time her father had kept the outer envelope as well. It bore Swiss stamps and a Basel postmark.

'What is this all about, Squirrel? This sort of thing can't help your state of mind.'

'My state of mind is fine.'

'I just hope you're not carrying on behind Alan's back.'

'Don't be ridiculous.'

She retreated to her bedroom to open the letter in private.

Dear Mrs Walcott,

Don't you remember we met in Paris and then afterwards in London? Anyway, after a lot of travelling, here I am now, safe and sound in Switzerland. But I still travel quite often and maybe we could meet again in Lyon. Sometime this autumn? Or whenever is convenient for you. Lyon would appear the most convenient. Only I cannot always get there at short notice because of other commitments but given time I can certainly make arrangements. Naturally I will do whatever you think best – just let me know.

Your friend,
Anton Albrecht

Lyon. It wasn't the city; it was the hotel where she had stayed in Paris that time. Hôtel Lyonnais. She read the letter through once more looking for other clues and it took her some minutes before she noticed his joke. Foolish, of course, because it compromised the security of the letter and rendered it vulnerable to all but the most cursory examination. But a joke, nevertheless, amid the fear. She laughed out loud, a laughter fed by relief and a kind of happiness – the knowledge that so far he had beaten them. They were blundering around looking for him while he was safe somewhere in Switzerland, and making jokes, dangerous jokes in the circumstances, in his letter.

Carefully she burned the paper in the ashtray in her bedroom, pulverised the ashes and flushed them down the lavatory.

The next morning she took a taxi to the station, wondering if they had followed her all the way to Oxford, wondering if they were following her now. You didn't always know, that was the trouble. Sometimes they were easy enough to spot; sometimes they managed to blend in with the crowds, like insects disguised as leaves or twigs. Perhaps that man on board the train who looked like an undergraduate going up to London for a job interview, or the other man who looked faintly down at heel, a travelling salesman with a leather case full of samples. Or that woman, who might have been a don's wife, with her unkempt clothes and a distant look in her eye. The possibility of their using women came as something of a shock, as though until now she had only considered the possibility of half the public being a potential threat but now she had to accept that anyone, man or woman alike, might be against her.

She posted a reply to Anton Albrecht the same day. We can meet in Lyon, she wrote, if that's convenient. But I need some time to prepare. I'll be in touch.

At least a month, she thought, because she had much to do.

'Anthony James Bright,' Fawley said. She had arranged the meeting, not because she wanted to see him but because she needed information. Know your enemy. He'd had a doctor talk to her, a young man with lank hair and a prominent Adam's apple, who had questioned her about what she remembered of that dreadful weekend, and talked about chloral hydrate in her gin and then an intramuscular injection, possibly of sodium thiopental. Later, he had suggested, they must have set up an intravenous line in her arm and maybe continued with the pentothal or maybe amytal or scopolamine. It was difficult to say at this distance. There was a new one called phencyclidine. All designed to lower the inhibitions and make you gabble the truth. At least, that was the intention although there was a great deal of debate about whether the things actually worked or not.

'Bright was a captain in the Intelligence Corps,' Fawley was saying. 'That much is true. He served first with the 11th Armoured Division and was at the liberation of Bergen-Belsen.'

'He told me that. I remember him telling me that in Hamburg.'

'And then he was transferred to the Control Commission at Bad Oeynhausen. By all accounts he did sterling work. But in May 1947 he went absent without leave. We believe that at that point he actually defected to East Germany.'

'*Defected?*'

'However, there was no definite evidence of this until his name appeared in an intelligence report in 1951. That's all we have, but it does seem that by then he was working for an organisation called the Institute for Economic Research. That's the Institut für Wirtschaftswissenschaftliche Forschung if you'll forgive my somewhat tortuous pronunciation. The IWF is a front organisation for the East German espionage agency.'

'So he's an East German agent?'

'It does look that way. Obviously it was useful that he knew you.'

'It was Bright who introduced me to Absolon.'

'Really?' Fawley's eyebrows were raised. 'Was this in Paris? You never mentioned it.'

'In Hamburg. The first time I met Absolon was in Hamburg. It was Bright who introduced us. We had a few drinks together.'

'Why didn't you tell me this before?'

'Because you never asked.'

Fawley looked disappointed in her. 'You should

have told me, Marian. You should have told me everything. Anyway, there's our connection: you were set up with Absolon as long ago as 1946 and you never realised it.' He shrugged, as if it were of no consequence, whereas in fact it had all the significance of a punch in the face. With a deprecating grunt he turned to the other matter, the mock Tudor house called The Vale. 'Officers from Special Branch have been to have a look at the place. As you say, it's just an empty house, although one of the upstairs rooms had basic furnishings, a bed with a mattress and some kind of coverlet, a wardrobe.'

'That was the room they kept me in.'

'There was also a stand for an intravenous drip and a medical cabinet. I'm surprised they abandoned those. Perhaps they left in a hurry. There was also evidence of recent use of the kitchen. Otherwise, nothing. No fingerprints, even, except yours all over the bedroom. Apparently the estate agent had handed over the keys to a new tenant a few days ago and never saw them again. The police have a description of the couple but I doubt it'll be of much use. They'll have been back in Berlin long ago, along with our friend Bright.' Admiration and a hint of envy crept into his otherwise impassive exterior. 'It looks as though it was a very slick operation.'

'And what were they after?' she asked, but it was a stupid question to ask because the answer was obvious. They were after Absolon.

'The question is,' Fawley remarked thoughtfully, 'how much did you tell them? And that rather depends on how much you know.'

She looked at him, thinking of all those years, from that first meeting in his Oxford college when he had hijacked her mission to France, to this final encounter. Had she trusted him at the beginning? She couldn't quite recall the motives and convictions of the naive girl she'd been then, but surely trust had been part of her armoury; now it wasn't. 'I've told you: I've received a postcard, posted from Munich, from someone I don't know. That's all. There's nothing to tell.'

PLAN

The things they taught her. In Scotland they taught her how to blow up a railway line, how to kill a man with a submachine gun, with a pistol, with a knife, and finally, with her bare hands. In Beaulieu they taught her how to pick locks and break into a house so that she left no trace behind her. They taught her how to open a safe and how to pick a pocket. They taught her about cover stories and false documents. They taught her to see and be unseen. *Pour vivre heureux, vivons cachés.* To live happily, live hidden. That was the motto of one of the instructors. And another of them, a Londoner with a sly smile and a wandering hand, had told them a little trick that you could use, in Britain at least, if you needed to become someone else. 'Dunno how it would work in France,' he'd said. 'But you could always give it a go.'

So on her next visit to Oxford she spent the morning trawling through the death notices in the archives of the *Oxford Mail*. She didn't find what she was looking for on that first occasion, nor on the next. It was on the third visit to the newspaper archive that she found what she needed, in an

504

edition of August 1921: the announcement of the passing of dearest Emily Jane Goodhew who was sadly missed by her loving parents, having died at the tragically early age of five months. No flowers, but donations to the paediatric unit of the John Radcliffe Hospital.

Miss Miller looked askance when she asked for yet more time off but she didn't give a damn. She didn't really care if they sacked her from the Peace Union now. She knew what she was doing and where she was going. The next time in Oxford she went through the birth notices of March 1921 to find the announcement of Emily's birth, the exact date and place. The happy event, to be followed with tragedy five months later, took place in a maternity clinic in Summertown, on the 27th March 1921. A subsequent visit to the Registry of Births and Deaths in the town hall yielded an official copy of Emily's birth certificate; a fortnight later, two photos and a visit to the passport office in Petty France provided a passport in the name of Emily Jane Goodhew, now aged thirty-two, single, secretary, hair colour brown, eye colour brown, no special peculiarities.

Names and cover names. At Beaulieu they'd taught her how to create a cover story, how to practise it and live with it. How to be, successively, Anne-Marie Laroche and Laurence Follette. Subsequently she had become Geneviève Marchal; and now she might be Emily Goodhew, known to her friends as Emmie.

BISTRO

And then one evening, after I had imbibed enough Dutch courage in the pub, I rang Marian's number. The very idea of having to speak to the Spitfire pilot who had never shot down a German almost put me off the project from the start, but to my relief it was Marian herself who answered. Her voice seemed distant and rather expressionless, as though she could barely be bothered to pick up the receiver let alone speak into it.

'It's Sam,' I said. 'Sam Wareham. I was just ringing to see how you were.'

'Oh, Sam. Yes, I'm fine. Why wouldn't I be?'

'Because I read about that business in the papers, and my mother told me—'

'Yes, well, that's all over now, isn't it? I'm fine now. Thank you.'

'Good. Well . . .'

The conversation, difficult enough when conducted over sixty miles of electric wire, stalled. 'Look, Sam,' she said, 'I can't talk now but I'll get in touch, OK? Soon. Promise.' And the line went dead.

What was I left with? The single word 'promise', which can seem so empty. The world of ordinary discourse is littered with the ghosts of promises. And yet she kept her promise, that was the remarkable thing. She did get in touch, two weeks later, with a phone call to my digs one evening, a call from a public phone box, which I thought strange at the time. I heard the operator telling the caller she was through and the coins going down in the machine and then Marian's voice sounding loudly in my ear, almost as though she were standing there beside me in the hallway and talking into my ear. Could we meet up for lunch somewhere? she asked. She wanted to talk things over. It'd be better if I came up to London. Could I manage that, perhaps next weekend?

Of course I could. And when we had finished I replaced the receiver with care, in case it might explode and take with it all my dreams.

We met in a restaurant that she suggested, in a side street off Shaftesbury Avenue, a small place that was, to my inexpert eye, the perfect simulacrum of a Parisian bistro. I had to follow strict instructions, to get there first and find the table booked in the name of Geneviève.

'Geneviève?'

'It doesn't matter why. That's the name.'

And I was to wait for her.

When she finally appeared she seemed out of breath, as if she'd been hurrying. She tossed her coat over an empty chair and sat down opposite me. 'Did anyone see you come in?' Her question sounded mad. I presumed dozens of people might have seen me enter the restaurant. It was a busy London street, for God's sake. But who would give a damn?

She gave a hurried smile. No one would give a damn. Of course not. Slowly she began to relax, glancing round at the place and beckoning the waiter over with a little blizzard of French that I could barely comprehend. We discussed the menu together and finally decided on onion soup and *magret de canard*, which was the first time in my life that I had eaten duck, and a bottle of Châteauneuf-du-Pape, which was the first time I knew that popes had castles in France.

'And now I must apologise,' she said when the soup had been served. 'For what happened last time. Sometimes things get out of control, don't they?'

'There's nothing to apologise for,' I assured her. 'I loved it. And—'

'And?'

I shrugged, not knowing quite what to say. 'No harm was done, was it?'

She, who knew so much about harm, wondered about that. She reached across the table to take my hand for a moment. 'I wouldn't want our friendship to be compromised, Sam.'

It hadn't, I insisted that it hadn't. And it wouldn't be, whatever happened.

'But you don't know if something is compromised until you discover it has been.'

Was she feeling guilty? It didn't seem to go with
the insouciant, audacious woman I knew. 'It's all
right,' I insisted. 'Everything's all right.'

Once that little difficulty was over, we talked,
ate, drank the wine of the Pope's new castle and
when I broached the subject of her recent
disappearance she batted the question away with
a dismissive wave, like someone executing a back-
hand at table tennis. 'Forget it. It's all over and
things are fine. Just forget it.' What she preferred
to talk about was what she was going to do in the
coming years – go to France, go to America, get
out of this grey, grim city – and what I might do
after I had finished my language course and gone
through university. 'I can see you as a diplomat,
Sam,' she said. 'Smooth and clever and maybe
cynical. Don't become cynical. You can be the
other things, but don't become a cynic.'

Cynic seemed a rather good option to me,
although I wasn't cynical about her when she
leaned forward and lowered her voice conspirator-
ially. 'Sam, I need your help.'

I felt a sudden jolt, something physical, almost
as though I had been punched in the stomach. Of
course she could have my help.

Apparently, she wanted a break, somewhere out
of the city. Her husband would be away shortly.
He was often away from home, travelling round
the damned country pursuing his sales targets, but

this time it was to Scotland and she was damned if she was going to hang around on her own. What about Furze Cottage? Could I get the key? Was anyone using it? That would be ideal, wouldn't it?

Furze Cottage? My instincts were suddenly awake to every possible implication.

'What do you think?' she asked.

I was, of course, stunned – almost literally: my senses confused, my mind slow to comprehend. I drank more wine and looked at the woman who sat across the tiny table in front of me (her lips were stained purple) and part of me thought that I was being readmitted through the portals of heaven. 'Am I invited?'

She laughed, holding her hand to hide her mouth. 'Of course you are. I need you to drive me. You can drive, can't you?'

Being able to drive, possessing a driving licence was a passport to adulthood; being able to admit that I could (I'd passed my test three months before) seemed to be an assertion of my maturity almost as great as losing my virginity. I'd drive her wherever she wanted.

'And when we're there?'

A wry little smile. 'We'll take things as they come. A fling, let's call it that. *Une passade.*'

A *passade* was all right by me. I was a pauper, prepared to beg for crumbs, and here she was offering me half the loaf. 'Tell no one,' she said. 'Let's keep it to ourselves. And for God's sake, not a word to your mother. She'd skin me alive.'

Then she paid the bill, gave me a kiss, *une bise* that strayed from cheek to the corner of my mouth, whispered '*à bientôt*,' and left.

I was, I'm ashamed to say, completely taken in. We were going away together for a weekend, that was enough. A weekend with the object of most of my dreams, the woman who had insisted I call her by her first name from the very beginning, who had treated me like an adult from the start, who had held my hand all the way to the hospital when I broke my collarbone, the woman who, on the very night she had attempted suicide, had sat with her arm around me, as though to bring me comfort. I watched her, heard her, loved every movement she made and, at that moment, believed everything she said.

Days passed in a state of priapic anticipation. It was easy enough to get the keys to Furze Cottage. A quick visit to my parents was sufficient, combined with some cock-and-bull story about a couple of mates from Cambridge going down to the cottage for a weekend of Pimm's and Pushkin. My mother thought that sounded ever such fun, having herself once been to C. S. Lewis's Beer and Beowulf evenings in Magdalen. Perhaps she thought I might be turning into a proto-academic rather than into the young goat I had already become.

The keys to the house were three in number, two Yales and an ancient mortise key all attached to a lump of cork in case they should be dropped from a boat. Throughout the following week they sat on the mantelshelf in my room, the keys to the gates of paradise rather than the keys to a rather rundown cottage by the sea with damp mattresses and sagging bedsprings. My imagination was rampant.

FURZE COTTAGE

In the meantime . . .

There's always a meantime, isn't there? The ordinary hours and days, even weeks, that fill out one's life between the scarce moments of interest. There's an awful lot of meantime in an agent's existence, believe me.

In the meantime . . . Marian Sutro pursued her work with the Peace Union as though nothing had changed. No hint was given of what was to come. No hint *could* be given, she knew that well enough. She dealt with her husband as she always dealt with him, with a distant affection and a certain intimate impatience. 'Oh darling, not *again*? Very well, if you must.' She went for her weekly talk to the psychiatrist in Oxford, staying that night with her parents as always. She went to visit her brother in the cottage near Harwell and told him that the connection with the Soviet side was irrevocably broken and the flow of information had ceased. They would never know whether it had been a success or not, nor even how to measure success. That was so often the way with the clandestine world – you never knew whether what you had done had made a jot of difference.

513

Ned was relieved to see it end, but sad for her. 'Does that mean he's gone for good, Squirrel? The man you were fucking?'

'I do wish you wouldn't use that language,' she said.

He laughed, that acid, malicious laugh. 'Poor Squirrel. Always trying to pretend.'

In the file entitled 'Trapeze' there's almost nothing about those days. Just a brief account of her abduction and interrogation by 'agents unknown, probably of the MGB' and then a final note that says simply, 'SWALLOW terminated'. It's signed 'Fawley'.

And so the Friday morning came, the day when we had scheduled our meeting, our little *passade* on the Sussex coast. It was one of those damp, chill days that England seems able to conjure up at any time of the year. The early train from Cambridge was full of commuters exuding a faint smell of damp cloth and stale armpits. I found a window seat where I could bury myself in an early collection of Akhmatova's poems and fancy that Marian was to me as Anna Akhmatova had been to her several lovers, a figure of tragedy, and triumph against the odds.

'What's that, then?' my neighbour asked, peering at the Cyrillic script.

'Russian,' I told him.

He looked at me with curiosity. 'You a Commie, then?'

'Was Bulgakov?' I responded. 'Is Pasternak?' He wouldn't have known either name but at least they shut him up.

From Liverpool Street the Underground trains were crowded as far as Embankment and Westminster but then most people got off and I was almost on my own until South Kensington. I walked through quiet, domestic streets as far as the block of flats where Marian lived. The building had something of the air of an ocean liner about it, of decks and railings and panoramic windows. The main doors even had circular lights, giving an impression of portholes. Memories of my last visit were rife as I climbed the travertine stairs but when she opened the door to her flat and hurried me in there was no laughter or excitement in her expression, nothing to hint at what had happened between us the last time I had been here. 'Did you see them?' she asked. 'Did you see them?'

'See whom?'

'I'll show you.' She took me to the sitting room, keeping back from the window, even instructing me to climb up on the sofa so that we could get a better angle of view down into the street. There was a car on the far pavement with the vague silhouette of someone sitting in the driver's seat. 'From the Russian embassy, I think. But they may be from the Security Service. I'm not sure.'

'They're *watching* you?'

'Don't you believe me?' There was a snap in her voice.

'Well, I—'

'I suppose if I said they were private detectives hired by my husband, it'd sound quite convincing, wouldn't it?'

I more or less agreed that it would.

'Well, they're not. They're from the Russian embassy and they're watching me.'

I admit I toyed with the idea that she might be mad. Lovely, certainly, but crazy. Maybe her experiences during the war had unhinged her. Perhaps this was some kind of shellshock, a form of paranoia induced by whatever had happened to her at the hands of her captors, another manifestation of whatever it was that had assaulted her when she had disappeared for those missing days. I remembered how she had been after that visit to the cinema with my parents to see *Odette*. The sobbing, shaking, hysterical wreck crouched in our sitting room like an overgrown foetus. Was this, I wondered for an instant, the woman I had before me now?

Keeping back from the window we went through to the kitchen to talk. There was a focused urgency about her manner, about the way she looked at me and the way she explained the plan, the same plan that she had outlined at our meeting in the restaurant but now embellished with baroque detail. Despite my initial doubts, I was swept up in it, carried along, convinced of its sanity and, more, its *necessity*. As though it was just normal, the kind of thing that happens, the sort of thing you do any day of the week when you live in the clandestine world.

'You'll help me, won't you, Sam?'

Of course I would.

'So, let's go.'

She gave me a kiss before she went, just a peck on each cheek. *Deux bisous*. And then she had closed the door behind her and, faintly through the heavy oak, I could hear her clipping down the stairs. I stood on the sofa at the back of the room to watch her cross the street, a bright, sharp figure in a red mackintosh and matching waterproof hat. Sure enough, exactly as she had predicted, the door of the waiting car opened and a man got out to follow her. He wore a fawn raincoat with the collar turned up and a trilby hat pulled down over his eyes. He followed her in the direction of the Fulham Road at which point I lost sight of the pair of them.

The car remained parked across the street. I waited. It was twenty minutes before it finally did what Marian had predicted and drove away.

As soon as it had gone I took my duffle bag and Marian's suitcase and left the flat. The stairs led down below the ground floor to the basement garage where, easily enough, I found her car. It was a black two-and-a-half-litre Riley saloon, powerful enough for the Spitfire pilot, I guess. Certainly it was the most powerful car I had ever sat in, never mind driven. I fiddled with the keys for a moment before I got the thing going. The engine seemed to boom and roar in the subterranean

517

confines of the garage but when I edged it out up the ramp into the aqueous daylight everything settled down to something more modest. Cautiously I turned left out of the entrance and headed towards the King's Road. I didn't really know my way around that part of London and certainly not by car, but her instructions had been clear enough and it wasn't difficult to follow the King's Road all the way to the river and Putney Bridge. As she had instructed me, I parked outside the Tube station and sat there watching people go in and out. It wouldn't be hard to spot her in that red mackintosh.

I must have waited for an hour or more but somehow I never doubted that she would be there sooner or later, only that when she did emerge from the station it wasn't the same figure that had left the flat earlier and I almost missed her. There was no red raincoat any longer, and no red hat. Instead she wore a thin black plastic mack and a nondescript headscarf. She ran across the road to the car, yanked open the door and slipped in beside me.

'Let's go!' There was a light in her eyes and a breathlessness about her manner, as though she had been running, as though she had been making love. I pulled away from the curb and out onto the main road, across the bridge over the grey slick of the river. Within a few minutes we found the Brighton Road and were heading south out of the city, Marian alight with excitement, explaining how she had led her follower a dance through the Tube, losing him among the crowds at Piccadilly Circus and dumping her coat as she did so. 'An old trick,' she said. 'I used it in Paris. Problem is, they'll be worried that I spotted them and deliberately threw them off. That's always the danger. If they do, then they'll go into full panic mode and throw everything at finding me. What I'm hoping is that they'll just head back to the flat and wait for me to return. You did remember to lock up after you?'

I remembered, of course I remembered. 'Why on earth are they following you?' I asked. She just smiled and shook her head. Her lips were blood red, her skin as pale as the moon and touched with grey shadows, and somehow she seemed more mysterious than ever.

'So you're not going to tell me what this is all about?'

She smiled faintly, smoking now, opening the quarter-light to blow smoke out. 'You'll have to trust me, Sam,' she said. 'You do trust me, don't you?'

'Of course I trust you.'

But I didn't. I'm not a complete fool. Either she was mad, in which case what I was doing was dangerous, or she was sane, in which case what we were both doing was dangerous. There didn't seem to be any other option. I thought about her disappearance a few weeks earlier. Was this another of those neurotic breakdowns, paranoia bursting out in her brain like an evil bloom?

'Just keep an eye on any cars behind us,' she said. 'If you think we're being followed, let me know.'

But there was no one behind us and for the last part of the journey, across the Weald under leaden skies, the roads seemed deserted. When we stopped at a village shop to buy some stuff for supper I had a devil of a job to rouse anyone to serve me. But finally I succeeded and we continued, now equipped with a loaf of bread, some butter, a pack of Mr Wall's best sausages and a rather muddy cabbage; no wine, but a couple of bottles of Ind Coope beer. And shortly we came to that point in the road where it runs along a high ridge and through the trees you can see the long, sleek cutting edge of the English Channel.

'The sea, the sea!' she exclaimed at the sight. I recalled her father saying the very same thing all those years ago when we all went down together. Perhaps she was quoting him as much as Xenophon. Perhaps there was something mocking in her tone. At the end of the high ground the road wound down and there was Furze Cottage waiting for us among the pines as it waited for any visitors, with a cool, damp indifference.

We parked round the back of the house – 'right out of sight,' she insisted – and hurried in through the drizzle. The first thing I did was light a fire in the sitting room with the kindling wood that was there. And the second thing was look to see if the jigsaw puzzle of Ophelia drowning was still in the old wooden trunk. It wasn't. Perhaps Amanda had taken it home; or perhaps one of the cousins. There was a moment of awkwardness when I picked up our luggage – her suitcase and my duffle bag – and glanced at her for guidance. 'Separate rooms, I think,' she said. 'That'd be better, wouldn't it?'

I supposed it would, although I didn't want it that way. If this were only a fling, I wanted as much of her as I could get. I wanted to sleep with her at my side and wake with her there in the morning. But I buried my disappointment, split the bags between neighbouring bedrooms, and went in search of sheets and blankets. We hung the sheets in the sitting room to air a bit and then made up the beds – a double bed for her, a single for me. There was something touchingly domestic about the scene. For a late lunch we made some sandwiches with a tin of Spam I found in the kitchen. Memories of lunch at the Tate. I'd turned the ancient radio on and we listened to the news. I half wondered if her absence would have been noticed and whether there would be one of those SOS messages one used to hear. But there was nothing more than the usual litany of bad news – a strike here, a calamity there, tension in Berlin, bloodshed in Indochina.

In the evening, like a pair of undergraduates in digs, we cooked up the sausages and cabbage, added a tin of beans that I discovered in the larder, opened the beer and ate our early supper in front of the fire. Afterwards I found a half bottle of whisky in a cupboard and we drank while sitting on the sofa. Outside, it rained. Inside, the firelight touched her with red and gold. It felt more like midwinter than summer, the kind of time you tell stories to children, and in recall that strange evening seems to last for ever, flickering in memory as it was lit at the time by the fire. An uncertain and deceptive illumination. In firelight features are meant to be softened, complexions flattered, age brushed away. But Marian looked older, much older. Her eyes seemed hollow, her cheeks sunken. Only her scent was unchanged, that blend of musk and earth with, underlying it all, something mordant that my sister had so disliked. I wanted to make love to her; she wanted only to talk. And so it was that she told me her story – not the recent stuff but what had happened during the war, which was half a lifetime for me but almost nothing for her. Curled up on the sofa and wrapped in a rug, we drank whisky and slipped into a strange state between sleeping and waking while she talked of things that seemed credible and things that I doubted, of Paris in the occupation and her killing two men, shooting them like something out of a cowboy film. She talked of betrayal, of the hard, damp cave of a prison cell and the slow, grinding death of the concentration camp. She talked of running through a forest with two other women, women she never saw again, whose names she never knew. Blurred with alcohol, she was incontinent with talk, spilling out things I had never imagined hearing and would never hear again. Her mood was sombre, as though this were a eulogy for someone who had recently died. 'I believed, you see, Sam? It was easy to believe in those days when the issues were black and white. Now we only have shades of grey. But then I believed.' And at the end she warned me, 'Whatever you do, Sam, don't get involved.'

I wasn't receptive to the older person's advice for the young but I'd have taken anything from her. 'Involved in what?'

'Your Russian course is pretty obvious, isn't it? You may talk about Pushkin and Tolstoy. Or even your poet lady – what's she called?'

'Akhmatova.'

'But tomorrow they'll be indoctrinating you into the secrets and rituals of their nasty little world. Just don't get involved, Sam.'

But I confess I found the idea rather exciting. The young man's easy dismissal of an elder's advice. 'Are you still involved?' I asked and she looked at me thoughtfully, her head on one side, her mouth twisted into a wry little smile.

'Up to my neck,' she said. 'And now I'm running away from them. First thing tomorrow, I'm going.'

'*Going?*'

'And you're going to help me. You'll do that, won't you, Sam?' Her tone was pleading. She needed help, she explained, someone she could trust not to say anything. Was I that person? All I had to do was drive her to Folkestone to catch the early morning ferry and then get rid of the car. She was going to France and she had no idea when she was coming back. She was sorry, so sorry not to have told me this earlier but it was need-to-know, wasn't it? I might have let something slip, to my mother or someone. You never knew, that was the problem, you never knew whom you could trust and who might betray you. 'During the war I was betrayed and I'm still uncertain who it was. Can you believe that? We never really found out. Anyway, I'm relying on you not to betray me. Will you do that?'

'Of course I won't betray you.'

'And am I forgiven for misleading you? You thought we were going away for a dirty weekend together, didn't you? And here I am running off without you.'

Of course she was forgiven. I had no claim on her whatsoever. But what about her husband, the Spitfire pilot who had never shot down a German?

A little shrug of indifference beneath the blanket. She was beyond understanding what damage she might do to others, beyond caring about anything else except what she had planned.

Did I believe the story she told me? I really don't know. It is perfectly possible to believe two contra-dictory things at one and the same time – that is one of the brilliant faculties of the human mind. Without it we'd have no war and no religion and precious little else that separates us from the other species. So I believed Marian Sutro and knew she was lying; thought she was sane and assumed she was deranged; trusted her and knew she would betray me in an instant; but I loved her and there was no negative counterpart to that. My love was total and desirous of nothing more than her presence. I suppose you could despise her for taking advantage of me but I can assure you that the possibility never crossed my mind. She wanted my help and I gave it unconditionally. I had never done such a thing before and certainly never since.

Dawn leached into the room like the insidious creep of floodwater, turning the depth and mystery of firelight into a cold, damp two-dimensional reality. We pulled apart and she went and washed while I made coffee. We'd found the coffee in a tin in the kitchen but it dated from the last time the house had been used and was stale. 'It'll do,' she said. She was packed now, standing with her suitcase like someone on the platform of a railway station snatching a hot drink before the train comes in. 'Let's go,' she said as she put her mug down.

The drive took an hour, a flatland journey across Pett Level, through the narrow lanes of Rye, past the towering Chain Home masts and across Romney Marsh. Folkestone lay beneath grey overcast, besieged by crying gulls and undermined by marine engines that rumbled almost beneath the level of human hearing. There was spray in the air and that pearly seaside light that looks as though it has been rinsed through chalk. I parked the car near the harbour station and retrieved her suitcase from the boot.

She handed me money. 'Get me an open return.'

Beside the ticket office there was a newspaper stand from which the Prime Minister frowned at the nation in an awful simulacrum of the manner in which he had conducted the war. But there was no such war now and he looked like nothing more than an old and wasted bull put out to grass. Behind the counter in the ticket office they were talking about films.

'He could kiss me like that on the beach any day,' one said.

'Not here, he couldn't. It'd be shingle, not sand and bloody cold with it,' said the other. She was reluctant to bother with my request for an open return to Boulogne, as though discussing Burt Lancaster and Deborah Kerr was her primary job and selling tickets was what she did in the moments in between, but eventually I persuaded her to take my money. When I emerged clutching the ticket, the boat train from London was edging slowly across the viaduct into the station. There was a discharge of steam into the dank air, a squealing of iron against iron, the banging of carriage doors as people climbed down onto the platform.

Marian was standing by the car with a headscarf on and her coat wrapped around her. Without make-up she looked like a refugee, one of the hundreds of thousands that haunted the European mainland for so many years in the aftermath of war. She turned and cupped her hands to light a cigarette. 'You know how they caught me in France?' she said. 'I was waiting on a platform and someone called out my name. My real name, not my cover name. "Marian?" she called out. "Marian Sutro?" And I looked round.' She made a little sound that might have been a laugh, might have been no more than a small cry of misery. Smoke made a little funeral pall around her mouth. 'Now I don't even know what my name is.'

Then she kissed me, once on each cheek – 'I'll be in touch sometime, Sam' – and walked away to where the foot passengers were boarding.

CLEARING UP

After she had boarded, I went ahead with the final part of her plan. First, I drove back to the cottage and cleared up. It didn't take much time. The impression she had made on the place was minimal. Then I drove on to Hastings, where I parked the car in the station car park. I took the first train back to London, crossed the city by Tube to Liverpool Street station and got the train back to Cambridge. At lunchtime I phoned the language school to tell them I had been sick on Friday but was getting better and expected to be in on Monday. Like some kind of petty criminal, I'd covered my traces, even, I confess it now, wiping the steering wheel and gear stick of the car to make sure I hadn't left any fingerprints. The key I dropped into the River Cam off St John's bridge. Maybe it's still there now, buried in the slime at the bottom of the river, rusted beyond recognition. Or maybe the anaerobic world of the silt means that it hasn't rusted and instead it's preserved, mint bright and ready for a car that no longer exists.

★　　★　　★

Time blurs the edges of memory. How much later was it that I got a phone call from my mother asking if I'd heard about Marian? Two days? Three?

No, I hadn't heard. What about her?

'Well, it seems she's gone missing again.'

I managed a nice little show of incredulity. '*Again?*'

Apparently the story was in the *News Chronicle*. 'The Disappearing Heroine' was the headline. Her husband had reported her disappearance to the police and a few days later her car had been found in the station car park at Hastings, a quarter-light smashed. Presumably that was just a piece of petty crime because people said that the car had been there for some days and it was only when the damage was seen that anyone bothered to report it. There was no sign of the owner. The cliff paths to the east of the town had been searched and the coastguard had scoured the shoreline and the inshore area. No trace of the missing person had been found. 'The cliff paths,' my mother repeated in a hollow voice. 'You know what that means, don't you?' And then she added: 'Weren't you down at the cottage then, with some of your friends?'

'We didn't see her, if that's what you mean. It was bloody awful weather and we stayed indoors most of the time.'

'Well, it's all very sad. We'd thought that she'd got over it all, that she was doing so well, working, settled down with Alan. And then that unfortunate business that got into the papers. When she disappeared. And now it's happened again.'

Later a journalist appeared at Wadham College and attempted to get an interview with her father, but Doctor Sutro was having none of it. Later there was another brief statement from her husband, who declared himself distraught at her disappearance and ever hopeful of her return. She had gone missing before and had turned up on those previous occasions. She had been, he was reported as saying, under a great deal of stress but he had not imagined, and could not imagine still, that she might do away with herself.

'Do away with herself'. Suicide was like homosexuality in those days – illegal and unmentionable in polite society.

A week later, when there was still no sign of her, a longer article appeared in the same newspaper, rehashing the 1945 story of 'Miss Anne-Marie S' whom they could now reveal was, in fact, the missing woman, Marian Walcott, née Sutro. A heroine of the resistance, decorated by both the British and the French governments, but also, tragically, a prisoner of the Nazis. What had been her fate? No answer was forthcoming and with nothing more to feed it the little flame of journalistic interest soon died out. Marian Sutro had vanished for good this time, popularly thought to have thrown herself off the cliffs, victim, some suggested, of the frightful experiences she had undergone during the war. I have the cuttings still, brown, brittle bits of newsprint squirrelled away inside some ignored book about the SOE. There's a photograph of her, probably taken for her identity card in 1943. Maybe it was the one used for Anne-Marie Laroche and Laurence Follette as well. But not Emily Jane Goodhew, known to her friends as Emmie.

GOODHEW

I leaned forward and turned the recorder off. 'That's it, then.'

She looked at the little device lying on the table between us. 'It's all in there?'

'All in there.'

'What will they do with it?'

I slipped the recorder into my pocket. 'I'll get it transcribed and then it'll be filed away in Registry.'

'And forgotten about?'

'Like so much else.'

She downed the last of her gin. I wondered whether to leave. I'd got everything they wanted but of course there was more, so much more. 'What happened to Absolon?' I asked.

'Off the record?'

'Off the record.'

'We lived together for a dozen years or more. Herr und Frau, although we were never married. We set up a translation agency. Albrecht and Goodhew. It has a good, reliable ring to it, doesn't it? Like a firm of solicitors. And then . . .' She shrugged. 'He grew old and resentful. Took to the booze. And my eye had already begun to wander.

New people, new experiences, new pains and new consolations. I've never been very faithful to one man, have I, Sam? You know that. After Absolon I was married for a few years but it wasn't a great success although it did get me Swiss citizenship. Which is ironical because Marian Sutro would have been entitled by birth whereas Emily Goodhew had to earn it the hard way. Absolon? He died over twenty years ago but at least he died in a Swiss hospital rather than a Soviet labour camp.'

'And your first husband?'

'Poor Alan. Do I sound very callous? I believe it took him years to get the courts to declare Marian Sutro dead but he managed eventually and settled down with a lady who made him a much better wife than I.' She pushed herself to her feet and went over to the sideboard to pour herself another drink. 'You know about my brother, I suppose?'

'Of course.'

'Poor Ned had a recurring nightmare that everything would end in a nuclear exchange between the Soviet Union and the Americans. But all that happened was a squad of policemen burst in and caught him in bed with his boyfriend.'

'It wouldn't happen today.'

'Neither would a nuclear war between East and West. So I suppose we've made some progress.' Then she was silent, staring at the glass in her hand. 'That was my only regret, leaving Ned behind.'

'You never let him know where you'd gone?'

She shook her head. 'Never break your cover.'

'Not even when they throw your brother in prison for gross indecency?'

I could see the emotion in her face, even through the mask of age. 'You don't understand, do you, Sam? That's why they betrayed him to the police, to flush me out.'

'The Soviets, you mean?'

'Whoever wanted Absolon enough.'

'And who was that?'

She considered my question thoughtfully. 'Tell me what happened to Fawley.'

'I imagined you knew.'

'Tell me.'

'They made him Director General. It was a bit of a stop-gap. Like making an old man Pope in the hope he won't last too long.'

Her smile made her look younger, gave a little glimpse of the woman I remembered. 'I always saw him like that. A priest.'

'He had just eighteen months in post, enough to earn him his K, and then he retired. Eastbourne or Brighton, somewhere like that. Grew prize dahlias and played golf.'

She nodded as if prize dahlias and golf were only to be expected. 'What was his Christian name?'

'Didn't you know? These days it's all first names. Reginald.'

That seemed to amuse her even more. She savoured the name. 'Sir Reginald Fawley. I fancied him a Cedric but Reginald isn't far off, is it? That's where I'd look, if I were you.'

'You believe that?'

'If not him, who? Someone in your beloved organisation betrayed Absolon to the Soviets. He told no one on his side what he was doing and yet they knew, the Soviets knew.'

She watched me with that ironical curiosity. 'I know a great deal about betrayal, Sam. I know its texture and I know its smell. It's pungent, exhilarating. Like sex.'

I thought of her own smell that had so captivated me and repulsed my young sister. If it still existed, it was buried now beneath the kind of florid perfume old ladies wear. 'It's not enough to have a nose for these things. You've got to have evidence. A paper trail.'

'What about Bright?' she said. 'What about him?'

I shrugged. 'There's virtually nothing on the record. A certain Anton Heiter worked in the British country section of the Stasi for a number of years. That might have been him.'

Perfect teeth, courtesy of some expert and expensive Swiss dentist, punctuated her laughter. 'Heiter, Bright. Surely he'd have done better with a cover name than that.' She went back to the sideboard. I thought she was going to insist I have another drink and listen to her theories about a mole in the upper echelons of the Security Service but instead she opened a drawer, took out a heap of typescript and handed it to me. 'Here,' she said.

'I thought you might like to read it. It's my story. Oh, not the post-war mess. What happened during the war. When I was a heroine,' she added with bitter irony. 'Perhaps you can do something with it, Sam. It's yours if you want to take it. A gift.'

I glanced at the title – An Agent's Life in France – and the first few lines:

> His name was Potter, which seemed unlikely to me at the time because it sounded false, like Smith or Jones – the kind of name you'd choose as a nom de guerre if you hadn't got much imagination. He had a querulous, fluting voice and a distant manner, as though perhaps he had already made up his mind that I was not really suitable for his requirements but he would see me anyway out of politeness.

'I'm sure it will be fascinating,' I said, getting up from my chair.

'At least it's true.'

'Unlike what you've just been telling me?'

Her laughter showed those even, white teeth to perfection – as much a lie as anything else about her. 'The strange thing is, it all meant so much at the time, didn't it – the Cold War, the Bomb, spies, traitors, all that kind of thing. And now? It's all irrelevant – just a dusty piece of history.'

We talked a bit more, that awkward kind of conversation when both of you know that this will be the very last time you'll ever meet, and one of you at least was in love with the other. '*Mon cher Sam*,' she said as we kissed farewell at the front door. '*T'as des regrets?*'

'No,' I assured her. 'None at all.'

'Then that's fine.'

'What about you?'

'Me?' She laughed dismissively, a throaty, knowing laugh. Apparently the question wasn't worth answering.

I walked towards the car. When I looked back, for a moment, just a moment – a trick of the light or something – she looked like the Marian Sutro I remembered. Then the illusion had gone and she was just an old lady standing unsteadily at the door of her apartment, holding up an arthritic hand in salute.